Cornelia Shields 1989

A MASTERFUL ACCOUNT, most compelling, exciting, and extremely difficult to put down until complete.

F. X. "Frank" DeAbreu, Teacher of History, Dayton, Washington

Seven for Oregon

recounts the stirring journey of the seven Sager children, orphaned on the Oregon Trail in 1844. Left with missionaries Marcus and Narcissa Whitman in Oregon Territory, they experienced the joys and hardships of pioneer life, and tragedy when hostile Indians attacked the mission in 1847. Their saga is a slice of American history, and an emotional reading experience not soon forgotten.

Cornelia Shields is a first-rate story teller. Her narrative of the Sager family's trek draws on extensive historical research to create a gem of a book that immerses the reader in 19th century frontier life.

John R. Jameson, Associate Professor, Department of History, Washington State University

A special book that makes history read like fiction.

Don Ross, Department of English, Washington State University

I would recommend this to anyone. I would read this again sometime. I learned a lot about human nature.

Mitchell Lockard, age 13, grade 8, Dayton, Washington

These events have always been known to me as a part of my heritage. Cornelia Shields, with her skill as a narrator and her sensitivity and faithfulness to historical accuracy, has at last portrayed all of the participants in this tragedy as the real people they were.

Elizabeth Miller Sullivan,
Great-granddaughter of Catherine Sager Pringle

Careful attention to details, a respect for historical accuracy, and an enormous amount of scholarly research make *Seven for Oregon* not only true to historical fact, but to the spirit of the time and place it covers. The reader is kept spellbound by the remarkably vivid scenes and the intensity of the action.

George T. Watkins, III, Professor Emeritus, American Studies,
Washington State University

Shields has been able to take us over the Oregon Trail with the Sagers, to enjoy their pleasant days at the mission, to suffer through the terrible day of the massacre and feel their terror in the long days afterward. Although it must be classified as a historical novel, *Seven for Oregon* is true history, very true to what really happened.

Robert E. Moody, Town of Gorham Historian, Rushville, New York
Authority on Marcus and Narcissa Whitman

What courage these children had—what spirit! I loved all of them. Their characters, so different, delighted me.

Mary Lou Williamson, Teacher of History,
Bryn Athyn, Pennsylvania

Seven for Oregon is very good. It held my attention clear through.... During the massacre, I cried. I felt like I was part of the family. After I was done reading it, I felt like I would never find a book that would hold my attention like *Seven for Oregon*.

Sherry Laib, age 11, grade 6, Dayton, Washington

Seven for Oregon

Cover photograph, by the author, shows Whitman Mission, now a national historic site, located near Walla Walla, Washington.

Printed in the United States of America by
Green Springs Press
217 East Oak Street
Dayton, Washington 99328-1595

FIRST EDITION...*1000 copies*...November, 1986
SECOND EDITION...*2000 copies*...March, 1989

Shields, Cornelia. 1961-
    Seven for Oregon.
    Bibliography: p. 310

SUMMARY: Fictionalized account of the seven orphaned Sager children's true adventures on the Oregon Trail and in the home of Northwest missionaries Marcus and Narcissa Whitman, 1844-1847.
ISBN 0-9617393-1-2

Seven for Oregon

A novel
Based on the Sager Family's
True Adventure

by

Cornelia Shields

Green Springs Press
DAYTON, WASHINGTON
1988

This book is dedicated to

Rosemary Sutcliff,

for all her books, especially *Knight's Fee*,
and to

William O. Steele,

for many happy hours of reading.
They taught me that learning history
could be enjoyable.

Foreword
To the Second Edition

Why write another book on the Sager family when so many exist? This question was asked, both by myself and others, many times in the six years I worked on the First Edition of *Seven for Oregon*, but when finished I could truthfully say I was glad I wrote the book, no matter how many came before.

The Sagers and I go back a long way. From the time Whitman Mission, near Walla Walla, Washington, became a national historic site in 1963, when I was two years old, my parents took me to see the grounds and hear the story of the Whitmans and the orphaned Sager children.

Visitors to Whitman Mission back then put on earphones to hear the story of the Whitman Massacre while looking at the diorama. With my head enclosed in those earphones, the events surrounded me, holding me rapt. The figure of John Sager never failed to captivate me, his face turned away so that no matter what angle I looked from I could never see it, his hand eternally frozen in the act of reaching for a gun.

After hearing the story came the somber moment of walking up the path to see John and his brother Francis's names carved in marble along with those of twelve others. Whitman Mission has changed since then, but the place and its story have not lost their appeal.

I first heard the story of the Sagers' wagon train journey in the third grade at Dayton Elementary School. Our teacher, Mrs. Edith Gowing, read us *The Valiant Seven*, by Netta Sheldon Phelps. In that way I was lucky, for Mrs. Phelps's book was far more accurate than the more widely read *On to Oregon!*, by Honoré Willsie Morrow.

I was caught up in the story of the pioneer family who left St. Joseph, Missouri, in 1844, with six children, the eldest in his early teens, the youngest born on the trail. The children met tragedy with the parents' deaths, and acceptance into the missionary home of Marcus and Narcissa

Whitman. For the first time in my life, the Sagers were not names carved in marble, but real children like myself. Though my life was very different from theirs, I felt a special closeness to them.

Five years later, when I was thirteen, a movie about the Sagers came to Walla Walla. Greatly excited, I read *The Valiant Seven* again, also checking out the second volume of Clifford M. Drury's *Marcus and Narcissa Whitman and the Opening of Old Oregon*, the finest book about the Whitmans. I wanted to confirm the movie's facts.

My disappointment in the movie *Seven Alone* was deep and long-lasting. It portrayed John Sager as an insolent brat forced to become a man when his parents died and the rest of the wagon train voted to go to California rather than Oregon. Insisting that Pa wanted them to go to Oregon, he smuggled his brother and sisters—including a tiny baby and a girl hobbling on a broken leg—away from the camp and into the wilderness alone.

William and Sally Shaw, who in real life helped the Sagers so far as to share their last loaf of bread with them, were portrayed as hindrances to the children, and Dr. Degen, the good man who personally looked after them, became in the movie Dr. Dutch, an incompetent, bumbling idiot.

The Whitman Massacre, which to me in many ways was the most interesting part of the story, dealing with the great courage of people facing death, was not even mentioned. The movie seemed to imply that after arriving at Whitman Mission, the children acquired a farm in Oregon's Willamette Valley and lived happily ever after.

For a while I wrote papers about the Sagers and talked about writing a book, but I had no idea of how to begin. After a while I decided that enough books had been written.

This idea changed in the fall of 1980 when I entered Walla Walla Community College. I had not thought of Mrs. Morrow's book *On to Oregon!*, the basis of *Seven Alone*, for years until I saw it on the reading rack at college. My composition teacher, Charles Cudney, hearing my complaints, suggested a paper for his class.

In the library, I found one excellent non-fiction study, *Shallow Grave at Waiilatpu: The Sagers' West*, by Erwin N. Thompson, two novels besides Mrs. Morrow's that were even more false than hers, and two novels based on fact, which I thought were still lacking. After my

First Edition was published, a reader pointed out yet another factual novel. I would be glad to hear from other readers who can help track these stories down. Anyone with information please see the note at the end of this volume.

My paper stated that a Sager book must be written with a successful combination of historical research and fiction technique, so that a wide general audience could learn the true story. Mr. Cudney said, "Very good. Why don't you write a book?" With this go-ahead, I immediately began researching the book I had wanted to write for five years.

If the main question before the First Edition was "Why write it?", the main question before the Second Edition, which I began in June of 1987, was "Why rewrite it? What's wrong with it?" In answer, I don't feel anything was seriously wrong with the First Edition of *Seven for Oregon*. In the Second Edition, I mainly shortened sentences and added information, telling more in less words.

It was suggested that my First Edition was biased against Native Americans, since it told many of the whites' motivations for their actions, and few of the Indians'. The Indians' main role in the story, it seemed, was to lurk menacingly in the background, then spring forward to massacre the Whitmans.

I felt bad until someone who has known the Whitman story longer than I've lived pointed out that diaries and other accounts don't detail everyday events. An observer such as Cyrus Walker was unlikely to write, "While I stayed with the Whitmans, Indian girls visited, playing nicely with the mission girls," while he was likely to write, and did, that he witnessed an Indian threaten to kill Elizabeth Sager. Unfortunately, one such isolated incident makes a more lasting impression than the many more times when Indians and whites cooperated.

In writing this Second Edition, I worked in a number of facts about local native tribes, speculating on their friendship with the Sagers and other mission children, and telling how the whites' arrival disrupted an ancient and continuous life cycle. The Indian words used are from accounts of local Northwest tribes, mostly Nez Perce. I do hope the native tribes had a fair shake this time around.

Readers familiar with the First Edition may notice that several incidents have been added or altered. Facts, of course, don't change, but the known facts can be interpreted in a number of ways, and each newly discovered source sheds different light on the previously known. A few new sources, and a fresh look at the old, led to revision.

Some people say that history should never be fictionalized. The Sager story was not only already fictionalized, but grossly distorted. The movie, and at least two false books, were internationally distributed, and the *Reader's Digest* published Mrs. Morrow's story twice. Surely no further harm could be done by fictionalizing within the boundaries of known fact.

What made me even angrier than the people who said history should never be fictionalized were those claiming the false story was "more interesting" than the true story. In Mrs. Morrow's book and the other false books and dramatizations, seven youngsters set out to accomplish what adults lacked faith and courage for. Certainly, some people argued, the truth could never be so stirring, so inspiring, so heroic?

I set out to prove them wrong, knowing that in the right hands, the true story could be much more interesting than the false. I learned that both Catherine Sager Pringle and Matilda Sager Delaney had expressed an interest in accurate novelization of their lives, which greatly encouraged me. I think this book would have pleased them.

Much of the material in *Seven for Oregon* agrees as closely as possible with fact as any historian could, taken as it is from diaries, letters, and interviews of the Sagers and others present at the events. Every person mentioned by name in this book actually lived.

Many conversations are, of course, invented, and in a few places I had to fill in for unknown facts, especially in the chapters dealing with Francis Sager running away to the Willamette Valley. Dr. Clifford M. Drury, foremost historian on the Whitman story, believed Francis left with someone named Perkins. John Perkins and family were the only ones of that name who stopped at Whitman Mission that year.

The information on the Perkins family and their land claims are taken from historical records. I have visited the site of John Perkins's claim, and many other sites in the story. The encounter with J. S. Griffin actually happened, although the exact date and place are not clear.

The sections dealing with Indian tribes, especially after the Sager children's arrival at the mission, are also improvised. No doubt John and

Francis Sager knew at least as much about the Cayuse and other local tribes as I have claimed, but unfortunately much of their knowledge died with them and with the Indians to perish during and after the 1847 measles epidemic.

Perrin Whitman, who knew even more than the Sager boys, seems not to have left many reminiscences—more's the pity. Much of the information I present in fictional form in this Second Edition came from Marjorie Williams, a full-blooded Native American, and other workers at the Whitman Mission National Historic Site well versed in native tribes.

The chapters dealing with the Whitman Massacre, however, are almost completely true. So many survivors told their stories in such detail that it was unneccessary to invent anything. Almost every sentence in those chapters can be documented somewhere. A bibliography is included in the back of the book.

Seven for Oregon was written both to strike back at the false stories, and in hopes of bringing another dimension to the telling of the Sager story than they and other previous authors did. I hope I have succeeded. In any case, I could not resist trying.

Cornelia Shields
Dayton, Washington
June 12, 1988

Acknowledgements

It's hard to know where to begin.

First of all, teachers who encouraged me were my third grade teacher, Edith Gowing, who first read our class the Sager story, my sixth grade teacher, Juanita Harting, who in broadening my reading habits started me on historical adventure, and my college composition teacher, Charles Cudney, who suggested I write my own Sager book.

Celista Collins Platz, a granddaughter of Catherine Sager Pringle, was patient in supplying me with family materials and tireless in her help. Her keen interest in the project helped carry me through. I also received kind encouragement from her sister, the late Sadie Collins Armin, and other family members, including a great-granddaughter of Catherine Sager Pringle, Elizabeth Sullivan, and her husband, Jack Sullivan.

Perhaps the one person who worked hardest on this book besides me was Jack Winchell of Whitman Mission National Historic Site, who guided me to historic locations and answered countless questions, particularly regarding flora and fauna. Thanks, Jack, you're a good help and a great friend. Roger Trick, Chief of Interpretation and Resource Management, June Cummins, and Cecelia Bearchum, all of Whitman Mission National Historic Site, offered valuable assistance. Another Whitman Mission employee, Marjorie Williams, a Native American raised in the old ways, kindly supplied many facts about Native American life, both before and after the white man.

People who helped in other ways were as follows:

Financial assistance: Robert W. Shields.

Location research assistants: Heidi and Grace Hotson Shields and the infamous rented car; Klara Shields; Ruth and Frank Younce and the late, great *Snuffleupagus*; Steven Kent Richter, navigator Stinky, and the good ship *Rocinante*; Sharon Maxwell; Bob Gray. Allan Lloyd and Dan and Melinda Allen deserve credit for getting me un-lost at South Pass.

Before the Second Edition, Laura McAnulty acted as faithful trail guide on a fascinating expedition which included Cole and Billee Reed, M. J. Crutchfield, and myself, to what we believe is Naomi Sager's grave site. Rex McAnulty, an Idaho old-timer, knew its location, way out in the hills by the now-dry Pilgrim Springs. It was the most exciting of all my research trips.

Readers: Dr. Don Ross, my Creative Writing teacher at Washington State University, encouraged me to start the actual writing after three years of research, and offered much good advice and a shoulder to cry on.

Dr. George T. Watkins, Professor Emeritus of American Studies at WSU, himself an Oregon Trail student, offered a number of well-taken suggestions.

Ruth and Frank Younce and Cathy Ensley also gave excellent, specific advice. Other readers were: Jack Winchell, Celista C. Platz, Nancy and Sherry Laib, Heidi and Jim Dull, Grace Hotson Shields, who also proofread, Dr. John R. Jameson, Joanna Lanning, Stuart Maxwell and his daughter, Sharon, Bob and Darbie Yates, Frank DeAbreu, Darlene Rima, Bonnie Anderson, Kara Bohlman, Doris Chaney, Denise Blankenbeker, Clif Jackson, Steve Carlson, and Sharon Himsl.

For the Second Edition, Maurice Brett, an Oregon Trail expert, who has flown over the trail and photographed it end to end, read *Seven for Oregon*, noting the slightest deviation in minutest detail. Thanks to him, Pacific Springs has been restored in these pages to its proper place, 2.7 miles west of South Pass, rather than thirty or forty miles down the trail. Where I picked up this piece of misinformation, also pointed out by George Watkins, I don't know. Mr. Brett also corrected minor errors regarding dates and distances.

Sources of information: My main sources were Dr. Clifford M. Drury's *Marcus and Narcissa Whitman and the Opening of Old Oregon*, in two volumes, Erwin N. Thompson's *Shallow Grave at Waiilatpu: The Sagers' West*, and *The Whitman Massacre of 1847* by Catherine, Elizabeth, and Matilda Sager, published by Glen Adams. Harry M. Majors's notes in the back of that book were most helpful.

Using primary sources listed in these three books, I discovered other primary sources in the archives of Eastern Washington State Historical Society, Spokane, Whitman Mission National Historic Site, and Washington State University. Most of my research came from books, magazines, and microfilm in Holland Library, Washington State University, Pullman.

Many of my sources were from Penrose Memorial Library, Whitman College, Walla Walla, Washington. The curator of the Eells Northwest Collection, Mr. Lawrence L. Dodd, was kind enough to let me examine Sager letters and other archival materials. Jim Rice, the Walla Walla Community College librarian, assisted my research.

The Oregon Historical Society in Portland, and the Oregon State Archives in Salem, also supplied information on various subjects. Besides these are newspapers, historical societies, and individuals too numerous to mention.

My little computer, Maximillian Macintosh, sat up late many nights, is faster, warmer, and more companionable than any typewriter, and best of all, smarter and more efficient. He set *Seven for Oregon*'s type and his friend, Big Mac, did some of the artwork. Without them this book would not have been finished, much less published, in time for the Whitman Sesquicentennial year, 1986. Now the Second Edition is ready in time for the Washington State Centennial in 1989.

I owe something to Netta Sheldon Phelps, author of *The Valiant Seven*, and Neta Lohnes Frazier, author of *The Stout-Hearted Seven*, for their influence.

Last—and perhaps not least—I must thank Honoré McCue Willsie Morrow. Her falsification of the Sager story has kept up interest in the real story, and my annoyance at the false stories which Mrs. Morrow started goaded me on to complete my work.

Cornelia Shields

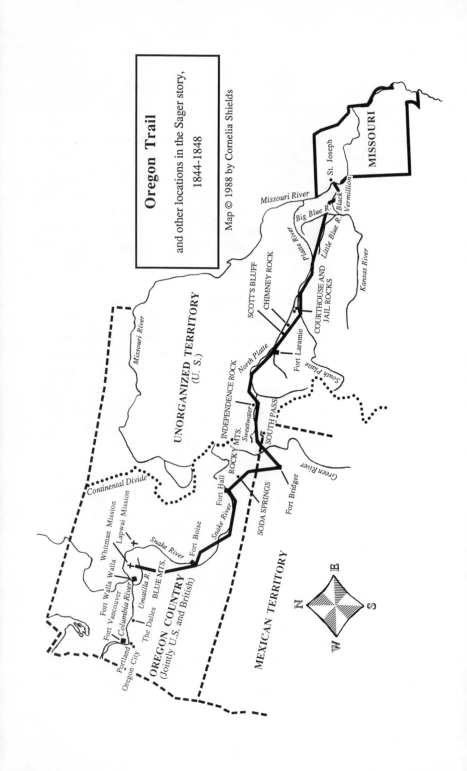

Oregon Trail

and other locations in the Sager story,
1844-1848

Map © 1988 by Cornelia Shields

Marcus and Narcissa Whitman's mission, Waiilatpu, in 1847, drawn by S. M. French under the direction of Elizabeth Sager Helm. The buildings are, from left: emigrant house, gristmill (in back, between the mill pond and the Walla Walla River), blacksmith shop, and mission house.

THE WHITMAN MISSION IN 1847

DRAWING BY S.M. FRENCH, ca.
IN 2-1947, 20574

ONE

The cool early morning wind rustled the ashes of dead campfires, gusted against rain-dampened tents and wagon canvas, whistled between dark, wet wheel spokes, shaking off the last raindrops, and broke free to soar over the wide river.

For days, wagons had crossed, leaving river and woods behind, rolling on to vast, empty prairies. A long line of wagons stretched back, moving ahead one by one as fast as the ramshackle ferryboats could row them over the Missouri.

In the darkness, one thirteen-year-old boy lay awake, hot with anticipation of the journey. John Sager almost set his blankets afire in his impatience to journey down the Oregon Trail. He heard the wind, still carrying the damp chill of the night's spring rain, blowing over the great sleeping camp. If only it would blow the sun over the edge of the sky. Today his family would cross the Missouri!

He thought back to the fall of 1842, two years before, when his parents began deciding to travel to Oregon.

One night as they talked of where to settle next, Pa said, "Texas. Now there's a place we could go. Hear tell it might be a state pretty soon." He could hear Pa's voice, see Pa and Ma sitting in front of the cabin fireplace. Logs popped, and John smelled wood smoke, saw firelight casting gold on Ma's light brown hair.

Pa leaned forward earnestly as he spoke, but Ma caught none of his eagerness.

"If we must go somewhere, let's go to Oregon," she answered. "I've heard so much about the healthful climate. Could be it'd do me good."

Her children listened intently. She worked on a piece of netting, and John felt a coldness in his heart as he noticed, not for the first time, the paleness of her hands. The flickering fire's warm glow could not lend

1

them enough color. Ma was not as well as she should be, and he felt sad and uneasy hearing her talk of her health.

"Oregon is a great place for farming...but we could stay in the states. I'd settle for Illinois." His last words lacked conviction. The Sager family, almost to the smallest, knew of Pa's excitement about the wagon trains trekking to the vast unsettled lands of Oregon Country, a wilderness jointly claimed by the United States and Great Britain, which had not negotiatied a boundary.

A few whites lived in Oregon, trappers, traders, and missionaries, of various nations, but most of its people were natives, called Indians by the whites, living in tribes. American farmers anticipated the U. S. government would soon donate land in Oregon, offering farmers land to encourage American settlement, and already hailed the expected free land as their promised land. "Oregon fever" was an epidemic, and ever-restless Henry Sager was one of its worst victims, but concern for his wife's health now made him hesitate.

"No, Henry." Ma did not pause in her work. "I want to go to Oregon. I feel sure I will grow strong and well in the Willamette Valley." She glanced up in momentary assurance, then back down to her netting. John wondered if she meant it, or if she spoke to please Pa.

"Oregon is a place I'd like to go, Naomi," said Pa slowly. "That rich farm land will either be settled by free Americans or fall to the British as another possession. The United States will claim its share of Oregon one day, and the first settlers will have the best choice. But it's a long, hard journey. Texas or Illinois would be a shorter trip."

Ma laid down her netting and looked at Pa. "I'm willing to go through the journey. It's worth it to enjoy the blessings of land and health."

Later, though, when she thought the children were not listening, John heard her tell Pa, "I don't think I can make it through."

"Don't say that, Naomi," Pa said. "You'll be fine. Everything will be."

Pa's plan of emigrating to Oregon became definite in February 1843, when a tall man dressed in fur, buckskins, and a buffalo overcoat rode through Missouri on his way east. He was Dr. Marcus Whitman, an Oregon missionary since 1836. Rushing through, he paused briefly to urge families to emigrate to Oregon, passing out a handbill describing its wonders, insisting families in wagons could make the overland journey, and the wagon train must start west at the first peep of grass.

Though they did not actually see Whitman, Henry and Naomi Sager saw his handbill many times. Better-educated than most frontier settlers, they were called on to read it repeatedly for neighbors who could not, until they memorized every word. After this glowing praise of Oregon from Dr. Whitman, who had actually traveled and lived there, Pa's mind was made up. He wouldn't have stayed in Missouri if he'd been nailed down. Marcus Whitman was a household name. He would join the 1843 emigration as a doctor and guide.

So they planned to emigrate to Oregon in the spring of 1843. But shortly before they were to leave, John's next to littlest sister got a white swelling on her leg. John felt a sinking inside him when Pa soberly examined the leg and said, "We'll have to give up going until she's well." John hankered so badly for the excitement of the long journey across the wild lands, for the arrival in Oregon, where Ma could be strong and well, it was an aching inside him.

All summer long, and through the winter, Pa worked to cure the little girl's leg, consulting his prized medical book. Henry Sager was practically a doctor, with his knowledge of healing with roots, barks, and herbs, and his knack for pulling teeth with a snacklebar or a turnkey. Rarely did one break, and hardly ever did the patient's jawbone crack. Usually the tooth came right out. Wherever he moved, Pa soon had a well-respected medical practice. Besides his medical knowledge, he was a legally acting Justice of the Peace back in Ohio. He had even performed his own wedding ceremony. The frontier needed learned, accomplished people.

By the spring of 1844, with his little daughter well, they were on their way to Oregon. Now they were camped at Capler's Landing, about twelve miles northwest of the tiny new community of St. Joseph. Today, May 14, they would cross the Missouri.

Thinking about the trip, John could no longer lie still. He crept out of the tent and, guided more by the mud smell and sound of rushing water than by the almost nonexistent light, made his way to the river's bank.

The Missouri River was their last link with their old life. John, filled with a fearful excitement, could hardly wait to see the other side. His blood pulsed strong inside him, matching the river's surging.

He stood among the bushes on the bank, close by the rushing water. In the cold and dark he smelled the sweetness of budding branches and sensed new life springing all around him. A delicate lacework of crisp new leaves brushed his cheek.

The rain that fell through the night had let up. Most likely the day would dawn clear. The black torrent raced past him into dark unknown regions. Behind him, the dim sound of voices and clatter of cookware told him the camp was waking. Realizing he was chilled clear through, he headed shivering towards the tent.

His brother Frank, who at ten was almost three years younger than John, was awake and ready, though his curly brown hair was still tousled. "You been out this morning and didn't take me!" he pouted, looking at John with wide, accusing bright blue eyes.

"Just took a little walk, that's all," said John, smiling. He tweaked one of Frank's curls, and Frank swung at him. John was glad to have straight brown hair like Pa's, though unlike his Pa he had no beard.

Now two of their sisters, Catherine, nine, and Elizabeth, six, stepped shivering from the tent into the early-morning chill. Elizabeth was running a comb through her fine, straight, light hair and saying, "You think you can have everything first, Katie. Just 'cause you're older!"

Here the sun isn't up and already they're scolding like a couple of birds, thought John. The two girls looked a lot alike—same kind of hair, same gray-blue eyes and delicate features, and now, similar scowls on their faces.

"Oh, for mercy's sake, Lizzie," Catherine snapped. "Just hurry up with the comb. I ain't got all day!"

At this last remark, Pa, a powerfully built man of medium height, with a large broad nose, appeared from nowhere, as John knew he would. "Catherine, what was that I heard?" He never called them "Katie" and "Lizzie," even when he was not angry.

Catherine glanced fearfully at her Pa, then stared at the ground. "For mercy's sake?" she whispered.

"You know that's very bad to say."

"Yes, Pa."

"Do you know why?"

Catherine took a deep breath. "Because we should be thankful for God's mercy, and not take it in vain."

"That's right. Now, if you ever say that again, I'm gonna have to give you a lickin'."

Catherine looked up with round, frightened eyes. "I'm sorry, Pa. Seems like I hear it so often since we been in camp, I plumb forgot."

"Well, you shouldn't, because God never forgets." He turned to the boys. "Francis, get the tent ready as soon as those girls are out."

John pulled rough branches and twigs from beneath the wagon, where he and Francis had left them to dry. He took the ax from the wagon's side and split the kindling, placing it in the ring of stones that had held last night's fire.

After shaving thin, dry bark into a fuzz with his knife, he took a damp rag—most everything was a little damp after these rains—and poured powder on it from the powder horn. Then he struck flint and steel together over the rag and tinder to create a spark. Before long, a campfire blazed.

Matilda, his four-year-old sister, came out of the tent and tugged on Catherine's skirts, begging her to help her get ready. Hannah Louise, the two-year-old, whose pet name was Louisa, was close behind. They looked much like their sisters, though Matilda's features were slightly thinner. If not for their different heights, one could hardly tell them apart.

"John," said Pa, "you help me."

In the wagon, Ma was securing things for the crossing. She moved slowly because she expected another little Sager very soon. John rushed to help her with everything. She set aside enough flour and bacon to cook the morning's slam-johns and sowbelly, and corn meal for mush. The rest of the provisions must be carefully packed away with the sugar, dried peas and beans, and other food supplies the wagon carried.

"You make sure my box of dishes won't rattle around now," said Ma. "It won't do for even one to break before we reach Oregon."

"Don't worry, Naomi," said Pa. "We already packed sacks of flour around it, and the forty yards of rag carpeting you wove." The carpeting was canvas-wrapped to keep it clean. Ma had wrapped her treasured camphor wood chest in an old quilt to prevent scratches.

They had to find secure places for the bedding, Pa's tools, the cooking things, the clothing, and Ma's sewing basket. Small items such as combs and brushes went in pockets sewn inside the canvas wagon cover. Things which could be hung, drinking gourds and such, dangled from hooks attached to the wagon bows. Pa's gun, which must always be within quick reach, was slung through cloth loops attached to two wagon bows.

Ma anxiously gave directions, making sure nothing was left behind, and John and Pa helped by moving things into place. They had all the corn meal, flour, and other foods they would need for the long journey, for no settlements were between here and the Willamette Valley, only a few outposts at which to lay in supplies, where prices would surely be high. That was why Ma bought dishes before leaving. They had Pa's gun to hunt fresh meat. John looked at it all and thought they had done proud. They were ready to cross the prairies and the plains beyond, to meet with anything that might happen on the way to Oregon.

The sky lightened. Dimly John could see the streak of river, with smudges of trees and brush on its banks. White mist steamed off the water. He knew the sun would rise faster if he pretended he was not interested in whether it showed itself. Smells of cooking corn meal mush, slam-johns, and sowbelly tempted his nose. Eating warmed his center, when all around was chill.

Frank and the girls kept up a merry chatter which John hardly heard. The sun hesitated at the sky' edge, then a clear red light showed in the east. It poured through John, starting with the top of his head and spilling down till it filled his boots, giving him strength for the long day ahead.

Several hours later, when it was near their turn to cross, Pa yoked four of his six oxen to the wagon and they drove to the river. John and Frank drove the cattle with neighbors who had come along to help, and kept their eyes wide open to all that was happening around them.

People hurried among the trees, raising a clattering racket while making last-minute preparations for the crossing, packing their wagons, which were not the massive, bowed Conestogas with arching covers at either side. Wagons meant to cross the rugged Blue Mountains in Oregon Country were light and square. Canvas covers rising straight from the wagon beds to curve over the top shaped them like treasure chests.

Near the river, little boys ran shouting, older ones acted important at their chores. Little girls stopped playing to help their mothers. The bank was a colorful moving mass of people, wagons, oxen, and a good helping of horses and mules. Here and there a dog ran barking and was roughly called back by its master.

Several long, flat ferryboats skimmed the water, bringing the wagons to the opposite side.

Not everyone there was going to Oregon. Some came to help drive stock and say good-bye to friends.

People on the bank wept openly. Those staying wept at the loss of friends, those going, at the thought of leaving everything for a long and uncertain journey. Watching them, John was sad for the first time since starting the trip.

Little children wept for fear of the mighty river which rushed by as if to sweep them away. A cool breeze from the water washed over those on the bank. Louisa, the youngest sister, ran crying to Catherine, the oldest, who held her, trying to look brave.

John looked at the roiling, muddy, foaming water sucking twigs and trash in its wake. The wet fur of some drowned animal bobbed to the surface momentarily, then was lost. He wondered if soon he and his family would be wet and drowned, but would not show his fear in front of Frank, who was grinning like anything. That boy seemed not to have sense to be afraid most of the time.

"It's our turn to cross!" cried Pa, watching as a ferryboat neared them. "Round up the girls!"

John shooed the girls into the wagon. The sisters wore crisp new matching dresses and aprons Ma had made. The younger ones hardly ever had new dresses, usually wearing hand-me-downs from the older girls or cut-down dresses of Ma's. They had plainer clothes for trail wear, but on this special occasion of leaving for Oregon, Ma wanted the family dressed in its finest. The girls looked fresh and clean in their new dresses and sunbonnets, while the boys wore coarse baggy trousers, new homespun shirts, and close-fitting short jackets called roundabouts. The colors were natural-looking earthy browns, yellows, and blues, since boughten dyes were expensive.

The dresses and pants were long, covering much of their bodies to protect from the blistering sun they would encounter on the trail. With the boys wearing wide-brimmed hats and the girls wearing bonnets, only their hands and a little of their faces showed. They all wore shoes, a luxury usually reserved for winter, all presenting a handsome picture.

Mrs. Sager, also wearing a fine new dress, held back tears as her friends embraced her, saying good-byes and presenting small gifts for the journey. The Sagers had been in Missouri for six years, after leaving Ohio when John was seven. Naomi Sager did fancy work for some of these women, wonderful netting and embroidering, besides reading and answering neighbors' letters, and teaching Sunday School.

As Mrs. Sager said good-bye to her friends, Catherine and Elizabeth leaned out the back of the wagon, chattering to several children whose folks were not going to Oregon.

St. Joseph, though it had only a few houses, was the first town the Sager children had seen. Six-year-old Elizabeth could not stop talking about it. "When we were in St. Joe, a man with a cookstove let Ma cook a meal on it. Maybe we'll have our own cookstove in Oregon. Bet you wish you were going," she said.

"Suits me fine right here," her little friend answered. "I don't know why you have to go."

"We just have to, that's all."

As the ferryboat docked, the girls wavered between fear and excitement. "It will be just like having our own little boat," Catherine told Elizabeth. Ma climbed into the wagon and made sure the canvas was drawn tight, leaving only a small hole at each end. John could hear the girls giggling, and Ma telling them to sit still.

After paying the ferrymen, Pa drove the oxen to the bank and unhitched them. He would swim them across with the cattle. John and Frank helped Pa and the other men push the wagon on to the ferryboat, then block the wheels securely so the wagon would not roll.

The ferryboat was a big, flimsy raft, which hardly looked sturdy enough for one more crossing. John and Frank stood on its creaking boards as their Pa's friends left the boat. The boys looked across the wide stretch of river. Sun glinted off the brown surface. Above the water, birds skimmed a perfectly blue sky. Small and far away on the opposite shore, people, cattle, and wagons moved west.

Three ferrymen would row them across. Two stood at one end of the boat, holding long, thin oars called sweeps, while the third stood at the other end with a sweep to serve as rudder.

Seeing that John and Frank intended to ride on the ferryboat instead of in the wagon, Pa said, "Take care you don't fall over the side!" and was off to see about the cattle.

With a lurch the ferryboat was on the river. As the boat heaved and creaked, John fixed his attention on the folks on the far bank. *They made it over, so can we.* The ferrymen swore and spat into the dirty brown water swirling around the boat. The trees on the opposite bank were small and far away. Then the spring breeze ruffled the water's surface, bringing the earthy smell of the river to his nostrils. John took a deep, satisfied breath.

A trampling and bellowing and splashing sounded on the bank behind them. John knew Pa and the other men were driving the cattle into the river. He tried to look, but the wagon blocked his view.

Frank ran towards the back of the boat.

"Hey! Watch whatcher doin'!" yelled one of the men.

"Frank!" John called. The space between the wagon and the edge of the boat was narrow, the railing low, the current swift, and Frank might easily be pitched over the side.

He barely caught himself by grabbing one of the wagon's wheels, and made his way more slowly to the back of the boat. "Here comes Pa and the others with the cattle!" he called jubilantly.

"That crazy kid," said one of the ferrymen. "He'll get hisself killed one day, see if he don't."

John looked away. Frank embarrassed him sometimes.

The opposite bank drew closer. Now they were safe. When the wagon was off the ferryboat, and Ma and the girls were out, they all watched Pa and the men drive the cattle to shore.

Ma looked at the camp on the other side of the river, and John saw her eyes mist up. "Say good-bye to the state of Missouri," she said. The State of Missouri—the United States—was separated from them by a vast expanse of water. They were now in wild country...Indian Territory.

John wished to comfort Ma. She was always so brave, it did not seem right to see her cry. In dread he remembered her words to Pa, "I don't think I can make it through." He opened his mouth to say, "We'll be all right, Ma," when Frank leaped high in the air and yelled, "Say hello to Oregon!"

TWO

The next morning, John was awakened by Pa gently shaking his shoulder. "John, you'll have to look after the family for a while. The cattle have gone back over the river."

John nodded sleepily, and when his Pa had gone, took over as head of the family, ordering right and left. If Frank or the girls dared to talk back, John answered, "Pa said I was in charge while he was gone."

Elizabeth went whimpering to Ma, who gently said, "John, I'm sure when your Pa said to look after the others, he didn't mean to boss them." Actually, Ma was in charge. John was ready to obey her orders. But for the most part, he enjoyed his power for all it was worth.

All that day and the next, wagons ferried across the river. Wagons, people, and stock moved past the Sagers' camp in the steadily falling rain, and still Pa did not return. The first night, wagons were still near the Sagers, but the second night, they were alone.

John worried as darkness approached. It was one thing to head the family in the midst of a camp, but another thing alone—especially at night, in the dismal rain. Not wanting the others to know how he fretted, all he said was, "Them cattle must have scattered all over the place. Put up the supper things, Frank."

"Put 'em up yourself," Frank muttered as he gathered them up.

The rain-dark sky grew darker. Bedding down in the tent with the others, John smelled the soaked earth and damp air and heard the falling rain, and the roar of the river beyond, never resting, always moving on— like Pa. He wondered if Ma was scared, all by herself in the wagon. But no, Ma was hardly ever scared.

Pa would be miles away on one side now, the other wagons miles away on the other side. John settled into uneasy sleep.

Late the next day, he heard Frank calling, "Oh, good, here comes Pa!

Now we don't have to be bossed by John anymore!"

John ran to the river bank, feet squishing on the wet ground, waterlogged britches clinging to his legs with each sloshing step. He peered through the curtain of warm rain at the men and cattle ferrying across.

"Oh, good," John mimicked Frank. "I'm glad not to have to look after you any more. Feel sorry for Pa, though." Water sprayed as Frank punched John's shoulder.

"Guess where those pesky cattle ran," said Pa when he joined them. "Clear back to the cabin where we spent last winter!"

The neighbors who helped drive the cattle camped with the Sagers that night. The next day, the men crossed the river in a drizzling rain.

"Let's get rolling," Mr. Sager said. "We got to catch up! Did John take good care of everyone while I was gone?"

"Tolerable, I guess," his wife replied.

The wagon ground through mud, miring once in a quag. John and Frank had to help Pa unload the dishes and other heavy things, yoke up with the four oxen the two whose turn it was to rest, and push. *So this is how our journey will be,* John thought, straining against the streaming end of the wagon, with the crosspieces pressing into him. For the next six months they would lean against the wild elements, and the elements would lean back, trying to crush them.

The wagon budged, and with a muddy sucking and splashing, they were rolling again. Shivering, John helped Pa and Frank reload. It was time to plunge farther into the wilderness.

At Wolf River, many Iowa Indians waited, with two canoes lashed together, charging the emigrants to be rowed across.

John stared curiously at the red men. He did not often have a chance to see Indians. They were a pure wonder. Hairy buffalo robes circled their waists, and bear claw necklaces fringed their necks. Their bare shoulders and dark faces were streaked and striped with red paint.

Red-painted hair thistle-tufted the tops of their heads. Many bound their heads with bright cloths. Beads like long narrow seeds were strung end to end, joined in circles. The bead circles, about the size and shape of ears, were strung through little holes punched in the sides of their ears, till the beads sticking out most hid the ears.

Catherine peeked from the wagon. "Ain't they a sight?" John quickly shushed her, not wanting to rile these wild-looking men. However, they seemed peaceable.

Pa paid them, and so many Indians helped the wagon across that they all got into each other's way. John thought they would never cross, but at last the wagon was safely on the opposite bank.

John was not the only one frightened by spending almost three days away from Pa and the other wagons. Although she had not said much, nine-year-old Catherine worried that Pa would not come back, or he would not come back in time.

She felt better when the wagon was moving, with Pa outside, walking with the oxen in the rain, while Ma sat on the bedding with Catherine and her sisters. The boys walked behind to keep the cattle from straying. It was safe and comfortable with all the family near, but one question still worried her.

"Ma," she asked, "we'll catch the other wagons, won't we?"

"Sure. Your Pa knows what he's doing."

Catherine leaned out the high front to call to Pa, "Reckon we'll ever catch the other wagons?"

"Why, naturally!"

"But they must be way ahead of us! Suppose they go to Oregon without us?"

Her father squinted at her through the rain. "Don't borrow trouble, Catherine. We'll catch them by night traveling, so don't you fret none."

Catherine was not used to riding in a covered wagon. The continuous, loud creaking of the moving timbers grated her ears and the cramped quarters made it hard to breathe. After hours of the wagon's rocking and screeching, her head felt swimmy and her stomach shifted around.

Rain on the wagon canvas caused a smothering mustiness. A cool smell would be bearable, but the warm showers made the odor unendurable. "Ma, can't we roll back the canvas and let in a little fresh air?"

"No, Katie. It would let the rain in." Soon the other children felt so sick that Ma opened the canvas in back, so anyone could lean out to vomit.

They traveled far into the night, camping in the road. Though wet from driving the oxen and cattle, Pa, John, and Frank felt better than those who had been shaken about in the wagon like cream in a churn.

It was a joyous moment when they spotted in the distance the group of canvas-topped wagons. Many men had gone to the nearby Great Nemaha Sub-Agency, where Sacs, Foxes, and Iowas lived, for blacksmithing. Pa decided to go, too. The children, excited by their first glimpse of Indians at Wolf River, begged to go with him, but he laughed and said, "You'll see plenty Indians soon enough."

Pa, an expert blacksmith, could do most anything well. Neighbors back in Missouri remarked, "Henry Sager can make anything from a figure-four trap to a sawmill." He had made everything in common use but a saddle, and they believed he could make that if he set his mind to it. He would make everything for the new home in Oregon—furniture, and a loom and spinning wheel for Ma.

"Since Pa's such a good blacksmith," Elizabeth mused, "do you think he could make a cookstove?"

Ma laughed. "I doubt that, but knowing your Pa, he just might try."

The blacksmithing done, the wagon train set about organizing. As Pa told John, the wagons had to be divided into companies. If they traveled together, the stock would not have enough grass.

Each company must elect officers. The Sagers were in the company of Captain William Shaw, Henry Sager's good friend. Henry Sager was elected a colonel, for the company was organized like an army, in case of Indian attack.

"I never saw such a crowd in all my born days," John told Frank. Their neighbors in Missouri lived far apart, and large gatherings were rare. This Oregon-bound throng was a sight. Their company alone had three hundred and twenty-three people in seventy-two wagons drawn by four hundred and ten oxen. The loose stock was one hundred and sixty-three cows, one hundred and forty-three young cattle, fifty-four horses, and forty-one mules. Mules were more expensive and ornery than oxen.

Whenever they had time, John, Frank, Catherine, and Elizabeth had games with the other children. They ran, laughing and shouting, between wagons and tents, skirting campfires, having the time of their lives.

Commanding all the companies was one general, Cornelius Gilliam. Frank howled with laughter at the name. "Some people think my name is funny, but I'd a heap rather be called Francisco than Cornelius!"

"That's why they call him Neil, and we call you Francis or Frank. I'm glad I have a regular name," said John.

At four a.m., the guards on duty fired their rifles. Then everyone rose, scrambling to get ready. The wagons were divided into eighteen platoons of four. Each platoon headed the column in turn, but any wagon not ready in time had to go to the rear. This made little difference now, in the rain, but would make a big difference on the plains, where wagons raised a powerful dust. No one wanted to develop the habit of tardiness.

The caravan traveled from early morning until late afternoon or early evening, resting at noon. The wagons rolled beneath rainy skies, through gray, treeless, grassy country, then stopped to graze the cattle. The oxen and the large cow column moved so slowly that the train made only about fifteen miles in ten or twelve hours' travel. Twenty or twenty-five miles was a good day's travel.

In the evening, they tried to camp near a river or creek, with water, wood, and grass. One of the men marked out a large circle, then rode the circle, the wagons following. As each came into position, the driver unyoked the team, turning them out to graze. Then the men used the yokes and chains to fasten each wagon tongue to the rear of the one before it. The last wagon perfectly completed the circle.

Catherine never failed to marvel at the strong barrier the seventy-two wagons created, protection against Indians, prowling wolves, or whatever danger might threaten.

After the men and boys set up camp, they drilled, at sundown sounding the drum to call out the guards. Catherine felt shivery at the thought of Indian attack, but safe knowing Pa, John, and Frank were there, the guards standing watch each night, even in the almost constant rain.

On May 22, when the Sagers had been with the wagon train only three days, Indians from the Great Nemaha Sub-Agency raided in the night, stealing a number of cattle and horses. The men of the wagon train pursued, recovering the cattle, taking six of the Indians' cows to replace six the Indians had butchered. The horses, however, were not to be found, so they took fourteen Indians as prisoners.

Returning to camp, the men learned the horses had wandered away from the Indians by themselves. Catherine thought that now they would let the Indians go, but they did not. Some boys from the wagon train wanted to kill the Indians and burn their village, but cooler heads prevailed, and the Indians were freed.

Catherine could not understand why those boys were so unfair to the Indians. Although she feared them a mite, she felt they should be treated as well as anyone. Several nights later, as the family sat down to supper around the campfire, Catherine blurted, "Pa, what will the Indians in Oregon be like?"

"What do you mean?"

"Well, first those nice Iowas at Wolf River all crowded to help us, then other Indians stole the cattle. So I wonder what the Indians in Oregon will be like."

Pa laughed. "Those Iowas at Wolf River weren't all so eager to help us. They were eager to be paid for helping us, and to hurry us through their country. Stealing the cattle was part of the same thing. They want payment from whites who cross their country."

"How about the Indians in Oregon? Will they want payment, too?"

"They'll be paid. The government will make treaties to decide which lands will be for the Indians and which for whites. Then everyone can settle without worrying."

It sounded simple, but Catherine was not completely satisfied. "I still don't understand why we're moving to Oregon."

"To farm, silly!" said Frank.

"But we farmed in Missouri, didn't we? Why must we go clear to Oregon to farm, Pa?"

"It's a father's job to decide what is best for his family. Little girls need to obey their parents, not wear them out with a string of questions." His tone was friendly, though, and, his point made, he continued, "Missouri was settling up too much, and besides we could barely make a living there. Folks like us live by our own sweat, and can't compete with slaveowners, who live by the sweat of others. I'll neither own nor be a slave, but in Oregon there will be no slaves, and we'll all start even."

In a few days, the children were over their wagon sickness. John and Frank were usually out, either driving the oxen or helping men and boys herd the cattle.

On the evening of May 29, the clouds lifted, and the sun set clear and yellow in the west. Catherine and Elizabeth were glad. They wanted to run and play, not be cramped in the wagon all day listening to the rain.

The next few days fulfilled their wish. The company stopped by a branch of the Nemaha river, about ninety miles west of the Missouri crossing, to dry rain-dampened provisions and build a bridge so the wagons could cross.

The country was unlike anything Catherine had seen. Back home, trees towered over the cabin. On the prairie, a little bit of land hung suspended beneath an enormous sky. As far as she could see, fresh, rain-washed green grass sparkled in the sun, waving in the wind. Only the trees by the river were taller than herself. The prairie's hugeness and the feeling of having nowhere to hide sometimes sent her running back to the shelter of the wagon, where Ma was.

Evenings after drill and supper, before the guards were called out, people sat around campfires, singing and talking. Fiddles made a lively sound. Folks danced, laughing. As darkness moved in, the wide, empty sky could no longer be seen, but was always felt. Catherine and Elizabeth loved wandering from campfire to campfire, standing at the edge of a circle of happy faces, but they must always be back when the drum sounded to call out the guards.

On May 31, the wagons crossed the bridge and camped on another branch of the Nemaha. That evening, Catherine and Elizabeth were nearing their wagon when an older girl, from the Page family, blocked their way. She had smallest Sagers, Matilda and Louisa, by the hand. "Your Ma says you're to come with me," the Page girl said.

Catherine did not understand. "Ma says we're always to be back when the drum sounds. If we're not, we'll catch it."

"Not tonight," said the girl shortly. "You're coming to my wagon."

Catherine stood first on one foot and then the other, not knowing what to do.

"Come on," said the girl in a tone allowing no nonsense. She headed towards her wagon, holding Louisa and Matilda's hands.

"What's going on?" cried Elizabeth. "Where are you taking us? Why can't we go to Ma?"

"She says you're to stay with me," the girl repeated. "Your Ma expects that baby any minute."

THREE

The girls' patience was near an end when Pa came to tell them they had a new little sister named Rosanna Sager. The boys, finished herding for the day, were with him.

"Mother and baby are both fine. Let's go tell everybody there's a new Sager!" said Pa.

Wading through the downpour, they stopped at wagons and tents with the news. Accepting folks' congratulations, the children grew merry, until one man who saw them wrote in his diary that night that there was a frolic in Mr. Sager's family.

The next day they met their new sister. Rosanna was red and blotchy, but Ma and Pa said she was beautiful. "None of you looked any better when you were born, and you turned out all right," said Pa.

Elizabeth admired the tiny hands that seemed too small to be real, while Matilda looked on, smiling shyly. Only Louisa was completely unhappy over the new baby. She howled until Catherine carried her from the wagon, and it was some time before she calmed down.

Ma was weak, but the other wagons advanced, and they must catch up. When they joined the others, Ma felt so ill the train waited a day. John worried as she lay on the bedding looking frail and sickly, drained and peaked, but Ma smiled and told him she only needed rest. On the morning of June 3, she was better, and the wagons moved westward again.

One evening a few days later, Catherine and Elizabeth sat wrapped in a blanket near the fire. They did not notice the blanket corner in the flames until it caught. The girls leaped up, entangled in the blazing blanket.

After a blur of screaming and flailing, the blanket was stripped off them, and Pa was stamping out the flames. "Well," he said, as the girls stood, shaking, before him. "What will you be into next? I guess I'll have to sleep in the tent with you kids from now on."

On June 7, they camped by the Black Vermillion River, where it set in to rain till it seemed to many in the emigrant party that only they and Noah's family had seen such a deluge. There was no way to cross the river in the downpour. After six days, the river overflowed its banks, forcing the wagon train back nearly a day's journey.

At night, Catherine lay between sodden blankets, listening to water trickling through the tent, thinking longingly of the dry corn shuck tick and soft covers she had shared with her sisters back in Missouri. She tried to think what a nice bed they would have in Oregon, instead of how wet and miserable she was now. She tried to be glad the rains were warm and not cold. Sometimes it worked.

The sun never shone to dry saturated belongings. Rain fell steadily, for ten days. The emigrants were restless at the delay. John heard mutterings of, "We could have reached and crossed the Black Vermillion June sixth, if the general hadn't held the whole train back because his daughter was sick," and, "Best to move every day, no matter what. A day's delay slackens folks. We've got to be across the Blue Mountains in Oregon Country before snow flies."

Since they were going nowhere, the emigrants explored the surrounding countryside. John and Frank rambled over grassy prairie, through ironwood and cottonwood thickets, Frank, having begged the use of Pa's gun, hoping to flush out game. Shooting at flocks of passenger pigeons flying southward, he wondered why they flew south in June.

"Most likely they're just flyin' a mite south, to find food. They are the beatin'est ones for gobblin' up everything in their path," said John.

The beautiful dark gray birds, their long necks tinted delicately pink, filled the sky, wings drumming thunder. Frank brought down a few, and Ma made pigeon pie.

John was content to enjoy the land's beauty and his own freedom to roam, away from his daily round of chores back in Missouri. He never cared much for killing, and in this beautiful country was even less of a mind to shoot critters. Two red deer Frank scared up were too fast for him. A few turkeys also escaped. John was secretly glad when Frank missed.

Rain still poured on June 17, but on June 18, the Black Vermillion was low enough to cross, using cottonwood canoes the men built, while others swam the cattle over. Captain Shaw's company, in which the

Sagers traveled, crossed the Black Vermillion that day, reaching the Big Blue's banks on June 21. The men hunted up canoes built by the previous company. After that, they could only wait for the river to recede. It was June 23 before Captain Shaw's company could cross.

The Big Blue was a sight larger than the Black Vermillion, and more dangerous, its swift waters unmerciful. Pa helped other men cross his wagon and theirs on canoes, while young unmarried men swum the cattle. John and Frank were too young for this dangerous task. In the best crossing place, funnel-shaped eddies as large as barrel heads swirled the surface.

After their wagon crossed, John and Frank watched the men swim the cattle, holding to strong oxen for support. The boys watched in horror as one man lost his hold, swept into a suck hole, and whirled in helpless circles. John's heart pounded as he seemed to feel the panic of being pulled under, having his breath choked off.

Spinning, the man bobbed into another eddy, his hands waving frantically above the water, searching for anything solid. An ox swam by, and John prayed for him to reach it. A moment later, holding to the ox, the man made it safely across.

All the cattle crossed finally, with no drownings, though it was a close call for many. Two days later, someone found in a thicket the bones of a traveler not so lucky. John went to see. The skeleton lay stretched on the damp, leafy ground, bits of mold clinging to its stripped bare bones, lonesome and forgotten. Nearby lay a broken arrow.

Several men stood looking at the dead man. "Go back to yer cows, boy, and quit yer gawkin'," one told him.

"Ain'tcha gonna bury this poor feller?"

"Could be. It's none of your lookout."

John looked again at the unknown, neglected bones, then turned from the damp thicket's shadows, chills coursing through him. Every day he realized more what a dangerous journey they were undertaking.

Ma and Pa both caught bad colds. Henry Sager was coughing, sometimes running a fever, but he would not complain. Oregon waited, so he hitched up the oxen and moved on.

On June 30, after another week's travel, the company camped by a river. Much discussion arose as to whether it was the Republican fork of the Kansas. The sky was clear, sunny enough to air and dry provisions and clothes. Catherine breathed freely the fresh, clean air, after being almost choked with damp.

That night the moon and stars shone bright. The children, bedded down in the tent, were startled by a shot. "Indians!" Catherine yelled. Her little sisters jumped up screaming. John and Frank tumbled from the tent. Pa rushed by, holding his gun.

Amid the camp's uproar, Ma was calling for the girls. Catherine picked up Louisa and took Matilda by the hand. "Come on, Elizabeth." Catherine lifted Louisa to her mother in the wagon and helped the others in. They huddled together, shivering, as the uproar died down.

When Pa and the boys returned, Ma asked what had happened.

"Oh, some young ladies were taking a moonlight stroll, and a guard thought they were Indians," said Pa.

"They weren't hurt, I hope?"

"No, no one hurt. That guard was scared half out of his wits, though."

"*We* weren't scared, though," said Elizabeth.

"Oh, you were so," said Catherine.

Each day John saw more prairie life. Often while following the cattle with the other boys, he saw an antelope, or two or three, on the horizon. No deer appeared since the two Frank scared up by the Black Vermillion. Deer showed themselves usually in early mornings and late evenings, but antelope, deer-like, pronghorned creatures with light brown backs, white throats and bellies, and spindly legs, stood boldly in plain sight, even at midday.

Antelope knew it was nigh impossible for hunters to shoot them. One only had to move toward an antelope, and it was gone. Those spindly legs carried them across the prairie faster than a bird's wings. They looked at the boys with stupid, pleased expressions in their dark brown, bugged-out eyes. Hunters managed to bring down one or two, and Pa was one of the few skilled enough to succeed in hunting the swift beasts.

The wagons were in tallgrass country now. The cattle relished the high grass and rushes, and it was a chore to keep them moving. They were not supposed to stop and eat until the end of the day. The boys yelled, slapping the cows' flanks, and after a while the lazy beasts plodded off, lowing complaints. Some cattle bullied others, and often one or more took it into their heads to wander, and had to be driven the right way.

The oxen were steadier than the pesky cattle in some ways. Once started, they would go on and on, if something did not stall them. Starting them was the problem. Henry Sager owned three yoke, or six oxen. Two were steady and well-broken, four young and unruly. He hitched four to the wagon while two rested. When it was time for the well-broken ones to rest, he had all sorts of trouble.

One day in early July, when the wagons were restarting after their noon stop, Mr. Sager's team refused to move. He tried everything short of lighting a fire under them. He had to start or lose his place in line. Other wagons lumbered by, chains jingling. Henry's face was turning red when his friend William Shaw, captain of the wagon train, offered to help.

First helping the mother and children from the wagon to a safe distance, he gathered a handful of stones and lit into the oxen, slinging stones, shouting in a voice full of authority. Thinking the team would bolt, Mr. Sager ran to his family, but Captain Shaw did not budge. Knowing they had met their match, the oxen soon were ready to travel.

Sally Shaw, the Captain's wife, came to Catherine as she and the others were about to climb into the wagon. "There's no need for you children to ride in the wagon all the time," she said. "If you try, you'll find you can walk many a mile in comfort."

Mrs. Shaw seemed kind. Catherine looked to Ma, who nodded, smiling approval, so Catherine said, "We'll try it." Soon she and Elizabeth found Mrs. Shaw was right. Sometimes they took Matilda, or even Louisa, on their walks.

Pa was nicest about stopping the wagon, since he was best with the oxen. John and Frank grumbled, but that was all right as Pa usually drove.

The girls rode in the wagon when tired, or in wet weather, though rainy days were scarcely more pleasant in the wagon than out. When they could, they enjoyed walking beneath the huge bowl of sky, looking for birds, rabbits, wild flowers, or anything interesting along the trail.

Often a billowing gray sky hung above, threatening to deluge the wagon train. Sometimes the threat was carried out in a sudden downpour.

On July 4, the train stopped to rest the cattle. Men hunted and women washed clothes—at least those who were strong enough did. Ma still felt weak, staying in the wagon much of the time. Mrs. Shaw, or "Aunt Sally," as the children now called her, and Nancy Morrison did the Sagers' wash, with Catherine helping.

Three days later, the wagon train reached the Platte River. Its tree-fringed sand islands were a gladsome sight after miles of prairie, causing the travelers to whoop and shout. They were nearing buffalo country, but had not sighted buffalo yet. They would be able to use dried buffalo droppings, or chips, to start their campfires, but until then they had to carry wood, gathered by creeks and rivers, in the wagons.

Looking at the Platte's shallow, shiny brown water winding between gold-brown sand bars, they made terrible jokes. "It's a mile wide and an inch deep." "Too thick to drink and too thin to plow." Noting the amount of mud in the river, Frank told Catherine, "I wanted a drink, so I took my knife and cut out a piece."

Elizabeth's seventh birthday was July 6, the day before they reached the Platte. She was learning much about the prairie. The first day they camped on the Platte's banks, she ran to Frank and Catherine shouting, "Oh, come look! It's just like in the Bible!"

Following her, they found a scattering of dry, bleached bones in the grass, not human bones like Ezekiel saw, but bones of all kinds of prairie-dwelling animals.

The children wandered beneath the cloudy, blue-gray sky. As they left the camp's clatter behind, prairie silence surrounded them. The wind played a mournful tune through the skull of a long-dead buffalo, blowing in through the eye sockets and out the jagged nose.

Delicate antelope skulls lay amid a confusion of arched white ribs and long, smooth leg bones. A skull with curved yellow incisors might have been a small rabbit or large rat. Elizabeth lifted a buffalo skull, holding a horn in each hand.

A broken strand of beads strung through the grass was a rattlesnake's skeleton.

"Listen," said Frank, beating a buffalo skull with a leg bone. It made a hollow sound in the blowing stillness.

Catherine shivered. "Oooh, Frank, don't."

Frank thumped a few more times and dropped the leg bone. "Lookee here! A coyote skull! It's perfect, with all the teeth and everything. Oh, I have to keep this!"

"Ma will never let you keep that old coyote skull," said Catherine. And she was right.

Three days farther along the trail, when Elizabeth was walking alone, two streaks of fur sprang out of a hole in the ground right beneath her feet. One chirped and jumped back in the hole, while the other sped off, lost among the grasses.

Before long she saw another standing on its hind legs, peering at her. Two others stood on all fours, watching intently. Slowly she crept up on the brownish-yellow animals, which looked like squirrels, except for their skinny little tails. These creatures were curious by nature as well as looks, for they let her approach almost near enough to touch them, seeming as interested in her as she was in them. As she closed in, however, they chattered and ducked into the ground.

She found the spot where they vanished—a hole with a dirt mound around it. Though she waited and waited by the opening, the little animals did not understand she meant them no harm.

She ran to tell Ma what she had seen, not asking Pa to stop the wagon. The children were practiced enough to hop on the tongue and scramble up the front, using the crosspieces as hand and foot holds.

Ma was resting with baby Rosanna cradled in her arms. "Ma, I saw the funniest squirrels! They live in the ground, but I guess they have to without trees."

"Why, those were prairie dogs."

"They seemed like squirrels."

"They are called dogs for their bark."

Then of course Matilda clamored to see the prairie dogs. Pa stopped the wagon, because she was too little to jump in and out like Catherine and Elizabeth. He had warned the older girls several times to be careful.

Elizabeth and Matilda found Catherine, and the three spotted a whole prairie dog town. They decided the prairie dogs did not so much bark as make a sharp chirp, almost like a bird. The girls loved watching and listening, though the strange little animals did their disappearing act when they drew too near.

FOUR

John, walking alongside Pa, helping drive the oxen, thought what a blessing the sun's heat was, after he had been so soggy for the last two months and three hundred and seventy-five miles that he thought he would never dry out. They still had sixteen hundred and fifty miles of travel, or thereabouts, to reach the Willamette Valley.

July 11 was nice and sunny, one of the first such days since beginning the journey. The column of wagons, cattle, and horses moved beneath a clear blue sky, the wagons following, when they could, two faint tracks left in the grass by last year's passing wheels. This was the Oregon Trail, but some called it "Burnett's trace" after Peter Burnett, a leader of the 1843 emigration.

An excited cry sounded ahead. The word, "Buffalo!" jerked John's gaze sharply forward. Several miles in the distance, a brown river ran up a rise. A solid moving mass of buffalo covered the green and tawny earth.

"You drive the oxen," Pa said, all fired up, voice charged with the same excitement John heard in the other voices sounding the cry from wagon to wagon. "Camp with the others." He was off for his horse and gun.

Other men saddled their horses in desperate haste. Each grabbed his gun and rode toward the buffalo, whooping and yelling.

Their fever caught John as they galloped by. Fire raced through him, while his heart beat hard and fast with the hoofbeats. This was his first buffalo sighting. He longed to ride with the men, to run with the vast herd across the prairie. But he must stay with the slow, creaking wagon, making sure the lumbering oxen did not stall.

The sun was low in the sky and the wagons were camped in a cottonwood grove on the bank of the Platte when Pa returned. John and Frank had set up the tent, and waited anxiously by the campfire with the girls. When Pa rode up, they rushed to him.

"Did you see lots of buffalo?" Elizabeth demanded.

"Did I see lots of buffalo? Hundreds, I guess. It's like looking at the sky and trying to count the stars."

"Never mind how many there were," Frank burst out just as John was about to speak. "Did you get one?"

"Ever know me to miss?" Pa was too happy to take account of Frank's rudeness. "Want to see it?"

"Oh, yes, yes, Pa!" the girls clamored.

"Whoa, there. You won't all fit on my horse. I think you little uns should stay with your Ma while I take John and Frank."

The little girls looked unhappy, but knew better than to contradict their Pa.

Pa, John, and Frank rode through the evening shadows to a brown mound jutting from the tawny grass: the buffalo, the hugest beast John had ever seen. They dismounted to look at it. Thick, black hair as shaggy as a bear's covered its head and front legs. Brown wool covered its shoulders, and short, smooth brown hair the rest of its body, down to the black tassel end of its tail. The sinking sun struck golden highlights on the still form, glinting on the wickedly curved horns.

Bloody froth matted the hair around its nose and mouth, and dried blood pooled beneath its gashed throat, darkly staining the grass stems. For a moment John was saddened that a rifle ball could bring down so majestic a creature.

Frank was all smiles. "Do we gut it now, Pa?"

"No, no. Gutting one of these things ain't as easy as gutting an antelope or a deer. It will take strong men and maybe a horse to pull the skin off."

John looked across the prairie in the dying light. As far as he could see were other dark mounds with small men clustered around them.

"More were killed than what you see," said Pa, noting John's gaze. "Over twenty, they say. We spread out a good bit during the chase. No one was thinking, I guess. But we have a lot of good meat for the journey. Come on, let's get back to camp. We'll need wagons to haul this meat."

The men gutted the buffalo, but no one returned with wagons, because on the way back after the gutting, a thunderstorm blew up. The men struggled back to camp through torrents of rain and gusts of wind.

The next morning, a thick white fog clung to the ground. Pa left Frank with the cattle. Aunt Sally and Mrs. Morrison could see to the family while he and John and the group of men and boys brought wagons to haul the meat.

Before they reached the first buffalo, a ghostly figure rode from the fog. "Go, back, it's no use!" it called. The group of men, boys, and oxen ground to a halt. The ghostly figure moved closer. It was General Gilliam on his horse. "The meat's spoiled," he told them. "Every last bit."

"Spoiled?" cried Pa, amidst shocked murmurings. "How can that be? We gutted them last night and left the skins on."

"The beasts were run in the hot sun all day, then left to lie. The meat's neither fit nor safe to eat."

Heavy silence settled upon the group. In the thick fog, John heard the creak of ox harness. Someone coughed. At last a man spoke softly. "How many thousand pounds of meat, all gone to waste."

John's heart went down as the sun had last night, dwelling on the dark mounds lying on the prairie.

"I guess we have something to learn about buffalo, besides they're easy to shoot," Pa said at last. "God forgive us."

"Amen," someone murmured. John said nothing, but felt ashamed for himself, and all of them.

When they returned, a cool breeze blew through the camp, chasing the fog. With it blew a hot wind of confusion and discontent. Some wanted to move on, saying enough time had been lost. Others wanted to stay and kill buffalo to make up for those spoiled. All were unhappy. Most of the complaints concerned General Gilliam's behavior.

At the word "buffalo," he lost his head. Calling a few orders to no one in particular, he flung himself into his saddle, leaving cooler-headed individuals to find a camp.

After much argument, those who wanted another day of hunting won out. This time the men brought in the meat soon after killing the buffalo, and cured it on scaffolds suspended over buffalo chip fires.

That evening, when the general called a meeting, John and Pa stood among a shifting, uneasy group. Some were sullen, some angry. No one wanted to be under General Gilliam's orders any more—a man who would rush unthinkingly towards waste and destruction.

Colonel Simmons, second in command, resigned, refusing to share responsibility with the general any longer. The general, still clutching at the power rapidly slipping from his fingers, called, in his most authoritative voice, for another election.

When it was over, and Jacob Hoover stood in Simmons's place, General Gilliam's wife and daughter helped him climb unsteadily on a barrel, where he surveyed his audience with a scowl. "From this moment on," he boomed, "no one is to leave camp without my permission. I'll hang upon the nearest tree the man who dares to leave the company." His hand shot up in threat, almost causing him to lose his balance.

A man named Daniel Clark rode by, calling, "If any of you men or boys intend going to Oregon, come on, I'm going." John laughed with the others.

"That's all the sense he has," said General Gilliam. Yet many in the company could not have crossed swollen streams without Daniel Clark's expert help.

Two days later, General Gilliam's brother-in-law went hunting without permission. At this, the general said, "They may all get to Oregon as they can, without me. I'll have nothing more to do with them."

His statement brought great relief. Now each captain headed his own company. Captain Shaw—Uncle Billy—led the Sagers' train. Captain Morrison's train traveled near them. They started as soon as possible after rising in the morning, depending on how long it took the boys to round up cattle scattered during the night.

A week after the buffalo hunt, the wagon train crossed the South Fork of the Platte. Mr. Sager had put a yoke of young, unbroken steers in the lead. Shortly after crossing, Catherine, inside the wagon, heard him yelling at the oxen, and leaned out to see what was happening. The oxen were headed toward an embankment, and Pa was trying desperately to turn them. Ma called for her to get back in the wagon.

The next moment, the world turned over. Catherine tumbled like cream in a churn, now hitting her elbow, now banging her knee. The contents of the wagon rumbled and flew. Rosanna gave one awful cry.

The wagon settled with a sickening lurch. Catherine lay in the half-light, quiet, hearing the cries of the others. Then, light: Pa was tearing off the wagon cover. From beneath a pile of bedding and a scattering of combs and brushes, pots and pans, she peered into his anxious face.

Other men gathered to help, one by one lifting the children out. Catherine, Elizabeth, Matilda, Louisa, even baby Rosanna were all unhurt.

Catherine's dress was torn off, leaving nothing but the waist and a strip hanging behind, but she was too worried about Ma to be embarrassed. She called, but Ma did not answer. The men were clearing things off her. Pa lifted Ma from the wagon. She did not move as he carried her toward the tent the other men were setting up.

"Come, dear, I'll help you find another dress." Aunt Sally had appeared from nowhere. The young man who had pulled Rosanna from the wagon stood holding her awkwardly, and Aunt Sally took the baby, thanking the man. "Help the others set the wagon up," she told him.

"But...Ma," said Catherine. "Will she be all right?"

"No one knows yet," she answered quietly, then turned to Elizabeth. "Sit down over there, and hold the baby carefully while I help Catherine find another dress." She took the four younger girls a little distance from the wagons, keeping an eye on them while she helped Catherine find and change into another dress.

As she pulled her arms through the sleeves, Catherine noticed for the first time that she was shaking. *Please, God, let Ma be all right,* she prayed. *And let none of the dishes be broken. Ma will feel bad if they are.*

Aunt Sally took the three younger girls to Mrs. Morrison, but Catherine and Elizabeth begged so to see Ma that Aunt Sally consented.

The wagon was upright and the men were repacking it. Pa came out of the tent. A streak of blood ran across one cheek.

"You're hurt!" Aunt Sally exclaimed.

"No." Pa shook his head impatiently. "That's just where the bows scraped me when the wagon went over. It's Naomi who's really hurt. She hasn't come to."

They entered the tent in a whisper of canvas. Catherine felt a cold pain in her heart, seeing Ma lie so still on the blankets, so pale, not moving at all. She looked to Aunt Sally.

"Get me something to wash her face with," Aunt Sally said, and Pa went.

He returned with a basin of water and a cloth, and Aunt Sally stayed by Ma a long time, gently washing her face and hands, while Pa went out to help repack the wagon. Catherine and Elizabeth sat, not speaking. Catherine wondered if she looked as frightened as Elizabeth, whose eyes were round and wide.

After a long time, Ma stirred and moaned. Her eyes shifted as if not seeing, then settled on Catherine. "Katie?"

"Yes, Ma?" said Catherine in a small voice.

"What happened? Where's your Pa?"

"The wagon tipped over, Naomi," Aunt Sally explained. "The men are reloading it."

Pa peered into the tent. "Naomi! Are you all right?"

"I'm well enough to go on, Henry. I'll get real strong in Oregon, you'll see."

The land stretched on in endless monotony. Once, when the company rested by a cool sweet stream flowing between shaded green banks, where wild roses sweetened the air, a place of unearthly beauty compared to the flat emptiness, four-year-old Matilda asked, "Is this Oregon?"

The others laughed at her. "It's a long hard haul yet, till we reach Oregon," Pa said.

They left the lovely hollow behind to travel across the prairie. In the cool morning hours, bird song filled the air. Meadowlarks perched on stalks of weed, making clear, warbling music.

"Their songs are a sight prettier than the larks out east make," said Ma. The birds looked a lot alike, with brown backs patterned light and dark, brilliant yellow breasts, and black V-shaped collars, but the western ones sang sweeter.

Squeaks and rustles sounded as ground squirrels, brown-and-white prairie chickens with orange neck sacs, and other small animals, scurried through the grass. The plain brown ground squirrels were like smaller, cuter prairie dogs. Catherine liked best the tiny ground squirrels with light brown stripes running the length of their dark brown bodies, and dots in between the stripes. She thought they were some of the prettiest creatures God ever made, and longed to stroke their soft fur.

The grass was shorter in this part of the country, it being drier than the tallgrass country. During the long, hot day, ground squirrels, antelope, and prairie dogs could be seen. Butterflies lit on round purple clovers, and fuzzy bumblebees weighted the blossoms. Many other animals hid during the hot hours.

In the evening, vesper sparrows sang of the day's closing. Owls and nighthawks skimmed the air, great wings outstretched, talons searching prey. Owls wanted juicy mice and gophers, but nighthawks craved insects. Coyotes howled high and shrill. Later at night, wolves sounded their deeper song, rich with authority and power. The animals continued an ancient life-and-death cycle visible from the wagons, but completely removed from them. To step away from the wagon train was to step into a vast quiet world with its own rules and concerns.

Out of sight, making themselves known only when they wished, the Indian tribes, another vital part of this land's nature, marked the wagon train's passage. Through this vast wilderness, the wagon train stretched, as thin and fragile as a spider's gossamer web, a tiny thread in the fabric of an infinite land. Had the emigrants vanished, the cycle of owl and prairie dog and coyote would flow on as if the aliens trekking over their land, with their worries about delays and supplies and snow in the mountains, had never existed.

Nights were cool, downright cold if it rained, days blazing hot. Sometimes a hot afternoon cooled, wind blew, and thunder rumbled. Catherine enjoyed the cool wall of air and first wet sprinkles, hoping the main shower would not hit. "Seems like it's 'most always too hot or too cold out here on the trail," she told Elizabeth.

Rainstorms were different out here. A long way off, they bruised the sky dark blue. Lightning zigzagged, thunder rolled, then rain pelted. The sun could be shining and rain falling, sunlight sparkling on the drops. Had someone told her such a thing, she would not believe it, but now she had seen for herself.

As she and Elizabeth walked beneath the endless empty blue sky on hot days, they saw big, stringy jackrabbits, or smaller, fluffy rabbits bounding through the grass. Sometimes a hawk winged overhead, hunting rabbits and ground squirrels. Day-flying hawks were not satisfied with insects. Yellow sunflowers on fuzzy stems, petals like bright sun rays, turned always towards the sun.

On July 25, Court House and Jail Rocks, two massive bluffs of clay, sandstone, and limestone, loomed in the distance. The sight of any rise was an occasion in this flat country, time to note progress made. They had traveled nearly five hundred and twenty-five miles since crossing the Missouri. Slowly, day by day, they were shortening the distance between themselves and Oregon.

The atmosphere was thin and perfectly clear, without a bit of haze, yet the strange air muffled sound. A rifle report a short distance away made a small pop, but its smoke could be seen for miles. The air smelled wild and lonesome.

Since judging distance was impossible when able to see forever, it was little wonder that at first sight of the tall spire of Chimney Rock, several men and boys thought they could reach it speedily. They returned late, saying it was miles away.

Chimney Rock was on the horizon for days, first as a thin line, then a reddish-tan column rising from a cone-shaped hill, as the wagons moved closer. The long finger pointing at the sky amazed and delighted Catherine, who felt a sense of loss the first day she could no longer see it.

As they moved farther into the wilderness, the grass grew shorter and scarcer. It was later in the season, and they were moving from prairie to plains.

Scott's Bluff was most wonderful. Oddly-shaped, sand-colored hills and ridges rose from desert-like earth, not quite white nor yellow nor brown, nor any real color. Winds had line-sculpted their sides, ringing the wide bases, circling the strange little caps on top. Set against pale delicate yellow-greens, with hollows of soft gray and pastel blue, the hills seemed unreal, a dream that would melt if looked at directly. Yet when Catherine looked again, they were still there.

Yucca plants, with dagger-shaped leaves and bulbous seed pods lined with grasshoppers, spiked the ground. Elizabeth found the first prickly pear cactus. Catherine wanted to bring the little spiny plant to Ma, but after trying to pick it, decided it was best left alone.

From a distance, she and Elizabeth sometimes saw a rattlesnake sunning itself, or slithering across the ground. Catherine learned not to mind the rattling she heard if she walked too far from the wagons. It was all right if she watched where she stepped.

The rattling, which might have been snakes or insects, was one of the few sounds away from the wagons during mid-day. She walked at a distance as much as she could, because of the dust they raised. She tried walking fast, to make her own breeze, hoping if she walked fast enough, the sun would not light on her long enough to burn, but it always did. With each step, grasshoppers fountained, snapping their wings as if annoyed.

The way through the odd sand hills was at a place called Robidoux Pass. After that came endless stretches of boredom when she saw nothing new or interesting. At these times, she had nothing to think about except how hot the sun was, how much her sunburn would hurt come evening, how thirsty she was. Then she fell to thinking about their new home in Oregon.

She saw a comfortable little cabin, Pa plowing, John chopping wood out back, Francis herding the cattle. She saw herself feeding chickens, Ma sitting by the door sewing, the little girls playing in the yard. She saw Ma's dishes in the cupboard Pa would make. Maybe they'd even have a cookstove. These visions became more real than the hot, dry, dusty air, the sun and the insects stinging her skin.

On the last day of July, the travelers nooned in a beautiful grove on the North Platte. After resting an hour, they left the river, moving over a level sandy plain covered with short, thin, dry grass. A few white, wispy clouds hung in the vast blue sky.

As the wagon clattered over the trail, Catherine climbed on to the boxes serving as a front seat. Looking down, she saw the wood and metal of the wagon tongue rattling close above the ground's bright glare. Holding tight to the wagon's front, she eased herself over the crosspieces and down on to the tongue, ready to leap free of the wheel.

Preparing to jump, she held to the wagon front with one hand, feeling the wagon tongue's hot metal and scratchy wood vibrating beneath her dusty bare feet, the shaking itching her legs. Dust went up her nose, making it itch, too, and her hand gripping the top of the rattling wagon front itched.

Something tugged at her dress, and she half-turned. Pa kept tools fastened to the wagon, and her dress was caught on an ax handle. She tried to pull herself free so it would not hold back her jump, lost her grip on the wagon front, and felt her feet slip from the tongue.

Her stomach contracted in fear as the ground rushed at her. The ax handle swung her in front of the wagon. Landing face down, she felt the shadow of the turning wheel the moment before it passed over her.

She screamed as the metal rim bit into her leg. Pa stopped the oxen before the back wheel reached her, and pulled her from beneath. Catherine had no time to breathe before the oxen bolted. She heard the other girls screaming as the wagon left the trail. With Catherine still in his arms, Pa ran after the wagon.

Looking through a haze of pain, she saw her left leg dangling at an odd angle. Pa saw, too, and put her on the ground. "My dear child," he said hoarsely, "your leg is broken all to pieces!"

FIVE

Henry looked down at Catherine, momentarily forgetting the others. When he looked up, Captain Shaw had stopped the runaway wagon. Mrs. Sager, Elizabeth, and Matilda jumped out to see about Catherine. "Set up the tent," said Henry to the people gathering around, and they did.

Catherine lay on the ground, eyes squeezed tight against the sun's glare, her whole body hurting. At the center of the hurt her leg throbbed in agony. She heard a man say, "Let me see that leg." Expecting more pain, she stiffened.

Henry elbowed the man back. "No! No one touches her leg but me!" In a quieter voice he added, "I have a doctor book and know about these things."

Catherine tried to tell herself Pa would make everything all right. Tears squeezed from her eyes. He carried her into the tent. She tried to lie still. Every move pained her. It even hurt to think.

Outside, the men argued over whether to go back to the river or on to Fort Laramie. They planned to reach the fort by nightfall. Some hated the thought of another delay, others were anxious for Catherine.

Giving the baby to one of the women, Ma sat by Catherine, stroking her brow, speaking soothing words. Racked by pain, Catherine soon lost track of the meaning, but hearing Ma's voice made her feel better.

Pa entered, carrying thin sticks which he kept for splints, and a sheet torn into strips. "I'm going to set your leg. You must be brave, Catherine."

She thought she would be able, but when Pa grabbed her leg to pull the bones back into position, she screamed. He quickly let go, tore a tiny piece from one of the strips of cloth, and wadded it into a ball. "Here. Bite down on this. Then it won't hurt so bad."

It was better to have something to bite on, but still Catherine could

34

hardly keep from crying aloud while Pa pulled her leg into position, binding it with the splint. "There," he said at last, "now I think in a few months your leg will be as good as new."

A few months! Was she not to walk to Oregon? It must be a mistake, but she was too aching and weary to think about it now.

Frank, Elizabeth, Matilda, and Louisa were in the tent with Catherine and Ma—John was still out with the cattle—when Pa came in again. Behind him was a man about his age, wearing a concerned look on his round, good-humored face.

"This is Dr. Theophilos Degen," said Pa. "A man from our train rode to another train for him. I told him I already set Catherine's leg, but he wants to look at it anyway." He looked at the doctor. "Since he came all this way I suppose he might as well."

The doctor approached Catherine, who watched through pain-dimmed eyes. The other children leaned forward breathlessly. Catherine winced as he touched her leg. Clucking sympathetically, he examined the splint with gentle care, then turned to Pa.

"Dot is fine," he said, "it is tchust so goot as I could do it myself."

Matilda and Elizabeth burst into giggles, while Frank stifled his laughter with his sleeve. Though she did not understand what was funny, little Louisa laughed because the others did. Ma shooed the older ones from the tent, and told Louisa to hush.

Outside the tent, Frank and the two girls laughed aloud as the doctor explained, in his funny accent, that he would stay near "in case you vere to needst help."

Frank even laughed at his name. "Theophilos! That's even funnier than Cornelius!"

Dr. Degen left the tent, and when he was gone, Pa, looking stern, confronted the children.

"You hadn't ought to laugh at the doctor," he told them. "He came to help your sister. Anyhow, your great-great grandfather George was from Germany, same as Dr. Degen, and he talked just like that."

"He did?"

"Our great-great grandfather talked like that?"

"He sure did. And since Dr. Degen is helping us for a while, you'll mind your manners."

A short while later, Pa laid Catherine on the bedding in the wagon, and packed the tent. The men had decided to go to Fort Laramie. Pa cushioned her leg with sacks and pillows. "When we get to the fort, I'll make a box for it to ride in," he promised. She gritted her teeth, trying to be brave.

A cheer broke out at dusk that evening as the travelers saw the fort's outlines. Sun-baked adobe bricks formed a rectangle of surrounding walls. Propped up on a roll of bedding, with the canvas pulled back a little at the side, Catherine could see three spiked towers, seemingly built in or near the walls, rising above them. Beyond the fort, hills rippled, soft golden in the fading light.

Except for Fort Bridger, this was the only American fort on the Oregon trail. All the others were British. Neither the Americans nor the British owned Oregon Country, but possessed it jointly.

There was merrymaking that night in the wagon camp two miles west of the fort. Catherine, lying in the wagon, having no part in the revelry, saw dusky light and heard fiddle notes drifting through the openings at the wagon's front and back. Ma and baby Rosanna slept on the bedding near her.

Aching rose in her throat as well as her leg. Tears stung her eyes as she thought, *If only I'd taken more care, I wouldn't be left out now.* She sniffled, feeling miserable and stupid and full of pain.

Pa's hands pulled back the canvas at the wagon's front, and Catherine quickly choked back tears as he looked in on her. Pa must not think she was not being brave. "How you feelin'?" he asked.

She said she reckoned she was doing all right, and asked wistfully what the fort was like. She had longed to see it.

He shrugged, trying to look casual. "Oh, 'tain't much," he said lightly. "There's a trading house and shops, and houses for the traders. I 'spect money's 'most useless there. Why, flour goes for twenty-five cents a pound, and sugar costs a dollar fifty a pint."

Catherine's mouth hung open.

Pa smiled at her amazement. "Guess how much a barrel of flour is? Give up? Forty dollars! Can you believe that? Forty dollars! Lucky we're packin' along plenty to last us. Try an' sleep now. The more you rest, the faster you'll heal."

The next day, August 1, John and Frank were minding the cows when far off over a rise they spotted a cloud of dust. After a while, the distant cloud turned into a band of Indians.

"Reckon they've come to attack?" Frank cried. "We ought to warn the camp!"

"Naw," said John. "Lookee how they're riding all slow like, and in broad daylight, too. If they meant to attack, they'd do it at night. And they wouldn't bring women and kids," he added as they drew closer and he saw women and children riding behind the men.

"What're they up to then? Reckon we could leave the cows?" asked Frank in a breath.

"Well, maybe just for a little while," said John without hesitation.

The Indians rode into camp, magnificent in buckskin fringes. Five men carried banners, which waved in the wind. Here were Indians such as they had dreamed of seeing. Each man, woman, and child was richly dressed. Even their moccasins were covered with beads or porcupine quill work. Beads sparkled, shining twin ladders of polished bone climbed the mens' chests.

Their hair was not spiked and reddened like that of the Iowas, but flowed long and black. Many wore braids. Most men wore a single eagle feather stuck straight up, but a few wore headdresses with slender curving horns, or eagle feathers circling their heads and draping down their backs. These were the warriors of the mighty Sioux.

The men of the wagon train presented them with powder, lead, and tobacco, making speeches of goodwill. Like Frank, they feared attack. The Indians received the presents and speeches with quiet dignity.

One opened a buckskin pouch decorated with bright quills and beads. From it he drew the longest, most elaborate pipe the boys had seen. Sun glinted on the red stone bowl. The Indian slowly filled and lit the pipe.

Several Indians wearing elaborate headdresses, who John reckoned were chiefs, sat cross-legged on the ground, the officers of the wagon train following suit. The other Indians and the pioneers watched as the chiefs and officers of the wagon train passed the pipe from hand to hand, each taking a puff.

John held his breath. The scene assumed a mystical quality, like a story, as ancient as earth and sky, springing to life. The chiefs, the officers, the quiet watchers, all were part of it. For this moment, they were something more than people, they were majestic figures enacting a splendid pageant, its meaning just beyond John's grasp.

When they had all smoked from the pipe, the ceremony ended. The Indians rode away, looking quietly pleased. The solemn mood faded with their going, and it was an ordinary day in camp. John and Frank returned to the cows, eagerly talking of the pipe ceremony, though John avoided mentioning the deep meaning which still eluded him.

Pa had built the box to steady Catherine's leg. The next day the wagons moved west again. With thirteen hundred and sixty miles still to go, there was no time to waste.

"Ma," said Frank one burning August day, "I feel slow and tired and my mouth is all sore."

"It's camp fever," said Ma. "Your Pa and I have a touch of it, too." Ma and Pa had never fully recovered from the colds caught during the long rains in June.

Soon John had the same symptoms. "Camp fever," or "mountain fever," a disease for which the travelers knew no other name, began with a sore mouth. A strong person could recover from it, but often the illness ended in death. One woman already lay by the trail, and another was not expected to live.

Theophilos Degen, the German doctor, offered to drive the oxen, but was of little help. He was worse than Henry at managing them, but Henry, John, and Frank were laid up sick in the wagon, crowded in with the ailing Naomi, baby Rosanna, toddler Louisa, and injured Catherine.

Mr. Sager hired a boy to mind the cattle. He and his boys had to take turns helping the doctor drive, when they were strong enough, and often when they were not. On the larger river crossings, such as that of the North Platte on August 12, the men used dugouts to float the wagons across. Other small streams and creeks had to be forded, which was a trial for Frank when Pa and John were too sick to help. During one crossing, Frank slogged across the sandy bottom, water swirling around him, shouting the oxen along, his throat sore and raw.

With the wagon safely on the other side, his wet clothes weighed him down, and he caught at the nearest ox's yoke to keep from falling. The doctor helped him into the wagon. "Tchust lie down, it vill be all right."

Ma leaned over him, her hand on his forehead, looking pale and worried. "I'm all right, Ma. You're probably sicker 'n I am, so lie down again."

Ma smiled a little. "Ain't much you can do to keep me from worrying. You lie still now."

The boy hired to tend the cattle said he had an awful time heading them away from alkali ponds. Frank went out to see the glaring, salt-looking white patches fringed by dark grasses, surrounding scummy, poisonous pools. If the cattle drank that dark water they would die for sure. That did not keep them from smelling and wanting it. Avoid the water as they would, the people still suffered from the poison. The white patches whipped up into a stinging dust which clung to hair and clothing and burned at the eyes. It smarted their noses and mouths, making them raw and red.

Now they were past grass country and into sagebrush country. Coarse, blue-green, scrubby plants dotted the sand for miles in all directions. On reaching the Sweetwater's banks the night of August 15, the cattle could drink all they wanted, for the Sweetwater was fresh and pure. By that time, another woman and a girl had died of camp fever.

The next day the train passed Independence Rock, a solid hump rising from the sand, with sides looking smooth and slick enough to slide off of, resembling a great scarred gray turtle shell scratched with travelers' and explorers' names. None of the Sagers had a close look. All were too young, or too sick.

The emigrants nooned on the Sweetwater. Matilda begged for a drink, so she and Elizabeth unhooked drinking gourds from their places on the wagon bows and headed towards the river. John and Frank went, too, to see a thing called Devil's Gate, that everyone was talking about. It was only a short walk from camp. They dragged along through the heat as best they could.

Devil's Gate, a sheer rock cliff, was amazing in itself to look at. Even more amazingly, the Sweetwater ran right through the rock, having carved a V hundreds of feet deep, but only as wide as the river.

Frank would normally have joined the children scrambling up the rocks, but felt just about strong enough to look at Devil's Gate and then dip a long, cool drink from the Sweetwater to soothe his aching throat. John, looking about gone in, slurped and gulped cold water from his dipper. Elizabeth drank, too, daintily dipping her hollow gourd into the water. Fresh green grass grew at the water's edge, unlike the dark, coarse stuff fringing the alkali ponds.

Matilda took a drink and screwed up her face in a sour look. "'Tain't sweet at all," she said. "It's just regular water."

Weak as he was, Frank laughed. She looked doubtfully at him, and he said, "They call it the Sweetwater 'cause it's good to drink—not like that nasty ol' alkali water."

Catherine's leg hurt less now. The household goods were shifted so everyone could lie down, or lie propped against something. At night they set up the tent. She found it best to sleep most of the time, waking gummed to the pillows, covered with a thin film of dust that dried her nose and mouth and made her teeth gritty. She shifted so the air cooled her sweat, sometimes sitting up to peep through a gap between canvas and wagon edge.

With Catherine laid up in the wagon, Elizabeth took Matilda out more often. They brought Catherine pretty rocks and pale delicate wild flowers, to try to keep her happy. Catherine liked best the bluebells, and the tiny frail asters with a purple fringe of petals around a bright orange center.

The rocks were like jewels. Glittering white quartz, smooth black basalt, and agates, red or clear, littered the sand. Catherine wished she might go treasure-hunting with Elizabeth and Matilda. It seemed unfair for the younger girls to do things she could not, but it was nice to be surprised by what they brought, too, to hold up to the light, and admire, a sparkling quartz or translucent agate.

At first the girls planned to take all their pretty rocks to Oregon, but once their pockets and sunbonnets were full, the treasure was too heavy to carry, and Ma said rocks would litter up the wagon. So they collected new rocks every few days, leaving the old in little piles along the trail, like jewel caches.

Other little piles now littered the trail—household belongings too heavy for the emigrants to carry. Only the most necessary items could be saved, to make the journey easier on the oxen.

Sometimes on their walks, Elizabeth grew impatient with Matilda, who almost always wanted to go back to the wagon first. Once, after they walked the whole long, hot way back, Matilda sat by Pa and asked, "Why do we have to *do* this?"

Her Pa looked quietly at her for a moment, wondering how to explain to a four-year-old. Matilda looked at him, waiting, and he said, "It's because if a thing is worth doing, it's worth going to some trouble for. Things are going to be better for us in Oregon, and maybe by going now, we'll make things better for others who'll come later. Get some rest now. You'll understand when you're older."

One August day, as Catherine lay half-awake in a sort of daze, she heard a rumbling away off to one side. Maybe it was a storm coming, but it was not a storm sound exactly, and there was no smell of wet dust.

Pa pulled himself up to look out the back of the wagon. A heavy force thundered past, shaking the ground and whipping the canvas, then the sound faded.

"What is it, Pa?"

"Buffalo!" Pa shouted. "Four buffalo just ran by the wagon, and I'm a-goin' to get me one!"

"You're too weak to get out of bed, let alone hunt," said his wife.

Pa would not listen. Catherine trembled as he got ready. Ma was never able to talk Pa out of something he was set on.

As he grabbed his gun, Catherine begged, "Please, Pa, don't go."

"Now, don't you worry. I'll be all right, and bring you back a fine big hunk of buffalo meat."

He left, returning after a long, anxious time. Dr. Degen had rolled back the wagon canvas at the side, so Catherine saw Pa approaching, sitting loosely in his saddle, not tall and straight as usual. The horse's every movement jostled him. As he stopped near the wagon, Dr. Degen stopped the oxen.

"Did you get the buffalo, Pa?" Catherine asked, anxious to hear him speak.

"No," he said in a faint voice, "they all got away." He slid from his horse, collapsing on the ground.

The doctor hurried to him. Exclaiming in English and German, he half-dragged Pa to the wagon and helped him lie down. Catherine kept looking at him as he lay, eyes closed. Ma leaned over him, speaking in soft, concerned tones, and Catherine felt more and more afraid.

On August 23, after nine hundred miles of grueling travel, the wagon train entered South Pass.

"Ma, will the wagon bump when we cross the Continental Divide?" Elizabeth asked.

"What?" Mrs. Sager, worried about her husband, only half-heard her daughter's question.

"I heard Alvira Eads saying we was going to cross the Continental Divide, and that it's a big line that runs all the way down. And I want to know if the wagon will bump when we go over it."

Ma smiled. "No, Elizabeth. It's an invisible line. We won't be able to tell when we've crossed it."

"Oh." Elizabeth was disappointed. "Then what's the use of crossing it?"

"The Continental Divide is where all the rivers and creeks start to run toward the Pacific Ocean instead of the Atlantic. It is called 'the backbone of the continent.' It's pretty near halfway to the Willamette Valley. When we cross it, we will be in Oregon Country."

Now the Rocky Mountains surrounded them, distant blue peaks rising high, cool, and refreshing, far above the parched sand. Spirits ran high as the emigrants celebrated crossing the Continental Divide at South Pass, and continued two miles west to Pacific Springs, the first water flowing towards the Pacific. "Halfway to Oregon!" they cried, and "Atlantic water gone, and Pacific water our drink forevermore!"

The Sagers were quieter than most. Pa was sick. John and Frank were better, but stayed close to the wagon most of the time. The family enjoyed its first drink of "Pacific Water." The children had expected South Pass to be a narrow trail high in the mountains, and Pacific Springs to be a bubbling fount. Instead, South Pass was a gradual ascent through flat country, with the mountains far distant, and Pacific Springs more like a marsh. Was Oregon to be so disappointing, after all?

Ma had all she could do with the cooking and care of the children, so she hired the Page girl, who had watched the children when Rosanna was born, to care for Pa. His stomach pained him, and people took turns sitting up with him at night.

The night they camped at Pacific Springs, the Page girl watched Pa, Catherine, still unable to hobble, little Louisa, and the baby, while Ma walked with the other children past wagons and tents, to where they could clearly view the sunset.

John, Frank, Elizabeth, and Matilda gathered close to their mother. All were silent as they watched the great orange ball sink towards the end of the trail, striking the clouds to brilliant color. Sunset was more beautiful with the blue peaks of the Wind River Range of the Rocky Mountains pale in the distance. The sun melted from circle into half-circle, far to the west, where their journey would take them.

Their mother spoke. "Children, look to the west. That is Oregon. That is where we are going to make our home."

The clouds flamed red in the deep blue sky, fading after a few minutes to pink. Blue shadows covered the pink, and at last a purple shadow overspread the land. The sun winked out beyond the next rise.

They turned. Campfires lit the evening darkness, bits of sun left behind. A fiddle's lively tune sounded lonely from far away. John and Frank hurried to light their fire.

SIX

Elizabeth shaded her eyes to look across miles of light brown sand and pale green sagebrush. The flat land ended in a sharp, clear line in blue-purple distance, so far away it made her dizzy. Clouds glowed white hot in the bright sky. She sighed. Walking was better than riding, with the wagon so crowded, but she grew hot, and her throat dry.

"Lizzie!" She looked back to see Alvira Eads. "Let's walk ahead of the train and find a good drink of water."

Elizabeth was proud to go with Alvira, a big girl, going on sixteen. Water sounded good, with choking clouds of dust rising around the wagons and cattle. The wagons spread out where the ground was flat, sometimes making a trail over a mile wide. They raised even more dust that way, but it was scattered.

Walking briskly, the girls soon passed the slow-moving oxen and their dust. Wagon sounds fell behind, shouts, cracking whips, creaking wheels and jolting wagon beds all lost in silence—the vast silence of the desert, broken only by their voices.

After walking a while, Alvira saw a little coulee. "There's bound to be water up there," she said.

They climbed into hot dry silence, beneath a blazing blue sky, and walked on and on, finding only dry gullies. The more she thought of water, the more Elizabeth's throat burned. Looking at the scorched dry sides of the gullies parched her mouth until she could hardly stand it.

"Well," said Alvira tiredly, "I suppose we might as well go on back to the train." They turned back, but before walking long a terrible realization hit them. They did not know in which direction the train was.

"We're lost," said Elizabeth.

"No," said Alvira, "It's just this way."

They climbed one rolling hill after another, but, as far as they knew, drew no closer to the wagons. They stopped speaking, and when they stood still to rest, deep silence settled upon them.

All around, as far as they could see, spread hot, dry, brown-white ground clumped with pale, scraggly sagebrush, its gray roots cracked and twisted. They could hear nothing. The surrounding silence held only the trace of a wind.

"Well, let's go on," said Alvira just as it seemed the silence would suck the breath from their mouths.

"Look," said Elizabeth after a while. "We must be getting close to the trail. We didn't pass that dead cow before."

Alvira looked. "That's not a cow. That's a bloated antelope."

Elizabeth began to tremble, her insides wobbly. "We're lost, and do you suppose we'll die out here?" She imagined two sets of bones picked bare, gray and cracked like the sagebrush roots.

"Oh, hush." Alvira's voice trembled.

"Reckon there's rattlesnakes out here?"

"Let's not talk about rattlesnakes right now."

"When shall we talk about them?"

"When we're back to the train. Now come on."

They walked till Elizabeth's hot legs dragged as if melting, and she asked Alvira to carry her.

"I'm tired myself. We'll have to keep going."

Elizabeth walked, muscles tight and pinched, till the girls topped another rise and yelled at the sight of white canvas wagon covers sewn with bright patches, crawling along the trail like snails. Forgetting their tiredness, they ran yelling down the slope to their own wagons.

Elizabeth was limping by the time she reached the wagon. "Stop," she called to Frank, who was driving. "I want up."

Frank regarded her calmly. "Wait till the top of this hill," he said as if she were being bothersome.

It was too much. Here she'd nearly died, and her own brother refused to stop the wagon. Elizabeth sank to the ground sobbing.

"All right, all right," said Frank, surprised. "Here, I'm stopping the wagon." He lifted her in. Elizabeth curled up on the bedding and slept.

When Pa got sick, John hoped if they took good care of him, he'd soon be well. But as the days went by, he grew steadily weaker. None of Dr. Degen's remedies helped.

Pa himself was the first to say what no one wanted to believe. "I will never live to see the Willamette Valley," he told them one night as he lay in the tent.

John, shocked, angry, and desperate, had his mouth open to say, "You don't mean that," when he caught sight of Ma's face. Her look told him she had known this for some time. John felt he should do something, but did not know what.

Pa spoke in a trembling voice. "I don't mind for myself so much. But it'll be hard for you all to go on—" His voice broke.

Dr. Degen said, "I look after your family. I take care of dem."

Pa looked at him without speaking, his eyes filled with tears.

John wanted to say he'd help, but no matter how he tried, he could not feel brave and helpful—only terrified and hopeless. He ached as he had with camp fever, only this was not an ache to be cured with rest, or anything John knew of.

August was ending. On the 27th, the wagon train camped on the silent banks of Green River, where it joined the Big Sandy, preparing to cross the next day.

Henry Sager lay in the tent with John and Catherine on either side of him. His wife had taken the other children for a walk so he could rest.

He was awake, eyes bright with tears. John looked at his Pa's face, sweat running in the lines that had deepened these last few weeks. All the comforting words he could think of were hollow, so he did not say them.

Hearing the crunch of footsteps, he looked out of the tent. Uncle Billy stood with his hat in his hands. "Can I see your Pa?" John nodded, and Uncle Billy stooped and entered the tent.

Talking and crying at the same time, Pa said, "I'm passing away, Billy. What is my family to do? My wife is sick, my children small, and one'll likely be crippled a long time."

Catherine took his hand and regarded him with large, serious gray-blue eyes. She had changed since her accident and Pa's illness. No longer the impatient little girl saying, "I ain't got all day!" she hardly ever complained. Riding in pain in the jolting wagon had resigned her to suffering. She frightened John almost as much as Pa did.

Uncle Billy's face lined with sadness as Pa continued, "My family has a long journey ahead. Please, Billy—you're my good friend. See 'em safe through."

"I'll do that, as best I can," said William Shaw softly.

"The missionaries at Whitman Mission might help. Will you take them there?"

"I give my word on it."

Henry Sager seemed satisfied. He looked at his friend and quietly closed his eyes. John held his breath till he saw Pa's chest move a little. Uncle Billy left with the slightest whisper of tent canvas.

Pa opened his eyes and looked at Catherine, who still held his limp, pale hand. His voice trembled as he said, "Poor child, what will become of you when your father dies?"

Next morning the wagon train crossed Green River on a narrow submerged gravel bar. John helped with the perilous crossing. Water rippled, swift and silvery, over his feet as he, Frank, and Dr. Degen, feeling their way through the current, struggled to keep the oxen on the gravel bar. Move a few feet either way, and disaster was sure.

When the wagon was safely on dry ground, John went to look in. Elizabeth looked out through the hole in the canvas, wide eyes dark in her pale face. "Pa's dead." Her whisper seemed unnaturally loud. "He sat up and grabbed the wagon's side and fell back dead." John pushed her roughly aside and looked in.

Pa lay still on his bedding. Ma was holding his hand, crying. Dr. Degen looked in to see if he was truly dead, but John knew he was. He left the wagon, wandering aimlessly until he blundered into someone and looked up through misted eyes to see Uncle Billy. "Pa's dead," he told him.

"I'm sorry. I'll take care of everything," said Uncle Billy, touching John's shoulder.

John did not know how much time passed in a haze. Someone chopped and hollowed a cottonwood trunk, laid Pa in the makeshift coffin, and it was time for the funeral. Ma did not want Catherine moved, but Catherine begged until she consented. Sitting on a blanket near the grave, her bandaged leg sticking out in front of her, she looked serious, solemn.

The men lowered the coffin in a trickling of brown sand. Uncle Billy read from the Bible as the family stood around the grave under the cloudy sky. A cool breeze off the river stirred their hair and clothing, riffling the Bible's pages.

John shivered. Through a mist of tears, he saw the river, the same color as the sky, gray and silvery white, running between banks of silver-green sagebrush. He smelled the coolness of rain waiting to fall.

The ceremony was done quickly. The wagons must move on. John took time to write in the family Bible. After "Henry Sager, born October 8, 1805, in Loudoun County, Virginia," he added, "died August 28, 1844, on west bank of Green River, aged 38 years, ten months, twenty days."

The part about the west bank was important. Pa had crossed Green River, traveling about nine hundred and fifty miles on his journey. He had reached Oregon Country, though he would never see the Willamette Valley. John would always remember he had tasted Pacific water before he died.

He went to look a last time at the freshly turned mound. The lowering sky showed no trace of sun, only roiling clouds, blue, white, gray. Fitful sprinkles pockmarked the loose shovel-turned earth. The wind that blew over the desert with nothing to stop it snatched a spray of dust from the grave and scattered it away.

SEVEN

When he was again able to think, John realized that Ma now headed the family, and he, thirteen-year-old John Sager, was man of the family. Not feeling big enough for the task, he wished it were all a terrible mistake, that he was playing boss until Pa returned, as at the journey's beginning.

The evening after Pa died, he and Ma sat together by the buffalo chip campfire. They had a little time alone because it was plain to the other women of the train that Naomi Sager felt poorly. Women nursing babies took turns with Rosanna. Sally Shaw, Mrs. Morrison, Mrs. Daniels, and others looked after the older children. Mrs. Nichols, who had lost a daughter to camp fever, showed great concern for their health. Almost everyone in the train was willing to do them a favor.

"John," said Ma, "I'm hiring a man to drive the oxen." She now consulted John about decisions as she used to consult Pa.

"Why, Ma?" John asked. "Dr. Degen ain't so bad. He's learning to handle the oxen."

"Maybe so, though he's yet to convince me. But I don't like some of his ways. Your Pa didn't approve of his language."

Dr. Degen cursed in English and German when things were not going well. The oxen in particular raised his ire when they stalled. He was gruff and impatient, but so gentle caring for sick folks John knew his heart was good.

"He's taken mighty good care of Katie," he said. The doctor checked Catherine's bandages regularly for signs of gangrene. If it set in, her leg would rot, and have to be amputated.

Ma stared into the fire, her face lined and weary. "He has been good, but Katie's healing up fine now. Somehow I just don't trust him, 'specially about driving."

49

"Reckon he could do with some help," John admitted, "at least with the driving."

She nodded briskly. "I've already talked to the young man. He'll start work tomorrow. Now all I have to do is tell Dr. Degen."

When Dr. Degen came to ask about Catherine's leg and Ma's health, she told him of her decision.

"I stay by you," the doctor said stoutly.

"There ain't no need, really." Her tone was gentle, but John could tell she wanted to be shut of the doctor. "You've been right kind, but don't worry yourself about us no more."

"No," said the doctor firmly, "I vill not leave till I see you safe in Villamette Valley."

Ma nodded briefly, mouth tight. Even in this time of grief, John had to try hard not to chuckle at the doctor's way of speaking. He was glad Dr. Degen was to stay with them.

The next day the young ox-driver arrived. John took an almost instant dislike to him. He bragged of his exploits on the trail, his hunting prowess, his girl in the train ahead, whom he planned to marry. He was a good driver, though, and Ma seemed to like him.

They reached Fort Bridger on the afternoon of August 30. Already snow covered the peaks of the Uinta mountains to the south, and the cool weather reminded them they faced more than a thousand miles' travel, including the hard road through the Blue Mountains.

Jim Bridger's fort, on the banks of Black's Fork of Green River, the last American fort they would pass on their journey, was built the previous year by Mr. Bridger and his partner, Louis Vasquez. The stockade of logs, set on end and sharpened to points, teemed with traffic of mountain men leading pack horses and mules. Indians, emigrants, and oxen also passed by the gates.

Mountain men and their Snake Indian wives lived in tipis, near which half-Indian children played. Like the Sioux, Snake Indians wore their hair long and black, sometimes in braids. Their clothes were of animal skins, but less elaborate than Sioux clothing.

Mountain men, whites who migrated west to trap and trade, wore long fringed buckskin shirts. Fringes ran down the sides of their buckskin pants. On their heads were fur hats, or wool hats with wide brims turned back. Their skin was rough and tanned, their hair and beards long, coarse, and wild. All carried a gun or two, a powder horn and shot pouch, and at least one big knife at his belt. They bathed seldom. John, who could smell them some distance away, knew he looked a little wild from his long journey, but the mountain men were the wildest folks he had seen. He viewed them with awe.

Plenty of timber, mostly cottonwood and willow, and good thick green grass, surrounded the fort. It had been a while since the travelers had seen good grass or timber.

"They call it Fort Bridger for courtesy," Aunt Sally Shaw, the captain's wife, told John, when she came to collect the family's washing. "'Bridger's shack' or 'Bridger's hovel' would be more fittin'. Why, it ain't in the least like a fort. There ain't so much as a knothole to shoot through."

"It sure ain't much to look at," John agreed.

Aunt Sally took stock of his clothes, as Ma had before falling ill. "I could patch them britches of yours with a deerskin. With three, I can fix your old britches 'most as good as new and make you a deerskin pair besides. Frank needs some, too. You can trade for them at the fort."

John's britches were thin in places, and sprung out at the knees. Clothes meant to last to Oregon had gone to tatters in three months on the trail. Shoe leather bleached, cracked, and flaked away in the sun and alkali. The girls' shoes were outgrown or worn to flinders. At this rate, they'd all be stark bare on reaching Oregon. The children, like others with them, were also dirty, going months between baths. Aunt Sally said the "Great Oregon Migration was more like the great unwashed and un-shaved."

"Yes, ma'am," he said. "Thank you kindly." Here was something he could do as man of the family, and to take his mind off things. Choosing a likely-looking calf from the herd, not too poor to trade nor too good to part with, he led it through the big wooden gate.

"Bridger's shack" would fit the place, as Aunt Sally said. The only buildings were two large log houses connected by a horse pen, crudely built and miserable-looking, with dirt-covered willow brush roofs. John tied his calf to a hitching post and one of the ragged mountain men laughed, "That's some saddle hoss you got thar!"

Ignoring him, John entered the building where Jim Bridger, the mountain man, tall, powerfully built, and sharp-eyed, with features lean and hard, stood behind a counter, trading. A large number of emigrants gathered in front of the counter, offering guns, plow irons, or whatever they had in exchange for Bridger's goods and blacksmithing services.

Bridger traded flour, bacon, and whiskey to the trappers and mountain men in exchange for furs, elk and antelope skins, buffalo robes, moccasins, and other Indian fixings. The emigrants were anxious for these, to replace their worn and tattered clothing.

Waiting his turn, John felt increasingly uncertain. Many of the men offered better things than a scraggly little calf, and did not receive much in trade. Jim Bridger seemed to disdain their offers. Maybe an important man like him would have no time to trade with a young boy. As the moments passed, John's courage drained, until he knew that if ever his turn came to trade with Jim Bridger, he would stand and stare like a fool, unable to speak.

Suddenly not feeling like the man of the family, but small and inadequate, John stole out and untied the calf, oblivious to his surroundings. Misery welled up in him as he tried to think of what he would tell Aunt Sally as an excuse for not bringing the deer skins.

A rough voice startled him. "Ho, young feller! You lookin' to trade that thar calf fer somethin'?" He looked around to see a bushy-bearded mountain man dressed in soiled skins, with a ratty old wool hat on his head, leading a mule loaded with packs.

For a moment John's voice stuck, then he said, "I need some deer skins."

"Well, boy, I can't do it. Deer don't offen happen by hy'ar. I got a nice heap of goat skins on this hy'ar mule, though." By goat skins, John knew he meant antelope skins.

"Those would do fine."

"Well, let's hev a look at yer critter." The mountain man walked around the calf, looking the little animal over, with the corners of his mouth turned down in distaste.

With a sinking feeling, John began to wish he had never started this trade. "You mean to tell me you want good goat skins for this mizzerble, half-starved thing?" the mountain man asked at last.

John looked at the calf. It was thin. The stock had grazed away most of the grass in the country they had just passed through. Ribs showed in its rough hide, and its pelvis stuck out. John swallowed and said, "This calf comes from good stock, and will fatten up real soon."

The mountain man looked disgusted. "How many skins you want?"

"How about...six?" That was how many Aunt Sally had said.

"Six! I can't give more than four fer sech a poor heap o' bones."

"I'll take it," said John. But when the man unpacked the skins from his mule's back, John saw their whiteness and said, "Why, those skins haven't been smoked! Think I'm too green to know the difference?" Unsmoked skins would harden if the least bit of water touched them.

"You sayin' I ain't a fair dealer?" The mountain man leveled a scowl that made John tremble, then drew a long hunting knife from his belt and slowly, deliberately raised it. He began to pick his teeth.

John remembered hearing stories about mountain men, how rough and mean they were. Not wanting to cross one and fall victim to his revenge, he hastily said, "I reckon I know how to smoke a skin. They'll do fine."

He took the four antelope skins, and as he carried them to Aunt Sally, he began to think he had done pretty well. When he handed her his purchase, he was pleased and proud.

His pleasure faded as Aunt Sally held up the skins one by one, her expression growing sadder with each one. "Honey, you've been robbed. Don't you know the difference between good dressed smoked deerskins, and dressed unsmoked antelope skins?"

"Yes, ma'am, but these were all the mountain man had," said John.

"And he only gave you four? I'm afraid you've been taken. I should have warned you not to go tradin' with these wild, hard-drinkin' mountain men. Why, the ones we passed t'other day wanted twenty-five cents a pound for flour. You should have gone to Mr. Bridger or Mr. Vasquez."

Crushed and ready to cry, John wanted to go right back and punch that mountain man in the nose. If only he had not lost his courage in Jim Bridger's trading post. If only he had been brave enough to defy the mountain man.

Aunt Sally smiled and touched his arm. "Don't worry. I'll smoke these and they'll do fine to make you and Frank each a pair of pants.

While I'm at it, I'll get my rag bag and patch the girls' dresses, too."

John and Frank helped Aunt Sally dig four holes, each about two feet across and one foot deep. They chopped wood, burning enough to make a thick bed of ashes and coals at the bottom of each hole.

"Hardwood would be better, but there ain't none to be had here," said Aunt Sally.

Draping each hide over four green boughs propped over the coals, she and the boys added green wood to make thick smoke. Frank and Aunt Sally tended the white skins, turning them until each one was an even shade of brown.

While they did that, John spent most of the rest of the day helping men and boys catch fish from the rocky river bottom, using wagon sheets as nets. They worked long under the cloudy sky, until wind blew and thunder rolled. Damp and chilled, John brought a fine catch of fish to cook over the campfire.

The young man Ma had hired ate till it seemed he would bust. Then he said to Ma, "Ma'am, if you wouldn't mind too much, I'd like to take your gun and go hunting. I'm a crackerjack hunter. Could be I'll bring back an antelope."

John was sure he was bragging. Pa had been able to shoot antelope, but they were too swift for most hunters. He was not sure he liked this stranger using his Pa's gun, but Ma was already taking it from the cloth loops attached to the wagon bows. The young man strode off whistling, the gun dangling carelessly from his hand. They never saw him again.

"He vas no goot, I knew," said Dr. Degen when he heard. "He has gone *mit* dat girl of his in da next train." Looking at Mrs. Sager, he said, "I take goot care of you."

She nodded, looking too weak to protest. Her quiet resignation alarmed John. Ma seemed to fight back a little less each day. The weather was setting in cold. Mornings were frosty, which John knew was bad for Ma. "I want one of you boys to stay by the wagon all the time," she told John when they were alone.

They left Fort Bridger, traveling through the Bear Mountains. On September 1 they nooned high upon a hill, with a grand view of a line of snow-covered peaks, and the Bear River Valley below. The drive down was steep. Mountains of blue, green, and brown, capped with white, rose beyond the valley. Lush blond-green grass covered the valley floor for miles. The pure water of the Bear River wound through the half-dry grass.

"This is Oregon, I know it!" Matilda cried.

"No, it ain't," John told her. "This here's good farming country, but too far away from everything to settle in. We'll tell you when we're in Oregon."

Lying on the bedding in the wagon, Ma told John of her plans to trade the oxen for horses at Fort Hall.

"Is that because horses will plow better?" John steadied himself as the wagon rolled from side to side on the rough trail. He knew a horse could plow clear down a field and be halfway back while an ox worked on its first furrow.

"Partly. And partly because our oxen are wearing out. I ain't sure they can drag this heavy wagon over the mountains. We can pack our gear on horses and ride from Fort Hall."

"But, Ma, you can hardly leave the wagon, let alone ride!"

A determined look showed on Ma's face. "I'll ride, if I have to be tied on. I can't stand much more of this wagon's jolting, anyhow." The determined look gave way to a troubled one. "I don't want to go to the Willamette Valley right away, John," she said quietly. "If we pack into Dr. Whitman's Mission for the winter, I'll have a chance to rest."

"We'll do that, Ma." John tried not to let fear edge his voice. "You rest up and we'll start us a fine farm in the spring."

The Bear River was great for fishing. While Frank stayed with the wagon, John caught two kinds of trout, one with red flesh, and the other white with a delicate flavor. A few were eighteen or twenty inches long. Frank had pretty good luck on his turn fishing, too.

Plenty of game lived along the river's banks. Once a rabbit bounded from a grass clump near John's feet. He did not need to shoot it, since his family had eaten enough, and even if they had needed the meat, he had no gun.

A wheeling hawk swooped from the sky. The rabbit bunched, hugging the ground. The bird winged upward, and the rabbit ran, a ripple of brown fur, until the bird swooped, when it balled tight again. This happened four or five times, as John watched. At last the rabbit huddled for safety in the cover of a sagebrush clump. The hawk rose with an angry scream.

For some reason, a lump came into John's throat. He was glad the little rabbit had escaped. They were all trying to survive, to reach a place of safety.

At Soda Springs, mineral springs of different colors and flavors bubbled from the ground, some gray or brown, others blood red. There were hot springs, warm springs, cold springs, fizzing springs tasting like soda water, others with a metallic taste, and one called Beer Spring.

By putting a tiny bit of sugar in a drinking gourd, then dipping up the soda water, the children made the tastiest drinks they had ever had. John and Frank took turns staying with the wagon. The boy not with the wagon watched the cows, but they found time to run, like Elizabeth and Matilda, trying to taste each spring. They made drinks for Ma, Catherine, and Louisa, but could never seem to reach the wagon before the drinks unfizzed.

Their favorite spring was the cone-shaped Steamboat Spring. Chuffing, chugging, and gurgling, it erupted in a mighty steaming geyser, three feet high. John had never seen such a wonderful thing. Pa would have enjoyed it. It was not too late for Catherine to see it. It was unfair for her to have to stay in the wagon all the time, missing the journey's fun.

When he told her about the Steamboat, she said, "I'm happy enough when the wagon stops, so I won't be jolted for a while. It hurts my leg to have to move."

"Oh, come on. I'll carry you on my back."

Catherine deliberated. "Well...I reckon that would be all right." Reaching Steamboat Spring, they waited for it to blow. When it did, Catherine shrieked with delight and declared it to be more wonderful than Chimney Rock. "Chimney Rock just sits there—it don't explode."

"Kind of reminds me of old Dr. Degen," said John, "the way he huffs and blusters and works himself up until he blows." Catherine laughed all the way back to the wagon.

Beyond Soda Springs lay vast, ancient, lava fields. Drifts of red volcanic rock, lightweight, jagged, and riddled with tiny holes, formed the landscape, with only a few hardy weeds showing through. Although the children's feet were toughened by now, the shards of rock were painful to walk on. This was the first rock they had walked on for any distance, all down the trail. Cold wind whipped over the rocks, lashing the weeds. Oxen and cattle had a hard time, foraging among the bare piles of rock.

The companies were splitting up now, wagons traveling farther apart, no longer camping in a huge circle. At night, each stood aloof, distant, close to its own tent and campfire, shut away from the others. Fiddle notes cried in the evening air. When different wagon trains traveled near each other, arguments arose as to whose company should be first. Always, though, Dr. Degen and the Shaws stayed close by the Sagers.

The weather stayed cold. Five miles from Fort Hall, John caught sight of its white adobe walls. Built on a dry, sandy plain near the Snake River, it was easy to spot. By the time they reached the fort, on September 11, Ma was much too sick to think of trading the oxen for horses as she had planned.

Dr. Degen was busy caring for her, and John had his daily work. The wagon train women could not watch the little ones every minute, and John had his hands full. At first Elizabeth and the younger ones had not seemed to realize that Pa was gone forever, but now they cried for him all the time, pestering John with questions about where he had gone. John got tired, listening to their crying.

Fort Hall was a real fort, surrounded by a high wall with a warped and uneven top. Towers stood on two corners diagonal from each other. Originally American, the fort now belonged to the British Hudson's Bay Company. Inside the wall were the Hudson's Bay men's houses and trading stores, and a two-story blockhouse. The buildings had the same white plastered look as the outside wall.

John wandered forlornly inside the high white walls, which were lined with square little portholes to shoot through. A lot of trading went on, but John had no part in it. After his experience at Fort Bridger, he did not think either he or Dr. Degen should do anything so important as trying to trade the oxen for horses. They might not make a good trade, and his pride balked at asking Uncle Billy. The Shaws were doing too much as it was.

John and Frank took turns staying with their mother. John wondered if the little girls realized how weak Ma was. Catherine must know. The oldest girl, and wise for her age, she rode in the wagon with Ma all the time.

The trail was rough and rocky, threading between dark basalt outcroppings high above the Snake River. Soon after leaving Fort Hall, John heard Ma tell Elizabeth, "Now I know why your father begged to be taken out of the wagon when he was sick. It seems as if it would be easier to die than to stand any more of this jolting."

When John heard her words, he wished desperately to make her better. He could no more do that than fetch her a drink from the Snake River. Far below the wagons, the green water turned the dry weeds and sagebrush a bright green where they touched its banks. But steep cliffs jagged with sharp rocks made it impossible to reach the water.

John, Frank, and Catherine knew Ma had camp fever. *But after all,* John told himself, *Frank and I had it and it didn't hurt us none. If Ma just don't do too much, like Pa....*

Then Ma worsened. She had not been bedridden, though she stayed near the wagon most of the time. She weakened until she could not rise from her bedding, and after a while would speak to no one, talking only of Pa.

They had eaten dust all down the trail, but this seemed the worst. Between the rocks, the thin light brown soil ground to fine white powder. A cloud covered the wagons all day. Aunt Sally hung a sheet before the hole in front to keep dust out, but then almost no air came in. Despite the cold, the wagon was close and suffocating.

Everything in this country was thin, and cold, and dry. The sparse vegetation was burnt yellow and brittle, the sagebrush was parched, and even the sky was dried to a thin cold pale blue. With nothing taller than sagebrush for shade, the glinting sun threw shards of light to hurt the eyes. Looking at the dull brown and black rocks gave scant relief. Dry, scaly lizards skittered their twiglike bodies over the rocks, as if seeking shelter. The grinding wheels kept bruising and breaking the sagebrush, and its pungent scent hovered in the nostrils, constant, sharp, and cloying. That and the lack of water added to dizziness and nausea. Near the wagon train, a white dust coating hid the plants' natural color. In the evening, the moon emerged, drained to a brittle, nearly transparent wafer.

Ma talked continually, asking for Pa, seeming to think he was listening, and begging him to relieve her suffering. A chill traveled up John's spine every time she called Pa's name. He tried to help her, but finally she could do nothing but moan.

When Aunt Sally or one of the other women came at the end of each day to wash Ma's face and make her as comfortable as possible, John was secretly relieved. It lightened his responsibility for a while.

They reached Rock Creek, a trickle bordered by willow brush, on September 21. The willows were flexible red-yellow switches as tall as John but thinner than his fingers, covered with long, pointed pale green yellowing leaves. Willow and sagebrush spread in a gray-green haze over the sand.

By the time camp was set up, Ma seemed better. She asked John to call Uncle Billy and the children. Uncle Billy rolled back the canvas at the side, and Ma sat in the wagon with Catherine, looking out at the rest of them. Her smile was weak, and terribly sweet. "You'll have to get along without me," she said. "I want you all to be as good as you can. Will you remember that?"

"Yes, Ma," they said softly.

She looked at John. "John, keep the children together."

John nodded, feeling as if he had swallowed something huge he could not cough up. Elizabeth, Matilda, and Louisa, uncharacteristically silent, looked on with wide, uncomprehending eyes.

"Frank," said Ma, "tomorrow you'll be eleven, old enough to help John take care of the girls."

"Yes, Ma," said Frank, voice husky. His lips trembled. John looked away from him, his own lips tight, to keep in the trembling he felt inside. The darkness of the evening sky pressed down upon him, wrapping him in chill.

"Always stay with them, boys, keep them together. Will you promise?"

"Yes, Ma," the boys said again, voices choked to ragged whispers.

To Uncle Billy, Ma said, "When I am gone, see that the children are taken to Dr. Whitman's mission. It was Henry's wish."

Uncle Billy promised he would.

Dr. Degen stood back a little ways. Ma looked at him, and for a long time John thought she would not speak. Then her expression softened. "Take care of them."

Dr. Degen came forward and took her hand. John saw tears in his eyes as he said, "Never fear, Mama, I vill da children care for as if my own dey vere."

Ma looked at him kindly. "Please bring my baby. I want to see her." As Dr. Degen hurried away, Ma lay back and closed her eyes.

After that she hardly spoke. The women who came at the end of the day asked if she wanted her face washed, and Ma said, "Yes," very weakly, but it was all she would say to anyone. The evening of September 25, while camped at a place called Pilgrim Springs, Aunt Sally asked her this question, but Ma did not answer.

"She must be asleep," she said softly to John. She washed Ma's face, then picked up her hand. "Her pulse is almost gone!" She ran to fetch Dr. Degen.

"Oh, Henry, if you only knew how we have suffered!" Ma cried.

Catherine looked at Ma with wide, frightened eyes. John put his arm around her, and the two sat, shivering, till Dr. Degen came and told them their mother was dead.

John was hardly even sad. He had known for a long time, though he tried to deny it, that Ma would die, even when she seemed better. Now she was with Pa, and he must write another name and date in the Bible.

The same sort of haze filled his mind as when Pa died. Certain things stood out, like writing the name and date in the Bible, and seeing Elizabeth and Matilda looking with Aunt Sally and Mrs. Morrison for a light-colored dress to bury Ma in. Unable to find one, they settled on a blue calico. The women dressed Ma and laid her in the tent. Early in the morning they called the children to take a last look at her.

Ma's white face stood out vividly above the blue calico dress, and the old patched quilt she lay on. The hands that would no longer embroider cloth, or soothe a sick child, were folded, stiff and white, on her breast. John looked hard at her face so as not to forget it, but she looked different somehow, so he looked away, head bowed.

Catherine, in Uncle Billy's arms, thought of another time when Ma lay in the tent and they did not know if she would rise again. This time there could be no hope. She must try, with Aunt Sally's help, to be a mother to the younger girls.

A short time later, Uncle Billy gave John a board for Ma's headstone. John concentrated on carving her name and age, trying not to hear the scrape of shovels in the background. Aunt Sally and Mrs. Morrison sewed the patched quilt around Ma, while the men cut willow brush and laid it in the grave.

John wished it were all a bad dream. Uncle Billy carried Catherine to the edge. The children watched men lower the quilt-wrapped form. Limp, yellow-green leaves shook; red-yellow branches bent under the burden.

John saw them lay on more willow brush, then his vision blurred. He did not see them fill in the grave. They read words from the Bible, and left Naomi Sager to her long sleep, in the desert by a little spring where willows grew. It was time for the living to move on.

EIGHT

Catherine was quiet most of the rest of that day, after seeing Ma laid in the ground. She had cried for Pa, but could not seem to cry for Ma yet. She could take no enjoyment in the country they were passing through, the striking rock formations and the waterfalls along the Snake filling the air with roaring.

When the wagon stopped and Uncle Billy looked in to say, "The oxen are tiring. We're unloading everything you can do without," she did not move or make a sound as he lifted her out.

She sat on a ragged quilt on the ground, looking at the oxen, which were poor and thin from pulling the wagon over dry, rocky hills. She watched in sorrow as Uncle Billy, the doctor, and the boys left by the side of the trail the forty yards of rag carpet Ma had worked hard to make.

She had to speak, though, when Dr. Degen picked up the crate of dishes. "Ma saved and saved so's we could have good dishes! What will we eat off when we get to Oregon?"

"Lucky you vill be to have food, vitout dishes to eat from," the doctor answered gently.

Catherine almost cried, looking at the dishes and carpet lying out of place among the rocks and sagebrush. It was not right. It would have broken Ma's heart.

Later that day, they reached a place where the Snake river, reflecting the sky's clear, cold blue, wound between yellow-brown hills speckled with sagebrush. The swift water ran across a bar leading from one bank to the other. Three islands, known as Three Island Crossing, rose near the bar. The water branched around them, crashing against the banks beyond with terrible force.

CAPTAIN WILLIAM SHAW
"Uncle Billy" in later years.

Photo courtesy of Northwest and Whitman College Archives.

The gaunt oxen still lagged. While men of the wagon train chained wagons together and negotiated with Snake Indians willing to guide them across, Uncle Billy decided, "The oxen can't pull any farther. We'll have to leave the wagon. The kids can stay with different families."

"You mean, split them up?" John demanded.

"Only till Whitman Mission."

"Not while I'm here, you don't." John faced Uncle Billy squarely, not caring that he was captain of the wagon train and a good bit larger. No one could make him break his promise to Ma. He would keep the children together, no matter what.

Uncle Billy's eyes flashed. He opened his mouth, snapped it shut. "Just what do you aim to do then, young man?"

"If we cut the wagon into a cart, we can stay together and keep part of our stuff."

"Henry Sager's boy, all right," said Uncle Billy under his breath. A little louder, he said, "Good enough."

Dr. Degen and the boys hammered and sawed while Uncle Billy sorted through the Sagers' possessions.

Catherine watched anxiously. "What will you do with the things, Uncle Billy?"

"Sell what I can. The rest will have to be left."

Catherine knew she must not complain. Uncle Billy was trying to help, but she wanted badly to keep their things. *Maybe we can keep most of them,* she told herself.

But pitifully little was left when Uncle Billy was done. After the sale of some things and abandonment of others, not much remained but the children's clothing and food supplies, little enough of the latter.

Beside the hind wheels and discarded wood of the wagon, they abandoned Mrs. Sager's treasured camphor wood chest. Catherine could hardly believe they were losing the things that had been near all her life. She still could not believe her parents were dead, and would never settle down in the little cabin in Oregon with their children and their things around them. The dream had been so real.

Nothing remained but the broken wagon by the trail, the abandoned belongings, the graves left behind forever. The aching hollowness inside her was unlike anything she had ever felt. She had little time to think before the doctor and the boys loaded the cart, and Uncle Billy lifted her in with Elizabeth, Matilda, and Louisa.

John helped Uncle Billy and the other men run a chain between the oxen in front of the cart, to attach to the back of a wagon, and in back to attach to the front of another wagon. The cart and nine wagons were chained together, because one wagon might be caught by the swift current and tumbled to pieces.

The Snake Indians, regarding the whites as a curiosity, happily traded their services for such poor goods as the emigrants possessed. One naked Indian would ride ahead of the first wagon to show where the shallowest water ran over the bar. Other naked Indians, stationed beside each team of oxen, motioned the emigrants to get in the wagons. John and Frank sat in the front of their cart, where they could watch.

The Indian on his horse started into the water. The long, creaking, jingling line of wagons followed, looking so frail and tenuous that John trembled inside. Suppose the oxen should stray from the bar into deep water?

He saw the backs of the four oxen pulling the cart, and the bare backs of two Indians, one on either side of the ox team, their long black hair hanging down. Whenever the oxen strayed to one side or the other, the Indians yelled and punched their sides, to keep them on the bar. The rippling green water pulled against the wagon's wheels.

The bar passed by the first island. John saw it over to the side. When the wagons reached the second island, the wheels ground briefly on dry land, then ventured again into the current. Again an island loomed before them. The wheels crossed land, then water. At last the wagons before them came up safe on dry land. The cart's wheels touched, then the wagons behind them reached the land. Once again, they had safely crossed a river. The Indians whooped jubilantly.

Ahead of the wagon train lay the Blue Mountains. Days were cold, nights colder, and provisions were running low. If they could not cross the Blues before the first snow, their doom was certain.

One evening a few days after crossing the islands, John found Catherine and Elizabeth sitting by the cart, talking quietly. "Look, John." Catherine pointed skyward. "We were just saying how Ma would have enjoyed them clouds."

John looked. A mass of pale pink, fluffy clouds, smeared with blue, hung suspended high in the cold, pale blue sky, looking heavy and light at the same time. Their strange beauty and the evening's chill sent a shiver through him.

"It don't seem worth it to go on, without Ma and Pa," said Catherine in a tight voice. Looking at her, John saw tears running down her face. His helplessness angered him.

Elizabeth began to cry, too. "I don't want to go on. I wish we'd stayed at home."

"Listen," said John, with a firmness that made the girls jump, surprising even himself. "Like it or not, we're going to Oregon. It's not something you can turn back on. Now dry up those tears." Turning on his heel, he walked away, feeling a choking in his throat, and a sudden need to be alone.

"Fight! Fight! Fight!" The wagon train children crowded in a circle, yelling, boys swinging their arms, girls jumping up and down. As the fight intensified, growing progressively louder, into the surging mass waded Uncle Billy Shaw, parting children like so much underbrush.

"What's going on?" he bellowed.

John and Frank Sager were screaming and flailing. Frank, taking the worst of the beating, refused to back down, arms circling in a continuous pummeling motion as John pounded on him. Uncle Billy grabbed each boy by the collar and hauled them apart.

"Say that again, and I'll pound you flatter'n a fryin' pan, hear?" John's voice was loud and hoarse. He and Frank lunged at each other, but Uncle Billy shook them.

"And I'll whale the tar out of the both of you!" he bellowed. "You're lucky I don't bash your heads together like a couple of rocks!"

Aunt Sally arrived, out of breath. "What in the world is going on?"

"I found these two young wildcats trying to tear each other to ribbons. What it's about I don't know, but it better stop right now."

Aunt Sally looked at the tearful, dusty boys. The other children were scattering. "Frank," she put an arm around him, "come over here by me. John, suppose you tell me what happened."

"He said he hated Pa!" John sobbed.

"So I do, and I hate Marcus Whitman!" yelled Frank. The boys sprang at each other, but Uncle Billy pinned John's arms and Aunt Sally pinned Frank's.

"That's enough!" Uncle Billy thundered. "I can give you both a beating that'll make your fight look like nothin'. Frank Sager, what ails you to speak so about your pa?"

"This stupid trip was all his fault, his and Marcus Whitman's! If it hadn't been for them, we coulda stayed in Missouri, and, and Ma would still be alive!" Frank broke down sobbing.

"Now, Frank," Aunt Sally soothed, "Your pa had no way of knowin' what would happen. He did the best he could for your ma and all of you. She told me herself that she hoped to regain her health in Oregon."

"They shouldn't have left us all alone out here."

"They didn't leave you all alone," Uncle Billy spoke up. "They left us to watch after you, and that we will, though I declare you are a handful, young Francis. Now if there's any more fightin'—"

"The boys will be good," Aunt Sally promised. "They're ready to shake hands an' make up." She pushed Frank forward.

Teeth clenched, John reluctantly extended his hand, clasping Frank's in a crushing grip. "You better not talk bad about Pa no more," he whispered.

"I still hate Marcus Whitman," Frank whispered back.

At times the children laughed. Dr. Degen was their main source of amusement. One day as he and John started the oxen, the doctor colored the air blue with curses while John struggled to suppress his laughter.

"*Gott im Himmel!* Vill dees schtubborn *Viecher* never move? Here!" the doctor called to John. "I sit inside holding reins, and you schtart *verückte Faultiere, ja?*"

The doctor climbed into the cart and sat on the boxes in front. John handed him the reins, and started the oxen with rough words and cuffs, but shortly they lay down again.

The doctor let loose a long stream of German and English curses, cut short by a surprised grunt. He leaned inside the cart, shaking his fist, words coming so thick and fast John could not understand a one.

"What's wrong?" he called.

Dr. Degen looked down at John, his face long with chagrin. "Dat Liesbet, oh, dat Liesbet, she has schneaked behind me and kicked me *im Hintern*."

The girls giggled wildly inside the cart. John could no longer contain his laughter. The doctor turned beet-red, shaking himself indignantly, puffed like a wet hen, while the children howled with laughter.

One evening Aunt Sally announced at supper, "Your flour is nigh about gone. Not much left but 'an handful of meal in a barrel,' as the Bible says. We have a little left, and you're welcome to it as long as it lasts."

"Don't worry, Aunt Sally," said John. "Frank and I'll butcher a steer tonight."

The boys stored the beef in the back of the cart. Next morning they watched as Dr. Degen loaded the bedding and cooking utensils. Humming and singing, the doctor slung things in as if not noticing the large load of beef in the back.

"He thinks the cart is still a wagon," said John to Frank. "We better say something before—"

"Don't tell him nothin'," said Frank. In a moment he was rewarded. The cart tipped slowly back. The doctor's startled cry was drowned by a thud and jangle and sliding clatter.

"Tchon! Frank! *Schnell!*" The canvas billowed as the doctor scrambled frantically, and things in the cart constantly rearranged themselves.

John and Frank stood laughing, jostling each other. Others, arrested by the spectacle, laughed too. The little girls shrieked with amusement.

"Tchon! Frank!" the doctor cried again, still trying to extricate himself. Doubled over with laughter, they staggered to the cart and opened the canvas. The doctor peered from beneath a pile of household belongings, the last of the flour whitening his face.

John tried to pull him out, and Frank helped by tipping things on top of him. Working this way, it took quite a while to get the doctor out. A circle of onlookers whooped with laughter. "Stay a spell and I'll fetch my team to haul him out," called one.

The doctor surged from the cart, brushing himself and exclaiming indignantly in two languages. John wiped tears of merriment from his eyes. Only Dr. Degen was not amused.

They crossed the Snake River for the last time on October 4 at Fort Boise, a Hudson's Bay fur trading post built like Fort Hall on a smaller scale, except that the buildings inside the adobe walls were wooden. Cottonwood trees were plentiful, refreshing to see after the four hundred miles of rocks and sagebrush they had passed through since leaving Fort Hall.

The Indians there kept the emigrants well supplied with fish, till all had their fill. The crossing was done in the same way as Three Island Crossing, by chaining the wagons together, but was not as dangerous.

They were nearing the Blue Mountains, the hardest part of the trail. Aunt Sally baked her last loaf of bread, and, true to her promise, shared it with the Sagers. After that, they had only meat. "Recollect what the Bible says," Aunt Sally reminded them. " 'Man shall not live by bread alone.' "

Frank was remembering something else—how funny the doctor looked when the cart tipped over on him. One morning while making coffee, Frank set aside a special cup for the doctor.

The doctor took one sip and his eyes bugged out like a bullfrog's. He sprayed out a mouthful of liquid. "*Du Bengel!*" He lunged at Frank, who ran laughing. A cupful of mud may look like coffee, but tastes different.

After that, the doctor might find a thistle or wad of burrs in his bed or boots, which Frank had carefully collected during every spare moment. Snakes were rare this late in the season, but Frank was skilled at finding small crawly things that might fit easily into a bedroll. The doctor learned to shake out his bedroll and any item of clothing he intended to put on, but he could count on Frank to strike when least expected, and he could never catch him. Frank ran dodging like a wild thing.

"You couldn't whup me, anyway," he bellowed from a distance. "You ain't my Pa!"

Uncle Billy spoke sternly about respecting one's elders. Frank crossed his arms and set his jaw. They weren't his Pa. Let any of them try to make him do something and they'd find out a thing or two. As long as he did his chores, though, they left him pretty much alone, though the doctor watched him warily.

They entered the Grande Ronde near the middle of October. Catherine called it the "Grand Round, because the mountains go all around."

In every direction, pale blue mountains rose on the horizon. It was beautiful, but cold. People huddled close to their campfires each evening.

Matilda, who passed her fifth birthday on October 16, turned herself by the campfire at night like meat on a spit. When her back was roasting and her front freezing, she turned around. One night as she turned towards the fire, a puff of breeze blew her skirt into the flames. She screamed and ran, fire clinging to her as she tried desperately to shake it off.

She felt herself thrown to the ground, and someone beating at her. At first she thought she was being spanked for being so naughty as to catch fire. Then a familiar voice said, "Dere now, you be all right." She opened her eyes. Dr. Degen was bending over her. A big, black, charred hole tattered her dress front, and the fire was gone.

John was at the doctor's shoulder, asking, "Is she all right? Are you hurt?"

"My hands dey are burnt, but better dem den da dear child."

Seeing Dr. Degen go about chores slowly and painfully, Frank was ashamed. The doctor did not find anything crawly in his bed until his hands were healed.

Chill winds swept from the mountains. The children huddled close at night. Dr. Degen propped the cart so it would not tip, and Catherine and Louise slept in it. He and the boys slept in the tent with the middle girls, Elizabeth and Matilda.

Rosanna was pindling, looking worse each time her older brothers and sisters saw her. Dr. Degen shook his head sadly when asked if she would live, saying only God knew.

One night in a camp at the base of the mountains, Captain Shaw awakened to a sound. At first, he thought it was the call of a wild animal among the pines. The sound came again, this time definitely a child's cry. He was almost asleep when he heard it once more. It had changed direction enough so that he could tell the child was not in a tent or wagon, as he supposed at first, but outside.

Lighting a lantern, he walked into the biting wind. The sound was steady, though weak. Near the Sagers' camp, his light showed a small, forlorn figure stumbling along.

"Louisa! Whatever are you doing out here?"

Tears were almost frozen to her red cheeks. Her nose was running, her lower lip trembling. He took a handkerchief from his coat pocket and wiped her face. Taking her in one arm and his lantern in the other hand, he walked to the tent and placed her in the warmth between the doctor and John. "See if the two of you together can take care of this baby," he said gruffly, and before they could answer, he was gone.

The wagons entered the Blue Mountains, and some in the company decided they had been without flour long enough. Several men volunteered to ride ahead to Whitman Mission and buy flour. Captain Shaw decided to go with them and ask if the Whitmans would take the seven orphans.

John came to him as he saddled up. "What if they don't want us?" he demanded.

For a long moment, Uncle Billy did not answer. Then he said, "Neither me nor anybody else in this train can take on seven kids, much as we'd like to." He clipped each word off short. "If they don't want you, we'll take you on to the valley." John looked at him steadily, and he pretended to tighten the already tight cinch. "We'll find good families for you." He mounted the horse.

Good *families.* Uncle Billy was riding away.

"You ain't a-gonna split us up!" John yelled. "Come back, you hear?" His breath shot out in white steam puffs on the thin, cold air.

Uncle Billy did not turn or answer. Tears hid him from John before he was fully out of sight.

The wagons crept painfully up wooded slopes, where crisp green pine scented the cold, thin air, and red-brown needles and dark cones and branches cushioned the forest floor. The crowded treetops rarely let in a glimpse of gray sky, but trees offered no protection against the biting wind. The travelers made their way haltingly, drawn in against the cold. Oxen and cattle, giving out, were left lying by the road.

When Uncle Billy returned with the flour, the children were afraid to ask what the Whitmans had said. Uncle Billy held his hat in his hands, turning it as he spoke. "I talked with Dr. Whitman's wife," he said. "She wants the baby. She says she'll take the girls, but...but she says she doesn't see how she can take the boys. Could be she'll change her mind," he said, looking at the children's stricken faces.

Frank turned it over in his head all day. The more he thought, the more lonely and unwanted he felt. After they made camp that evening, he curled himself into a miserable ball at the foot of a pine, away from the camp, out of the wind. Shivering, he pulled his feet, so cold they were almost numb from mid-calf down, stained with dirt and pine pitch as they were, close under himself for warmth, hunched over, and wept bitterly, wishing he were old enough to show pickety missionary ladies what he thought of them. Most of all, though, he raged at Marcus Whitman, him with the handbill and the talk of paradise in Oregon.

A voice startled him. "Ach, do not take it so hard. You still have me to play your tricks on. I be goot father, yes?"

Frank glared at Dr. Degen. "I don't aim to leave my sisters with those people long. Just the minute John and I can hold a claim, we'll take the girls, and if the missionaries won't give them up, we'll make them sorry!"

The doctor nodded gravely. Frank knew he was thinking that John would have to be twenty-one to hold a claim, and that was more than seven years away. Frank knew it, but maybe he'd think of a way to reunite the family before then. He clenched his fists, his heart smoldering. He *had* to think of a way!

NINE

Cold wind tore at the canvas, roaring and shrieking. Catherine, holding Louisa tight while Matilda huddled close for warmth, looked up at the madly flapping wagon cover, thin, weak, patched, and spotted green with mold, clinging tenuously. Gray sky showed through the frayed, ragged holes. She was afraid that the wind would shred the canvas and snatch away the pieces.

The lightweight cart, which could easily outdistance the wagons, now paused on the crest of a hill, waiting for the rest of the train.

"Down hill ve go and fire ve schtart, yes?" Dr. Degen called. The cart creaked into motion.

Catherine's splint was off now, and she could move herself, hobbling on a rag-padded pine crutch. She pulled herself to the cart's front where she could watch the others.

Abandoned pieces of wagons lay strewn in the wind-tossed grass and weeds. Elizabeth and the boys tore at them until they had enough to start a fire, using dried moss and pine shavings as kindling. Catherine, Matilda, and Louisa, peering from the cart, watched Dr. Degen grow red with cold and frustration, working over the damp pile. One thin gray curl of smoke rewarded his efforts.

"*Verdamt nochamal!* Dis vood she is too vet. I findt better."

He crossed the meadow, disappearing in a stand of pines. Frank bent over the fire, opening the powder horn. Catherine had her mouth open to say he hadn't ought to do that when a roar split the air. Frank somersaulted backwards in a flash of light, and sprawled in the grass. For a heart-stopping moment, Catherine feared he was dead. Then he was up and running to a nearby creek, falling to his knees, and frantically scrubbing at his face.

By the time Dr. Degen crashed bellowing through the trees, Frank was on his way back to the cart, blue eyes peering from a mask of solid black. His eyebrows and eyelashes were gone, his hair singed. "Are my eyes red?" he asked the doctor.

Catherine held her breath as Dr. Degen peered at Frank's eyes. Then he whooped with laughter. "You play jokes on me, play goot vun on yourself, *ja?* Never you pour gunpowder on da fire! First get rag, *ja?* Den make vet da rag, *und* only den do you make *mit* gunpowder da fire. Funny joke on you! Oh, I feel some even now!"

Suddenly it was funny, and Catherine and the others laughed, too. Frank glared at them, but the angry expression on the comical face only made them laugh the harder.

Soon afterwards they left the Blue Mountains. They had made it through before the snows. *If only Ma and Pa could have lived a little longer,* thought Catherine. The children had come one thousand, seven hundred and fifty miles along their journey. The Whitman Mission, which they talked of by day and dreamed of by night, was only about a week's journey away. Captain Shaw had arranged for the children's arrival there, and the children knew when the missionaries expected them.

Stopping by the Umatilla River in October's last chill gray days, they met many Cayuse, Umatilla, and Walla Walla Indians. The Cayuses were the dominant tribe of this area, having conquered the Umatillas and Walla Wallas, holding them in a certain degree of subjection, though all except slaves taken in raids were free to wander as they pleased.

Nez Perces, a large and important tribe, and Teninos also roamed Cayuse land at times, though the Snakes and Northern Paiutes were unwelcome. These tribes, though familiar with the Hudson's Bay Company and other explorers and traders, had not seen a large emigration of whites until the year before, when Dr. Whitman arrived with a wagon train of American settlers bound for the Willamette Valley.

Disputes between whites and Indians had risen here, but not all-out battles, as in the East. The Indians returned to the owners oxen and cattle left in the mountains, which had needed only rest, and traded pumpkins, potatoes, and horses to the emigrants. The Cayuses and Nez Perces were immensely proud of their magnificent bands of small, strong, swift horses, the dashing mounts of many colors, the pinto war horses, and the spotted Appaloosas, which were difficult to manage and often used as pack animals. The Indians measured their wealth in horses. Because of the Cayuses' expert horsemanship, the emigrants called any especially fine horse a 'cayuse.'

Certain Indians had learned some English from the missionaries; most used a trade language composed of signs, gesturing towards their offered goods, roots, berries, and dried deer and elk, and towards the emigrants' offers, indicating "more" or "enough." The potatoes and pumpkins, the first the emigrants had seen since beginning the journey, were mighty good. Hot baked potatoes and stewed pumpkin helped chase the chill from inside them.

Men, both white and Indian, traded most often, women trading seldom. If a white man got the best of a trade, he proclaimed these Indians to be perfectly peaceable. If an Indian got the best of a trade, the white man muttered that you had to watch out for these tricky redskins.

These Indians, like the Sioux, had long black hair and wore fringed buckskins. The children saw Indian women wearing long black braids, fringed buckskin dresses, and moccasins, and men and boys wearing moccasins and breechclouts. Since it was late fall, many also wore woolen blankets. Men sometimes wore a single eagle feather sticking straight up; women, hats woven of grass fiber, resembling baskets. Unlike the Sioux, their faces were not hawklike; many were round-featured. Their skin was a brownish cast, their eyes rather slanted. They praised the missionaries, calling themselves "Dr. Whitman's Indians."

"Maybe the Whitmans ain't so bad, if the Indians like them so much," John told Frank.

"Aw, what do Indians know?"

"As much as anyone," said John. He suspicioned Frank had nothing against the Indians. Even before Pa and Ma died, he was sometimes contrary, but now he muttered and sulked and acted ornery about most everything.

The night before they were to leave the Umatilla for Whitman Mission, John said, "I reckon you girls ought to look presentable when we bring you to the mission. I'll cut your hair. Oldest first, Katie."

He held Ma's sewing scissors, and Catherine sat obediently. John tried, patiently at first, to comb the knots from her matted hair. After working for some time, with Catherine wailing, "You're pulling every hair from my head!" and three little sisters still to do, he hacked through the tangled places.

After Catherine came Elizabeth, and Matilda, who could hardly sit still, then Louise, whose wails could be heard all over the camp before the ordeal was over. John stood back and surveyed his work.

"Well...I reckon you do look some better."

Catherine looked at her sisters, whose hair hung in ragged, uneven strands, as if rat-chewed, and hoped she didn't look as bad.

"Shall I cut your hair now, Frank?" John was so proud of his work he did not realize how unkempt the girls looked.

"You ain't *touchin'* my hair!" said Frank with deep finality.

The next day, Aunt Sally washed the girls' faces and put their best dresses on them. Catherine had helped her scrub the dresses, and thought they looked right fine, though considerable worn. All the while she helped them, tears ran down Aunt Sally's face. Catherine was sorry for her, but more frightened for herself and the others.

Baby Rosanna would not be coming with them to Whitman Mission. She was behind in the Perkins wagon, and whoever took her next would bring her to the mission, if she lived. Dr. Degen saw her every day, and doubted she would recover.

Catherine thought of a sad lullaby she had heard Aunt Sally singing to Rosanna, one time when she did not realize Catherine was listening. It was so mournful it made Catherine lonesome even thinking of it. Some of the words went:

> Hush, little baby, don't you cry,
> You know your Mama was born to die.
> All my trials, Lord,
> Soon be over....
> There grows a tree in Paradise,
> And the Pilgrims call it the tree of life.

It made Catherine think of Pilgrim Springs, the place where Ma was buried. Her trials, and Pa's, were over. Perhaps Rosanna's would soon be over, too. Catherine and the others, however, now had to leave their friends seeking a home among strangers. Maybe their trials were just beginning.

The six children sat in the cart. No longer did the boys drive the cattle behind. They had eaten many of their beef animals. Besides the three yoke of oxen hitched to the cart, all they had was a milk cow and a steer, tied behind. Pa's horse was long since traded.

The cart was open, the ragged moldy canvas folded for the girls to sit on. Aunt Sally said, "I wonder what fate has in store for you poor little orphans."

Catherine's heart dropped like a stone in cold water, sinking, sinking.

The doctor cracked his frayed whip, the tired oxen started once again. Uncle Billy rode alongside of the cart. The six children looked back at Aunt Sally, and she at them, till they lost sight of each other.

That evening as Catherine sat by the fire, Frank appeared, carrying a small, flat, rough, light-brown object that looked like a rock. Catherine might have thought it was a buffalo chip, if they were not past buffalo country. He broke off a piece and held it towards her. "Lookee here what I got. Have some."

"What is it?"

"Camas-root bread. Got it from an old Indian lady. Gave her one of Ma's best tablecloths for it. She was mighty happy to—"

"You gave away one of Ma's best tablecloths?" Catherine's voice sounded dangerous, and a storm brewed in her look.

Had Frank had eyebrows, they would have raised in surprise. As it was, his forehead went up questioningly. "Sure. We gotta eat."

Catherine wanted to slap the blank look from his face. He did not understand, and the thing was done. Now she could only be mad about it. "Don't you reckon we could save a few of our mother's things without you and Uncle Billy giving away every last one to strangers? I won't eat your old bread! There!" She flung it as hard and far as she could.

Frank shot her a smoldering glance and took one step toward her, then whirled and ran after the piece of bread. Rations were too short to be wasted that way.

Catherine watched him search through the grass where it had fallen. She turned over with her face on her arms and cried as long and hard as she could.

When she stopped, out of breath, Uncle Billy and Dr. Degen coaxed her to eat a piece of the camas-root bread. But Catherine refused to touch it, so the others divided it without giving her any.

The last part of the trail to Whitman Mission crossed flat land, where steep, round-shouldered hills and ridges rose abruptly, looking as if they belonged in a different landscape. Tawny bunches of grass, with spears rising twice as tall as John, made a dense curtain across the land. Often they saw Indian horses of brown, black, gray, roan, and white, bearing their owner's marks. Once they saw a brave racing, his horse a light gray streak beneath dark gray sky. A few miles from the mission, Uncle Billy spurred ahead to alert the missionaries to the children's approach.

Even the the Walla Walla River looked gray today. They passed an Indian village near one of its curves. Long hills of poles and mats stood dark brown against gray sky. Smoke drifted from holes in the roofs. Distant human figures moved by the lodges. Women looked up from weaving. An old man sitting on the ground glanced in their direction, a boy stood still as stone to watch. Dogs barked fretfully, the sound chopping the still air.

The oxen trudged leadenly, as if not wanting the journey to end in this cheerless land among strangers. *I wish they'd hurry and get it over,* Catherine thought. *No, I wish Dr. Degen would change his mind and keep us.*

They followed the crest of a hill and came around the other side. Far down the trail, Catherine saw buildings unlike Indian lodges. That was Whitman Mission.

A wide loop of river ran into a mill pond. She heard the water pouring through the millrace. Ducks called faintly in the chill, misty air. The cart passed low fences of short rails piled like corn shocks, with long rails laid between them.

She had expected a log fort, but the three buildings were adobe. Only the mill was wood. The biggest building, a story and a half high, stood at the end of the yard, T-shaped, corners square. The houses were startlingly white in the gray and brown landscape. A round stockade fence of dark, damp wood was in the middle of the yard, but no stockade surrounded the mission, only a small section of high board fence, and the rail fences. Smoke scent pierced the air.

The cart passed an abrupt ridge on the right and neared the buildings. Deep, grass-fringed ditches cut through the mission grounds. One ran by the fence on their left. Now the first white building, big and square, was on their left and a large alkali pond on their right. Mud pattered from the wheels as they cut into the dark brown trail ruts.

Opposite the big T-shaped house, Dr. Degen drove across a small wooden bridge over the irrigation ditch, and stopped. The oxen folded their legs, settling wearily to the ground.

A dark little girl Catherine's age stepped out the door and flung a pan of dishwater. She looked curiously at the children in the cart, then disappeared into the house, closing the door.

A moment later it opened again, and Uncle Billy came towards them. The children sat up, alert, wary, not knowing what to expect. He spoke to the boys. "Help the girls out and find their bonnets."

Catherine looked toward the big house with dread. Frank climbed wearily from the cart, and John handed Catherine and the other girls to Uncle Billy. Then he rummaged blindly through the cart, finding two bonnets. No time remained to look for more. The missionary woman was approaching.

John sank down in the front of the cart, weeping bitterly. On the other side, with the cart between him and the house, Frank leaned on the muddy wheel, head cradled in his arms, sobbing aloud. After one thousand, eight hundred miles of struggle, their long, heartbreaking journey was ending. For the last half year they had toiled through every kind of danger, only to be torn from their sisters in this forbidding place.

On the side nearest the house stood the girls, Catherine and Matilda each holding a limp bonnet. Catherine looked at the boys in horror, then at the woman. All four girls stared at the approaching woman with wide, frightened eyes.

TEN

Narcissa Whitman wore a dark calico dress and gingham sunbonnet. Blond hair with a coppery tinge showed beneath the bonnet. She regarded the children with large, light-blue eyes. *She's the one who doesn't want the boys,* thought Catherine hotly.

Even in her resentment, she considered the woman the most beautiful she had ever seen, more beautiful than Ma, or Aunt Sally, or anyone. It was not mainly her features that were beautiful, but a certain proud and noble bearing that set her apart, a reserved and mysterious air surrounding her.

Mrs. Whitman smiled a welcome. "So these are my new children. Come to the house and we will get acquainted," she said to the girls. Elizabeth, Matilda, and Louise scurried behind the cart. Catherine limped behind as quickly as she could.

Looking a little flustered, Mrs. Whitman turned to the boys. "Why are you crying?" she asked. Seeming to sense their distress, she added, "Poor boys, no wonder you weep."

Catherine looked at Dr. Degen, who stood, whip in hand, by the oxen, trying hard not to cry. For a moment Uncle Billy looked ready to cry, too. Then he began to unload the cart. "John, Frank, hand these things out," he ordered. John and Frank wiped their faces on their sleeves, and, still sniffling, helped him.

An old Indian woman sat nearby, asking questions about the children. Mrs. Whitman, a large woman with a take-charge air, answered while arranging the things Uncle Billy and the boys handed down. The firmness in her voice and manner, her quick, crisp movements as she handled the worn possessions, told Catherine, cowering with her sisters behind the cart in an agony of shyness, that this woman would stand for no nonsense. How were they to live with her, proud and serious as she was, when they were used to simple, kind Aunt Sally?

Catherine saw a girl Elizabeth's age standing beside Mrs. Whitman. The girl wore a green dress and matching sunbonnet, pushed back to reveal glossy black hair. Looking at the girl's clean dress and crisp white apron, Catherine was painfully aware of how dirty, ragged, and sun-burned she and the others were. Their dresses were thin and worn. The bonnet Matilda clutched had belonged with the dress that was spoiled when she caught fire. Catherine's bonnet did not match her dress, either. She had never felt so shabby.

Mrs. Whitman placed her hand on the shoulder of the little girl standing by her. "This is Helen Mar Meek. Helen, show the girls into the house."

Catherine and the others crept from behind the cart, looking, she knew, like a bunch of scared rabbits. The dark-haired girl turned to lead them toward the T-shaped house.

Mrs. Whitman spoke to Dr. Degen. "You and the boys can carry the things into the sitting room. Mr. Shaw will show you where it is."

People usually called Uncle Billy Captain Shaw, but Catherine realized with a start that with no wagon train, he was no longer a Captain. She tried her best to follow the girls, but her leg was stiff, and she was far too shy to say anything. Then Mrs. Whitman was taking her arm to assist her. With her free hand, she took Louisa's, and led them to the house.

At the door, Uncle Billy asked her if she had any children. The two little girls they had seen could not be hers. She had light coloring, and the girls were dark and appeared to be part Indian.

She turned to face the steep hill bordering the alkali pond, and pointed. Catherine saw a little wooden marker at the foot of the hill. "All the child I ever had sleeps there." Her large blue eyes were lost in distance a moment. "It is a great comfort to be able to see the grave from the door."

Catherine thought of the graves in the desert she would never see again, and knew she could feel no comfort.

Then Mrs. Whitman led them through the door into the kitchen. Elizabeth clutched Catherine's hand as the doctor and boys brushed past them, carrying things. "Katie," she whispered with deep fervor, "a cookstove! They have a cookstove!"

It was true. The kitchen was elegant. Besides the square black stove, radiating delicious warmth, two tables stood against the walls, another, with chairs around it, in the middle of the floor, a real wooden floor and not a dirt one. The windows had glass panes, through which Catherine could see the yard and the miles of grass beyond. Silver and gold glinted from pitchers and candlesticks on shelves mounted on the white walls. A frying pan, a ladle, a cleaver, and other kitchen tools hung for ready use.

Behind the stove was a settee where people might warm themselves, and by the settee a door which led into a neat little pantry, lined with baskets that must contain all sorts of good things to eat. Catherine saw onions hanging in bunches from the ceiling beams. Her mouth watered.

The little girl she had seen emptying a pan of water stood by the table, washing dishes in a basin. A pot on the stove bubbled more hot water.

"This is Mary Ann Bridger," Mrs. Whitman said to the girls. "Well, Mary Ann, how do you think you will like all these sisters?"

Mary Ann smiled shyly.

The boys came through the kitchen again, and Mrs. Whitman told them and Dr. Degen to go to the emigrant house. "I'll show you to it," said Uncle Billy. The boys took a last sad look at the girls and left.

"Helen," said Mrs. Whitman, "go out to the mill and tell Doctor to come in and see his new children." The girl in the green dress jumped to obey.

Mrs. Whitman took chairs from around the table for the girls and sat herself in an armchair with Louise in her lap. "Sit down and tell me your names and all about your journey," she said. Catherine, Elizabeth, and Matilda sat and told her. "Poor children," she said as they related one hardship after another.

Catherine was telling about breaking her leg when Dr. Whitman came to the door. He was tall, broad-shouldered, and muscular. His dark blue eyes, deeply sunk beneath bushy brows, showed surprise at the sight of the ragged little girls, and he ran a work-roughened hand through his dark brown, gray-tinged hair.

His wife laughed at his expression and said, "Come in, Doctor, and see your children."

He tried to take Louise in his arms, but she jumped from Mrs. Whitman's lap and ran screaming to Catherine. Mrs. Whitman again laughed at her husband's chagrined expression. She grew serious as she told him, "I wanted the baby most of all. She has not yet arrived, and they tell me she is very sick and may die. It was the baby I wanted most of all," she repeated.

"Wife, you know my feelings about taking in that baby. We have obligations to the natives here. It is enough to take in these older children, without a young baby to care for."

Catherine looked at him in alarm. This was the first she had heard about not being allowed to stay with her baby sister. Were they to lose Rosanna as well as the boys?

Mrs. Whitman sighed. "I know, but I had special hopes for that baby." In the small silence that followed, the doctor sat, looking resigned. Then his wife said, "The oldest girl, Catherine, was just telling me about how she fell under the wagon wheel and broke her leg."

Catherine shrank as Dr. Whitman turned his gaze on her. Elizabeth was not so hesitant. "Pa done a fine job of setting it, and Dr. Degen said it was just as good as he coulda done himself."

"I'm sure Dr. Degen is very skilled," Marcus Whitman said. He beckoned to Matilda, who went to him without hesitation. "Why, you're as light as a feather," he said as he lifted her into his lap. She smiled up at him.

Mary Ann left her dishes to answer a knock at the door. Uncle Billy stepped in.

"Well, Mr. Shaw, these seem like fine girls, and we should get along well together," said Dr. Whitman.

"I'm glad you like them," said Uncle Billy. "Their parents were good friends of mine." He paused a moment. "They asked that the children not be separated. Won't you consider taking the boys as well?"

Dr. Whitman shook his head. "I was sent out here as a missionary to the Indians. As it is, the Board will probably object to my taking in white children, and won't allow me any support for them."

"These orphans are surely objects for missionary charity," Uncle Billy argued. "Whatever missionary work comes your way should be your duty, whether to natives or whites."

They argued for some time, while the girls listened, not daring to move, hardly daring to breathe. Might John and Frank be allowed to stay with them after all? With each argument of Uncle Billy's, Dr. Whitman weakened. At last he consented. Turning to his wife, he said, "Well, Mother, where are the boys?"

"I sent them to the emigrant house, and as far as I'm concerned they can go on to the valley. I simply won't have them, Marcus."

"If you are to have the girls—and the baby—" he looked at her meaningfully—"I must have the boys," he said with decision. "Helen, run over to the emigrant house and bring the boys over."

In the emigrant house, Frank was in tears. "She's an old cow," he sobbed, hardly able to catch his breath from crying so hard. "She's a big-eyed fat old cow, and I won't let my sisters stay with her!"

"Don't you talk about my mother that way!" cried a shrill voice behind him. Frank, John, and the doctor turned, startled, to face a little girl with dark, snapping eyes, whose scowl, which might have stopped a clock, put a stop to Frank's crying. "Mother and Father say you boys can stay with us, so you just better mind your manners."

"*Ach*, he meant not to speak ill of your mother," protested the doctor gently.

The girl's frown diminished, and she said in softer tones, "Father says to come to the house." She marched off past the stockade yard and rail fences.

As the boys stepped into the house behind her, Frank felt uncomfortable with so many pairs of eyes fixed on him. He also grew warm with anger. Here they'd been sitting out in that old mud house waiting, while, he knew very well, they argued over whether he and John were worth keeping. Uncle Billy probably had to beg that old cow to keep them. It wasn't fair.

So, when Dr. Whitman asked if they would like to stay with him, Frank raised his head and looked at him boldly. "John and I was aiming to go on down to the valley and stay till we're old enough to hold a claim."

"That's right," said John fiercely. "Then we're going to send for the girls and take care of them ourselves."

The doctor looked at them calmly, without anger. "Your parents wanted you kept together, and I must honor their wishes. If you don't want to stay with me, I'm afraid I can't take the girls, either."

Frank heard a little gasp from one of the girls. The cold knot in his stomach drew tight as he gazed at the doctor's steady blue eyes. He saw no cruelty in them. The doctor smiled encouragement. "Well, boys, how about it? Don't you want to stay here and be my boys?"

For the moment, Frank and John were defeated. They nodded their heads and said, "Yes."

Dr. Whitman smiled at them. "I have something for you," he said. He left the room and returned holding it.

"Pa's gun!" John exclaimed. "Wherever did you get it?" Dr. Whitman handed it to him, and he turned it over unbelievingly. Frank stared in wonder.

"A young man left it, asking me to keep it until the owner should come for it," Dr. Whitman explained. "It's yours now."

"I'm mighty proud to have it," said John softly.

Before supper, Mrs. Whitman washed the girls in a tin tub by the stove in the sitting room. This was not a cookstove, but a little, round, black heating stove. The sitting room was peaceful, lined with the Whitmans' books, and glinting bottles of brown, blue, and clear, which held the doctor's medicines.

Cold as it was, the boys scorned the sitting room and washed in the river. Then Mrs. Whitman gave them all an even haircut. Everyone looked presentable to come to table. Mrs. Whitman sent Mary Ann and Helen out with food for Dr. Degen and Uncle Billy in the emigrant house.

Besides the two little girls, they were joined by a dark-haired boy John's age, who looked like a younger Dr. Whitman. The doctor introduced him as his nephew, Perrin Whitman.

"And this is David Malin," said Mrs. Whitman, putting her arm around a little dark boy Matilda's age.

"His mother was an Indian and his father Spanish," said Dr. Whitman. "His real name is Cortez, but we call him David Malin after a friend from New York. Well," he said as they all crowded around the table, "looks like we're going to have to make the table bigger." The Whitmans' family laughed. The Sagers smiled shyly.

"Such wonderful dishes," murmured Catherine with longing, picking up a shiny blue-patterned white plate. She remembered her mother's dishes which had been left by Three Island Crossing.

Dr. Whitman walked around the table, serving up baked ham and lady finger potatoes, while Mrs. Whitman sliced some dark stuff.

"What's that?" asked Matilda as Mrs. Whitman put a piece on her plate.

"It's bread," Frank answered.

"No, that ain't the color of bread."

It did look awfully dark, but Frank was sure it was bread. He had his mouth open to say so when Mrs. Whitman snapped, "It isn't polite to complain about the food." Matilda wilted under her gaze. Frank swelled with indignation, but said nothing.

"It looks dark because it's made from unbolted flour," Dr. Whitman explained more kindly. "Give them a chance, Mother."

"Leave the discipline to me, Father," Mrs. Whitman returned smartly. "These children are going to learn manners. First of all, they must not gobble their food."

"You're right about that." He spoke to the children, who were stuffing in their first good meal in months as if afraid it would be snatched away. "Often I find nothing wrong with a sick person but overeating. If you children keep gobbling your food, you will endanger your health."

The children slowed for a moment, but it was so good to have food in front of them that they soon began to wolf it down as fast as ever, passing their plates for second helpings.

When Dr. Whitman and Uncle Billy agreed on what to do with the orphans, Dr. Whitman said he would send the boys to Tshimakain.

"What's Shim-uh-kain?" Uncle Billy wanted to know. "I want to make sure those boys are in good hands."

"Tshimakain is a mission like my own, about one hundred and seventy miles to the north, run by two families named Walker and Eells. They are good Christian people," Dr. Whitman explained.

Uncle Billy agreed it sounded like a good enough place.

One hundred and seventy miles! thought John in despair. That was a good week's ride away, and they would be living with strangers in an unsettled land to the north, instead of going south to the Willamette Valley, where they might be close to people from their own wagon train. They would never have a home with the girls. They would be lucky even to see them.

"So he doesn't want to keep us. He'll pack us off soon as he can." Frank voiced the thoughts John was also thinking, when they were alone.

Uncle Billy, satisfied the children were well provided for, rode to meet his family.

Dr. Whitman proved right about their eating habits. They all had stomach aches from the change in diet. The smallest, Matilda and Louise, suffered the most, and had to be put to bed for a few days.

Nothing could stop Elizabeth from being out the next day. Mary Ann and Helen got Mrs. Whitman's consent to show her around the mission. The three girls went out through the kitchen door, walking past the woodpile and a length of rail fence. Behind the fence, Elizabeth could see the circular stockade yard. In front of her was a small building smelling of smoke. Elizabeth heard the ring of a hammer on metal and the hiss of hot metal in water. "That's the blacksmith shop," said Helen.

"And over there is the emigrant house," Mary Ann told her, pointing to a square white building a little farther on, near the mill pond. "That's where the emigrants stay every year."

Elizabeth marveled at the tall grass, and Helen told her, "That's rye grass. The Indian name of this place is Waiilatpu, the place of the rye grass."

"Wye-ee-lat-pu," Elizabeth repeated softly.

The mission house and emigrant house were connected with a long fence, and another long fence joined the other end of the mission house, so that they had to go back through the kitchen door and out a back door to find themselves behind the house. Elizabeth saw that the rail fence which connected with the emigrant house went around the back of the mission house, making an enclosed yard. Farther back, near the river, were an apple orchard and a garden patch.

"Here's where we have our garden in the summer," said Helen. "Mother lets us plant all kinds of flowers."

Turning slowly around, Elizabeth looked at the steep tawny hill beyond the dark brown stockade fence and white buildings, then past the mill pond to the mountains rising misty and blue in the distance. She looked at the mill by the river, then at the bare apple trees and brown field beyond them. Rolling hills covered with rye grass stretched as far as she could see. She began to think she was going to like it here at Waiilatpu.

Unlike Elizabeth, John and Frank felt awkward and out of place,

DR. MARCUS WHITMAN   **NARCISSA WHITMAN**

Paintings by Drury Haight, based on sketches by Paul Kane believed to be of Marcus and Narcissa Whitman. Courtesy of National Park Service, Whitman Mission National Historic Site.

WHITMAN HOME AT WAIILATPU

Paul Kane sketch believed to show the Whitman home. Courtesy of Royal Ontario Museum, Toronto.

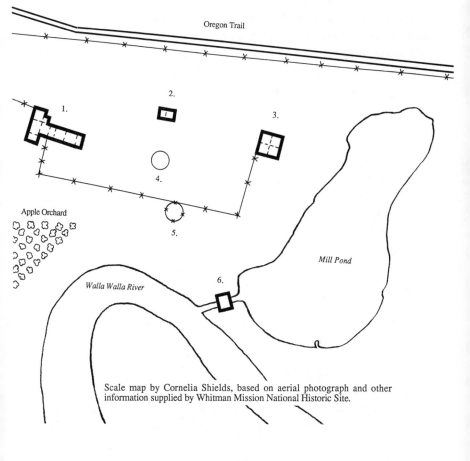

Scale map by Cornelia Shields, based on aerial photograph and other information supplied by Whitman Mission National Historic Site.

89

smoldering with bitter resentment towards the four loved and wanted children the Whitmans had taken in, Perrin, Mary Ann, Helen, and David. Two days after their arrival, John and Frank sat warming themselves by the kitchen stove in the evening after chores, while the two older Sager girls and the two mission girls played nearby. Matilda was still not well, and David Malin, who was also about five, eagerly awaited her recovery so he could have a playmate. Mary Ann mentioned to Catherine that her father ran Bridger's Fort.

That was enough to set John off. "Bridger's Fort! You mean that dumpy little trading post where a crooked mountain man cheated me out of a good calf for a couple of antelope skins? If your pa lets cheats like that around his place, he must be one himself."

Mary Ann, normally shy and quiet, flashed back in anger, "That's a lie, John Sager! My father is not a cheat! You take that back!"

"I won't take back the truth. He's a cheat and more. If he's a good father, why're you 'way out here 'stead of with him?"

Mary Ann's face froze in shock, and John felt a small degree of mean satisfaction. *His* Pa wouldn't go and leave *him,* leastways not if he could help it.

"Please, John, don't be so hateful," Catherine begged.

Mary Ann recovered her power of speech. "My father sent me here for an education, which I can see is more than you have! He is a good and brave man. Why, once Doctor Whitman dug a three-inch arrowhead from his back, that had been there three years, grown into the bone, and my father didn't so much as flinch. *Your* father would have been yelling his head off!"

John, Frank, Catherine, and Elizabeth raised their voices all at once in protest. Helen rushed to defend Mary Ann. John was yelling, "So the arrowhead was in his back, was it? *That* should tell you how brave he is!" when the kitchen door burst open. Dr. Whitman silenced the children with a thunderous look.

"We'll have no bad talk about anyone's father!" he ordered when the room was quiet. "Jim Bridger was brave during that operation, and, John, I'm sure your father was a brave man, too. We should never speak ill of the mountain men. Without their help, my wife and I could not have reached our mission. I've made an important decision concerning you boys."

John felt sick. *Now I've done it,* he thought. *He'll send us off and we won't see our sisters again for years, maybe never.*

Looking steadily at John and Frank with serious blue eyes, Dr. Whitman said, "My father died when I was eight. I had to live with my uncle because my mother couldn't afford to keep me.

"Many times I wished I was with my mother, brothers, and sister, and I think you children should be together, too. I'm going to catch up with your Uncle Billy and tell him everything is fine, and not to worry about you any more."

John could have sobbed with relief. He was to have a home, a real home, with his brother and sisters! He looked joyfully at Frank, but Frank's face was hard and unbelieving. Looking back at Dr. Whitman, who met his gaze squarely, John knew he would keep his word.

The next day, Dr. Whitman left to catch Uncle Billy, and Rosanna arrived in the arms of a thin, ragged, evil-smelling old woman named Louisa Eads.

Catherine had not seen Rosanna much since before Ma died, when she was being passed around to different women in the train. Now as she lay in Mrs. Whitman's arms, Catherine viewed her with shock. She was pale and shrunken, her arms thin, fingers tiny and weak. She lay very still in her rag wrappings, not responding as her brothers and sisters crowded round.

A cradle stood ready in the corner. Mary Ann drew Mrs. Whitman's armchair near it, and she sat, holding Rosanna. "Mary Ann, bring some milk from the pantry and warm it on the stove."

When the milk was the right temperature, Mrs. Whitman fed it to Rosanna, who drank hungrily.

If she can drink like that, she'll soon be well, thought Catherine. But shortly Rosanna vomited all she had drunk.

"You children, run outside," said Mrs. Whitman. "I'm busy with the baby now." They all left but Catherine, whose leg allowed her only to hobble. She tried to make herself small as she watched Mrs. Whitman wash the thin little body in warm water and dress her in clean clothes.

When Dr. Degen came in, he said, "I see I need not to vorry about da little one. I vorry so about dese childrens, I have become as poor as a schnake. I sink it time I should be going."

No, Dr. Degen! No! Catherine wanted to cry, but was too afraid to speak in front of Mrs. Whitman.

The doctor saw her distressed look. "Vorry not," he told her gently. "Dis lady, she take goodt care of you."

Dr. Degen saddled his horse. The children gathered to say good-bye. For Catherine, it was worse than saying good-bye to Aunt Sally. Dr. Degen had been with them every moment since her accident, always taking care of them. Now he was leaving them alone in this strange place with people they did not know.

Before he left, he gave Mrs. Whitman an account of each child. He told how brave John and Catherine were, how John especially took on responsibility after his parents died. Frank looked at the doctor anxiously as he began to speak about him, but when he said only good things, they exchanged a secret, understanding glance.

Coming to Elizabeth, the doctor laughed. "Oh, but Liesbet! You tchust look out for dat Liesbet! She so full of mischief! She goodt girl, but so tricky! You tchust look out for dat Liesbet!"

Mrs. Whitman smiled and said, "Elizabeth and I will get along fine."

After saying a few words about Matilda and Louise, he said a final good-bye. Catherine felt a strange, insistent pain tugging at her heart as she watched him ride away.

ELEVEN

The next few weeks were lonely for Catherine. For a week or two, the Whitmans were busy with emigrants stopping at the mission. Some would stay until spring, but many would buy supplies, finish blacksmithing, and go on to the Willamette Valley. Mrs. Whitman paid little attention to the children, except to care for the baby and see that the older ones obeyed the rules.

One evening, Elizabeth and Matilda came in after the others had started supper. Elizabeth looked hurt and said, "Why didn't you call us?"

"It isn't our business to call little girls who have wandered away without permission," said Mrs. Whitman. "It is your business to be on time for meals. For your disobedience, you can go without supper tonight."

Catherine thought this very mean until she talked to Mary Ann. Catherine mostly stayed in the kitchen corner by Rosanna's cradle, sewing the few simple stitches she knew, wondering if she could ever sew fancy work like Ma's. Mrs. Whitman came in periodically to bring the baby her milk, but Catherine was too shy to speak to her, much. Timid in the presence of these new strangers, Catherine devoted her attention, with some success, to winning over the cats the Whitmans kept as pets and pest killers.

Catherine was sewing in the corner one day when Mary Ann came in to wash dishes. Summoning her courage, which grew fainter each day, as if deserting her, Catherine said, "Why is your mother so set on people being at a certain place at a certain time?"

Mary Ann regarded her seriously. "Mother and Father think it's very important for us to be regular about when we get up, eat, bathe, and so on."

"But why are they so angry when someone goes somewhere without permission?"

"That's the rules. I think it's because of what happened to their little girl."

"The little girl buried out by the hill?" Catherine thought of the wooden marker she had seen the first day.

"Of course. That's the only little girl they ever had. Helen and I are adopted. Anyway, her name was Alice Clarissa. One day when she was about two, she wandered off, not for very long." She paused thoughtfully.

"She went to the river, where they'd told her not to go. They didn't even know she was there till they found two little cups belonging to Alice, floating on the water. Then Chief Umtippe found Alice in the river. I think that's why Mother and Father want to know where everybody is all the time." She went back to washing dishes.

Catherine remembered when Louisa had wandered away and nearly frozen. It would have been terrible losing her. She quickly turned her face to the wall, so Mary Ann would not see her cry.

That was one of the few times Mary Ann spoke to her. She and the others were too busy running outside, playing with their dolls, and having a good time generally, to pay much attention to Catherine, who could only sit in the corner, often weeping alone. How could she ever be happy here where things were so strange, so different from the cabin back in Missouri?

She saw John and Frank only at meals. At noon, they might have beef, mutton, chicken, or very rarely pork or duck, along with bread, cheese, eggs, potatoes, corn, or other vegetables, or fish, which, along with wild fruits and berries, the Whitmans bought from the Indians. Supper was usually corn meal mush and milk, because the Whitmans were against big meals before bed.

A change had come over the boys. If the doctor had no chores for him, John asked permission to go out. Taking Pa's gun—his gun now—he stayed out as long as the doctor allowed. John had never much cared for hunting before. It was as if, with Pa gone, he was trying to be like him.

Frank also kept as much away from the Whitmans as possible, and so seldom saw his sisters, who were usually around the house.

Without Dr. Degen, Uncle Billy, Aunt Sally, or even her brothers to protect her, Catherine was frightened. The kitchen corner was her haven, but even there she felt threatened. If Dr. Whitman, or any adult, spoke to her, she lowered her head, and tears welled in her eyes.

She had to attend school in one of the rooms of the mission house, with the Whitmans' children and emigrant children staying the winter. The teacher's name was Alanson Hinman. Catherine soon saw through him. With the Whitmans, he was sweet as could be. He could do no wrong in Mrs. Whitman's eyes. But the moment he was alone with the children, he became a brutal tyrant.

The first morning of school, he made Catherine stand in front of the class to read. As she looked at the other children's expectant faces, terror overwhelmed her. The words on the page dissolved as she bowed her head and cried.

"I'll not have this behavior in my classroom!" Mr. Hinman cried. "Miss Sager, hold out your hand."

Looking through a film of tears, she saw him holding a long ruler, and put her hands behind her back. Grabbing her by the shoulder so that his fingers bit in deeply, he growled, "Why, I'll—"

John and Frank were on their feet. "Touch my sister and I'll knock yer head off!" Frank yelled.

"You impudent young whelp!" Shoving Catherine aside, he lunged at Frank. The only door led outside. Frank ran for it, but the teacher caught him and struck again and again with the ruler, while Frank curled into a ball with his arms over his head.

Catherine stood helpless, crying as she watched John try to pull the teacher off Frank. Hinman beat him back and continued to whip Frank. Finally he stood, breathing harshly, hair standing in spikes. Sweat trickled down his forehead.

"You may go to your seat. Go on," he prodded Frank with the ruler. Frank pulled himself up, trying hard not to cry, a few tears spilling over despite his best efforts. "John and Catherine Sager," the teacher continued, "you sit down, too. You're all very wicked children. Mary Ann Bridger, come to the front of the class and read."

After that, it was always the same. If Frank came a little late, he was whipped for that. If he came on time, Mr. Hinman surely found something to whip him for before the day's lessons were over. He whipped John and some of the others, too, usually for no good reason.

They were in school five days a week, and a half day on Saturday.

None of the children dared to tell Dr. or Mrs. Whitman what the teacher was like in their absence. They would refuse to believe it, and if Mr. Hinman found out, it would go hard on whoever told. So the children were silent, learning very little in that classroom. Frank, especially, thought mainly of how to protect himself from the next attack.

He still resented Whitman Mission and its people, so early one morning after chores, when Perrin offered to take him and John to the nearby Indian lodges, Frank hesitated.

"Aren't you interested in meeting the Indian tribes?" Perrin asked. "They're not here all year round, you know. They start to move out in spring, are gone most of the summer, and don't come back until fall. After the first winter snow, they tell great stories and legends, but they won't let you hear them until they know you well, so if you want to meet them, you should start now."

Frank viewed with suspicion the boy's good-natured face, but John spoke. "Sure, we're interested. Beats being stuck at the mission all day."

Perrin's fallen face showed this was not the enthusiastic response he had hoped for, but still, after gaining permission from his uncle, he led them a few miles to a group of lodges near the Walla Walla River. "They always camp near wood and water," Perrin explained. "They can camp closer to the river in winter, because no insects are around and the river doesn't rise too much this time of year."

Frank followed in sullen silence, but John asked questions. When they were within sight of the dwellings, he asked, "Is this the Indian village?"

"You could call it that. In winter they usually camp in larger groups and in summer in smaller groups. Families stay together, and each main Cayuse chief has his own band, but they don't have a settlement or town. They carry their mat lodges with them, and can set them up anywhere they want in Cayuse country."

"Do the same groups always stay together?"

"No. Sometimes a family travels by itself. Tribes intermarry, so each family has many relatives."

"Doesn't the chief tell them when and where they can go?"

"No, they're free to decide. There are different kinds of leaders. A war chief has authority in war, a home chief at home, but not the other way

CAYUSE MAT LODGES

Courtesy of National Park Service, Whitman Mission National Historic Site.

around, and they mostly give advice, not orders. The medicine men, or *te-wats*, are also important, but they don't order people around."

Frank looked at the lodges. The structures resembled tipis he had seen on his journey, but were the length of several tipis, oval at the bottom, and made of reed mats, not skins. The sides sloped to a sharp ridge where support poles formed a series of V's. The long reeds in the mats pointed up, so that the lodge grew from the ground like the rye grass. Except for the pointed top, it was shaped like one of the ridges that rose from the land, nothing like the Whitmans' white house with its square corners.

Near the river was a rounded, mud-plastered mound. Wisps of steam escaped from it. As he watched, a group of Indians emerged, first old men, then younger men, followed by boys, the smallest last. All of them plunged into the river, wetting themselves all over.

"What are they doing?" Frank blurted. "It's November! They'll freeze!"

"Sweat baths are their regular practice every single day. The willow frame of the *etemas*—the sweat house—is one of the first things the men build at any camp. They cover it with mud or horse blankets, then pour water on hot rocks inside for a thick steam. They stay in a long, long time, till they work up a good lather, then they jump in the river."

"Whatever for?" John asked.

"It's part of their *wash-ut*."

"Well, I wash up, too, but not in a cold river after a hot sweat."

Perrin laughed softly. "The *wash-ut* is their religion. It's their way of life because they practice it every day. They believe the sweat bath cleanses them of all ills. It's their way of thanking the Creator by starting the day with a clean mind and body. When they don't have a sweat house, they'll jump in the river even if they have to lower themselves through a hole in the ice."

"Why bother with the sweat house, then, when they have the river?" Frank asked.

"In the sweat house they receive a lot of their important teachings."

"Like what?"

"I don't know. You have to be in the tribe. See, now the women are taking the girls in. They'll have to stay in while the older ones have their say. The young ones can't leave till the old ones are good and ready."

Several boys Perrin's age, now clothed, spotted the white boys and approached them. Perrin spoke, and the boys replied.

"What language is that?" John asked.

"Nez Perce. All the tribes around here speak it. The Cayuses speak their own language as well."

One boy, with a round, friendly face, spoke a sentence, and Perrin translated: "He says to follow him and he will teach you the game of hoop-and-pole." They followed the boy into a lodge, which had fires for several families. Animal skins, woven baskets, and other possessions were neatly stored.

The Indian boy picked up a wooden hoop wrapped in buckskin, and Frank picked up a stick leaning against the wall nearby. "Is this the pole?"

Perrin translated his remark, and the Indian boy laughed and gestured towards a younger boy, speaking again in Nez Perce, which was mostly unaccented and guttural sounding. As he spoke, an unhappy look overspread the younger boy's face.

"He says whip man brought that stick for his younger brother. When children are naughty, whip man or whip woman hears of their deeds and brings them a switch. The oldest relative lectures the child. Sometimes they say, 'the hoo-hoots will come for you.' Then the child must lie down and be switched seven times. Whip man switches boys, whip woman, girls. The child must keep the switch as a reminder to be good."

"Ol' Hinman switches me a lot more than seven times, but at least I don't have to keep his ol' ruler around," Frank muttered to John.

The boys walked to a level place and played several games of hoop-and-pole, Perrin, John, and Frank each competing with an Indian boy, one rolling the hoop while the other tried throwing a pole through it. The Indian boys always won, but the white boys improved. Frank was sure he could win next game, but school started at 9:00, and the Indian boys had their own tasks to attend, so they reluctantly left the Indian village, Frank in better spirits than when he came. He was sure he could befriend the Indians. The Indian boys had already given him a name. It meant "No Eyebrows," because his eyebrows, missing since his gunpowder accident, had not yet grown back.

After most of the emigrants were on their way to the valley, Mrs. Whitman asked John if he had any relatives. "Yes, ma'am. I can name off all my aunts and uncles."

"Good. Do you know how I might write them?"

"Why...no. I know what states they live in, but not where exactly."

"That's too bad," said Mrs. Whitman. "I would like to let your relatives know you are here."

"John," said Elizabeth after overhearing this conversation, "will you tell me our aunts' and uncles' names again?"

John took her on his knee as always, and recited, one by one, every relative's name that he knew. "And don't forget, they're our family. No one else is." The children the Whitmans had taken in called them "Mother" and "Father," and lately John was disturbed to hear his sisters using the same names.

Catherine, especially, was close to Mrs. Whitman. Being confined to the house, she spent much time near her. Mrs. Whitman told her of plans and fears for the children, and Catherine could tell she cared about them. Mrs. Whitman told of her own family, left far behind in New York state, almost as far east of Missouri as Missouri was of Oregon—almost twice the distance Catherine had traveled.

Soon Catherine knew the story of the founding of the Oregon missions. In 1831, a delegation of four Nez Perce Indians traveled east to St. Louis, Missouri, to visit General William Clark, one of the leaders of the Lewis and Clark expedition, which had returned from the west twenty-five years earlier. The Indians were anxious to learn about the "white man's Book of Heaven."

Missionaries, hearing of their wish, sent out an appeal for volunteers to establish missions in Oregon. Marcus Whitman and Narcissa Prentiss both wished to go west and teach the Indians of white religion and culture. They were married on February 18, 1836, in Angelica, New York.

Catherine was well-acquainted with the details of the wedding. Narcissa's wedding dress was black bombazine, and all of her family wore black. Their daughter was going so far away they knew they would never see her again, so the wedding was like a funeral.

The congregation sang a missionary hymn, "Yes, my native land! I love thee." As the song spoke of the joys of home and the sadness of leaving, one by one, the friends and family gathered in the church were overcome by emotion. By the last verse, all were sobbing, save one. Narcissa Prentiss Whitman sang as a solo:

> In the deserts let me labor,
> On the mountains let me tell,
> How he died—the blessed Savior—
> To redeem a world from hell!
> Let me hasten, let me hasten,
> Far in heathen lands to dwell.

Hearing the story gave Catherine a strange, sad, wonderful feeling. Now she knew that Mrs. Whitman felt as homesick as herself.

The Whitmans started west on March 3, 1836, and were soon joined by another couple, Henry and Eliza Spalding, and a mechanic, William Henry Gray. Mrs. Whitman and Mrs. Spalding were the first white women to cross the Rocky Mountains, at South Pass. The missionaries traveled with the mountain men of the American Fur Company, without whose help they could not have survived the grueling journey.

By taking their wagon, reduced to a cart, as far as Fort Boise, they proved it was possible for wagons to cross the desert between the Rockies and the Blue Mountains, opening a way for others to follow. The party arrived in the Walla Walla Valley on August 31, 1836. The missions the Whitmans and Spaldings established were among the first in Oregon.

Mrs. Whitman missed her home and family so much that, when Indians were baptized, she named them after family members. There were Indians called Richard, Deborah, and Edward. Deborah she called "Cousin Deborah," since she was named for a favorite cousin.

The children at Whitman Mission slept in a loft above the sitting room, the four boys in one room, the seven girls in another. Evenings after it became too dark to see, John and Frank stayed in the loft while the other children were downstairs with the Whitmans. Mrs. Whitman was teaching them to sing, and often the sound of a hymn drifted upstairs.

One evening, John wanted to clean his gun and discovered he did not have enough clean cloths. He would have to ask the doctor for some. Dr. Whitman was easier to talk to than his wife.

As he started down the stairs, he heard Mrs. Whitman say, "Elizabeth, you knew it was wrong to grab that piece of calico from Matilda. Now you will have to give me back your string of beads."

John stepped far enough down the stairs to see what was going on, without calling attention to himself.

The girls sat on settees. On the end of one was a pile of odd scraps and a sewing box. Elizabeth faced Mrs. Whitman, one hand clutching a piece of calico and the other a string of beads around her neck. The other girls wore similar strings of beads.

"But I wanted it first!" Elizabeth protested.

"Don't argue with me. Think of your parents. What would they have me do? Wouldn't they want you to be kind to your younger sister?"

Anger flashed inside John. She always had to mention their parents when she was about to punish them.

Elizabeth's stubborn look changed to an unhappy one as she handed back the beads and calico and sat down. Mrs. Whitman began to show Matilda how to make a rag doll. Catherine was busy on one, and Mary Ann and Helen were making clothes for dolls they already had. The Sager girls' playthings were lost or abandoned on the Oregon Trail. Mrs. Whitman had to do most of the work on Matilda's doll. She had made one for Louise, who played near the others.

Well, the girls would do what they'd a mind to. It was no use standing here steaming, John realized. He'd ask for rags from Dr. Whitman, who was reading in a corner, and nip back upstairs.

He entered the sitting room, taking a few rapid steps toward Dr. Whitman before Mrs. Whitman intercepted him. John stopped in chagrin.

"We're just about to sing. We'd love it if you'd join us." Her tone and expression were hopeful.

"No, thank you, ma'am," he said, hoping he sounded more polite than he felt. "I want to clean my gun and I need some rags."

"Rags? Perhaps I can find you some." She rummaged among the scraps of cloth and held out several. "Will these do?"

"Thank you, ma'am," said John, taking them.

"You're sure you won't sing with us?"

"No, thank you, ma'am," he answered, by now quite wretched. He could feel his sisters looking at him. He knew they enjoyed singing with Mrs. Whitman and wanted him and Frank to, too. He turned quickly and started up the stairs.

Frank sat on the bed, looking at Pa's medical book, one of the few possessions they had saved, by candlelight. "What took you so long?" he asked as John entered the loft.

"Mrs. Whitman tried to turn me into one of her little songbirds."

"That old cow!" The girls thought it awful when Frank called her that, but with her large eyes and ample figure, John could see the resemblance. "Isn't it enough she's treating our sisters like they belong to her?"

"They'll forget her soon enough when we have our own place in the valley. We don't have to stay here forever."

"Just seems like forever," said Frank, returning to his book.

It began to seem longer when Catherine came to him one day in early December, visibly upset. He asked what was wrong.

"Oh, it's just awful! You know, Mother—I mean, Mrs. Whitman," she said, catching sight of his scowl, "Mrs. Whitman hasn't said anything about making Christmas presents. I thought she forgot, and I'd better remind her before it was too late. And she said...she said...." Catherine paused, as if not believing what she was about to say. "Mrs. Whitman said it ain't right to make a mockery of Christ's birthday by havin' a party. She says we're not to pay any mind to Christmas."

"She said *that?*"

"Yes!" Catherine began to cry.

Frank was too upset to cry. *No Christmas?* Every year Ma and Pa made sure to have some kind of a Christmas. Ma baked pies or cakes, Pa carved wooden toys. One year Ma made them all new tippets and mittens. When the children were old enough, they made each other presents in secret.

He burned in resentment against the Whitmans. It was bad enough, them trying to take his parents' place. Dr. Whitman was all right sometimes, but he was a far cry from Pa. Mrs. Whitman couldn't compare to Ma in the least. Ma cared about him. If he came to her with his back all bruised, saying, "Ma, my teacher's beating me," she'd tend to his bruises, then take a good big piece out of that teacher, and so would Pa.

But Ma and Pa, in leaving him unprotected, showed they weren't as strong as he thought.

On the first Monday in December, they had to attend a prayer meeting. Mrs. Whitman explained that a prayer meeting the first Monday in each month was to read about, and pray for, missions.

Frank would not have minded that so much. But at Whitman Mission, prayers were ceaseless.

Saturday nights was Bible class meeting. Each child had to prove a subject from the Bible. After everyone made his or her proof and the others commented, they took turns reading verses of a Bible chapter. The Whitmans had the children comment on what they read to make sure they understood it. Frank tried to say things to please them, though most times his heart was not in it. He believed in the Bible all right, but this constant studying nearly wore him out.

After this, they all sang a hymn together. These times John and Frank did not escape singing.

Saturday night was only practice for Sunday morning's ordeal. On the Sabbath, no one dared work, or make a noise. They scarcely dared breathe. A silent pall hung over the house.

When they came downstairs Sunday morning, the Whitmans reminded each one that it was the Sabbath, and gave them books, or pictures for the younger ones. Although not yet in school, even little Louise could read words of three letters, a remarkable accomplishment for a three-year-old girl. Frank sat with the others, reading until breakfast. He dared not do otherwise.

Rosanna was much better now. Mrs. Whitman's care had put meat on her bones, and she was able to play, but on the Sabbath even her toys were put away. They never ate a hot meal on Sunday. Mrs. Whitman cooked the night before, and after they ate, she set aside the dishes for one of the girls to wash on Monday.

After breakfast, they dressed for Sunday School, which Mrs. Whitman held at 11:00 in the schoolroom, while the doctor conducted worship service with the Indians. Frank and the other children read notes and expositions on the lesson. Sunday School lasted an hour, then it was time for lunch and two more hours of silent reading.

By 3:00 Frank thought they could be free of so much silent meditation, but then it was time for another worship service, this one in English. Dr. Whitman read a sermon, and woe unto the child who could not remember the text. The rest of the evening they spent reading, and talking with Dr. Whitman about what they had read. Sunday nights at family prayers, the children repeated Bible verses learned before breakfast each morning. Frank always pretended interest. He hated it when they made him feel like a sinner, and he did not need more trouble.

On Thursday evenings, during a prayer meeting with the children, Mrs. Whitman discussed the salvation of their souls. John and Frank, who were baptized, were saved as far as they were concerned. Frank was tired of hearing about it all the time. It made him angry. He was angry at his parents for dying, angry at God for letting it happen, angry at the Whitmans for harping on about death all the time, and he knew if he said anything everyone would be angry at him. He still believed that if not for Marcus Whitman's handbill, his family might now be safe and whole in Missouri.

Adults had different ideas about where his parents had gone. He reckoned he believed that Ma and Pa were in Heaven, or sleeping until Judgment Day, or in the Land of the Dead the Indians spoke of, from which none returned, but where the living, after death, met those who had gone before. It was all scant comfort. He didn't have to like any of it.

Catherine thrived on religious instruction. Frank admitted to himself that the teachings helped her to live better. She prayed earnestly and aloud, without embarrassment or hesitation, excelling at repeating her verses. Frank, however, found memorization difficult. He remembered general ideas, but exact words often escaped him.

One Sunday, Frank was reciting his verses. He searched frantically for the words to Wednesday's verse. It was something about lines and precepts.

"For precept...must be...upon line," he faltered.

"That is incorrect, Francis," said Dr. Whitman. "Try again."

"For line must be upon precept—" he began desperately.

Dr. Whitman stilled him with a look. "'For precept must be upon precept, precept upon precept; line upon line, line upon line; here a little, and there a little.' Isaiah twenty-eight, verse ten," he recited smoothly. "I thought you could learn a simple one like that."

Frank felt himself redden.

Mrs. Whitman said, "That is how we try to teach you, precept upon precept, line upon line. Why do you find it so difficult to follow the rules we set forth?"

Frank was too choked with anger and humiliation to answer. His injured pride burned hotly inside him as he recited the rest of his verses. He was not sure yet what to do about it, but he had passed his boiling point, and wanted to escape this place.

TWELVE

Winter weather and his growing fascination with the Indian tribes temporarily cooled Frank's simmering escape plans. Unable to flee the Whitmans, he instead immersed himself in the Indians' way of life.

In November, groups of Cayuses, Walla Wallas, and Umatillas began gathering on the Walla Walla River's banks in loose formation, in large enough numbers by December to be called villages. All over the area near rivers, these winter villages collected. With or without John and Perrin, Frank frequented villages, learning Indian words and skills.

He asked tribal members about the other tribes, but could only gather certain information. When it came to anything negative, the Indians believed, "All things travel in circles. Speak ill of someone, and the bad will return to you in a circle." So Frank learned by watching how the tribes related.

The Cayuses were the imperial lords of the valley, generally aggressive and demanding, having conquered the Walla Wallas and Umatillas in raids and battles. Indians of other tribes, captured in raids, lived as slaves. Slaves, however, could work their way into the tribe by strength of deed.

Most other Indians feared the Cayuses. A Cayuse could ride into a Walla Walla or Umatilla camp, demand food or clothing, and receive them with little resistance. The Walla Wallas and Umatillas avoided angering the Cayuses. The Cayuses were the wealthiest tribe, gaining through force. Unlike landlords, they only demanded possessions from certain others, not taxing every member of another tribe. All the Indians believed that no one owned the land, which Hon-ea-woat, the Creator or Great Spirit, ordained for use by all.

The Cayuses called themselves *Te-taw-ken* (we, the people). They believed that the Nez Perces, Cayuses, and Walla Wallas came into being from pieces of a great beaver (Pieka) which became trapped in the Palouse River while retreating from the larger Snake River. This beaver created Palouse Falls and the area's people.

The Cayuses, having sprung from the beaver's heart, were braver, stronger, and more successful than neighboring tribes. Due to their superiority, they guarded their customs closer than other tribes, refusing to answer certain of Frank's questions.

Perrin spoke Nez Perce fairly well, and John and Frank were learning, but when the Cayuses did not want the boys to understand them, they spoke in their own language, a harsh sound like sticks breaking. It was unlike Nez Perce, English, German, or any language the boys had heard.

The Indians often laughed as Frank struggled to learn Nez Perce. He remembered his laughter when he first heard Dr. Degen speak. The Indians' language seemed more backwards in sentence order, its words less pronounceable, than English was for Dr. Degen.

At first none of it made sense, then one by one words assumed meaning, till familiar words jumped out at him as the Indians spoke. Frank imitated the words he knew, but learned to be careful. A slight change of accent meant he was speaking nonsense, or worse, saying something indecent.

Even after learning the language well enough to follow conversations, Frank had great difficulty speaking. Understanding was one thing, forming sentences and pronouncing words quite another. Cayuse was a much more difficult language. Even some Cayuse children did not understand it, and the whites did not attempt it at all.

December closed around Waiilatpu. Days grew shorter and darker, snow fell, and the Indians gathered in their mat lodges, shutting out the cold, deepening preparations for the great turning of the season—the Indian New Year. This fell a few days before the white people's celebration, Christmas.

As this season approached, the Indians gathered around their fires. While smoke holes funneled dark gray smoke into light gray air, tribal elders taught the young through stories. "These stories must not be told until snow falls, and then only during winter," they said. "In winter your mind is set, and you are ready to receive these teachings. Listen carefully and understand. When your elders die, they will take all they know. You must keep this knowledge with you." Unlike the whites with their "Book of Heaven," the Indians lacked written language.

Long knotted strings recorded past deeds and events, recounted by one who knew how to read the strings. Songs, feasts, and stories marked the year's turning. Grandmothers and grandfathers told of ancient days and how things came into being. Almost all the stories taught a lesson, very few entertaining only. All of this was part of the Indians' religion.

The stories were many, and though some were repeated, the young were expected to learn the first time. Frank soon found that asking for instruction after once receiving it brought a long stern lecture. "Teachings drift from your mind as the smoke drifts from the hole! How do you expect to live after your ancestors have passed on? You cannot dig them up to ask questions! Learn to listen not only with your ears, but with your heart." In the wild, one mistake could mean death. Only after the youth understood this would the story or fact be repeated, and then only once. Like the whites, Indian children learned "precept upon precept, line upon line."

One story told of how the Cayuse gained fire. At one time Mount Hood contained all the fire in the world. Fire and smoke spewed from it, and inside Fire Demons guarded a vast lake of fire.

Two brave young men, Takhstspul and Ipskayt, decided to steal fire for their people. They cleverly evaded the Fire Demons, but at the last moment were chased, Takhstspul running so fast his path melted the snow and carved out a great river.

The Great Spirit, Hon-ea-woat, permitting his children to keep the stolen fire, changed the Fire Demons into pine trees, which is why pine trees are so thick high on the mountain. Takhstspul became a beaver, Ipskayt a woodpecker. The beaver spat the fire into a willow log, and to this day the willow log is used to start fire. The woodpecker taps at it to show the fire is in the wood.

Besides stories told around fires in mat lodges, other stories were imparted in the sweat lodges, the elder men teaching the boys and the elder women, the girls. Inside the lodges, in temperatures much more intense than on a hot summer day, the young conditioned their bodies and minds, gaining strength to withstand the heat while concentrating on the teachings. Obedience and proper behavior were expected, not rewarded, while disobedience and misbehavior drew shame and punishment. Ostracism was the penalty for resisting society's codes.

Frank learned so quickly, at first with Perrin translating and later on his own, that the Indians gave him a name meaning "Quick Learner." He was curious about everything of the Indians', fascinated by their pipe tomahawks with metal heads and wooden handles. Some were plain, others elaborately curlicued and decorated with beadwork. The tomahawks were pipes in time of peace, weapons in time of war, or hatchet-like tools any time.

"I wonder how they work this metal without blacksmithing tools?" he asked Perrin.

"They soften it real well with spit and pound it with rocks." At Frank's openmouthed expression, he laughed. "They're trade items made in England or France. The Indians trade with the Hudson's Bay Company for them."

Frank was astonished. To think of Indian tools being made clear over in England and France, then shipped here!

He wanted to learn to make real Indian weapons and fire, to hunt the Indian way, which was the main use of bow and arrow, since guns scared animals, how to ambush the eagle for its feathers, then release it. Umatillas and Walla Wallas offered to teach him some of what he wanted.

He had less luck with the Cayuses. Most of the Indians laboring for Dr. Whitman, digging ditches, herding sheep, and other heavy work, were Walla Wallas. Cayuse men were too proud to work much, acquiring necessities through raiding and trading. Their women seemed like slaves compared to white women or even other Indian women, though all women worked very hard, but the thought of their women and children working for outsiders alarmed Cayuse men, and Dr. Whitman knew not to expect it.

Certain knowledge belonged only to the tribe. Each boy and girl must quest on a night vigil for their guardian spirit. They could never reveal their spirit, or, in some tribes, it would desert them, in others it would return causing illness. After acquiring their spirit and its powers and song, and learning the proper tasks of men or women, the children were ready to be initiated into the tribe.

The Whitmans, having established their mission to discourage the Indians of "superstitions," as they called them, would be horrified at the thought of their foster boy going on a spirit quest. Besides, school and daily chores filled much of his time, and he was not allowed to stay out overnight.

Frank had to content himself with learning games, skills the Indians were willing to share, and racing with the boys. John entered in to a lesser extent. Even with the elders' strictness towards the young, Frank found the Indians' society easier than that of the Whitmans.

"We are here to teach them our ways, not learn theirs," Marcus Whitman warned. "Be careful what games you play. The stick and bone game is gambling, which is a sin."

"I don't like my children associating too much with Indians," said Mrs. Whitman. "Their language is coarse and crude, and you may pick up lice in their houses. Lodge living is unsanitary. I don't know what I'd do in this country without fine-toothed combs. I call them louse traps."

But, learning from the Indians, Frank thought it would be fine living in a lodge, growing his hair long, wearing breechclouts and blankets, and swimming, hunting, and fishing when he pleased. The Indians struggled to survive, but seemed free. When he left Whitman Mission he would be free, too, even if he never lived like the Indians.

Frank found one friend at the mission. John Perkins, hired by Dr. Whitman to repair and run the gristmill, took an interest in him.

Glad for someone to confide in, Frank saw him as often as he could. The mill's squeaking, grinding machinery and racing water made a background to their conversation, so Frank was not afraid of being overheard. He was even able to tell of the beatings Mr. Hinman inflicted at every turn. After showing the marks on his back, Frank made Mr. Perkins promise not to tell about Mr. Hinman.

Soon Mr. Perkins was talking to John, and found he, too, was unhappy. He asked if the girls were happy, and when the boys said yes, he said, "Then why don't you two come to the valley with me in the spring? Leave your sisters here, if they're happy, but you shouldn't stay and be treated this way."

John shook his head. "Our Ma told us to keep the girls together. We can't go without them, and if we took them, they'd be split up. I reckon we'll have to stick it out."

Mr. Perkins looked at Frank, who avoided his gaze. John's words made him remember Ma's face as she said he was old enough to help keep the girls together.

As winter clouds lifted, the Whitmans prepared for a missionary meeting in May. The Spaldings, who had come west with the Whitmans in 1836, and other missionary families who had arrived in 1838, would attend. One night Mrs. Whitman asked the children how they felt about being baptized at the meeting. Catherine, Elizabeth, and Matilda wanted to, and the Whitmans decided for Louise and Rosanna.

The boys shook their heads. "We've already been baptized," said John. "I reckon we don't need to again."

The Whitmans looked unhappy, but did not try to force them.

With spring, the year entered another phase in its eternal circle. Food stored in summer and autumn began to run low around February. For whites, spring meant long hours in the fields, plowing, sowing, and weeding. For Indians, as Mother Earth turned green, she prepared to yield food for them to gather, and new generations of all living things. This was an important time, not to be taken for granted.

Around the time of the whites' celebration of Easter, the Indians celebrated the First Foods Feast. Women, the custodians of food, prepared it and laid it out, each food in its order, within the lodge. A leader, chief or priest, rose before the assembled people to remind his listeners of the Great Spirit who had created the land and its foods for all. Prophecy stated that the First Foods ritual and gathering cycle would be carried out each spring throughout eternity.

After the leader thanked the Great Spirit for providing food to nourish all creatures, and the people chanted the Song of Thanksgiving seven times, the leader tasted each food in order.

"*Nasau*," he would say, lifting salmon to his lips, "*choos*," before drinking water.

Salmon always came first, then dried meat, deer or elk, then roots in order, first kouse (pronounced khouch with a sound the whites could not imitate), bitterroot, and others, lastly huckleberries and chokecherries.

This procession of foods was the Indians' circle. Only after partaking the First Foods Feast could the women dig for roots and the men hunt animals; before then only food stored from the previous year could be used.

Boys and girls from the age of eight or nine learned their separate tasks. For boys, making weapons and stalking animals, learning which animals to hunt at what times so as not to disturb their cycle. For girls, gathering and drying roots, preparing and storing the fish and animals the boys captured, or, as the Indians said, "taking care of the food." If food was not properly cared for each spring, it would not return the following spring. Roots must be dug, so many taken and so many left, animals hunted, so many taken and so many left, or else they would depart the land. The harvesting and leaving were equally important. The Indians must respect Mother Earth if they expected to be welcomed back to her bosom when they died.

Frank's Indian friends were shocked when he told them of the buffalo hunt on the Oregon Trail, where tons of meat spoiled. "The right way to hunt is to take only what one needs, and to use every part of the animal. Nothing must be wasted. Nature is pure and must not be violated. The white man slaughters the buffalo and would change the rivers themselves if they did not suit him." They spoke of Dr. Whitman's diverting the Walla Walla River for use in his mill pond and irrigation ditches. "If Nature is not taken care of, it will never return as it was, and the Indian will perish with the buffalo."

During this gathering season, one of the main differences between whites and Indians surfaced. Marcus Whitman, like most whites, marked off his fields and planted by his own labor crops, within his fences, which he considered his. The Indians believed the land was made for all, and Cayuses were entitled to anything growing on Cayuse land. Marcus Whitman might plant crops, but the Great Spirit grew them through Mother Earth. A fence was only a horizontal piece of wood, and Whitman's lectures on stealing futile. Nothing could be stolen unless owned in the first place, and no one person owned the land and its harvest.

To add to this problem, Whitman was supposed to be paying them for use of their land, but his payments were in arrears. He claimed a Cayuse chief, Umtippe, gave him the section of land where the mission stood. The Cayuses argued that a chief could not give away land which belonged to the tribe as a whole. The lending of Umtippe's section to Whitman ended with the chief's death, and the land reverted to the tribe. Keeping the Indians out of the crops was difficult. They did not reject farming themselves, but their nomadic life conflicted with raising crops.

Men and women of the tribes each had distinctive tasks. According to their religion, one must not perform another's task or disaster would befall the tribes. As in white society, a strict order of life prevailed at all times. Thus, if a boy felled a deer or speared a fish, it was a girl's job to carry it home and prepare it. Women did almost all the carrying, also packing the family home and possessions when it was time to move, and many things the whites considered man's work. Women rarely expressed an opinion to men. Public speaking especially was forbidden, being solely a man's province.

In contrast, Narcissa Whitman had great say in how Whitman Mission operated. The children's tasks varied, only certain ones being girls' or boys' jobs. It was not against their religion, nor would disaster befall, if the children traded chores now and then. The disaster would befall the children if they shirked a chore assigned to them.

The Indians wondered why Marcus Whitman listened to his wife so much, and why he had only one, when with many wives, everyone had more to eat. Grandmothers stayed home, cared for babies, and cooked, while mothers foraged. Walla Walla and Umatilla men were generally less strict with their wives, sometimes listening to them or helping them. The food and home were considered the woman's property, while in the Cayuse tribe, who held themselves superior to others, everything belonged to the men, and women's words were rarely heeded.

The Sager girls, like the Indian girls, must clothe the family, the mission girls dyeing and knitting the wool Mrs. Whitman spun and sewing cloth, the Indian girls tanning hides and sewing moccasins. Little David Malin, too young for field work, had his own household duties.

Mrs. Whitman and the Indian mothers both taught, "There is a time for work and a time for play. Work is important, play is not. Only after finishing work comes the time for play, and the times are separate. Responsibilities always come first." The adults made sure the children understood why work was important. Without it, no one would survive.

The children would have enjoyed lightening tasks by treating them as games, but work was too important to be disguised as play. Children must never avoid work, or interrupt a busy adult.

When play time came, the Sager girls, Mary Ann, Helen, and David could play with nearby Indian youngsters. The white, half-Indian, and Indian children treated each other the same. As long as companionship and laughter were shared, no room was left for prejudice. The Indian girls, with wonderfully crafted dolls in toy cradleboards, enjoyed many games with Mrs. Whitman's children. The girls, being younger than the boys, found it easier to learn each other's languages. John and Frank, however, had more opportunity to mix with Indians their own age, being older and able to leave the mission grounds for longer times and farther distances, and so learned more than their sisters.

Both the boys and girls were allowed to attend feasts of celebration with the Indian children. These ceremonies, open to all, celebrated the children's maturing by marking an Indian boy's first kill, or an Indian girl's first gathering of roots or berries. At the feast, the food was served, and elders advised, encouraging the youngsters to continue providing food. "Your back is strong, your legs are strong," they said. "You are younger, and must work harder to feed your people." When special maturity surfaced, family elders renamed the child, bestowing adulthood in the Indian way.

Spring showers passed away. The sun shone warm and bright, sparkling on new green grass and falling golden on the few remnants of last year's dusty brown grass that escaped the fires the Indians set in late fall. Tiny light green spikes fringed the wagon tracks. Beyond the mill pond, across miles of land mounded with new rye grass clumps, the half-circle of mountains was a delicate, clear blue patched with white. The apple orchard behind the house was a mass of tender green leaves and white blossoms.

Shortly before the missionaries arrived for the meeting, John said to Frank, "About this baptism business...Rosanna should be christened to honor Ma and Pa."

Frank thought this would be fine. "What would we call her?" he asked.

"Henrietta Naomi." John savored the name.

"Henrietta Naomi," said Frank in contentment. It was perfect. They kept the name secret until the last moment.

"I don't know if it's best to change her name from what your parents gave her—" began Mrs. Whitman. Then, seeing their intent faces, she said, "But I believe you are right."

"Besides," smiled Dr. Whitman, "Henrietta's a prettier name than Rosanna. At least you didn't call her Narcissa. I can't think of a homelier name." He called his wife "Wife" or "Mother," often teasing her while she smiled through pretended annoyance.

The Whitmans' missionary associates came to the mission to pray, and discuss business. The Walker and Eells families, with six little children, and a girl the Walkers were caring for, rode the one hundred and seventy miles from Tshimakain, and John and Frank had a chance to meet the people they almost had to live with.

The Reverend Henry Spalding came from his mission, Lapwai, one hundred and twenty miles northeast of Waiilatpu. His wife was at home caring for their smaller children, and he brought his daughter Eliza, who like Elizabeth was seven years old. Rev. Spalding had a wild dark beard and a wilder eye. The boys were a little afraid of him.

The third day of the meeting, Sunday, May 11, 1845, Rev. Spalding baptized six children: Mary Ann Bridger, Catherine Carney Sager, her sisters Elizabeth Maria, Matilda Jane, Hannah Louise, and the baby, christened Henrietta Naomi. Frank and John exchanged a pleased glance as Rev. Spalding pronounced her new name.

They were unhappy about the other person baptized: their teacher, Alanson Hinman. He received membership in the First Presbyterian Church of Oregon. Frank bristled as the other adults fussed over him, and Mr. Hinman smiled ingratiatingly.

What irked him was that to be baptized by Rev. Spalding, a person must pass a test of faith almost as rigorous as the Indians' initiation. How could Mr. Hinman claim Christianity after the way he'd treated the children all winter, and how could they believe him? Frank could see by John's face that he felt the same.

"And the next day he had fits," Frank told Mr. Perkins later, with disgust. "Jerked around and rolled his eyes. They said he was probably excited about being baptized and all. They still think he's so all-fired holy." He used the swear word knowing Mrs. Whitman would be angry if she heard it.

"He may have a medical condition causing fits," said Mr. Perkins, "And don't be so sure that Christianity won't do him some good. Let's hope he learns to do unto others as he would be done unto. Won't be too long and I'll go to the valley," he added temptingly, "and you, and your brother if he wants to, can come along. My oldest child is only eight. I could use two fine big strong boys to help me."

Frank nodded seriously, trying not to show how pleased he was to be called "fine." The Whitmans did not think he was "fine."

The meeting ended May 14, 1845, and many of the emigrant families who had stayed the winter left soon after the visiting missionaries. The Perkins family and a few others stayed. Not long afterwards, Mr. Hinman let school out for the summer. He would spend the last of his time at Waiilatpu preparing for a journey, accompanying Dr. Whitman and Emma Hobson, the little girl who had been staying with the Walkers, to the Willamette Valley.

Frank was relieved to see Mr. Hinman go, but even that could not convince him to stay longer at Waiilatpu. He would go with Mr. Perkins to a place where he would be better treated, where he would be wanted.

The others went about their usual routine, not noticing Frank's feelings. Mrs. Whitman took the younger children on nature walks. They climbed the steep hill close by. Catherine's leg was well enough to do some walking now, and her shyness was disappearing, especially now that she did not have Mr. Hinman to worry about.

Frank could tell his sisters enjoyed their activities at Whitman Mission. They planted a vegetable garden near the house, and each had her own flower garden. In the morning they had household duties, and they rarely needed to be told. Mrs. Whitman pointed at the task, and the girl to do it. When that finger pointed, they jumped as if it were a gun.

Dr. Whitman's and the boys' before noon work was mostly outside. The boys tended stock and milked the cows and they all worked in the fields. At noon everyone came in for dinner. Afterwards the doctor and boys rested till 1:00 and the girls sewed while one read aloud. Dr. Whitman, John, Frank, and Perrin went back to work until 5:00, when everyone ate supper.

After supper, the girls worked in their garden, then came free time. Daily swimming for the girls was in the hour before lunch. The three older boys took David swimming evenings. Mrs. Whitman was very particular that they wait an hour after dinner.

Peeling off his sweaty clothes and plunging into the cool waters of the Walla Walla River was one of the few things Frank enjoyed about their daily routine. Sometimes before going to the river, they brought the horses so Mrs. Whitman and the girls could ride. Mrs. Whitman was teaching the girls to ride sidesaddle, like her.

Occasionally Indian boys joined them at the swimming hole, but summer was nearing and it was time for the Indian villages to break up as the Indians ranged wide in search of food. Early spring brought salmon, then roots to gather in the foothills of the Blue Mountains. In summer, the Indians prepared these foods for winter use, gathered the hemp and tule reeds for their winter lodges, and scraped and tanned hides.

Spending part of early spring and summer around Whitman Mission, later in the season they neared the Blue Mountains for deer and elk hunting. They did not move as a large group or even by tribes, but individually, often a single family traveling alone. By constant moving, they left behind many of the fleas and lice that plagued campsites, and provided grazing for the thousands of horses by which they measured their wealth.

In the fall, they moved down the Columbia to Celilo Falls, near the Dalles, for a huge trade fair, the finale of the gathering season. Indians of many tribes traded food, clothing, materials, and companionship before establishing winter camps. To the Indians, this meant the completion of their circle, the constant seasonal order established at the beginning of time and continued each year. To Frank, it merely meant he would be without friends for much of the summer. Restlessness stirred within him.

Frank felt almost free when he and John were allowed to ride over the countryside, gathering flowers in a tin box for Mrs. Whitman to press. She was an eager student and teacher of botany.

Beneath the wide sweep of cloud-tossed sky, they searched the grass for heavy yellow sunflowers, tall red stalks of Indian Paintbrush, and white constellations of Queen Anne's Lace, each tuft of blossoms like delicately mounded snow that might melt at a touch. One tiny dark red-purple flower at the center was its heart. The flowers softly thumped the box's sides and lay wilting.

The hobbled horses snuffed delicately and cropped grass a little distance away. "I sure hope they don't gobble the best flowers," said John. "Oh, here's something good!" His hand grasped a stem of buttercups as bright as if they had just been waxed. They waved in the breeze a moment, then Frank saw them shining softly on the bottom of the tin box.

Serviceberry bushes, commonplace shrubs through most of the year, now showed forth delicate white blossoms to tell all the world it was spring. Sparrows laced the sky, flipping their wings in the cool air. Frank felt a heavy weight pressing between his shoulders as he viewed the bright land and sky. He wished he might find a place where he could bloom instead of wilt, where he would be happy enough to sing and show the world he was glad he lived.

A few Indians still camped near the mission, and one day Dr. Whitman left John and Perrin in charge of the chores and took Frank and the girls to help give them a farming lesson.

One of the emigrants still at the mission was an Irishman named O'Kelley. He drove the wagon the girls rode in. Frank and Dr. Whitman rode mares, each with a colt trotting behind.

"I'll give ye a foin big dinner," O'Kelley promised. "I've a big chunk of bafe to bile, and I'll make drap dumplings."

"What's bafe?" Matilda wanted to know.

"Beef! That's how he says beef," Frank hissed at her.

"But what are drap dumplings?"

That Frank could not answer, and, though the girls pestered him, O'Kelley only smiled and looked mysterious. Frank wondered, but was too proud to make a fool of himself, like the girls.

"Here's the first lodge where we'll help the Indians cultivate their garden," said Dr. Whitman. He indicated a mat lodge near a miserable little weed-choked garden patch.

"Sure, and there's not much cultivation here," said O'Kelley.

Dr. Whitman laughed. "The Indians will learn to farm, and eventually be civilized. They've been hunters for years. They are gone much of the summer, and sometimes the men go to buffalo country for two or three years. They must learn to understand the importance of staying in one place, farming."

Frank, who had not meant to speak, suddenly found himself saying, "Why should they farm, when they're used to hunting?" Maybe the Indians, like himself, wanted to be left alone.

"Don't you think the emigrants will farm?" Dr. Whitman asked.

"I reckon so."

"More farmers will come west every year," Dr. Whitman explained. "The Indians can't preserve their old ways, riding here and there to hunt. If they become farmers, everyone can settle peacefully together."

The Indians assembled, and Dr. Whitman spoke earnestly in their tongue about the importance and care of a garden.

From that lodge, they went on to others. At last it was time for the beef and "drap" dumplings. Frank always thought dumplings were supposed to float. No doubt these were "drap" dumplings, for they sank to the bottom of the kettle and stayed there till the children fished them out.

After visiting more lodges with miserable little garden patches, Dr. Whitman said it was time to leave. Matilda ran to Frank as he mounted his horse. "Take me back, Frank, please?" She smiled up at him.

He smiled. One of his sisters still cared for him, and didn't think the Whitmans were their only family. "Sure," he said, lifting her.

They crossed the Walla Walla River at a different place on their way back. It looked swifter and deeper, but O'Kelley forded the oxen and wagon, and Dr. Whitman said the horses would be all right. He started into the stream, Frank and Matilda close behind.

Halfway across, the river grew deep and swift. It tugged at the horses, but they managed to hold their own. The colts, though, were too small to swim across and began to float downstream. Hearing their frantic neighs, their mothers neighed in answer and tried to go after them.

Taking a tight grip on the wet reins, Frank turned his mare desperately toward the opposite bank. "Hang on, Matilda! Hang on!"

"I am!" She squeezed his ribs so tight he could hardly breathe. As the mare plunged through the water, Frank saw the colts bobbing like corks, tossing their heads and rolling terrified eyes. A bit of color disappeared beneath the current; Matilda had lost her sunbonnet. She wailed. "I'll take care of you!" yelled Frank over the churning water and frantic neighs.

Then they were across. The shaking mare scrambled up the bank and stood dripping. Dr. Whitman handed his reins to Frank. "Hold my horse. Mr. O'Kelley and I are going after the colts."

The colts had rounded a bend, but they could still hear them. Catherine and Mary Ann helped Frank hold the horses, which kept starting after their colts until Dr. Whitman and Mr. O'Kelley brought them back.

"I'm sorry," said Dr. Whitman. "I judged in error that time."

"Oh, now, don't worry about it," said Mr. O'Kelley. "We're all allowed mistakes."

As they headed toward the mission, wet and tired, the colts again trotting behind, Frank said to Matilda, "Like I told you, I'll always take care of you."

"If I hadn't a hung on to you, I woulda gone right down the river," said Matilda.

Dr. Whitman, Mr. Hinman, and Emma Hobson left for the valley near the end of May. The others had Henrietta's first birthday celebration on the last day of May. When Frank came in at noon, the girls were fixing lunch and Mrs. Whitman the cake.

Henrietta was a fine big baby now, and could stand, with something to hang on to. While Mrs. Whitman frosted her cake, Henrietta crawled on to a chair next to her. She was a funny kid, Frank thought. Even though she couldn't walk, she could climb.

She was interested in the cake, and no wonder. Pies and cakes were rarities at Waiilatpu—Mrs. Whitman thought too many sweets bad for children. They had pies for Thanksgiving and New Year's, and a cake for Louisa's third birthday in January, and pies for John's fourteenth in March and Catherine's tenth in April, and those were the only such treats they had since coming here. Ma had baked sweet things much more often, not only for special occasions.

Henrietta seemed to know the cake was hers. She reached for it. "No, no," said Mrs. Whitman forcefully, lifting her down. Henrietta climbed the chair again, and in a moment was reaching once more for the cake. This time Mrs. Whitman did not stop to ask what her parents would have done. She turned her over her knee and spanked her, setting her bawling on the floor.

Frank trembled with rage. How could Mrs. Whitman be so mean as to spank Henrietta for admiring her own cake on her own birthday? He didn't dare speak, or she'd spank him, too. Oh, he couldn't stay in a place where people could mistreat his little sister and he could do nothing about it. He stalked out. Crossing the yard in throbbing rage, he almost ran into Mr. Perkins, who said, "I'm leaving Monday." His tone said, "This is your last chance."

"I'll go," said Frank. "I'll sneak everything I need to you, then make a run for it at the last minute."

Mr. Perkins smiled. "I'll have a horse ready for you."

"Thanks," said Frank, cooling off. "I better go in to lunch. I won't get none if I'm late."

After supper that evening, without asking permission, he climbed the steep hill. It was quite a scramble, clinging to weeds and grass clumps, with dirt trickles cascading beneath his feet. He didn't know how that old cow Mrs. Whitman ever made it up this hill. At last he stood on top.

Nothing was above him but the clear blue sky touched with white wisps of cloud. From here, the emigrant house was a small box he could have held in his palm. The fences were tiny sticks. The blacksmith shop, mill, and mission house were small neat squares and rectangles. Tiny girls worked in a tiny garden. Apple trees were little knots in orderly rows.

He looked at the mill pond, shining in the late-afternoon sun, at the curving loop of river running behind the house. It all seemed small and unimportant from here. The mill pond was a mud puddle, the mission with all its activity an anthill, or maybe a beehive.

He looked far into the distance, trying to sight his way to the Willamette Valley. He would be glad to go there. He would be glad to leave this place.

THIRTEEN

Frank came down from the hill and discovered that no one had missed him. They were preparing for the Sabbath. *At least I won't have to go through that after tomorrow,* he thought, trying to feel happy about it.

Sunday evening, in their loft room, he told John of his decision.

"But you *can't* leave!" John wailed.

Frank motioned frantically. "Shush! You want them to hear?"

John went on in an undertone tinged with desperation. "Ma said for us to keep the girls together. She said—"

"She said to take them to Whitman Mission, and we done that," snapped Frank.

"But we promised to always stay with them and take care of them!"

"Those Whitmans won't let us do anything for the girls. They want to be boss, but they ain't *my* boss. I don't have to stay."

John's eyes filled with tears. "Stay for me, Frank. *Stay for me.*"

"You have Perrin." Frank turned away. They both knew Perrin was a friend to John, but not a brother. *But it's his own fault if he don't want to go with me,* thought Frank fiercely as he left the room.

He stood a moment in indecision. Should he say good-bye to the girls? No, the little ones would only take on and run to Mrs. Whitman, who would find a way to keep him here. But he could tell Catherine, who was in the girls' room alone, in bed early with chills and fever.

Frank entered the room softly. Catherine's head lay on the pillow, her light hair spread across it. Her eyes were closed. A candle flickered on a table beside the bed, with an open book face down near it.

"Katie," he said softly, "You asleep?"

Catherine's blue-gray eyes opened. "Naw," she said, "I was reading, but my eyes are plumb tuckered out."

"Well," he said gruffly, "blow out that candle if you ain't usin' it. It's dangerous."

"I will," she said, and kept looking at him as if to ask, "Is that all you came in to say?"

Frank braced himself, drew a deep breath, and said, "If I tell you something real important, will you promise not to tell?"

She nodded solemnly.

Drawing a deep breath, he said, "I've decided to leave."

"Whatever for? Mr. Hinman's gone. He ain't coming back."

"He wasn't the only one who bothered me."

"Who else does, then?"

"Mrs. Whitman!"

"She ain't a bother! Why, she loves us like a mother! Almost like a mother," she corrected hastily as Frank took a menacing step forward.

"She isn't nice to the children. She even spanked Henrietta for trying to touch her own birthday cake."

"Well, I think she was pretty nice to make Henrietta a cake at all. If she does correct us or spank us, it's for our own good."

"Ha!"

"Anyhow, you wouldn't run away. You wouldn't be brave enough to go off and leave us." Her voice was not pleading, like John's, but full of conviction. She closed her eyes again.

Frank walked to the door, turned in the doorway and said, "You just watch me."

He woke the next morning with a strange feeling, half-heavy, half-light. John was downstairs, David and Perrin were dressing. Frank put on his clothes. Mr. Perkins had the rest of what he was taking. Instead of heading downstairs, he sat on the bed.

"Aren't you coming to breakfast?" Perrin said. David had already started down.

"In a minute," Frank lied, having no intention of eating breakfast as if nothing were wrong.

After a while, Elizabeth entered the room. "Everyone else is down to breakfast," she said. "Mother says to come."

"I ain't coming," he snapped, turning his back.

As he heard her go downstairs, his heart pounded and his stomach squirmed. His palms were sweating, and he stuck them under his armpits, hugging himself. He would just sit right here until Mr. Perkins was ready to go.

He heard someone else come upstairs, then Mrs. Whitman's voice said softly from the doorway, "Come to breakfast, Francis."

Frank followed her downstairs. The last thing he needed right now was an argument with Mrs. Whitman. Besides, breakfast might not be such a bad idea.

When they entered the kitchen, his first good look at Mrs. Whitman's face startled Frank. By her red-rimmed, dark-circled eyes, she seemed to have stayed awake crying. John, crying soundlessly, looked away when Frank entered. Frank was sorry a moment, then pushed the feeling away. John had told Mrs. Whitman his plan. That was all *he* cared about keeping his brother's secrets.

Frank ate the fried mush Mrs. Whitman placed before him, though his stomach was jumping, his throat so dry he could hardly swallow. He kept his eyes firmly on his plate, but knew all the others were watching him, except for John, who sat hunched over his meal with his tears falling on his food. Talk was sparse during breakfast. Louise and Helen ventured a few remarks. Even Matilda seemed subdued.

When Frank finished eating, he stood, and, acting casual, took his hat and walked slowly towards the door.

Mrs. Whitman started from her seat. "Francis," she said in a firm but not entirely steady voice, "you must not go. You must stay with me." The statement was half order, half entreaty.

Frank backed toward the door. His voice came out high. "I got to go. I can't stay."

Seeing her motion John to bolt the door, Frank rushed out in a desperate dash across the yard for the wagons. Tied nearby was the horse Mr. Perkins had promised him.

With John close behind, Frank pounded towards the horse, untied it, and leaped into the saddle. John reached for him, only brushing his moccasin. Frank wheeled and galloped down the trail.

John watched him go. He would remember this day, June 2, 1845, as the one on which Pa and Ma's worst fears were realized. The family was split up. He had failed. Blinded by tears, he started for the house.

Mrs. Whitman looked close to tears herself, the little girls uncertain and frightened. Mrs. Whitman said, "Don't worry. I'll write a letter to the doctor and Francisco will return with him."

John tried to believe this, or at least stop crying, but could do neither.

A few hours later, a boy from one of the wagons returned for a forgotten calf. Mrs. Whitman asked if Francis had come up with the wagons, and the boy answered no.

Just after the noon meal, a tall Indian with a long scar on his left cheek came to the door. Mrs. Whitman stepped out to speak to him, and John and the others stood in the doorway listening.

"Me see your boy in woods," the Indian told Mrs. Whitman. "He lost, crying. Ask way to wagon road. Not tell him. Say, 'Go home to your family.'"

"Then maybe he's still in the woods," said Mrs. Whitman. "Thank you for being so helpful. Will you go with John to look for him?"

The Indian nodded assent, and John started out with him.

All day they searched, calling, John growing more hoarse and hopeless with each passing hour. After dark a cool damp wind swept up, indicating a rain storm. "Francis!" John shouted. "Frank! Come home!"

Then the Indian was at his side. "We go back now," he said. "Storm come."

The storm swept down upon them before they reached the house. They straggled into the kitchen soaking wet. Mrs. Whitman sat in an armchair by the stove. The Indian warmed himself in silence, then went out into the storm.

Mrs. Whitman said to John, "Get some sleep. You can look for Francis tomorrow." John went to bed weary and discouraged.

The next morning, Mrs. Whitman still sat in her armchair, looking as if she had not slept. John wanted to look for Frank immediately, but she urged him to eat first.

His hunt through the sodden woods failed to turn up a trace of Francis, but he did not give up until dark. Then he returned and told Mrs. Whitman Frank must have caught up with the wagons.

When he rode away, Frank fully expected the wagons would catch up to him sooner or later. He would wait in the woods, where no one at the mission would find him.

Reaching the cool dark woods, Frank leaped from the saddle and quickly led the horse in among leafy shadows. Farther and farther they went, until Frank realized that every tree resembled every other. He had explored these woods, but had never crashed into them in such a panic. He had no idea where he was going.

Hawthorns spread their thorny branches as if to catch him, blackberry runners lay across his path to trip him. Alders, with their green leaves and small green cones, leaned over him as if examining a strange intruder. Panic rose, though he tried to resist, telling himself to be calm. If he kept going, these woods must end. But suppose he kept circling until he was plumb wore out? Maybe they would never find him. Maybe he would starve here among the hawthorns and alders and looming ponderosa pine.

A tight lump bound his throat. If only they hadn't been so cruel, forcing him to run, he wouldn't be out here now, waiting to die. Choking back a sob, he plunged recklessly through crackling underbrush. He had to keep going.

Suddenly he gasped. The tall Indian in front of him seemed almost a part of the woods. Frank was so blinded by tears he did not see him until he was right in front of him.

Frank did not know what to expect, momentarily remembering the Indians who had stolen their cattle on the Oregon Trail. He might want Frank's horse and gear. This Indian had a long scar on his left cheek, as if used to battle. Now Frank recognized him, having seen and spoken to him a few times. The man knew a little English. Trying to look brave, Frank wiped away his tears and said, "C-could you show me to the wagon road? I done lost my way."

Wasting no words, the Indian turned and Frank followed, leading his horse. At last light filtered through the trees. The woods were thinning. The Indian pointed. In the distance, the wagons rolled.

"Oh, thank you, thank you!" cried Frank, leaping on the horse and pounding towards the wagons. He reined back as he neared the Perkins wagon, and drew up by Mr. Perkins, who was driving the oxen.

"Well, I see you made it, boy. You sure took a long time gettin' here, considerin' you started before us. That horse of mine is slower than I thought. It's a mighty slow horse that's slower than an ox team."

"I got lost in the woods," Frank admitted, turning his face away. His cheeks were burning, and he wondered if tears still showed on his face.

"Well, you're here now, and that's what counts. I'm glad you came. You're a sight better off with us than with those mission people."

"I reckon so," said Frank half-heartedly, trying to think how happy he would be away from ol' Narcissa, and not about how sad she had looked, or how he would miss John and the girls. Most especially, he tried not to think about breaking his promise to his mother. He could hear her still, telling him he was old enough to help John take care of the girls, and saying, "Always stay with them, boys, keep them together. Will you promise?" And he had said, "Yes, Ma."

But, he thought, *she couldn't be mad at me for leaving if she knew the reason.*

Mr. Perkins saw Frank's agitated frown. "Don't worry, Francis," he said. "You did right by coming with us."

FOURTEEN

"Did they really beat you, Francis?"

The voice belonged to Mrs. Brewer, the Methodist missionary's wife. Their mission was at the Dalles on the Columbia, about halfway between Whitman Mission and the Willamette Valley, near Celilo Falls, where the Indian trading fair heralded each summer's end. When Mr. Perkins told Mrs. Brewer about the Whitmans' treatment of Frank, she invited the travelers to dinner.

"Well...." Frank stopped to swallow so as not to talk with his mouth full. "The Whitmans didn't beat us, so much, though Mrs. Whitman spanks my little sisters, even Henrietta, who is only one. The person who really beat us was the teacher, Mr. Hinman."

"Did he beat you awful hard?"

"To within an inch of his life," said Mr. Perkins. "Ain't that right, Frank?"

"That's right. He beat me, my brother, and all the children in the school."

"And the Whitmans wouldn't do a thing about it?" Mrs. Brewer's eyes were large and round. She was finding the talk much more interesting than the meal.

"They don't seem to care," said Mr. Perkins.

"Oh, you poor little things." Mrs. Brewer turned a sympathetic gaze on Frank. "What did they say when you told them the teacher beat you?"

Frank felt swelled up with importance, receiving so much attention from an adult. He was a little embarrassed to answer directly, so he said, "They wouldn't listen if we told them. They think everything a teacher does is right," and left out the part about being afraid to tell the Whitmans about Mr. Hinman.

"The Whitmans aren't the most amiable folks," said Mr. Perkins.

WASKOPUM

The Methodist mission at the Dalles. 1849 painting by William H. Tappan.
Courtesy, Oregon Historical Society.

"That's what I always thought." Mrs. Brewer nodded. "That Mrs. Whitman is nothing but a stuck-up redhead."

Mr. Perkins continued. "And the prices Dr. Whitman charges for his supplies—why, it's robbery. Five cents a pound for flour, and twenty for sugar! Well, I never."

Frank remembered seeing flour for twenty-five cents a pound last year at Fort Laramie, but it was impolite to contradict, so he said nothing.

"How terrible," said Mrs. Brewer. "I'm glad this poor little lamb is out of their clutches, but sorry for the others. I'll do something about this. It's truly awful."

The next day the travelers moved on towards the Willamette Valley. After seven months of being mostly cooped up inside, Frank was in the open air again, traveling by day and camping by night. He soon became a big brother to John and Sarah Perkins's five children: Sarah, eight, Eli,

six, Joe, four, Alvira, three, and the baby, Lizzie, who was born on the
Oregon Trail.

They passed through dry country at first, where tall gray round
slopes, studded with dark basalt outcroppings, were ridged around their
sides as if with cow paths. Bunch grass, growing in knots, gave them a
woolly appearance, like sheep's backs.

As they neared the coast, spruce, hemlock, cedar, and larch covered
the slopes. Pines sprayed forth starry needle clusters, and sloping fir
branches looked soft in the June sunlight. Great spreading, moss-covered
white oaks graced the woods. Cool water dripped among the airy, light
green fronds of enormous, delicate ferns.

The evergreens held dark branches against the clear blue sky.
Sometimes one or two towered alone above the earth, majestic. Out of
the woods, mountains almost always rose in view, blue and green in the
distance. Many slopes were bare because the Indians burned off grass and
brush each fall to clear the land for spring. Grass grew up in the spring,
but trees could not gain a foothold.

Once in a great while they passed a peaceful little farm with a log
cabin and barn, and cattle grazing and hogs rooting nearby. In clear
places were ripening fields of grain. Mostly, though, they passed through
wild country, settlers being few and far between. *This is the Oregon Pa
dreamed of,* thought Frank. *This is where John and I will farm and live
with the girls, as soon as ever we can.* He was the first of his family to
reach the valley his parents died dreaming of.

They arrived in an area called Yamhill, and stayed for a while with
Mr. Perkins's parents, who had come west with their sons and daughters.

Frank asked Mr. Perkins's father why this place was called Yamhill.
"It's because this is such good farm country, the yams grow as big as
hills," the old man replied seriously. "Even the little ones grow as big
around as my leg and as long as my arm."

"I see that's just something for the green ones to chew on," said
Frank. "I'd have to have a cow's stomach to digest that one."

The Perkinses laughed. "You're still pretty green yet," John Perkins
said.

John's brother Joel had bought improvements on a claim from a man
who was leaving. Claims could not be sold, but improvements, such as

a cabin, could. John Perkins must stake out a claim.

Frank rode with him over rolling hills as he surveyed the country. Some days were sunny, the blues and greens so vivid Frank caught his breath. On other days, rain drizzled, wrapping the landscape in gray, softening everything. Frank's buckskins clung to him, clammy and miserable.

Mr. Perkins seemed to like the rain, though. "Feel that. It will make the crops grow. This is God's country, the most beautiful I've seen." After that, Frank felt better about the rain.

"The place we pick has to be near the river," Mr. Perkins told him, "with wood enough to build a house and fuel the fire, but enough clear land to plant wheat and oats and barley." Wheat was all-important in Oregon. The settlers used it for money.

One day Mr. Perkins said, "This is the place. Look at that meadow rolling off away to the mountains. We'll have the river running down the side of our claim, all the wood and water and grass we need—not to mention the prettiest view of the mountains in all Yamhill."

He picked an area he figured was about six hundred and forty acres, the allotted size for a claim. The river and one of its branches made two sides of the boundary. Two ash trees, one on the river and one on the branch, served as natural markers for the claim's corners. Then Mr. Perkins drove two stakes at the other ends of the claim to show people this land was taken.

"Now it's time to build a cabin."

Mr. Perkins's father, brother, and three brothers-in-law would help build. His brother's claim came with a cabin. The others had built cabins when they came to the valley last fall.

First they sawed off sections of a huge Douglas fir, to use as wheels for a "truck" to haul logs. They drilled holes in the middles and ran axles through them. Then it was time to cut the logs.

Frank wanted to help, but Mr. Perkins said he was more useful hauling water, tending stock, and keeping tools sharpened. "You're also pretty good at amusing the young ones," he said with a wink.

One day Frank was sitting on a section of log sharpening an ax. Mr. Perkins's father and three brothers-in-law were cutting and hauling logs, great, sweet-smelling lengths of Douglas fir. The screech of the "truck" was awful. At first Frank tried sitting as far away as possible, but that only intensified the noise. It was better to sit close, but not so close something might fall on him.

John Perkins and his brother Joel would not allow the children too close while they worked. They were building up the walls, starting by laying two logs in troughs in the ground, notching the logs' ends. Then they notched two more logs and fit them into the notches of the first two to form a square. They went on up this way, cutting notches and fitting logs till the square was high enough to form the cabin walls.

Eight-year-old Sarah sat by Frank with a sigh, bored with keeping an eye on the little ones for her Ma. Eli and Joe and Alvira capered nearby. "I wish to goodness they'd get that old cabin done."

"You ought to be glad there ain't no hoop snakes 'round here," said Frank.

He waited for her to ask, "What's a hoop snake?"

When she did, he continued: "A hoop snake's one of the deadliest critters in creation. We had them back in Missouri. When a hoop snake puts his tail in his mouth he can roll faster than a man can run.

"Once a hoop snake chased one of our neighbors. When he saw he couldn't outrun it, he slipped behind a tree. The snake bit into the tree and all the leaves withered and died.

"A few days later, a settler came by and found an enormous tree, so big he built a whole cabin from it. He went off hunting, and when he came back he found a little thing the size of a dollhouse. He found out later the tree had been snake-bit and all the swelling from the bite had gone out of the wood."

Sarah stared wide-eyed. Then she laughed and said, "Oh, Frank, you're a born tall-tale teller."

One hot day, Frank was returning with water from the river. When he left the cool shade of the trees, his shirt wilted against him and his hair stuck to his forehead with perspiration. It was not as hot here as at Whitman Mission, but the temperature could rise pretty high. His feet whispered through the tall grass. As he neared the cabin, he saw a lone rider approaching.

A visitor! Who could it be and what could he want? His steps quickened. On closer view, his spirits sank. The man on horseback was Marcus Whitman!

Frank considered leaving the bucket and heading back the way he had come, but it was too late. Dr. Whitman saw him. Frank sighed in resignation and went towards him.

"Hello, Francis. How are you?" The doctor's tone was friendly.

"All right, I guess," Frank muttered, not wanting to commit himself. What did Dr. Whitman want? Had he come to take him away?

"How do you like it here in the valley? Do you like living with the Perkinses?"

"Everything's fine," said Frank.

"I came to see how you were doing, and to show you this." He held out a paper.

Frank took it. It looked important. "Klackamas District, 3d June, 1845, J. W. Nesmith, Judge," it began. The paper told about his father dying, and Captain Shaw taking his children and possessions to Dr. Whitman. Henry Sager's estate had been appraised at $262.50.

The paragraph at the bottom read:

> Whereupon the said Marcus Whitman gave bond for double the above sum and was appointed guardian of the above named children, subject to, and accountable to, the probate judge of Oregon.
>
> (Signed) J. W. Nesmith
> Probate Judge of Oregon.

Frank looked up at Dr. Whitman.

"That paper makes me your legal guardian," the doctor said. "I thought you should know. We're all very sorry you left the mission. Since you like it here, you can stay as long as you want. I'm going back soon." He took the paper from Frank.

"Good-bye," said Frank, hardly able to believe that Dr. Whitman would not force him to return. In a way, he wished he would. It would give him an excuse. Now he was committed to staying away.

"Good-bye," said Dr. Whitman, mounting his horse and riding away.

That night, Frank lay awake for a long time thinking. It would be years before he and John could have their own farm. Suppose he did not see John and the girls until then? Loneliness washed over him in waves. Home had never seemed so far away. He lay, eyes burning, throat tight, thinking, *I ain't gonna cry, I ain't gonna cry, I ain't gonna cry....*

Matilda wandered contentedly behind Elizabeth as they drove the cows to pasture in the day's first light, swishing through tall dew-cool grass. Bird song drifted on the breeze, and the scent of grass and flowers and earth. A magpie flew by, so black its wings looked blue and its tail looked green. Its wings and body were white-patched, its tail so long it was a wonder it could fly at all. Standing out a moment against the blue sky, it dropped into the grass, hidden.

In a stand of rye grass, Matilda spotted a band of Indian horses. Dark manes showed above the tall green grass, which rustled when manes shook or tails switched. She heard them munching mouthfuls of the good fresh grass.

Every so often the girls had to chase an ornery cow, but mostly they watched the big, lazy beasts lumber ahead, and tried to think of something new and interesting to do.

"Let's find some of the herbs the Indians eat," Elizabeth suggested.

Matilda was doubtful. "Do you know what they are?"

"Oh, sure," said Elizabeth. "I've seen them."

"Where do they grow?"

"Some are down by the river."

At the river tall stalks grew in the mud, branching out in tufts of delicate white flower. Elizabeth said, "Here's one. Try it."

Matilda broke off a stalk. "Are you sure these are good? I think they're poison."

"The Indians eat them."

The little bunches of white flowers were soft and feathery against her face, smelling cool and fresh. Elizabeth, being older, should know what she was talking about. Matilda bit into the stalk and chewed. "It doesn't taste very good," she said at last. "I don't like it, even if the Indians do eat it." She threw the rest away.

They sat by the river, throwing sticks into the current, watching them bob downstream. Sun glared off the moving surface. Matilda watched the ripples, now up, now down, now light, now dark. Her head was swimming, pain gripped her stomach. She thought she might be sick. "My gut's painin' me," she told Elizabeth. "I'm going back to the house."

She started to walk, but her legs were slow. She lumbered along, slower and heavier than the cows. Her feet felt caked in mud, so heavy her small, weak legs could hardly drag them along. She might have been walking through water. Elizabeth ran up beside her. Matilda knew she should be able to run, too, but could not. She did not know what was happening.

An eternity of dragging steps, then the house. She was almost to the door when her muscles locked, and she collapsed.

Elizabeth ran in, calling, "Mother! Mother!"

Mrs. Whitman rushed out and picked Matilda up. "What happened? Did a snake bite her?"

"No, nothing really happened—"

Matilda could hear, but could not speak. She was in such terror her heart must be beating very fast, but it felt slower...and slower....

"Has she been eating some strange plant?"

"Well, we found an herb by the river, and she took a bite of it."

"Did you bring some?"

"No. It's just an herb the Indians eat."

"Well, go get some. Hurry!"

Elizabeth ran off.

The other girls crowded around. "What's wrong with Matilda?"

"I'd best put her to bed." She took Matilda upstairs. Matilda wanted to ask, "Will I be all right?" but was too sick to speak. Her stomach pains were worsening.

Mrs. Whitman stayed by her, sending Catherine for a bowl in case Matilda was sick, which she was. Matilda thought she should feel better after throwing up, but did not, much. She was weak and limp as a wrung-out dishrag.

Elizabeth returned with a plant stalk. Mrs. Whitman looked grave when she saw it. "She's been eating wild parsnip. She must have thought it was wild carrot."

"Will she be all right?" asked Elizabeth, almost crying.

"Only the Lord knows." Mrs. Whitman would say no more.

When John came home for supper, Helen ran to meet him. "Matilda's real sick!" she announced. "She ate a poison plant. Mother says she might die!"

Heart pounding, John ran past her through the kitchen and sitting room and up the stairs. In the girls' room Matilda lay in bed, pale and still. Mrs. Whitman bent over her.

"Is she...?" he began.

"Hush," said Mrs. Whitman. "She's sleeping. I keep checking to make sure she's still breathing. Her pulse is slow and weak."

John saw how pale and worried Mrs. Whitman looked. He had not expected this, but had no time to wonder about it.

Suddenly Matilda's back arched. Her face contorted in pain. She thrashed horribly in a tangle of covers, then lay still again. Mrs. Whitman stroked her brow, speaking soothingly.

John had been holding his breath. When he could speak again, he asked, "Is she going to die?"

"Perhaps. She's very sick. We can only do our best, and pray. I'll need your help in taking care of her."

"Of course," said John, forgetting to sound distant or guarded as he usually did with Mrs. Whitman.

That evening as he sat by Matilda, Elizabeth came in while Mrs. Whitman was out of the room a moment.

"Will Matilda die?"

"Mrs. Whitman says she doesn't know if she'll live." Then, seeing she was about to cry, he said, "But don't cry, Lizzie. We're doing all we can."

"But...but...," Elizabeth burst out, "I told her to eat that plant! I thought it was an herb the Indians ate! I'm older and should look after her. If she dies it'll be all my fault!" She began to sob.

"Come here," said John.

Elizabeth came slowly to him. John pulled her into his lap and held her close. "Don't feel so bad. You didn't do it a-purpose."

"Oh, I shouldn'ta done it at all. I was just so *sure*."

"We can't always be sure of things." He wished he could say more. At last he said, "She might live. And she might die. But don't blame yourself, either way." He held Elizabeth until her sobs quieted.

John had little chance to be distant or guarded with Mrs. Whitman in the next days. He was around her constantly as they cared for Matilda. She showed such concern, doing everything to make Matilda comfortable and well, he could not feel badly toward her. When she told John to do something, he did it. Anything to save Matilda's life.

While John and Mrs. Whitman were busy taking care of Matilda, Mrs. Brewer made good on her promise to "do something." She wrote Mrs. Whitman a letter informing her that Francis and the Perkinses had stopped by, that she understood the Whitmans beat their children, and a good many other things. Mrs. Whitman was too busy to answer until later.

One morning when John went in to see her, Matilda said, "I want up. I think I could walk if you was to help me."

He picked her up and helped her stand. He was going to hold her, but she said, "I can walk by myself."

He let go reluctantly, thinking she would collapse. Instead, she took a few wobbling steps and smiled at him.

"Mother!" John called. "Come quick!"

Mrs. Whitman rushed upstairs, expecting, by the look on her face, that Matilda had worsened. When she saw her swaying weakly on her feet, she cried, "Our prayers have been answered! Thank you, Lord!"

"I want to lie down now," Matilda said. John helped her back into bed.

Mrs. Whitman stood smiling at John until he began to wonder. Then she said, "You called me Mother for the first time."

One day, hearing hoofbeats on the trail, John looked out the window to see Dr. Whitman approaching. He started for the door, but Helen was out like a shot, running to tell him about Matilda's illness.

The doctor started toward the girls' room without speaking to John or any of the others. Matilda held up her arms when she saw him, and he swept her up.

"Are you all right?" he asked. "How do you feel?"

"I feel some better," she told him. She could get around the house now, feebly.

"Rest, and you'll soon be well." He gently placed her back in bed and went down to greet the others.

"I saw Francis in the valley," he told John.

"Did you ask him to come home?" It was the first time he had called the mission "home" in front of the doctor. Dr. Whitman said nothing, but a flicker of interest in his eyes showed he had heard.

"No, I want him to be well satisfied with his visit below."

"Did you bring us anything, Father?" Helen demanded.

"Helen, what atrociously bad manners!" Mrs. Whitman exclaimed. "For that you'll get yours last."

Dr. Whitman had a gift for each of them, and sent Perrin and the little ones off happy. He kept John behind, saying, "I want to talk to you."

They went outside where they could be alone, and as they walked, Dr. Whitman said, "In the valley, I had a paper drawn up making me your legal guardian. The farmers there talk quite a bit about you children. They've heard of you from Mr. Shaw and others who were on the trail with you. Since Francis left, many rumors have started that Mrs. Whitman and I don't treat you well."

John felt uncomfortably warm. "I know. Mrs. Brewer at the Dalles wrote us an awful letter. Mother read it to me. I didn't agree."

"That's what I want to ask you about. Are you happy here? Are you willing to stay with us?"

At one time, John would have wanted to answer differently. But now Mr. Hinman was gone, and he no longer resented Mrs. Whitman. Dr. Whitman seemed concerned for the children, the way he ran up to see Matilda just now. So John answered, "Yes, I want to stay."

Dr. Whitman smiled. "Good. I can give you and Francis horses and stock to raise a herd to take to the valley when you're ready to go—which I hope won't be for some time. How does that sound?"

"Fine! Thank you, sir."

Dr. Whitman's blue eyes were friendly. "Now if you'll write Francis, I'll have someone take your letter to the valley."

John wrote the letter, telling of Mrs. Whitman's kindness when Matilda was sick, and the doctor's offer about the stock. Now they must wait until one of the men working for the doctor could take the letter to the valley.

FIFTEEN

At harvest time in Yamhill, that late summer of 1845, wheat and oats and barley hung heavy and gold on slender stalks. The sun on a field of grain gave it a soft look, like some great beast's golden fur. To the farmers, the grain meant food and money, but most of all right now, work to exhaustion.

John Perkins's cabin had taken weeks to build, complete with attic, door, windows, and a mud and stick chimney. The floor, called a puncheon floor, was of logs split endwise, laid side by side. To cover the roof, the men split off shingle-like wooden wedges called shakes. The shakes needed drying, one reason the building took so long. Now Mr. Perkins was harvesting in return for enough grain to feed his family all winter. Frank helped him.

One day Frank sat at the edge of a field, humming to himself over the high sound of stone on metal as he sharpened a scythe with a smooth whetstone while Mr. Perkins and the others cut grain.

Every so often, he poured water over the blade. Thin black mud formed on the whetstone, sticking to his hands. The blade's sharp edge gleamed. Frank looked up when he heard a horse approaching. A man in his late thirties rode up, tied his horse to a nearby tree, and went to Frank.

"Are you Francis Sager?"

"Yes, sir."

"I'm the Reverend John Griffin," the stranger said. "I've heard a lot about you."

Frank gave him a questioning look.

"Your parents died on the plains last year. People in your wagon train took you and your brother and sisters to Dr. Whitman's mission. But you thought their discipline too strict, so you ran away."

"That's right," said Frank.

"There is more," said Rev. Griffin. "Before your mother died, she asked you to care for your sisters and keep the family together, and you promised you would. Do you think you've kept that promise?"

Looking into the stern face, Frank, unable to speak, felt suddenly dizzy and ill.

"Soon afterwards, your mother became delirious and died, thinking you intended to keep your promise. Could she be proud of you now?"

Frank ran into the woods, stomach churning. Trees rushed at him until he hit one, and held on to it, gagging. The contents of his stomach heaved forth. He leaned against the tree, spitting, but a bitterness that was more than an aftertaste remained.

I didn't promise to stay anyplace where they'd treat me like that! he thought.

But you promised to take care of the girls! the stranger seemed to say. *You left them with those people,* he thought the stranger told him. Or was it his own conscience speaking? He did not know. He turned to look at the stranger, and could see only his outline at the edge of the trees. Then Rev. Griffin untied his horse, and rode away.

Frank hardly had time to plan his return to the mission. It was work, work, work, from dawn till dusk, under a blazing blue sky. The soft-looking grain was really scratchy and dusty. Frank could never avoid chaff down his shirt, which stuck to his sweaty skin, making him itch. Sweat rivers ran through the dirt on his body. At night he sank down exhausted, asleep almost at once. After harvest, he promised himself, he would return to the mission.

One evening when he and Mr. Perkins returned from the fields, Mrs. Perkins told Frank, "A man left this for you."

A letter lay on the table. Frank reached for it. "Not so fast! Wash your grubby hands first!"

Frank did, then opened the letter, which was in John's writing. It said Matilda had been sick—like to die—but Mrs. Whitman had nursed her and she was much better, though weak. It also told of things Dr. Whitman would do if Frank came back, but Frank hardly saw that part. Matilda was sick!

A weakness not from hard work made his hands tremble on the letter. "It's...it's from my brother," he said. "One of my little sisters has been real sick. I promised Ma I'd take care of them, and now she's sick, and I've got to get back to the mission right away!"

Mrs. Perkins nodded. "Dr. Whitman sent a man, who has a horse for you. I'll fix vittles."

Mr. Perkins put his arm around Frank. "You've been a real help these past months. We'll miss you."

Sarah and Eli and Joe and Alvira crowded around with long faces. "We want you to stay, Frank," said Sarah.

"We want you for our big brother," Eli chimed in. Joe and Alvira pouted.

"Sorry, but my real little sisters need me." *I got a promise to keep,* he thought.

When they neared the mission, he spurred ahead of the man who had brought him. As he rode into the yard, Helen rushed out, shouting, "Frank's home! Frank's home!" Close behind her was Catherine, running with hardly a limp. Elizabeth passed them, flinging herself on Frank as he jumped from the horse, gave the reins to Helen, and said, "I want to see Matilda."

Seeing her walking towards him, he shook off Elizabeth and swept up Matilda. "You all right? John said you were real sick."

"Yes, I'm all better now," she said, clinging to him.

"Remember the day we nearly washed down the river on the horse, and I said I'd always take care of you?"

"Yes." She laid her head on his shoulder.

"Well, I meant what I said, and I'll never leave you or the others again."

"Even me, Frank?" three-year-old Louisa wanted to know, holding out her arms to be picked up.

"Yes, even you," he said, putting down Matilda and picking up Louisa.

John ran towards him then, laughing and slapping him on the back. Then all the children were silent as Mrs. Whitman came out the door.

She walked to Frank and said quietly, "We're very happy to have you home, Francis. When you left I felt as if someone had died." Then she added, "I think we'll have a special supper tonight, in honor of your coming home."

The little girls jumped up and down.

"But you girls will have to help."

"We'll be glad to," said Catherine, putting her arm around Frank. A happy glow rose inside him like a flame.

At supper that night, the others told Frank of the Indian with the long scar on his left cheek, who came to the mission the day he left and told about trying to persuade him to return. Frank told what really happened, and they all laughed.

"Sounds like that Indian was trying to please everyone at once," said Perrin.

"I reckon so," said Frank.

The fall of 1845 brought nearly 3,000 emigrants to Oregon, almost twice as many as the year before. Some, who could go no farther, stopped at Whitman Mission before going on. The weather had been good on the trail this year, so the emigrants crossed the Blue Mountains earlier and fewer had to stop on their way to the Willamette Valley.

One Sunday morning, a tall, slender man of about twenty-five, with sandy yellow hair and a mild manner, arrived at the mission. His name was Andrew Rodgers, and he inquired about lodging a friend sick with consumption, and buying supplies. Dr. Whitman said he would put the friend in the emigrant house, and sell them supplies.

"Is there a millwright in your train?" asked Dr. Whitman. "When the Indians set fire to the grass this year, my gristmill burned." Burning off old grass was a practice with the Indians each fall, so that strong new green grass would cover the land in spring. The millrace had kept the fire from reaching the house, but the gristmill was ruined.

"One of my companions is a millwright."

Delighted, the doctor invited Mr. Rodgers to spend the day. The children gathered round on settees in the sitting room, while Dr. and Mrs. Whitman questioned Mr. Rodgers. He was from Illinois, and had belonged to the Associate Presbyterian Church, "But I was excommunicated," he told them.

Elizabeth sidled up to John. "What's 'excommunicated'?" she

demanded.

"It means turned out," John whispered, "now hush."

Turned out! Now she remembered what excommunicated meant. She had overheard them talking at the mission meeting last May about excommunicating a man named James Conner for Sabbath breaking, fighting, liquor vending, and other things she did not even understand. She looked at Mr. Rodgers aghast.

He had heard her question and was trying to look serious, but his face beamed with good humor as he continued, "I was excommunicated for singing hymns."

This was too much. Elizabeth burst into giggles.

Mrs. Whitman glowered. "Elizabeth, show our guest some respect."

"It's all right," said Mr. Rodgers. "I suppose it was a funny church. You see," he explained to Elizabeth, "they didn't believe in singing man-made hymns. They could only sing the Psalms."

Elizabeth looked at him with her mouth wide open.

"Close your mouth, Elizabeth," said Mrs. Whitman. "Mr. Rodgers, it's wonderful you sing! I've tried to teach my husband, but he can't sing a note. Do you know 'Rock of Ages'?"

"One of my favorites."

She named many favorites. Did he know this, and that, and such a hymn? He knew them all. Mrs. Whitman was glowing.

"Mr. Rodgers," the doctor asked at last, "how would you like to teach our school this fall?"

"I would love it," said Mr. Rodgers, smiling.

"You're hired!"

Mrs. Whitman beamed. "A music teacher will be wonderful for the children," she said.

Mr. Rodgers stayed the night, leaving Monday morning for the Umatilla to bring his sick friend. They returned late Monday night.

The sick man's name was Joseph Finley. At the journey's beginning, he was carried from his bed to the wagon, but was now well enough to ride. Mr. Rodgers stayed close by him, looking after him anxiously, making sure he was comfortable. Their close friendship put Catherine in mind of Jonathan and David.

With Mr. Finley were his cousins, Josiah and Margaret Osborn. Mr.

Osborn, the millwright Mr. Rodgers had spoken of, would soon build a fine new mill. He and his wife had four small children, whose company delighted the younger Sagers.

Dr. Whitman and Mr. Osborn went out to see what could be salvaged of the mill. Catherine was outside by the corral, a high fence of pointed logs, when they headed back, and overheard Mr. Osborn ask, "What is the last name of these seven children you have taken in?"

"Their name is Sager."

Catherine, rid of most of her shyness, was still bashful when talked about. Dodging behind the stockade fence, she pressed herself against the logs so Mr. Osborn would not see her.

"Their father is buried by Green River, isn't he?" Mr. Osborn asked Dr. Whitman.

"Yes, how did you know?"

"We found an open grave to the right of the trail, just after crossing. The name on the marker was Henry Sager. Indians must have opened it, because the poles that covered the body were standing straight up. Coyotes had scattered the bones and they were bleaching in the sun. We buried him again."

Catherine slipped away, cold shivers running up her spine, seeing again the desolate, windswept desert where Pa lay among the sagebrush, imagining too well those lonely, forsaken bones left bare to sun and rain. Had the same thing happened to Ma? It was a terrible knowledge to bear.

That night they all gathered in the mission house. Elizabeth noticed Mr. Rodgers brought an odd-shaped case. He smiled mysteriously as he opened it.

"Why," said Mrs. Whitman, "you never told us...." She was smiling and very pink.

"The other reason I was excommunicated."

"It's a fiddle!" Elizabeth exclaimed.

"No, child," said Mr. Rodgers. "This is a violin."

He picked it up and tuned it a moment. Elizabeth noticed he tucked it lovingly under his chin, rather than holding it across his arm, as she had seen fiddlers do. In a moment he began to play "Rock of Ages," and they all joined in.

When they finished, Elizabeth asked very shyly, "Do you know 'Come Thou Fount of Every Blessing'?" She and Matilda had heard an old Baptist believer sing it the Sunday before, and she thought it the prettiest hymn she ever heard, especially the high part, which soared through the air.

Mr. Rodgers began to play, and all who knew it joined in:

> Come, Thou Fount of every blessing,
> Tune my heart to sing Thy grace;
> Streams of mercy, never ceasing,
> Call for songs of loudest praise.
> Teach me some melodious sonnet,
> Sung by flaming tongues above;
> Praise the mount—I'm fixed upon it—
> Mount of Thy redeeming love.

Mr. Rodgers had a beautiful voice. At last Mrs. Whitman had a kindred spirit to join her in song.

She was not the only happy one. Frank's long ordeal was over. He did not have to worry about whether the new teacher would be as bad as the old one. Mr. Rodgers was mild and reasonable, and soon the children loved him so much that no one was inclined to disobey him. As they had called Frank "No Eyebrows" when he first arrived, the Indians called Mr. Rodgers "Hushus Moxmox," or "Yellow Head," *moxmox* meaning yellow.

The four older Sagers, Perrin, Mary Ann, and Helen were continuing school this year. Matilda Sager, David Malin, and Nancy, the Osborns' oldest, were starting. The Walkers from Tshimakain sent their oldest son, Cyrus, age six, the Spaldings from Lapwai sent their daughter Eliza, who was seven, and three emigrant children attended, totaling fifteen in the mission school.

Besides their usual lessons, Mr. Rodgers taught music, and often the schoolroom rang with song. Sometimes, to entertain emigrants or other visitors, Mrs. Whitman lined up all her children, from largest to smallest, and led them in song, Mr. Rodgers accompanying on the violin. She called the long line of children, from tall Perrin to little Henrietta, her "family stairway." People often remarked that Mrs. Whitman was the best singer they had ever heard.

One day soon after school started, Catherine, Elizabeth, and Eliza
Spalding were ironing as Cyrus Walker looked on. An Indian burst into
the kitchen, without so much as knocking. Elizabeth recognized him as
one Mrs. Whitman called Frank Eskaloom. He was coming straight
towards her.

He grabbed her iron. She resisted, but he ripped it from her grasp and
started ironing his handkerchief.

"You give me back my iron!" Elizabeth yelled.

"You can't barge in here and take peoples' irons!" Eliza chimed in.

"Why don't you give Elizabeth her iron and leave us alone?"
Catherine added, in softer tones.

Frank Eskaloom turned, scowling, towards Elizabeth. He raised the
iron high over his head, slowly advancing, his face and upraised hand
twitching and trembling with rage.

Elizabeth's indignation turned to fear, and she shrank back, shaking,
but still he pressed forward. "I kill you!" he said. His eyes were wide and
menacing. The iron was poised, ready to come down.

Suddenly Mrs. Whitman was between them. "Don't pay any
attention to them, Frank," she said, "they're only girls. You can iron your
handkerchief if you wish."

Still scowling, Frank Eskaloom finished ironing his handkerchief,
thumped the iron down with such force the children jumped, and stalked
out. Mrs. Whitman said briskly, "Continue with your chores," as if
nothing had happened.

Mrs. Whitman was busy much of the time talking to the sick man,
Mr. Finley. He told her of his life, between increasingly worse coughing
bouts. She felt he could not live. He was not a Christian, and often told
her he could not forgive his family's treatment of him. Mrs. Whitman,
much concerned by his words, worked to convince him of his need for the
Savior. He soon began to show an interest, especially since his friend, Mr.
Rodgers, was a strong Christian.

One fine fall day, Catherine stood near the mill watching Mr. Osborn
and the doctor grind corn for the Indians.

"Who is that wise-looking old one?" she heard Mr. Osborn ask Dr.
Whitman.

"That's Tiloukaikt, the head chief."

TOMAHAS

by Paul Kane.   Courtesy of Royal
Ontario Museum, Toronto.

TILOUKAIKT
or "Act of Lightning"

by Paul Kane. Courtesy of Stark Foun-
dation, Orange, Texas.

"Till-a-kite?"

"Yes. In their language, that means 'Act of Lightning.'"

"He sure cuts a fine figure."

Catherine agreed. Tiloukaikt's thin, wrinkled face was knowing, the
nose a sharp curving beak, the cheeks sunken, craggy hollows, the eyes
alert, watchful, holding the lore of many years. Gray-black hair, parted
in the middle, touched his shoulders. His blanket was a mysterious cloak,
like mist wrapping the mountains on a rainy day. He and the mountains
had been in this land a long time, retaining many secrets.

Tomahas, Frank Eskaloom's brother, galloped up on a magnificent
horse, almost running the others down. He had shoulder-length black
hair, a long, sharp nose, small, angry eyes, and a thick, downturned
mouth. He slung his sack of corn at the doctor, saying, "You. Grind my
corn now."

"You'll have to wait your turn," Dr. Whitman said. "These others
are before you. Besides, it's dinner time." He went in, Catherine

following, while the Indians waited outside.

During dinner, the family was startled by strange grinding noises.

"That must be coming from the mill," said the doctor, starting out. The others crowded to the door. Mr. Osborn was already on his way to the mill, but Tomahas met him, blocked his way, and knocked him down.

Tomahas then rushed at the doctor, but Chief Tiloukaikt seized him around the waist. Tomahas roared, foamed, and twisted like an enraged cougar, but could not escape the old man's firm grasp.

At last he said he would leave if Tiloukaikt let him. When he let go, Tomahas leaped on his horse and galloped away.

Catherine and the others went to Dr. Whitman and Mr. Osborn. Dr. Whitman was asking Mr. Osborn what made the grinding noise.

"He put sticks in the hopper. He is the most fractious fellow I've ever seen."

They did not see Tomahas again for some time, but the anxiety he caused was a long time in going away.

SIXTEEN

Elizabeth was hungry, and could do nothing about it. She sat looking out the doorway of one of the sawmill cabins, thinking.

It began as a pleasure trip. Now that school was out, the Spaldings came from Lapwai for Eliza, and Mrs. Whitman decided to return partway with them. She and the children traveled six or eight miles, to see where the sawmill was being built.

The four log cabins, with their large fireplaces and stick chimneys, were bare and uninteresting, but the surrounding land was beautiful.

Silver-white clouds swept across the sky. Below them was the dark blue line of mountains, descending into the folds of buff green hills. From her place in the cabin door, Elizabeth could see distinctly tall green pine and fir trees on the mountains, instead of seeing the mountains as a blue haze as she did at the mission. In the shadowed places lay white spreads of snow.

Near their camp grew stands of stiff-needled ponderosa pine, and a plain covered with lush green grass. Winter had been mild, and though it was only March, wild flowers waved in the grass. Graceful yellow glacier lilies arched by the cold, clear, sweet, blue creek waters.

A thunderstorm blew up on the afternoon they came, which was why they stayed overnight. Now the grass and flowers sparkled in the sun. Elizabeth wished she could eat them. Horses belonging to a band of Indians camped across the creek were grazing contentedly. Her mouth watered at the thought of food.

All the food was gone. Not expecting to stay, they had brought only lunch yesterday. Then this morning they found the oxen gone. Dr. Whitman rode back to the mission to attend the sick man, and to send John to recover the oxen and bring food. Elizabeth wished he would hurry.

She wandered from the cabin door to the creek. Nearby, Catherine and Mary Ann made doll houses in the tall grass. Matilda, Helen, Cyrus Walker, and David were playing, but slowed down more each minute. Every so often one said, "When's John coming? I hope he gets here before we all starve." Mrs. Whitman stayed by Louise and Henrietta, who were curled in the grass after crying themselves to sleep.

Elizabeth plucked a strand of rye grass, trailing it in the water. A glint of motion caught her eye, and she stopped. The biggest salmon she had ever seen was trying to swim upstream, but was caught in a shallow place. She shouted for the others, and not minding the cold water, plunged in after the fish.

Her shout brought the others running, along with a few Indian boys. In a moment the children, Elizabeth in the lead, were pursuing the wriggling fish, which they trapped against the muddy bank. It slid from Elizabeth's hands, but did not slide against her apron when she used that to scoop it up. The dark, mottled fish flopped wildly, but she held it tight. Then someone took it.

An Indian boy of about fourteen was climbing the bank, holding her fish. Elizabeth grabbed for the fish, but he dangled it just out of her grasp, smiling as if to say, "This is my land, and you would not have caught this fish without my help. Make me give it back."

There was a wordless standoff. Elizabeth was furious. She had seen the fish first, and did most of the work catching it. But the Indian boys were bigger than the children, gathering around the boy with the fish, seeming to think he had the most right to it.

Another Indian, a grown man, came towards them and spoke scoldingly to the boys. The children did not understand all his words, but the result was that the boy with the fish looked shamefaced and handed it to him. The older man mercifully tomahawked the gasping creature and gave it to Elizabeth. She and the man exchanged smiles. The Indians headed for camp, and Elizabeth, wet, smelling fishy, holding the dead salmon, waded across the creek to the others.

When John arrived, carrying saddlebags of food, he found them all sitting on the grass, eagerly devouring salmon soup Mrs. Whitman had made. Elizabeth laughed and said, "Slowpoke! What took you so long?"

One morning not long after their return, Elizabeth was sweeping the kitchen floor when Mrs. Whitman came from Mr. Finley's bedside in the parlor, and said, "Run for the boys. Mr. Finley is dying, and wants to see you all."

Elizabeth ran, heart pounding, afraid Mr. Finley would be dead before they returned. The children entered the parlor with noiseless steps. Joseph Finley had become part of their lives these past months. Lately, his disease worsening, he coughed blood. The doctor and Mrs. Whitman, his good friend Mr. Rodgers, John, and Perrin, all took turns watching at the sick bed. Rev. Spalding, newly arrived, now stood by Mr. Finley.

Mr. Finley, pale, weak, and gasping, had only strength to whisper to Rev. Spalding, who told the children of his happiness at being saved, and how they must all be prepared for death. The children stood at the bed foot, silent, solemn.

Mrs. Whitman sat nearby, weeping softly. The doctor held his fingers on the dying man's pulse.

"Do you feel your prospect to be bright?" Rev. Spalding asked.

Elizabeth could barely hear the whispered answer, "I hope so." He said good-bye to the Whitmans and the children, thanking them for their care. Elizabeth felt strange, as if she should be sad, but could not when Mr. Finley seemed so happy, somehow. In these last few moments his pale, drawn face had illuminated.

He reached for Mr. Rodgers, who took his hand. They looked at each other a few moments, then Mr. Finley closed his eyes.

The funeral was on the following day, the Sabbath, March 29, 1846. After the men buried Mr. Finley in the mission cemetery, the children heaped wild flowers upon the raw turned earth of the grave. The night after the burial, as Elizabeth lay wakeful, very late a mournful wailing rose outside. Shivering close to Catherine, she asked, "Katie, what is it? What is it?"

"The Indians are singing the death chant," Catherine whispered. "He died a perfect death, I think."

"What do you mean?"

"Well, the way he said good-bye to us all, looking so happy. And the letter he wrote to his family before he died, forgiving them, and the way everyone gathered around the grave crying. And now, the Indians singing

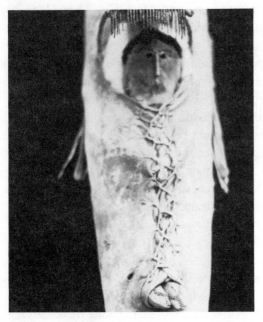

INDIAN DOLL

Owned by Whitman Mission National Historic Site, believed to have been Elizabeth Sager's.

Courtesy of National Park Service, Whitman Mission National Historic Site.

the death chant."

The mournful sound, unlike any other, wailed over the March wind, sometimes louder, sometimes softer. One voice called, others answered, blending like the wind's voices.

"I wish we'd had time for a funeral and all when Ma and Pa died, 'stead of hurrying on like we did," said Catherine. "Good night."

She drifted off to sleep, but Elizabeth could not until long after the last of the death chant faded away.

The doctor and older boys were breaking up land and planting crops for the Indians much of the time. Mrs. Whitman took the girls and David on nature walks to learn of wildlife and botany. Often the doctor and boys brought in various plants found between home and the fields.

One day Elizabeth, finished with chores and allowed out, was playing with her favorite doll, Eddie. Eddie and his clothes and cradleboard were soft dressed deerskin, not made of rags like the other dolls. His hair was black sheep's wool, and his black eyes were trade beads. A sunshade of sturdy grass stems edged with beads was over his head, when he was in the cradleboard, and a bead fringe swung in front of his eyes. Even his tiny buckskin moccasins sparkled with beads.

The rag dolls were named after Mrs. Whitman's sisters, so Elizabeth named her leather doll after Mrs. Whitman's brother, Edward, but he was a baby still, so she called him Eddie. An Indian woman made him, not for Elizabeth's birthday, but from friendship.

Dr. Whitman approached, walking quickly and purposefully as always. It was neither noon nor evening. She did not know why he was back at this time of day. His jaw was set hard and firm.

He seemed not to notice as she followed him to the back of the house. He went to the mill and did something to the machinery. In a moment he turned back, clutching an iron bar, and noticed her for the first time.

"Father, what is it?" she asked.

"Trouble. Go to the house."

Clutching Eddie, she ran across the yard, past the rail fence enclosing the back of the house. Three doors, one on the end of the house and two on walls at right angles, led in, two into the parlor and one into the kitchen. Catherine stood in the open kitchen door. "What's going—" she began, and stopped. Tomahas was riding to the mill, with a sack of corn slung over his horse's back.

Squeals of protest came from the machinery as he worked over it, and noises of frustration from Tomahas. He was having no luck starting the mill. Dr. Whitman never allowed Indians to run the mill, so none of them knew how. He always made them pay a small amount of their corn for his work in grinding it, to show that he was not their servant. What was more, he had adjusted the machinery just now, so Tomahas could not have started the mill, had he known how.

Tomahas rushed at the doctor, who sat on the rail fence nearby. The doctor brandished the iron bar, and Tomahas hesitated, club in hand.

"Put that down," he ordered.

"I will when you put yours down."

Tomahas dropped his club. Dr. Whitman dropped the iron bar, and Tomahas seized the club and ran at him. Dr. Whitman jumped from the fence, with just time to grab the iron bar and swing it, warding off Tomahas's club blow.

Tomahas, driven back, nearly dropped his club. Recovering his balance, he charged the doctor, raining blows fast and furious, which the doctor blocked with the iron bar. Finally Tomahas stopped trying to hit the doctor and stood staring him down. Elizabeth felt the fierceness of his look, and shrank back against Catherine.

"You will leave this country!" Tomahas bellowed. "I do not want you here!"

"I'll leave," Dr. Whitman replied steadily, "when all the Indians ask me to. I will not leave because one asks. If you will behave as a friend, I will grind your corn."

Elizabeth held her breath. To her surprise, Tomahas made a short noise of assent. They went to the mill together. Catherine and Elizabeth went into the house.

Dr. Whitman burst in a short while later. In the sitting room, he threw himself on a settee, telling Mrs. Whitman and the others what had happened. "I'd gladly leave if all the Indians asked, but so many ask me to stay. Tomahas and some of the others try me almost beyond endurance."

Summer was happy at the mission. As early as April, the girls began swimming every day except the Sabbath. Under Mrs. Whitman's watchful eye, they dipped themselves in the cool waters of the Walla Walla River where it flowed over smooth, round, gray rocks.

They caught periwinkles, tubular shells encrusted with rock fragments of black, red, and green, clinging to the rocks with feathery black legs, and they watched tiny greenish-gray fish darting about. Swimming was their favorite activity. "They love it so well that they would as soon do without dinner as without that," Mrs. Whitman wrote in a letter to one of her sisters.

The children were allowed to sail boats made from watermelons cut in two and hollowed out, but an older girl must always watch the younger ones. Dr. Whitman would tan their hides if the little ones played by the irrigation ditches or the mill pond alone.

The house was lively, with the children at work or play, cats running in and out, Dr. Whitman and Mr. Rodgers in earnest discussion about Mr. Rodgers's decision to study the ministry, Indians coming and going to sell dried berries or obtain medicine, and Mrs. Whitman in the middle of it all, trying to write home between duties.

Mrs. Whitman never missed an opportunity to correct the children. None of the Sagers had received the kind of education she had, and she tried to have the children speak correctly. If Matilda said, "The mosquitos are mighty thick tonight," Mrs. Whitman said, "You mean they are very numerous," or if Catherine asked, "Shall I peel the potatoes, Mother?" Mrs. Whitman replied, "No, I would pare them if I were you."

One day when the girls came from their baths at the river into the coolness of the house, Dr. Whitman told them, "Remember this, girls. Marry at sixteen; don't wait till you are old maids as your mother did."

Mrs. Whitman said, "I waited until I was twenty-seven because it took that long to find anyone meeting my standards, and my girls, also, will wait until they are ready." Her husband smiled at her, and a small smile played around Mrs. Whitman's mouth. They were teasing again.

Day to day work kept the mission residents busy, as well as the special days when they dipped candles or washed clothes. On wash day, they rose early and were in the kitchen by four o'clock a. m. Mrs. Whitman supervised as the doctor and boys, wrapped in long aprons, hauled tubs of water from the river.

She and the girls scrubbed the clothes with rough lye soap they had made from beef tallow and lye drained from wood ashes, the same soap they used on their hands and hair. Dr. Whitman and the boys, who had most of the hard work, pounded the clothes, everyone laughing, joking, and singing as they worked. Catherine, who was frail, and David, who was small, fixed breakfast for the others. By nine o'clock a.m., the clothes hung fresh and clean on the line.

The children did their chores with no thought of disobeying, so the doctor and boys were surprised one afternoon while resting before returning to the fields, when Matilda burst in clutching an empty bucket, which she was supposed to have filled at the river, and stood before them, panting as if she had run all the way.

"What is it?" the doctor asked.

"I saw the strangest animal at the river!"

"What was it like?"

"Like nothing I ever seen!" Matilda still used bad grammar when excited.

"What color?" John demanded.

"Gray, sort of, with yellow eyes."

"A wolf!"

"'Tain't no wolf," she began, but he was bounding upstairs, returning in a moment with his gun.

"Must be a mad wolf, out in the day like that," said Frank. "Let's get 'im."

"You're not going anywhere," said Dr. Whitman. "Let John take care of it."

"All right." Frank smiled. "Perrin and I'll protect the womenfolks." He put his arm around Matilda.

After a while, hearing no report of a gun, they went into the parlor, on the corner of the house. From the door they could look towards the river.

John was coming back, laughing fit to bust. Every so often his laughter doubled him over so he could hardly walk. Matilda had the uneasy feeling she had done something foolish she would soon hear about.

John came in the parlor door, wiping his eyes. "Was the animal you saw about so big?" He gestured.

"Ye-es."

"Why, that was nothin' but a big toad! You don't mean to tell me in six years of livin' you ain't never seen a toad before?"

Furious, she refused to speak.

The others laughed, and "the time we had to save Matilda from the toad" became a running joke.

Matilda did not think the joke very funny. She knew she was brave, but when things were new and different she sometimes forgot, like the time Mrs. Whitman took her to Fort Walla Walla.

Fort Walla Walla was a Hudson's Bay trading post, twenty miles away on the Columbia River. When Mrs. Whitman visited, she sometimes took one of the children. The time Matilda was allowed to go, she was terribly excited. It was so long since she had seen a fort with a stockade, she scarcely remembered what one was like. She and Mrs. Whitman stood together on the river bank to watch the boats come in.

Matilda saw them far down the river, between high barren rocky hills. Suddenly a great booming shook the hills, echoing far down the wide river. Matilda jumped and cowered against Mrs. Whitman, whimpering.

Mrs. Whitman stroked her head. "Hush, child. They are firing the cannons to salute the boats. Everything is all right."

Summer rainstorms cooled; light skies turned the heavy rich blue of fall, moving closer to earth. Starry white clematis flowers on the vines draping the rail fences sprouted long silky beards. Hot, dry air turned sweet and cool, then nippy. Smoke drifted from the Indians' fires. Near their lodges, the children could smell tanned buckskin.

Sprays of leaves on the crooked twigs of sumac shrubs turned a light, clear red to go with the deep crimson of their cone-shaped seed clusters. The sumacs were bright spots of blood in the brown grass. Great, black, charred-smelling patches spread across the land, where the Indians had burned the ground to cleanse it of grass and brush. One morning frost ridged the mud, sparkling on the grass stems by the wagon tracks. Thin crisp ice edged the puddles in the wagon ruts.

With fall came the emigrants, not as many as the year before, but enough to keep Mrs. Whitman busy serving three meals a day to over twenty people. Besides those, people stayed in the emigrant house and sawmill cabins.

Eight men lived at the sawmill. "The Indians can't farm well without good fences," said Dr. Whitman. "Animals destroy their crops. When the animals are ours, the Indians blame us. We'll help them plow, and split fence rails to protect their fields."

Mrs. Whitman hired two women to help around the house. A nineteen-year-old named Mary Johnson was the children's favorite. They loved to tease her, and so did Dr. Whitman. Once Elizabeth was washing dishes in the kitchen as Mary, wearing Mrs. Whitman's wrapper, worked at the stove. The doctor looked in from the sitting room, motioned Elizabeth to silence, and sneaked behind Mary, giving her a big hug. Embarrassed and scandalized, she could only splutter in protest. Elizabeth giggled without restraint.

"Why, Mary," said Dr. Whitman, "I would never have dreamed of such a thing. Since you had on my wife's wrapper, I thought you were she." His voice was solemn, but his blue eyes twinkled.

Since Mr. Rodgers was busy studying the ministry and the Nez Perce language, also spoken by the Cayuses, Dr. Whitman hired a new teacher, William Geiger. The children did not like him as well as Mr. Rodgers, but those who remembered Mr. Hinman agreed that at least Mr. Geiger was not that bad. "I don't think anyone *could* be as bad as ol' Hinman," said Frank.

The Spaldings sent their daughter, Eliza, age nine, and son, Henry, seven. Nine emigrant children brought the school's enrollment to twenty. Four-year-old Louisa and two-year-old Henrietta were too young to attend.

In early December, 1846, Dr. Whitman went to Lapwai to deliver Mrs. Spalding's baby. While he was gone, Catherine, Mrs. Whitman's companion and confidante, slept by her side. One night Mrs. Whitman said, "I'm glad the doctor is attending the Spaldings this time. It frightens me every time he is called to attend an Indian."

"Why?"

"Because of their custom regarding medicine men, or *te-wats*, as they call them. If a sick person dies, the relatives have the right to kill the medicine man. They have killed a number during our time here."

"Frank told me about that. He says they don't kill the medicine man for not curing the sick person, but only when the relatives think the medicine man bewitched the sick person."

"There's no guarantee they won't think that about the doctor. Their beliefs are different than ours, and they are hard to convince. The more white people they meet, the less they believe them."

Catherine was frightened, but said, "Some of Father's patients have died, and nothing happened."

"I know, but I can't help being afraid for him anyway."

The deep blue sky went gray, then white. Pale yellow grass and brown snow-tufted weeds showed through a thin delicate coating. Tiny snow spikes clung to the feathery grass stems, fuzzed the sod roof, and frosted the dried clematis vines clinging to the fences.

One day the weeds and grass were gone. In their place lay a soft, smooth white layer. Fields and trail and sky were one great motionless whiteness. Soft ropes of snow draped the fence rails, breaking into pieces and showering to earth when the children touched them.

Dr. Whitman, back from Lapwai, amused the children on cold winter nights with games and stories. One night he sat near the small heating stove in the sitting room, casting shadow pictures on the wall as he held two-year-old Henrietta in his lap while the other children gathered around him.

As his fingers twisted into shapes, the black shadows of rabbits, ducks, assorted animals, and faces, leapt on the white wall. Elizabeth noticed his fingers were crooked and asked why.

The doctor held them out, looking at them. "They are pretty crooked, aren't they? They froze when I rode back east in the winter of 1842. That's why they're not straight, like yours."

"Why did you ride east in the winter, Father?" It was unthinkable, to ride across vast wilderness wastes, alone, in freezing weather.

"I rode because the mission board wanted to close my station and Mr. Spalding's, and to move your mother and me north to Tshimakain. That country isn't as good for farming as here, and it is not a good location from which to help emigrants.

"Some day the United States and Britain will set a boundary dividing Oregon Country between the two nations. Your mother and I knew that if we kept our station open, we could help the American emigrants who would surely pour in. I couldn't wait a year for my letter to cross the continent, and a year for their reply. I had to make the ride."

Frank, sitting at his feet, gazed up at him in silent thought. If not for Marcus Whitman's ride, Pa might not have decided to move his family to Oregon. Frank remembered how he had hated the doctor for that. He could never have imagined then that only two years later he would regard Marcus Whitman as a second father. Life worked in odd ways sometimes.

The cold tightened its grip on Oregon Country. The soft white snow turned to brittle grains of powder. Day after day, the bitter cold hung on, as if trying to squeeze the warmth from the people and animals at Whitman Mission.

One December morning, John, Frank, and Perrin came into the

kitchen after milking the cows. They shivered and stomped snow from their boots.

"I've never been so cold in all my born days!" Frank exclaimed. "Did you ever hear of snow three feet deep staying on the ground two weeks?" He inhaled deeply the good smell of steaming corn meal mush. "An' talk about the wolf at the door! You should have seen the big critter by the house when we went out. They're plumb starved. Father'll have to put out more poison."

"If these boots hadn't come in the missionary barrel, my toes would be froze plumb solid," said John. "I think they are anyways."

"I wish there'd been a pair to fit me," said Perrin. "My moccasins are frozen stiff."

"Take them off, then, and warm your feet at the stove," said Mrs. Whitman. "You don't want frostbite."

Perrin put their share of the milk in the pantry. They had already taken the emigrant families' share to them.

The girls were setting the table. Frank leaned to whisper in Matilda's ear, "I thought my fingers were gonna freeze on to one of them cows." He rolled his mischievous bright blue eyes at her.

Matilda turned pink. It was all she could do not to giggle.

Mrs. Whitman said severely, "Francis, it's not polite to whisper."

"Sorry, Mother." He always called her Mother now. The first time he had used the name, Helen teased him, and Frank laughingly replied that it was "as good a name as any." Now, quickly changing the subject, he said, "The Injuns say this is the coldest winter ever to hit these parts. The oldest in the tribe can't remember such cold."

"You talk to Indians too much. You know I don't like it."

"I'm sorry, Mother, but they know so much. You ought to hear what they say." He paused, and when she did not tell him to be quiet, went on, "They say it was never this cold before white people came."

"Some say the cold is the white peoples' fault," said Perrin.

"They don't remember that we suffer, too," said Mrs. Whitman.

"Still an' all," said John, "they've lost more stock than we have. Some say an Indian named Old Jimmy brought the cold to punish them. If it keeps up, they'll pay him for a thaw."

"That's enough idle talk," said Mrs. Whitman. "Eat your breakfasts."

Dr. Whitman entered and sat. "The mill is frozen solid. We have no way to grind corn."

"We'll make do with boiling wheat and corn for a while, then," said Mrs. Whitman as cheerfully as she could.

"The whole river is frozen," he continued. "After breakfast, we must chop holes in the ice so the animals can drink."

The next day when Matilda entered the kitchen for the noon meal, she found Mrs. Whitman standing over the doctor, who was wrapping a bedraggled sheep in an old blanket. Four more blanketed sheep milled around the kitchen, bleating loudly.

"Really, this is too much," Mrs. Whitman scolded. "Turning my kitchen into a sheep pen, and right before dinner, too! Look at the mess they are making."

"They must live, Mother," said Dr. Whitman mildly. "We can't afford to lose any more stock."

"What happened?" Matilda asked. The others crowded in, staring.

"They fell through the holes we chopped in the river, and I rescued them," said Dr. Whitman.

Mrs. Whitman sighed. "We'll survive this winter, one way or another."

SEVENTEEN

It seemed spring would never follow such a hard winter. A thaw came, but in two days the weather was as cold as before. John said the Indians had paid Old Jimmy to bring about the thaw, but he told them they had not paid enough.

They heaped gifts upon him, and one night instead of a cold, biting wind, a chinook swept down, pushing against the roof thatch and turning the fine powdered snow into a heavy wet mass. Mrs. Whitman said it would have happened anyway. Spring was bound to come every year.

In February, the sun turned the river to silver and the bare brown tree branches along its banks to gold. Brown birds flashed gold in a clear blue sky. In March, a bright green spray of leaves misted the trees and bushes, beautiful against the blue of the mountains.

That March of 1847, welcome news reached the mission with the spring. The United States and Great Britain, nine months earlier, had settled their boundary question, by dividing Oregon Country at the 49th parallel. Now both had a large share of that fertile land known as Oregon.

By May, the weather was warm enough for travel. The Presbyterian missionaries planned a meeting at Tshimakain. Dr. and Mrs. Whitman and Mr. Rodgers would attend, as would Catherine, her reward for help and companionship to Mrs. Whitman. A group of Cayuse Indians accompanied them to help with the packing and care of the animals.

The high point of the journey was stopping at Palouse Falls on the Palouse River. They rode through dry, rocky hills where only grass, weeds, and sagebrush grew. Brittle sprigs of peppergrass, thin flat round leaves surrounding their stems, trembled in the breeze. It was hard to believe in anything worth seeing in this remote, desolate place. Then suddenly the hills dropped away. A deep gorge split the earth, a torrent rushing through it.

The falls shot through a narrow cleft into a basin far below. At first Catherine hung back from the edge, afraid of being sucked down, tossed into the eddying flotsam and jetsam. Spray danced on the air where white, foaming water splashed into dark green. With Mr. Rodgers's encouragement, Catherine drew close enough to look down on the rocks a dizzying distance below.

Bare shoulders of gray-brown rock jutted above the falls. Directly to the left rose a thin ridge of stone formed in delicate fairy castle towers. From the basin at the foot of the falls, the river wound through a maze of terraced hills. Bright green sagebrush showed in the brown coating of grass. Gray cascades of gravel littered the steeper places.

For a long moment, no one spoke. Then Mr. Rodgers said, "Truly we should thank God for this magnificent sight."

Tshimakain, a mission of several log cabins, was situated amid pines and blue mountains. A rail fence like Whitman Mission's enclosed a yard, and a high board fence surrounded the chicken yard. Catherine watched the children while the adults held meetings. The Methodist missionaries at Waskopum on the Dalles, where Frank stopped after running away, had given their mission to the Presbyterians, who must decide at this meeting who should run it. The Whitmans were excited about expanding their missionary efforts.

They returned to a particularly busy summer. John and a hired man each drove a team of oxen to the Dalles to bring up a threshing machine, cornsheller, plows for the Indians, and other mission goods from the mission board in the east. These goods had made a long journey by sea and up the Columbia River. This was a man's task, and John, successfully completing it, went to Lapwai to stay with the Spaldings.

Frank built himself a hand wagon, asking a blacksmith Dr. Whitman had hired to make the wheels. On July 4, his old enemy, Alanson Hinman, showed up unexpectedly, all smiles and friendliness. He told Dr. Whitman he was now married, with a child. Frank felt sorry for the child. Mr. Hinman wanted to borrow the mission press "for the purpose of printing another paper in the Willamette." That sounded all right to Dr. Whitman, but he said he should ask the other missionaries first. Returning with news of their approval, Mr. Hinman left for the Dalles, with the press, in August.

Another visitor, a Canadian artist named Paul Kane, arrived in July and drew pictures of the mission. One day he was sketching in the yard as the children cleaned up. To make her work more interesting, Matilda balanced a rake on one finger, but it kept wobbling and toppling over. Just as she almost had it, Mrs. Whitman called, "Matilda, stop that nonsense. I don't want a picture of my little girl acting silly when she should be working."

Mrs. Whitman was not cross, though, actually seeming to be in a good mood lately. One summer day, Elizabeth found her giving the house an unusually thorough cleaning.

"Why are you cleaning, Mother? It isn't spring."

Mrs. Whitman looked up from shaking out settee cushions long enough to say, "Don't you know your Aunt Jane is coming?"

Mother's sister was coming all the way from New York! "Will she live with us?" Elizabeth cried.

"No, she'll go on to the Dalles and teach at the new mission."

When the children were alone, Perrin said, "I heard Aunt and Uncle talking, and I think they plan to fix something up between Aunt Jane and Mr. Rodgers."

"What do you mean, fix something up?" Elizabeth demanded.

Perrin looked as if her stupidity tried his patience. "I mean they hope Mr. Rodgers and Aunt Jane will fall in love and get married. I heard Aunt Narcissa say they are just right for each other. After all, they both love to sing."

Near the middle of August, Perrin and Dr. Whitman left for the Willamette Valley. Perrin, who could speak Nez Perce, and had held church services with the Indians, had volunteered to manage the new mission at the Dalles. He was not afraid of Mr. Hinman. "I'm big enough now to whip *him*, if he tried to whip me," he said.

John's and Perrin's absence did not leave a gap in the family. John Manson, age thirteen, and his eleven-year-old brother, Stephen, sons of a British Hudson's Bay Company employee and an Indian woman, came to study at the mission school.

Mother's good mood held. Talking of Aunt Jane brought back memories of life in New York, never far from her mind. She talked of picnics and parties in days gone by, reading the children stories of picnics.

PERRIN WHITMAN AND CHIEF TIMOTHY

Perrin Whitman, Marcus and Narcissa Whitman's nephew, who came to Waiilatpu the year before the Sagers, stands with Chief Timothy of the Nez Perces on an 1868 visit to Washington, D.C. Courtesy of Smithsonian Institution.

"You should have a picnic some time," she decided, and promised one if lessons and behavior went well for a certain amount of time.

In August that time ended, and Mrs. Whitman sent Frank and David out one day to find a good picnic spot. When they returned, she was busy preparing a large variety of food. "Frank, bring your little wagon. David, find something for us to sit on."

Frank returned with his wagon and David with some old blankets and a bearskin. Mrs. Whitman loaded food and dishes into the wagon with care. The chattering, excited girls, and John and Stephen Manson, gathered together and started off.

Catherine rode on the horse behind Mrs. Whitman, and the others walked, Frank pulling his wagon. Helen, Matilda, and Louisa carried rag dolls, and Elizabeth carried Eddie, her little Indian baby, in his cradle-board. When the girls tired, the dolls rode in the wagon, except for Eddie, who stayed on Elizabeth's back always.

Everyone came except three-year-old Henrietta, who was sick. Mr. Rodgers stayed with her, assuring the others he had been on plenty of picnics.

They traveled about a mile and a half upriver to the place Frank and David had found. Balm of Gilead trees stood a little distance from the water, not crowding the bank. The young trees' trunks were smooth and gray; the old ones deeply grooved.

Soft-leaved orange honeysuckle vines streamed from the trees, weighting and decorating, sweetening the air, tangled green thread on a loom of branches. Leaves fluttered in the breeze. Clusters of delicate-fuzzed white clematis vine flowers were shining stars in a sky of dark green.

Between river and trees, the grass was deep and green but not swampy. In the fresh-scented grass delicate purple, yellow, and white flowers waved.

"It's a lovely bower," said Mrs. Whitman. "A perfect place for a picnic. Let's have a game before we eat."

They played tag. Afterwards, the little girls played with their dolls while the older children ran races, till everyone was hungry.

Mrs. Whitman spread a tablecloth on the grass, and she, Catherine, and Mary Ann covered it with bread and butter, cheese and cold meat, several kinds of pies, cakes, preserves, and Mrs. Whitman's special Irish moss custard.

At Mrs. Whitman's word, Frank said the blessing. Mrs. Whitman served the children, heaping the blue and white patterned dishes, and sent David to the river to fill the pitcher. When they were all full and the leftovers and dishes put away, they had more games.

"At the picnic parties I attended in New York, we crowned a boy king and a girl queen. Which boy and girl most deserve this honor?"

"How about David for king?" Frank suggested. "He found this spot."

They agreed it would not be a perfect picnic without the perfect spot. Elizabeth twisted a thin willow branch into a crown of leaves, while Frank cut strips from the bearskin and tied them around David's head to roughly resemble a beard and moustache. "King David!" he exulted. "Just like in the Bible!"

David grinned behind his makeshift beard. "Now," said Mrs. Whitman, as David adjusted his crown and fidgeted with his bearskin beard, "which girl shall be queen?"

After a spirited debate, she said, "Louise has shown herself very helpful and well-behaved lately. It was not always so. When she first came to me, she was willful and disobedient. She still is sometimes, but I think she should be queen."

Five-year-old Louise smiled, squirming delightedly under all the attention. Catherine hastily wove a wreath of tiny white daisies. "I crown thee Queen Louise the first," she said, placing it on her head. The children cheered and clapped.

"Let's hurry home and show Mr. Rodgers the king and queen." Mrs. Whitman mounted the horse, which had been enjoying the lush green grass while the children enjoyed their food. Catherine decided to walk. "I'd feel too joggly on the horse after all that food," she explained.

Frank started out with the wagon, dishes, dolls, leftovers and all. The Manson brothers walked with him. Mrs. Whitman on the horse soon passed them, riding at a leisurely pace. Behind them, in stately procession, were King David and Queen Louise, walking side by side, and Matilda with them, all in high spirits. After them came Catherine and Mary Ann. Elizabeth and Helen lagged at the rear.

"Look at that," said Elizabeth when the others were some distance ahead. She pointed at a round, gray object in a tree.

"A hornets' nest!" said Helen.

"Wonder what would happen if we threw something at it?"

Without answering, Helen gathered a handful of dirt clods. Elizabeth did the same.

Whack! Helen's clod struck the nest and bounced off. Crack! Elizabeth's heavier, harder-flung clod burst the flaky, hollow shell and out swarmed a buzzing, angry horde.

"Run!" Elizabeth shrieked. Helen did not have to be told. They soon caught up with the others and began to pass them, Eddie in his cradleboard thumping against Elizabeth's back as she ran.

Mrs. Whitman's horse reared and plunged; Mrs. Whitman cried out and they knew the hornets had attacked her and the horse. Catherine and Mary Ann dived screaming for the bushes, while the youthful king and queen, with Matilda, streaked down the trail, clutching their crowns.

John and Stephen were soon far ahead. Frank, however, was hampered by the wagon. In panic he clutched the handle and ran. The wagon bounced and rattled over the rough trail and two of Mrs. Whitman's china plates jumped out and broke. No time to think of that now. The hornets were attacking! They caught up with Frank and let him know what they thought of invaders to their territory.

A bit farther down the trail, the hornets retreated and hysteria died down. It was time to regroup and count losses. Mrs. Whitman had been stung in several places. Helen and Frank had also been stung. Louisa's daisy crown was broken, but Catherine fixed it with flowers from the side of the trail, and also rearranged David's beard and crown. The worst loss was the dishes. Mary Ann brought the pieces to Mrs. Whitman. "Well, never mind," she said, looking at them sadly. "Let's go home."

Seeing the way Mother looked at the pieces of her dishes, Elizabeth wanted to weep tears of shame. But fearing the terrible punishment Mrs. Whitman would inflict, she dared say nothing. They trailed behind the others, Helen crying over her stings as well as the dishes.

Notes from Mr. Rodgers's violin drifted to them on the summer air before they could see the house. When he heard them coming, he came out. Mrs. Whitman introduced King David and Queen Louise, and he greeted the royal pair with respect, bowing deeply. The others gathered around him, eagerly telling everything about the picnic, not forgetting the hornet attack—far from it! They all had something to tell, except Helen and Elizabeth, usually among the most talkative, who now hung back, strangely silent.

When Mr. Rodgers went in to check on Henrietta, Mrs. Whitman turned to the children with a stern look. "It's time for someone to confess," she said. "Which of you children disturbed the hornets' nest?" Eight faces looked back in blank innocence, while two were miserable with shame.

Helen spoke in a tiny quavering voice. "Elizabeth and I did, but I threw first."

Mrs. Whitman pointed at them. "Go to bed right now, and you'll have no supper tonight."

Not having supper wasn't such a terrible punishment, Elizabeth reflected as they climbed the stairs. She, at least, would not miss a little corn meal mush and milk after all that food at the picnic. But the shame was truly terrible, and having to spend the rest of the long, sunny afternoon in bed was the worst of all.

EIGHTEEN

"John's home, John's home!" Helen shouted.

Catherine bounded out, saw John on his horse, and ran to him. The Spaldings rode with him. It was now late September of 1847, and she had not seen him since he left to spend the summer at Lapwai.

Farther back on the trail, Indians led heavily laden horses. Before Catherine could say more than a few words, the others crowded around John, trying all at once to tell about their summer and introduce him to the Manson boys.

Amid the flurry of excitement, Rev. Spalding explained to Mrs. Whitman, "I have a pack train of wheat I want to sell to the emigrants while they're along the Umatilla."

"I'd like to come along to find a young lady to teach the children. My sister Jane was going to, but is not coming after all."

Dr. Whitman had returned from the Willamette Valley about the middle of September, leaving again to guide emigrants along a new route he had discovered. The emigration of 1847 was the largest yet to pour into Oregon Country. Mrs. Whitman had to turn many away. "My husband says he cannot winter many because provisions are lower than usual, and will only winter those who arrive late in the season," she explained.

Mrs. Whitman, Catherine, John, and the Manson boys traveled to the Umatilla with the Spaldings, meeting after a few days Dr. Whitman and Perrin. They were ready to go home when the doctor learned of a young emigrant man who was having trouble breathing. He and Mrs. Whitman and Perrin stayed to help while the others went back to Waiilatpu.

Arriving on Monday, October 4, they found a visitor who introduced himself as John Mix Stanley, an artist hailing from New York and Ohio, touring the Great Plains and Far West to paint portraits of Indians.

He had been at the mission a few days, making friends with Mr.

Rodgers and the children, and painting magnificent portraits of several Cayuses. He was disappointed to hear the Whitmans had not returned, and left promising to return in November and perhaps paint their portraits. The younger children, who had grown quite fond of him, were sorry to see him go.

Dr. and Mrs. Whitman and Perrin returned. The doctor brought each child a small gift, also bringing the unwelcome news that measles and whooping cough were spreading through the wagon trains. "None of you children has had measles, and very few whooping cough. I'm afraid this is going to be bad," he said.

In a day or two, he and Perrin departed to show the emigrants the new route. This time Perrin would not return, but go straight to the Dalles.

The Spaldings prepared to leave, and take John with them. Catherine did not want him to go, and the others felt the same.

Now sixteen, John had changed since leaving at the beginning of the summer. Though still ready for games, he seemed more grown-up, taller, responsible, as if he had gone from boy to man during his absence. Instead of wandering with his gun as before, he now read, more often than not.

Mysteriously, he rose before 4:00 in the morning, spending the hours before breakfast writing. No matter how the younger children teased or begged, he would never tell what he wrote—not even to Mother and Father.

The morning he was to leave, Catherine watched miserably as he led his saddled horse from the pasture. Around his neck was the nice new tippet Mother had knitted to keep him warm that winter. Catherine could think of nothing to say. It seemed hard to be separated from him again.

John looked to where the Spaldings waited with the Indians and horses, ready to go. He turned to Catherine. "I reckon you'll get along fine without me," he said, as if reading her thoughts. "You did all summer."

"It would have been better with you here, to be with us at the picnic and all. Mother says she'll give a better one next summer."

"Maybe I'll be here for that," said John. Jamming his hat on, adjusting his tippet, he moved to join the Spaldings.

Mrs. Whitman hurried from the house. "John, I wish you'd stay. The measles started with the emigrants and are already among the Indians. It's hard enough now, and soon will be worse. Even when the doctor returns, there won't be enough help, especially if measles spreads among the children, which I'm afraid it must. Please stay and help us."

"All right, Mother." John smiled. "I can see you need me more than the Spaldings do."

When Catherine realized he had not wanted to go, any more than she wanted him to, her heart felt suddenly light. John would be here to take care of things!

"Here, Sis, take my horse." Handing her the reins, he walked across the yard to tell the Spaldings he would be staying at Waiilatpu.

Returning from the Umatilla, Dr. Whitman brought a family named Saunders with five children. He had hired Mr. Saunders, a judge, to teach the mission school. With the Saunders family was a tailor, Isaac Gilliland. The doctor promised him work, as well. Mrs. Whitman was glad to finally have a teacher, but still wanted a young lady to help her with the girls.

After them came the Osborn family, who had visited two years before. Mr. Osborn's mechanical ability would greatly help Dr. Whitman. Nancy, the oldest of the four children, was now seven. Mrs. Osborn expected another child soon.

Judge Saunders opened school on October 19th. He proved a much better teacher than Mr. Geiger, having been a peacemaker in his wagon train.

The emigrants kept blowing in like the pale yellow autumn leaves from the trees along the river. The doctor took in those who would work for him, and those too sick and destitute to travel farther.

Lorinda Bewley, a graceful blonde in her early twenties, attracted Mrs. Whitman's attention, and Mrs. Whitman, delighted at having found a young lady to help with the girls, persuaded her to stay. At twelve, Catherine and Mary Ann would soon be young ladies, and must learn genteel manners like Miss Bewley's. Lorinda's older brother, Crockett, also stayed, along with their friend, Amos Sales, the rest of the family traveling on.

Besides the emigrants were Nicholas Finley, a half-Indian who understood French, living in a nearby lodge with his Indian wife, and Joseph Stanfield, a husky French Canadian hired by Dr. Whitman the previous fall. Waiilatpu was full to bursting. The Canfield family, last to arrive, had to camp in the blacksmith shop.

Shortly afterward, another emigrant arrived—one Dr. Whitman soon decided he did not want at the mission. Calling himself Joe Lewis, the man looked like an Eastern Indian, perhaps a Delaware, and was probably half-white.

The ill, feverish man's pants were torn, his feet wrapped in rags, and he clutched a ragged, miserable coat around himself, which he opened to show the doctor he had no shirt. Although he could take in no more people, the doctor could turn away no one in that condition. He clothed him, cared for him until he was well, and planned to send him with emigrants to the Willamette Valley.

All the emigrants refused to take him. His evil reputation had spread through the train with the measles. No one wanted to spend a minute with him. At last, the doctor found one family willing to travel with Lewis, and sent him with them.

Three days later he returned, and though the doctor tried everything short of force, Lewis would not leave. Finally Dr. Whitman said, "If you insist on staying, you must make yourself useful. Will you work for me?"

Lewis said he would. He stayed on, moving into Nicholas Finley's lodge, building coffins for the Indians dying of measles. His presence made everyone uneasy.

The Osborn family stayed in the Indian room, a big room with a fireplace, adjoining the sitting room of the mission house. It had been an Indian schoolroom and meeting place until so many emigrants arrived. Some of the Indians resented whites occupying their room, and Dr. Whitman, supposed to be their missionary, devoting much of his attention to whites, Frank had learned. Mrs. Osborn had measles. Her baby girl, born on November 14, died the same day. Ten days later, her six-year-old, Salvijane, also died of measles.

Mrs. Whitman tried to comfort Mrs. Osborn. "The Indians are angry because their children die while ours recover. Perhaps it will do them good to see that white children can also die." When she brought in several Indians to see the dead white child, they looked at the small body, laughed, and walked out. One dead white child was pitiful after scores of dead Indian children.

Indians were dying in such numbers that Joe Lewis and the others could not make coffins fast enough. While coffins were being made, dead Indians, large and small, hung over the fence, like so many sacks of wheat. The doctor presided over a funeral service every day, sometimes burying five or six before hurrying back to attend the sick, both Indians and his own household.

The Indian camps were places of constant wailing. Measles mainly struck down children. How would the tribes survive without the young with their strong legs and backs, to learn the old ways and gather food and provide for their people?

Dr. Whitman tried in vain to persuade the Indians that their custom of sweat baths was causing their children to die. The Indians persisted in steaming until lathered with sweat, then jumping in the cold river, intending, as always, to drive the ills from their bodies. Dr. Whitman tried to explain that measles was a disease which caused an outbreak on the flesh. Any shock to the system was harmful during disease, but the sweat bath drove measles inside the body, where its effects were disastrous. Indians trying the sweat cure usually died the next day.

This was the state of things at Whitman Mission on November 22, 1847, when Henry Spalding brought his ten-year-old, Eliza, to attend the mission school, not realizing the serious situation until their arrival. School was closed because of measles, but Mr. Saunders thought he could reopen it in a week or so.

One by one, the mission children caught the disease, different children suffering different stages at the same time. Some were miserable with fever, coughing, runny nose, and red eyes. Others had tiny white spots like salt grains inside their mouths, and in the next day or two, a rash of pink dots, sometimes joined in clumps, covered their heads and bodies.

Still others were over the first symptoms, but weak. Louise's and Helen's condition was most serious. Frank, one of the first to become ill because he circulated widely among both whites and Indians, now well into recovery, was worried about them. The only thing that worried him more was Joe Lewis's actions.

The Cayuse tribe, once a band of four hundred, lost over half its members to measles when the wagon train passed through. They were half-crazed with fear and grief, and Joe Lewis was taking advantage of it, trying to set the Indians against the doctor by lying.

Frank had befriended many in the tribes, observing both at the mission and the Indian villages. He warned Dr. Whitman of Joe Lewis's tales, but the doctor made light of it. "Don't worry about all this talk. Most of the Indians are our friends. We've been among them eleven years. They don't want to hurt us."

As November drew to a close, angry words buzzed like hornets through Chief Tiloukaikt's band of Cayuses. The Cayuses at first were not alarmed by the trickle of whites passing through their land. They would go on to the Willamette Valley, not stop in Cayuse country. Then the trickle became a tide, and Joe Lewis came with his tales of white treachery in the East, of sickness and wars and broken treaties. From these evil places in the East came strange shipments for Marcus Whitman, bottles and bundles with poison and power to destroy all of the Cayuse tribe. As more died, Lewis's words appeared true.

On Saturday, November 27th, Frank confronted Dr. Whitman, determined to make him listen. He caught him during a rare relaxed moment, as he sat reading.

"Joe Lewis is telling the Indians you're a bad medicine man. They're saying you once poisoned watermelons, making Indians sick."

Dr. Whitman glanced up from his book. "My associate Mr. Gray did that six years ago. It was not poison he used. His plan was not to kill the Indians, but to give them an experience to prevent them from stealing watermelons."

"They're saying three Indians took the meat you put out for the wolves, and nearly died. Joe Lewis says if you'd poison a wolf, you'd poison an Indian. He tells them you and Mr. Spalding plan to poison all the Indians to steal their cattle and horses and land. They're having another council tonight with Joe."

Dr. Whitman sighed, laying the book down. "I know. This isn't my first warning, though I didn't like to worry you children. Tonight, Mr. Spalding and I will ride to the Umatilla to see some Catholic missionaries staying at Young Chief's lodge. They plan to establish a mission, and I may sell my buildings and other mission property to them. Perhaps it will appease the Indians if we show signs of leaving."

The doctor and Mr. Spalding did not wait for supper that evening, but ate hastily and rode away. The steady, regular routine at the mission was disrupted by the measles. For several weeks, Joe Lewis and the doctor were the only ones well enough to prepare supper. The doctor worked the most.

In the kitchen that evening, Frank heard a knock. Tomahas entered asking for medicine, and Frank brought a bottle from the sitting room cabinet. Tomahas stood for a moment as if wanting to say something. By the look on his face, it was not good.

Catherine came in, recovered enough by today to be up and about. During her illness, Mrs. Whitman had cut her long hair off round her neck. Cutting hair was a sign of mourning among the Indians, Frank knew. Tomahas's eyes widened with interest, and he demanded of Frank, "Are any of the children dead?"

"Only the little girls who died earlier, though Louise and Helen are mighty low," Frank answered.

Tomahas's eyes burned, and Frank was momentarily afraid he would strike him. He left in a fierce, quick motion, slamming the door.

Trembling, Catherine touched her mouth. Then she seemed to collect herself, and began to fix supper.

Joe Lewis came in and sat on the settee behind the stove. He and Frank eyed each other with deep hatred. Joe turned his attention to Catherine.

"I heard your two little sisters might not live," he said.

Catherine glanced at him, but did not answer.

"Too bad about them." Joe almost smiled. Frank wished for a gun. "I'm glad someone's well enough to fix supper," he went on. "I'm so starved on the doctor's swill I've gone crazy."

He looked crazy. His wild, bloodshot stare sickened and frightened Frank. "Nothing like a pretty little girl fixing supper," Joe said.

Frank made a quick move toward him, stopped himself. He did not want to worsen things, and anyway he could not take on Joe. He burned with helpless, desperate rage.

Joe put his arms behind his head, leaning against the wall. A row of rotten teeth showed beneath the sharp nose and insane, glittering eyes.

"What's the matter, boy? Ain't I right?" He chuckled. The sound caught in his throat, rasping, wheezing.

Frank clenched his fists, tight, feeling he was squeezing his heart in his hands. If only they could rid themselves of this man in time.

Sunday night, Frank and John were in the sitting room watching the sick children when Dr. Whitman came in, wet and tired.

"Why are you back so soon?" John asked, worry etched on his face. "We thought you'd be a while talking with the missionaries."

"The children are too sick to be left long."

"Where's Mr. Spalding?" Frank asked.

"He fell from his horse. He'll be all right, but was unable to ride back with me. I'll take over for you. You've stayed up long enough."

John and Frank went upstairs. Their voices awakened Catherine, who lay watching Dr. Whitman. His weary movements and lined, haggard face showed he was much troubled. *It must be because Louise and Helen are so sick,* she thought.

He looked one by one at the children. Catherine pretended to sleep when he passed her. Coming to Helen last, he sat by her side. "Mother, I'm afraid Helen is dying."

Mrs. Whitman, who lay on a bed near the small black heating stove, did not move or reply. Exhausted, she probably had not heard.

Catherine felt it was best to lie quiet. For some half-fathomed reason, she did not want the doctor to know she was awake.

The doctor sat a long time by Helen's side. At last he said, as if speaking to himself, "I was wrong. She is better." He took a chair near his wife's bed. "Mother," he said softly. "I wish to speak with you."

Now, why doesn't he let her rest? Catherine wondered. *It must be serious.*

Mrs. Whitman pulled herself slowly, wearily up, and sat in a chair by him.

"Mr. Spalding and I stayed at Stickus's lodge last night. Stickus told me what Frank has...that the Indians hold councils, planning my death."

Catherine went cold inside. She knew the Indians were angry, but the possibility they might kill Father had not entered her mind.

By the light of the candle near Mother's bed, she saw Mother pull her chair closer and take Father's hands. They sat with heads close together. "What shall we do?" Mother asked.

"I've seen a Catholic bishop and two priests who started a new mission in Young Chief's lodge. They promise to visit us. If they want the mission, and the Indians want them, it could solve our problems."

A heavy silence fell between them. "If only we can reach an understanding in time," Father said. "If it comes to the worst, I think they will kill only Mr. Spalding and me, no one else." He put his arms around her, rocking her as if she were one of the children.

"We can do nothing else?" she asked, leaning her head against his shoulder.

"Nothing but pray."

They talked low while Catherine tried to make sense of what she heard. It was all too impossible to imagine.

After a long time Father said, "Go into the parlor and sleep. No, don't argue. I'll watch the children."

"You must call me if there is any change for the worse."

"I will, I promise."

He watched her go into the parlor, then went to the bed where she had lain, blew out the candle, and sat on the edge of the bed, resting his head in his hands. A single lamp, which burned low all night so the adults could keep watch on the children, lighted the room.

Catherine could not sleep while he looked so worried. The conversation kept repeating itself in her mind. When he looked in her direction, his gaze remained on her and she knew he saw she was awake. After a moment, he crossed the room and sat on the end of her settee.

"Why don't you run?" Catherine asked. "Stay away until it's safe."

In the dimness she saw an expression of gentle amusement cross his face. "Run, where? To the valley? To Fort Walla Walla? The fort won't hold all these people, and I can't leave them seeking my own safety. I'm responsible to you children, the emigrants, all the sick ones." He took her hand. "Don't worry. The only sure thing is God's will. Trusting Him, we don't have to worry."

He sat by her until she was able to sleep, a long time later.

NINETEEN

Matilda's eyes flew wide. Waking with a jump, too fear-stiffened to sit up, she looked around moving only her eyes.

It was Monday, November 29, 1847. She was alone in the girls' upstairs room. Catherine and Mary Ann, Elizabeth and Helen, Louise and Henrietta were all so sick that they slept on settees downstairs. With one of them in sight, she would be brave enough to move out of bed, but as it was, she lay still in the cold aftershock of a horrible dream.

She tested her arms and legs, which after a nightmare always dragged as they had when she ate the poison plant—as if they would not move right. Everything worked, everything was right, for now. Staying upstairs in the gloomy loft alone would only frighten her more, so she crept down in the cold early-morning darkness, seeking the warmth and comfort of her family.

In the sitting room the low-burning lantern cast its light over the sick girls' settees. Louise tossed, moaning a little. Helen and Henrietta lay perfectly still, their flushed faces covered with little red points. The boys, not so sick now, slept in their own room. Catherine, Elizabeth, and Mary Ann, still weak, lay on settees pushed against the walls.

The little heating stove warmed the room. Rows of brown-backed books leaned against each other in the bookcase, each holding the next one up. Medicine bottles glinted dully brown and clear and blue in the cabinet under the stairs. She tried to feel relieved that things were not as they had been in her dream. Passing quietly and carefully past the sleeping girls into the kitchen, she found Dr. Whitman on a chair by the cookstove, broiling steak for breakfast.

"Good morning, Father." Matilda climbed into his lap, put her arms around his neck and kissed him. She leaned against him, listening to the steady comforting beat of his heart. His warmth, the stove's warmth, and the good smell of the steak made her feel a little better.

"Good morning, Matilda." He spoke wearily but without irritation. She leaned against him another moment before speaking.

"I had such a bad dream, and I was frightened."

"What was your dream?"

She hesitated. "I dreamed the Indians killed you and a lot of others."

Dr. Whitman sighed. "That was a bad dream, but I hope it will not occur."

The family members well enough came to the table. Dr. Whitman had spoken only to John, Frank, and Catherine about the trouble hanging over them, but everyone was silent and gloomy.

Joe Lewis, who usually ate at their table, was gone this morning. Catherine glanced nervously at the empty place, but was silent, as was everyone.

Mrs. Whitman was also missing, too busy lately to eat. After Dr. Whitman said the blessing, Elizabeth asked, "Where is Mother?"

"She doesn't feel well," replied the doctor. "She is not coming to breakfast."

Catherine noticed how calm he seemed. The blue eyes peering from beneath the overhanging brows showed a quiet sadness, nothing else. Last night, even while comforting her, he was preoccupied, agitated. Now he was more serious than usual—that was all.

"Shall I take her some breakfast?" Elizabeth asked.

"Yes, if you wish. Eat your own breakfast first."

After breakfast, Dr. Whitman sat in the sitting room with the sick children, reading a paper, keeping watch over Louise and Helen. School had been closed because so many children were sick, but today at 9:00 Mr. Saunders was opening it again. Frank, Matilda, and David readied, Frank, especially, hurrying. He was to shoot a steer which Joe Stanfield, the French Canadian hired man, had brought in that morning.

Mr. Rodgers came in. He and the doctor talked in low voices. Elizabeth knew they discussed the Indians' discontent, but did not know the exact trouble. She had only overheard disturbing snatches of conversation these last days.

In the kitchen she filled a plate with steak, baked potatoes, and toast, and took it and a cup of coffee into Mrs. Whitman's room. Coffee was a special treat, chosen to make her feel better.

Mrs. Whitman sat in bed, her head bowed. Her usually neat red-gold hair hung in a tangled mess over her face. She was weeping.

Elizabeth did not know what to do. "I've brought you some food," she said, her voice coming out a whisper.

Mrs. Whitman looked up with red, swollen eyes. "Oh, thank you," she said weakly. "Set it on the stand and run along." Her hands, her steady capable hands, were shaking. Elizabeth ran away.

She took Catherine aside into a corner. "Mother was crying when I went in. I reckon Louisa and Helen are going to die."

Catherine looked into Elizabeth's face, then told what she had heard last night.

A chill raced the length of Elizabeth's spine. So that was the trouble! "Oh, Sis! Would the Indians really kill Father?"

"I don't know," said Catherine. Her trembling voice filled Elizabeth with dread.

"Let's go to John," said Elizabeth. "He always knows what to do."

They found John working as on any ordinary day. His next task was making brooms, and he methodically gathered twigs and poles as if that were the most important thing to do right now. "We must all be brave," he told them.

"It's easy for you to be brave," said Catherine. "You've always been brave and I never have. Dr. Degen and everyone said how brave you were after Ma and Pa died, when all I could do was sit and cry."

John snorted. "As if I had any choice! Some said it was courage, but all I did was what had to be done for us to go on. What else can anyone do?" The girls had no answer.

At 11:00, Dr. Whitman buried three children from Chief Tiloukaikt's lodge. Before leaving for the funeral, he instructed Mrs. Whitman about caring for the sick. She was now dressed, her hair neatly combed, and, seemingly recovered from her earlier grief, she looked after the children calmly.

When the doctor returned, he told his wife, "No Indians attended the funeral except Chief Tiloukaikt and a few others. The rest of them must be waiting for the men to butcher that steer Francis shot this morning."

Elizabeth looked out the sash door that led from the sitting room to the back yard. Its top half set with glass panes, it faced the river. In the yard, a crowd of Indians surrounded a dead steer hanging by its heels. Jacob Hoffman, William Canfield, and Nathan Kimball, three emigrant men, were butchering the steer. Mr. Hoffman was pulling out its entrails. Elizabeth turned away, never liking to see an animal butchered.

Around noon, Elizabeth went into the kitchen. Dr. Whitman sat at the table. Nathan Kimball, one of the emigrant men helping butcher the steer, was warming himself on the settee behind the cookstove.

Catherine swept the floor with an old, worn-out broom. John sat on a high stool at a table near the door that opened towards the river, setting out twine and twigs to make new brooms.

"Yes, the situation looks pretty dark," Dr. Whitman was telling Mr. Kimball, "but I think I shall be able to quell any trouble. If things do not clear up by spring, I will move my family to the valley."

Move to the valley? It did not seem possible. Whitman Mission had lasted eleven years. Elizabeth was full of questions, but little girls must be seen and not heard, so she did not ask.

"I wish you luck," said Mr. Kimball. He went out the door past John, into the yard.

When Mr. Saunders let Matilda and the other girls out of school for afternoon recess, they went into the kitchen.

John sat on a stool by the door, untangling a mess of rough brown twine. The girls tried to attract his attention and make him smile, but he refused to look up. His face was set, clouded over with gloom, so downcast that at last the girls fell silent. He spoke only to Matilda. When he saw her dipping a drink, he said, "Would you bring me a drink, too?"

She brought the full the dipper to him. A dull gleam caught her eye, and she saw a pistol lying on the shelf just above his head. Though over the fright of her dream, she was suddenly uneasy again. Why did John need a pistol? It was hard for an eight-year-old to understand all that was happening. She wished he would say something to make her feel better, but all he said was, "Won't you hold the twine for me?"

She wanted to stay, knew she could not. "It's only recess," she said. "I'll hold it after school."

The bell rang to call the girls in, signaling the boys' recess. Frank and the others went out in the yard to watch the emigrant men butchering the steer. A group of Indians stood near, some sitting on the fence rails, each with a blanket fastened closely around him.

"What do you suppose all these Indians are doing around here with their blankets on?" Frank heard Mr. Canfield ask.

"Some of their devilment," snapped Mr. Hoffman, taking up his ax.

Elizabeth was in the sitting room with Mrs. Whitman, Catherine, and the other sick children when Mrs. Whitman said to her husband, "I wish you would go see Miss Bewley. She's very sick."

Dr. Whitman went upstairs, returning after a while not with his usual quick, purposeful step, but slowly, almost hesitantly. His face was deeply lined with trouble as he walked to the sash door and stood looking out its window, drumming his fingers on the glass, while Elizabeth waited in an agony of suspense.

"Poor Lorinda is in trouble and does not know why," he said at last. "I found her weeping. She said a presentiment of evil was on her mind that she could not overcome. I must get her some medicine. You take it to her and try to comfort her. I have failed in my attempt." He walked to the medicine case under the stairs.

A presentiment of evil. That's how we've all felt, thought Elizabeth. What did it all mean, and how would it end?

"I'll bring her the medicine as soon as I give Henrietta her milk," said Mrs. Whitman. "Here it is almost two o'clock in the afternoon and I haven't even bathed the children yet." The children always bathed at 11:00 a.m., summer or winter. She headed towards the pantry after the milk. Elizabeth followed her into the kitchen.

A crowd of Indians milled, loud voices reverberating off the walls. They often entered without knocking, but Elizabeth had never seen so many in the house, and they had never behaved so rudely. She could see their manner alarmed Mrs. Whitman, who was trying hard to keep her composure. Mary Ann was heating dishwater in a big pot on the stove. She looked fearfully about at the dark, angry faces above the blankets.

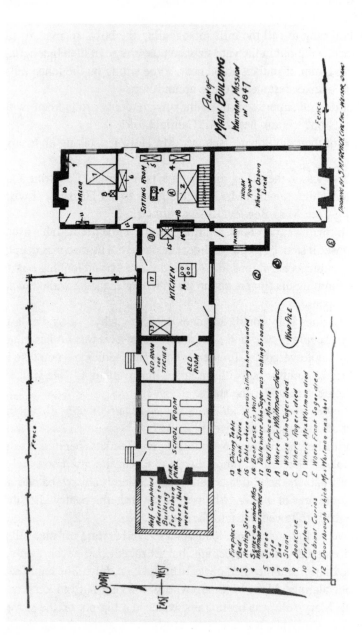

Floor plan of the first floor rooms of the mission house, where the Whitmans and Sagers lived. Drawn by S. M. French under the direction of Elizabeth Sager Helm.

John, winding twine into a ball, seemed to be trying to ignore the Indians. Elizabeth leaned on his knee to steady herself. To a ten-year old girl, a sixteen-year-old brother seemed grown up, sometimes even older than grown up. Sunk deep in some private sorrow, John wound the twine, around and around, never looking up, only looking at the twine coming off the floor, the end growing shorter as he wound it tight.

A kitten sat under the table, safe from the moccasins walking back and forth, trying to catch the ever-moving end as John wound it. Normally Elizabeth would have laughed at her antics, but now she felt strangely like crying.

The pantry was a little room off the kitchen. Mrs. Whitman squeezed between the Indians and in a moment came out carrying a pitcher of milk.

An Indian grabbed her sleeve. "Give me."

"Wait until I give my baby some."

"Give me milk, now!" the man yelled. Elizabeth shrank from his furious look.

Mrs. Whitman pulled free and grabbed the handle of the sitting room door. As she passed into the sitting room, the Indian tried to force his way through, but Mrs. Whitman closed the door and Elizabeth heard the lock click. She had never seen Mrs. Whitman lock the door between the sitting room and the kitchen, and it amazed and frightened her.

An Indian grabbed John. "You. Give me milk! Bring medicine!"

John pulled loose. "Leave me be." He went back to winding twine.

The sitting room door cracked open and Mrs. Whitman peered in. "Elizabeth, come along. It's almost time for your bath."

The doctor looked up from his reading as they entered and said, "Catherine took medicine and water to Miss Bewley, but can't seem to comfort her." He paid no mind to the noise in the kitchen, though he must hear it.

"I'll see what I can do for her soon." Mrs. Whitman crossed to the settee where Henrietta was lying. A cup lay nearby and she filled it, took Henrietta in her arms and gave her the milk. Once sure she was comfortable, she took Catherine to a large wooden tub by the heating stove, and helped her undress and bathe.

The Indians were pounding on the kitchen door, still calling for milk and medicine. "You'll be all right by yourself for a moment, won't you, while I give them the milk?" Mrs. Whitman asked Catherine.

Feeling a little weak, as she often had since catching the measles, Elizabeth lay down on the sofa near the stove, built like the settees only a bit larger, and watched Catherine swirling water in the tub.

Mrs. Osborn entered from the Indian room.

"It's good to see you on your feet," Mrs. Whitman said. This was the first time Mrs. Osborn had been up since catching the measles.

"Thank you." She sank onto a chair, looking drained and sad from the measles and the loss of her two little girls.

Mrs. Whitman reached for the kitchen door handle. The Indians in the kitchen shouted for the doctor. Mrs. Whitman turned to her husband, saying, "Doctor, you are wanted."

The doctor went first to the medicine cabinet under the stairs for a bottle, his face, sad, troubled, but somehow calm. Stopping at the kitchen door, he said, "Bolt the door behind me, Mother." She bolted the door as soon as he was through it.

When Catherine finished her bath, she dried herself and began to dress. Elizabeth undressed and lowered herself into the warm water. She was still a little weak, so Mrs. Whitman helped her bathe.

In the kitchen, John wound twine and Mary Ann washed dishes, both assuming a calm air. The crowd of Indians was increasingly rough in manner.

Dr. Whitman gave the medicine to the Indian who wanted it and sat on the settee behind the cookstove. Chief Tiloukaikt stood in front of him and began to discuss a sick woman the doctor was caring for.

John felt sorry for Tiloukaikt. Three of his grandchildren were buried that morning. When the women wailed for the dead, their keening cut through him worse than the chill November wind. Grief must be making Tiloukaikt so argumentative. He was louder and angrier with each word. Dr. Whitman kept answering him in a soft, steady voice.

Suddenly Tomahas, who had stolen up beside Dr. Whitman, drew a tomahawk from beneath his blanket. Before John could warn the doctor, Tomahas drove his weapon full force against the back of his head. Dr. Whitman staggered forward, but Tomahas struck again, and the doctor fell to the floor.

His heart beating wildly, John grabbed for the pistol he had left on the shelf above him and fired at Tomahas, but the shot went wild as an Indian grabbed his arm. John turned in horror and saw a gun pointing straight at him.

Shots exploded in the kitchen, glass shattered. Elizabeth jumped from the tub to run, she knew not where.

"Mrs. Whitman, what is the matter?" cried Mrs. Osborn.

"The Indians are killing us!"

Catherine yanked open the outside door and she and Elizabeth raced through.

"Girls, come back," called Mrs. Whitman. They were standing in the yard, Catherine half-dressed, Elizabeth shivering, wet and naked, turning around, not knowing where to run. They came back in.

"Mrs. Osborn," said Mrs. Whitman, "go to your room and fasten your door. Catherine, finish dressing." Mrs. Whitman started to fasten the doors and windows, then caught sight of Elizabeth. "Poor child, you must have your clothes on," she said.

She dressed Elizabeth in dreadful haste, pulling her clothes on over her wet skin so that they clung to her. Catherine and Elizabeth followed Mrs. Whitman as she rushed around the room, checking the bolts on each door and window. Mrs. Osborn hurried into the Indian room and shut the door.

Mary Ann burst in through the west door. "The Indians are killing Father and John!" she cried.

"Is the doctor dead?" asked Mrs. Whitman.

"Yes!"

"My husband is killed and I am left a widow!"

When the Indians by the beef heard the shots in the kitchen, they dropped their blankets, revealing knives, tomahawks, and guns. Frank and the other boys, still out at recess, raced into the schoolroom. "Mr. Saunders, the Indians are killing the men at the beef!"

Mr. Saunders rushed to the window. The children, crowding behind, saw Mr. Hoffman fighting off six Indians with his ax, used moments ago to split the beef. Mr. Canfield and Mr. Kimball were running. Mr. Marsh ran only a few steps from the mill before an Indian shot him.

Mr. Canfield scrambled over a rail fence, trying to reach his family in the blacksmith shop. An Indian shot at him and he tumbled from the fence, wounded in the back. He pulled himself to his feet and ran.

The schoolroom had a window on each end, and they saw him grab his little children from their play by the blacksmith shop, and run in.

Peter Hall, another emigrant, laying a floor for the new addition, leaped from the mission house's second story and raced towards the river. An Indian on horseback chased him, swinging his tomahawk. Mr. Hall disappeared into the brush at the river's edge.

"They're killing Mr. Hoffman," said Mr. Saunders. "I must go to my family." He ran out. As he opened the door an Indian dived at him. He shook him off and ran for the emigrant house, where his family was staying. Soon two Indians were upon him with butcher knives. As soon as he fought one off, the other grabbed him.

His daughter Helen, who like Frank was fourteen, ran for the door. Frank threw his arms around her waist, clinging despite her desperate struggles. "Let me go! Let me help my father!"

"You can't! You'll only be killed! John and Steve," he called to the Manson boys, "bolt the door! We must hide," he told the others.

Nathan Kimball burst through the west door into the sitting room. His arm, broken at the elbow, swinging at an odd angle, spilled blood over his white shirt.

Mrs. Whitman was in the sitting room with Catherine, Elizabeth, Mary Ann, and the sick children. At first she had cried out in despair, but now moved about as calmly as if doing ordinary housework.

"The Indians are killing us!" Mr. Kimball yelled. "I don't know what the damned Indians want to kill me for. I never did anything to them. Get me some water." He staggered a few steps and sank to the floor, leaning weakly against the wall near the sofa.

Elizabeth clapped her hands to her mouth, giggling at the very idea of anyone saying "damned" in front of Mrs. Whitman. She expected Mrs. Whitman to reprove him for swearing in front of the children, and also to reprove her for giggling. But Mrs. Whitman went to the Indian room without a word and carried back a pitcher of water. She poured water on a rag from her sewing box and washed Mr. Kimball's arm.

He raised the pitcher unsteadily with his good arm, but his spurting wound darkened the water. He put the pitcher down quickly saying, "I can't drink bloody water."

Mrs. Whitman could not clean his arm too well. The wound was too fresh. She bolted the west door.

The kitchen seemed quiet now, so Mrs. Whitman opened the door. Eliza Hall, the wife of the man who had been flooring the second story, and Rebecca Hays, a widow, rushed in, each holding a baby and with a three- or four-year-old child clinging to her skirts. Mrs. Hall's six-year-old girl ran in, too. All were screaming and crying with fright.

"Oh, don't take on so," growled Mr. Kimball. "Why don't you help Mrs. Whitman?"

Mrs. Hall said she would, and she and Mrs. Whitman dragged the doctor into the sitting room, Mrs. Hall taking his shoulders and Mrs. Whitman his feet. Elizabeth watched anxiously. Though his head was injured, he was still alive.

"What about John?" she demanded.

"We can do nothing for John," Mrs. Whitman said quietly.

Elizabeth started to protest. They must help John! Then she saw Mrs. Whitman's drawn face and was silent.

Mrs. Whitman fastened the kitchen door, slid a settee pillow under the doctor's head, then hurried into the Indian room, returning with fireplace ashes, wrapped in a towel. She sponged the doctor's head with the bag of ashes. Elizabeth's blood ran cold when Mrs. Whitman lifted the reddened towel. The pillow beneath his head was also soaked.

"Do you know me?" Mrs. Whitman asked him.

"Yes."

"Are you much hurt?"

"Yes."

"Can I do anything to stop this blood from flowing?"

"No."

"Can you speak to me?"

"No."

"Is your mind at peace?"

"Yes."

"Is the doctor dead?" asked Mr. Kimball after a moment.

"No," Dr. Whitman said.

Feeling cold and sick, Elizabeth looked out the sash door to avoid seeing the pool forming around Dr. Whitman and Mr. Kimball. The yard was a scene of blood, too. Catherine joined her, and they looked out, silent. Mr. Hoffman, or pieces of him, lay by the butchered steer, both shredded. Near the mill lay the miller, Walter Marsh, unmoving.

Mrs. Whitman left the doctor a moment to look out each window. "I wonder where Mr. Rodgers is," she said.

Elizabeth called, "Mother, I see him!"

He was running from the river, with three Indians after him. One closed in, tomahawking him behind the ear, but he kept running. The other two shot at him, smoke exploding from their guns. *Please, if he can only reach the house,* Elizabeth prayed.

Unable to stop at the sash door, he sprang against the window, breaking two panes. Elizabeth and Catherine jumped back. Mrs. Whitman let him in and bolted the door. With a bloodcurdling yell, his pursuers turned to find other victims. His shoulder was red from a tomahawk wound behind his ear, his wrist dripping from a bullet hole.

Mr. Kimball still slumped against the wall, his wounded arm dangling limply. Mr. Rodgers stood trembling, holding his wrist. They looked at the doctor lying on the floor. Mr. Kimball turned away and squeezed his eyes shut, looking sick. Mr. Rodgers stared blankly, eyes round, mouth slack, face pale. Mrs. Whitman knelt by the doctor, applying the sponge. The blood would not stop flowing.

Louise, Helen, and Henrietta lay on the settees, unmoving and unaware. The emigrant women were silent. One little Hall girl whimpered. Catherine, Elizabeth, and Mary Ann waited to be told what to do.

Elizabeth, shaking all over, was still standing near the sash door when Joe Lewis came with a gun in his hand and tried the handle. Mrs. Whitman went to the door. "What do you want, Joe?" she asked him through the broken panes. Joe turned abruptly and left. "Oh, that Joe Lewis is doing all this!" Mrs. Whitman exclaimed.

After a while Mr. Rodgers asked, "Is the doctor dead?"

"No," answered Dr. Whitman. After that no one tried to speak to him, and he did not speak again.

TWENTY

After Frank said, "We must hide," he and John Manson moved a table underneath the opening to the schoolroom's loft. Piling books on the table, Frank managed to reach the trap door in the ceiling, slide it aside, and pull himself through.

John Manson climbed on the table and handed up his brother Stephen. "You help Frank haul up the others."

John helped Matilda, David, and Mary Hall, who were eight, Eliza Spalding and Gertrude Hall, who were ten, and Helen Saunders, Mary Smith, Ellen Canfield, and Susan Kimball, who were all between fourteen and sixteen. Frank and Stephen hauled them into the loft, last of all hauling up John.

The loft was sometimes used as a teacher's bedroom, but now the dark, dusty space held only rubbish, old broken tools, and bits and pieces. Below, the children heard windows and doors smashing. Above the noise sometimes rose the voice of Old Beardy, the only bearded Indian, crying and begging the others to stop the destruction.

"Let's pray," said Frank. The children knelt and Frank implored God to spare them. He was still not much on praying, but now his desperation lent him eloquence. It seemed to Matilda, kneeling beside him, that Frank's prayers were the most beautiful she had ever heard.

By now all the sitting room doors and the outside parlor door were firmly bolted. The Osborns had shut the Indian room doors.

Elizabeth saw Joe Lewis at the sash door again, seeming to think no one was looking, reaching furtively through one of the broken panes, trying to undo the bolt. Too frightened to speak, Elizabeth plucked at Mrs. Whitman's sleeve. Mrs. Whitman went to the sash door.

"What do you want, Joe?" she asked, her voice shaking with

agitation.

Joe looked at her with his bloodshot eyes, turned, and left. Mrs. Whitman and Elizabeth stayed at the door, looking out.

Frank Eskaloom, the Indian who had threatened to kill Elizabeth two years back, stood on the schoolroom steps. He raised his gun. Another window pane shattered and Mrs. Whitman cried, "Oh! Oh!"

It happened too suddenly for Elizabeth to move. Mrs. Whitman lay on the floor with a rifle ball piercing her left breast.

Elizabeth looked to Mr. Rodgers, who only stood looking dazed. "I am wounded, hold me tight," said Mrs. Whitman. Elizabeth watched, powerless, unable to cry or move, as the stain spread across Mrs. Whitman's dress. Dr. Whitman lay breathing harshly, not speaking.

Catherine ran and kneeled by Mrs. Whitman. "Child, you cannot help me; save yourself," she said. Mary Ann came and Mrs. Whitman said, "Never mind me; attend to the sick ones." It was too much to bear. Mary Ann and Catherine began to cry, but Elizabeth was somehow unable.

"Lord, save these little ones!" cried Mrs. Whitman, breathing hard, nearly sobbing the words. "This will kill my poor mother. Please, give my mother strength to bear this. Lord, save these little ones!"

Mrs. Hays and Mrs. Hall helped her into a chair. A crash from the next room meant the Indians were breaking the kitchen windows. Undoubtedly the sitting room windows would follow, under which Helen, Louise, and Henrietta lay helpless on settees. "Mr. Rodgers, take them all upstairs!" Mrs. Whitman ordered. Mrs. Hays and Mrs. Hall took their children upstairs.

Mr. Rodgers snapped out of his daze. Much too excited to speak, he started to push Catherine and Mary Ann up the stairs, but Catherine held back. "Who will take care of the sick children? Let me take them up, too. Don't leave them here alone."

Mr. Rodgers grabbed Helen and handed her to Mrs. Hays, who had come halfway back down the stairs. He took Louise upstairs and Catherine carried Henrietta up.

Mr. Rodgers went back down and helped Mrs. Whitman upstairs. Everyone seemed to forget Elizabeth, who stood by the sash door, not knowing what to do, unable to think after so many dreadful sights.

Mr. Rodgers came back downstairs. "What will we do now?" Elizabeth asked him.

"We can't do anything except trust in God."

Elizabeth thought it might be better to find guns and kill the Indians and trust in God when things were quieter, but Mr. Rodgers was saying, "Run upstairs," and she must obey and not contradict her elders. He fastened the door at the foot of the stairs, and when he came back up, the seventeen frightened people huddled together in dread.

With a horrid crash, the Indians broke down an outside door. Mr. Rodgers and Mrs. Whitman were in prayer when an ax splintered the stairway door.

"We must prepare for death!" said Mrs. Whitman.

"Yes, we must all prepare for death." Mr. Rodgers was cool and deliberate. Fear seemed to have left him.

Mr. Kimball would not give up so easily. "You can prepare for death all you want," he said as the Indians swung their axes against the door. "I say we find a gun and put it over the railing." The door was splintering, pieces flying inward and hitting the stairs.

"An old gun barrel is in the corner," said Mrs. Whitman. The words had barely left her mouth when Miss Bewley thrust the old broken gun into Mr. Rodgers's hands.

The Indians had the door down and started up the stairs, but the sight of the gun barrel turned them back. One ventured up again, but Mr. Rodgers shook the gun barrel at him. All the Indians retreated, and silence settled for a while.

When the group of schoolchildren had been in the loft for some time, they heard someone forcing the schoolroom door and entering.

"Frank!" called a voice. "Frank Sager!" It was Joe Lewis.

Frank's stomach gave a sickening twist. "Ask Joe if he'll kill me," he whispered to John Manson when he could speak.

"I think it's best if we don't say anything about you being up here," John answered softly. "Don't answer or make a noise," he breathed, with a stern look to the younger children. After a moment, they heard Joe leave. "If he comes back," said John, "I guess you younger kids will have to go. I don't think he'll hurt you. But don't mention anything about

Stephen and me being here, and especially *don't mention Frank!*"

More footsteps entered the schoolroom, crossing the floor, stopping almost directly beneath the loft. "John and Stephen Manson!" Joe's voice called.

Frank jumped and then desperately stilled himself. None of them must make a sound.

"I know you're up there. I see your table and your pile of books." With a crash Joe pushed the books to the floor. "Come down; you won't be hurt. We aren't mad at the Hudson's Bay people. We're only against the doctor and his people."

The children were silent. John frowned, biting his lower lip. All of them knew it was worse than useless to be contrary with Joe and the Indians. "All right, we're coming," he said after a moment.

Frank stole into a far corner and pressed against the wall. His hammering heart seemed loud enough to betray him, its beating shuddering inside his stomach. His palms sweated and he dared not move enough to wipe them.

A square of gray light appeared as Joe Lewis thrust aside the trap door. John Manson went to the edge and jumped to the table, Stephen following. Frank saw their legs and shoulders and last of all their black hair disappearing through the trap door and heard their moccasins hitting the table. Joe Stanfield was in the schoolroom. Frank heard him say, "Take the other half-breed boy, too." The Mansons and Joe Lewis helped David Malin down.

"I'll take you three to Finley's lodge," Frank heard Joe Stanfield say. "We don't want any half-Indians, especially Hudson's Bay people, to be hurt." Nicholas Finley was half-Indian, and lived in a lodge with his Indian wife. Like Joe Stanfield, he spoke both French and English, as well as the Indian tongue.

"The rest of you kids come down, too!" Joe Lewis ordered. "The Indians are going to burn the house." A scraping noise told Frank he had pushed the table away.

Eliza Spalding was first at the opening. "Won't you put the table back?"

"Oh, come on and jump!" Joe Lewis yelled. Eliza jumped, and one by one the other children followed. Matilda went last. She looked down at Joe Lewis and a group of Indians looking up at her. The Indians had the children rounded up like so many sheep.

"I'm afraid to jump," Matilda said. The floor was a long way down. Maybe they would let her stay up here with Frank.

"Put your feet over the edge and let go and I'll catch you," Joe Lewis told her.

Matilda did as he said, but as she let go, Joe stepped back. She struck the floor hard, pain shooting through her head. Furious at Joe, she wanted to kick and bite him. He grabbed her by the arms and shook her. "Where is Frank? Where's your brother?"

Mrs. Whitman and her own mother had always taught her it was an awful sin to lie. Dazed and frightened, she almost spit out the words, "In the loft." Stopping herself in time, she said, "I don't know."

Joe looked hard at her, then said, "Where do you want to go?"

"I want to go to the kitchen where John is."

"John is dead and the rest of them."

She looked at him in horror, expecting him to take the hateful words back. He looked down at her with an odd little half-smile. He must be lying, as when he said he would catch her, and then let her fall. "I don't believe it," she said stoutly. "He was there when I went in for recess."

Joe took Matilda's hand in his hideous cold clammy one. She tried to pull loose, but he squeezed her fingers until she almost cried out. He grinned into her face, and she turned from the foul stench of his breath. "There is no one in the kitchen," he said, "and your brother is dead." He dragged her outside and the Indians herded the other children behind them.

The kitchen door was nearby as they left the schoolroom, but the rail fence touched the outside wall between the two doors, separating school from home as much as possible. They had to go around the end of the building, past the skeleton second story Mr. Hall had been building, past the woodpile on the other side of the house, until they were outside the opposite kitchen door.

During Matilda's three years at the mission, the kitchen had been the heart and center of family life. There they shared meals around the large table, and warmed themselves in chill winter weather.

Joe opened the door and Matilda looked in. What she saw filled her with such revulsion she quickly looked away and did not want to look again, but her head turned back towards the sight against her will.

Her brother John seemed to float on his back in a dark red pool. One arm was thrown up and back and the other outstretched. The twine he had been winding entangled his knees, web-like. The white wall was red-spattered, the floor stained, red moccasin prints connecting the pools. For the first time she realized that no matter how this day ended, her life would never be the same again. They were all caught in an inescapable web.

She could not believe what she saw at the first glance, and kept staring as Joe pushed her in. John's soaked tippet, its ends trailing, was stuffed into a gaping wound in his throat. His shirt and hair were soaking up blood, as if trying to draw it back into his body. He did not move. He must be dead. Matilda, cold inside, wished Joe had been lying.

Indians filled the room. One, named Clockamus, wore the straw hat John had been proud of. He cut and braided the straw last summer while cutting wild grass for the Spaldings, and Mrs. Spalding sewed it for him.

The Indians pointed their guns at the children, asking, "Shall we shoot?" Matilda shrank back, but the Indians behind her pushed the children in, crowding Matilda closer to the Indians in the kitchen.

A few waved tomahawks over the children's heads, crying, "Kill them! Tomahawk them!" One of the Indians wanted to line the children up before shooting them, so they took them back out the door and lined them up in the corner made by the pantry and the Indian room.

The children stood in a row, some weeping, others meekly awaiting death. Matilda looked at the Indians, most of them boys John's age, leaning on their guns, faces stern and still. Maybe it was best this way. John was dead, and the rest of them could die together. No, she did not believe that. It might be selfish, but she wanted to live.

She looked away from the Indians, over the alkali pond, a faint light patch in the darkening evening. Tall stands of dead rye grass dwindled into the distance, ending in black burned patches. The hill, with Alice Clarissa's grave at its foot, was a black mound against dark sky. Indians stood silhouetted on its crest, watching that none escaped. The November evening was cold, and chill sweat ran down her back, making her shiver.

Chief Tiloukaikt stood before the children. The Indian boys looked towards him as if awaiting his advice. Poised to shoot, they wanted to know first what he thought. Matilda could read nothing in his expression, neither anger nor pity.

Old Beardy, a grizzled fellow with hair half gray and half black and short graying bristles sticking from his chin, came to the chief's side. None of the other Indians had whiskers like Beardy, who now spoke earnestly to the chief.

Eliza Spalding, who spoke Nez Perce as well as she did English, stood next to Matilda. Matilda knew some words, but not enough to understand all they said. "What does he say?" she whispered.

"He says," Eliza whispered back, "'The children have not come to take away our land. The children have not poisoned us. They have done nothing to be killed for. Why should they who have done no harm be killed? Don't kill them. If you do, we will suffer for it.'"

Chief Tiloukaikt stood impassive for a long moment. Matilda did not breathe. Finally he spoke.

Eliza whispered in her ear again, "He says, 'It is enough. No more blood must be shed. The doctor is dead and the men are dead. These women and children have not hurt us. They must not be hurt.'"

Dr. Whitman, dead! It could not be! But it must be. Not all the blood in the kitchen had been John's.

Old Beardy, looking relieved, took the children back into the kitchen, speaking soothingly. He motioned them to sit on the settee behind the cookstove, but seeing the bloodstained cushion, they balked. Beardy looked, removed the cushion, and Matilda and some others sat down.

The Indian women were plundering the pantry. Matilda heard the rattle of dried berries on the floor as they emptied the cans and pans so they could carry them away. They must think the food poisoned, for they were not taking it.

Directly in front of her, on a low bench by the table, Mary Ann's dishwater grew flat and cold. On the floor nearby lay a crumpled dishrag and the halves of a broken dish. She looked at the stitches in her moccasins so she would not have to see John, the floor, and the Indians who still might kill them. She heard the Indian women pouring beans on the floor, and remembered how much she hated to pick up beans.

When Dr. Whitman pulled up the white bean vines in the fall, he gave each child a tin cup and they had to pick up beans. Every bean must be saved, as if they would starve for the want of that one bean. And now he was dead and she would never have to pick up another bean. Suddenly things that had seemed bad before did not now. Before, she had not known what bad really was. Perhaps the worst was still to come.

The kettle of meat Frank had set to boil was still on the stove. Joe Lewis saw it and seemed to recollect his manners. "You children haven't had any dinner," he said, took out a piece of meat, and sliced it on the kettle lid. He passed it in front of each child, drawing it temptingly beneath their noses, but none of them could eat. They turned away, but not one spoke or even made a sound.

"Is that any way to act? You have to eat to grow up big and strong." He laughed harshly at his bitter joke, and went into the sitting room. He must have gone into the parlor and broken into the large wooden chest of Mrs. Whitman's keepsakes, because he returned carrying five of her fancy gauze kerchiefs, which he handed to the chief and some head men.

Frank huddled shivering in the loft, remembering early this morning when he had walked, carrying a gun, into the shroud of mist hanging over the mission grounds.

He chose the right spot to aim, the gun exploded, and a hole appeared in the steer's head. Its legs buckled, it rolled on its side, and lay still. "Good shot," said Mr. Kimball, who had come to help him.

(*Mr. Kimball, running with his arm swinging and blood on his sleeve.*)

Frank slit the steer's throat, feeling the warm liquid pour over his hands, then they strung the animal up by its hind legs.

Mr. Hoffman disemboweled it and the Indians did the same to him. Frank saw. And now, what were they doing to Matilda? If only he still had that gun!

He was safe, if they did not burn the house. But was she safe in the hands of Joe Lewis, who let her fall from the loft, and now might stand by while the Indians killed her? Frank had heard them crying, "Kill them! Tomahawk them!"

(*But if I go down, they'll kill me.*) He remembered Mr. Hoffman swinging his ax, and how they closed in on him and then...but it was too horrible to think about.

(*I'm safe as long as I stay here.*) What was happening below? He must know. He dared not find out. He paced, trembling and sweating. Past memories surfaced at random. The ferryboatman the day they crossed the Missouri saying, "That crazy kid! He'll get hisself killed one day, see if he don't." His mother saying, "Always stay with them, boys, keep them together. Will you promise?"

"Yes, Ma," his own answer echoed back.

That decided him. He did not want to stay up here, safe, if the others were killed. And he could not stay still with so much happening below. The suspense made his skin crawl. It would be better to take action and meet his fate than stay here wondering and let fate come to him. Besides, he must go down and take care of Matilda, who had lied to protect him, as best he could. What use would it be to live if he let something happen to her? He must face the outcome with his family. His fright-stiffened arms and legs would hardly obey him, but he willed them to work, made himself jump from the loft, and hurried toward the kitchen.

Matilda felt her heart sink as Frank came in. She wanted to yell, "No, go back, stay hidden!" His face was set, grimly determined, as if he had made a hard decision he would stick to, no matter what.

He stopped when he saw John lying on the floor, walked to him, and stood a long moment. Matilda could not understand why, but he bent over him and pulled the tippet from the wound. To her horror, John opened his eyes, and his lips moved weakly. He had been alive all this time. He tried to speak, then his eyes closed and he did not move again.

Matilda felt as if a cold hand gripped her scalp, raising her hair and sending shivers all down her body. She could not cry. It was too hideous.

Frank turned to the schoolchildren, eyes brimming with tears. "I will soon follow him," he said.

Wiping his eyes, he sat beside Matilda. His shoulder against hers felt strong and real, although he was shaking. His jacket was cool and smelled of outdoors. "I came to find you," he said. "I don't want to live if the others are killed. John is dead and we don't know about the rest of the family. The Indians will kill me. What will become of you, my poor little sister?"

Indians stood over them. Motioning the children outside, they lined them up again in the same place. Frank, standing between Matilda and Eliza Spalding, put his arm around his little sister. "The Indians will kill me, but if you are spared, be a good girl and meet me in heaven."

"No," Matilda protested, in a high, tight voice. "The chief told them not to kill any of the children."

Frank did not reply.

Elizabeth sat by Mrs. Whitman on the bed upstairs. Louise and Henrietta lay on the same bed and Helen on the other. They were all delirious and calling, "Mother! Mother!"

"Oh, the poor little things," said Mrs. Whitman. "Hold me tight," she said to Elizabeth.

Elizabeth put her arm around her. Her wound ran warm and sticky on Elizabeth's hand and on to the bed where the children lay. Elizabeth was terrified she would die. Saying anything would only make it worse.

Downstairs, a voice called for Mr. Rodgers.

"The Indians wish me to come down," Mr. Rodgers whispered to Mrs. Whitman.

"Don't do it! It may be a trap." During the pause that followed, the people upstairs had time to consider their position. Three were wounded, eleven were children, some small, or sick, or both. Mr. Rodgers sat closest to the stairs, still holding the broken gun. Mr. Kimball lay in a far corner, moaning faintly. The voice called again for Mr. Rodgers.

"Answer him," said Mrs. Whitman at last. "God may have raised us up a friend."

"Yes," Mr. Rodgers called down the stairs, in the Indian language. Elizabeth did not know it well, but in three years of living here she had picked up enough to make out what he said. "I'm here. What do you want?"

The Indian spoke in slow simple sentences so the white man would understand him. "I have just arrived. I did not know about the killing. I have not killed the whites. I want to help. I want you to come down."

"No, I won't."

"Ask him who he is," said Mrs. Whitman.

"Who are you?"

"Tamsucky."

"I didn't see him among the Indians who were killing the men," said Mrs. Whitman.

"Don't trust him, Mother," said Catherine. "I saw him trying to kill Mr. Saunders."

"I think you are mistaken. It must have been another Indian who looked like him."

"Why don't you come up here?" Mr. Rodgers called.

"You have white men up there who will kill me."

"No one's going to kill you. Come up."

"Send down Mrs. Whitman."

"She's badly wounded. She can't come down."

"Then you come down."

Mr. Rodgers turned to Mrs. Whitman. "Should I go?"

"No, I'm afraid they want to get you down to kill you."

"Maybe they really want to help. I ought to talk to them."

She took his hand. "The Lord bless you, go!"

Mr. Rodgers went almost down to the stairway door. They could hear him and Tamsucky talking. Elizabeth shuddered when she recognized Joe Lewis's voice. "All of you come down," he said.

"No," said Mr. Rodgers. "You want to get us down to kill us." He went back to talking to Tamsucky. "Should we let them come up?" he called to Mrs. Whitman.

"Let Tamsucky come up," she said.

Tamsucky came up and shook hands all around. As if to show his friendliness, he spoke English. "Very sorry you are hurt," he said to Mrs. Whitman. "Very sorry about doctor and white men. Injuns will burn house tonight. You come to Injun's house, ten miles away. Must start now. It is nearly night."

"We can't go ten miles tonight," said Mrs. Whitman. "Some of us are hurt, and the children are sick."

"Go to other house; stay there tonight." He meant the emigrant house. He looked down at Mr. Kimball. "Injun shoot," he said, "bad Injun shoot." He turned to the others. "You leave now."

They had no choice but to go. If they went out, they might be killed, but if they stayed, they would surely die when the house burned.

Catherine wrapped Henrietta in a blanket and held her out to Tamsucky. "Will you carry my little sister?"

He pushed her away. She had forgotten that one never asked a Cayuse man to carry anything. "You stay here. We come back for you."

"Don't worry, Catherine," said Mr. Rodgers, "we'll come back for you children as soon as we get Mrs. Whitman to the emigrant house."

Mrs. Hall and Mrs. Hays went down first, with their children. Tamsucky followed. After them came Mr. Rodgers and Lorinda Bewley, helping Mrs. Whitman. Mrs. Whitman looked over her shoulder and said, "Come with me, Elizabeth."

When they reached the sitting room, the doctor was still breathing raggedly. On his face were three new long gashes. Elizabeth shuddered. Mrs. Whitman turned away and said she wanted air. Mr. Rodgers and Miss Bewley led her to a settee where she lay down.

Mrs. Whitman said, "Get all the things you need from the press." *Maybe we are going to live after all,* thought Elizabeth as she hurried, regardless of her stained hands, to collect dresses for Mrs. Whitman.

Mrs. Hall and Mrs. Hays gathered as much as they could hold and still carry their babies. The rest of the things they put on the settee with Mrs. Whitman, on top of a blanket Lorinda Bewley spread over her. Lorinda and Elizabeth each had an armload of clothes.

Mr. Rodgers, though wounded in the wrist, went to pick up one end of the settee. Joe Lewis took the other end. "Oh, Joe, you, too?" said Mrs. Whitman.

Several Indians came in and shook their blankets, saying, "We have no guns. Don't be afraid." Elizabeth was still afraid.

Mrs. Hall and Mrs. Hays went out, carrying their babies and the clothes, with their little children following behind. Lorinda Bewley walked after them. Close behind came Mr. Rodgers and Joe Lewis carrying the settee where Mrs. Whitman lay, with Elizabeth following.

As they entered the kitchen, Elizabeth recoiled at the sight of John lying facedown in the doorway, surrounded by blood. She stepped tremblingly over him.

Outside the open kitchen door, the children from the schoolroom stood lined up in the corner where the pantry joined the Indian room. An Indian pointed to Mrs. Whitman and said to Frank, "Go along with her."

Frank took a hesitant step. Joe Lewis dropped his end of the settee in the mud. Mr. Rodgers looked up in alarm, and at that moment the Indian boys pulled guns from beneath their blankets and fired. Elizabeth saw a bullet hit Mrs. Whitman's cheek, then a whole volley of bullets struck Mrs. Whitman and Mr. Rodgers. Mr. Rodgers threw up his hands, cried, "Oh, my God!" and fell.

Elizabeth stood frozen on the doorstep a moment. Mr. Rodgers lay crumpled in the mud, moaning. Mrs. Whitman lay motionless on the settee with her wounded cheek against it, other wounds seeping. In the growing darkness, the quick glimpse Elizabeth had of her still face was white and beautiful.

An Indian holding a tomahawk ran at Elizabeth. Before she realized it, she was running, tightly clutching Mrs. Whitman's dresses. She skidded in a pool of blood, rebounded off the wall, and, leaping over John, raced through the sitting room. As she disappeared up the stairs, the Indian gave a howl of rage and disappointment.

Upstairs, Elizabeth told the others what had happened, but there was no need. They had given up hope when they heard the shots. "Treachery! Treachery!" Mr. Kimball exclaimed. "Children, prepare for the worst." They listened, hardly daring to breathe in their fright. A single shot rang out, then came the sound of the Indians taking kindling from the woodpile, preparing to burn the house.

Catherine took Louise and Henrietta on to the bed with Helen. The other bed was covered with Mrs. Whitman's blood, and their clothes were saturated from lying beside her. "Go to sleep now, don't worry," Catherine told them. They were suffering for water, and kept crying for a drink.

"Mr. Kimball, don't you have some water in your pitcher?" Catherine asked.

"Yes, but it's not fit to drink, it has so much blood in it."

The children kept crying. Catherine tried desperately to think of a way to get them water. "Elizabeth," she said, "earlier today I brought up some medicine and water for Miss Bewley. The water ought to be on the shelf by her bed. Go over and get it."

Elizabeth groped her way to Miss Bewley's bed. Fumbling around in the dark, she found the water, but only after spilling it on herself, so the sick children had to go without. They began to cry harder.

"I wonder if Frank is still alive," Elizabeth said after they had sat a long while. "I saw him outside when they were killing Mother and Mr. Rodgers." No one answered. All was quiet except for the mournful wind. Since the Indians had killed John, they might kill Frank, too. The Indian who spoke to Frank when she last saw him told him to go along with Mrs. Whitman, as if they planned the same fate for both.

"The Indians always liked Frank," said Mary Ann without conviction.

"I wonder where Matilda is. Could be she's sitting in the dark somewhere."

"Maybe she's wandering around, hunting for the rest of us," Mary Ann suggested.

"Maybe she's outside," said Catherine. At that horrible thought, she started up. "I have to find her."

"It's no use," said Mr. Kimball. "If she's alive, she's likely doing as well as we are, maybe better."

Elizabeth thought of the Indian boys who might still be waiting with guns. She grabbed Catherine's dress with both hands. "Please don't leave us!" At this, Catherine sank back down on the bed.

Silence fell, broken only by the yowls and snarls of cats fighting below, which made everything more dismal and awful. Not even the cats could live in peace.

Mary Ann and Elizabeth fell asleep. The three sicker children wore themselves out crying for water, and slept, too. Downstairs, the cats cried to be fed. Catherine sat alone. Every once in a while Mr. Kimball asked if she were asleep. At last she lay on the edge of the bed and drifted off.

She woke with a start to feel a head leaning against her. An Indian must have stolen in and was waiting for her to wake up. She reached down cautiously, felt shaggy hair, and shrieked.

"It's only me," said Mr. Kimball. "I'm sorry to startle you. I got tired and cold lying on the floor, and sat up against the bed to rest myself. But I'm too weak to raise my head."

Catherine felt a stab of pity for him. The sick children woke and kept up their pathetic cry for water until day dawned.

TWENTY-ONE

At daybreak, Catherine and Mr. Kimball were still awake. Often during the night, Catherine had wished it might always stay dark, or that the roof would collapse and crush them so they would not have to face the coming day. Why had the Indians not burned the house when they said they would?

Darkness, with the wind whistling and shrieking over the roof, intensified her terrible fears. Hideous scenes loomed before her, eerie and distorted. The awful awareness of those still forms wrapped in darkness below pressed on her like a cold weight, rendering her motionless. The first light of early morning did little to dispel her dread, and the three sick children cried for water, keeping Elizabeth and Mary Ann awake.

"Catherine," said Mr. Kimball, "if you'll bind my arm, I'll try to fetch the children some water."

Catherine arose, stiff and cold, with a dazed, uncertain feeling.

"Take a sheet off a bed and bind my arm with it," Mr. Kimball told her.

Catherine looked at him and nothing seemed real. Not even his face seemed real as she looked at it. "Mother wouldn't like the sheets torn up," she said.

The face before her frowned, its expression more worried than angry. "Child, don't you know your mother is dead, and will never need sheets?"

Catherine seemed to be dreaming.

"If you want the sick children to have any water, you'll have to do as I say."

This roused her from her dream somewhat. She folded back the blankets on the bed Miss Bewley had been using and pulled off the top sheet.

"Now tear it into strips."

Catherine began to, and even the sheet in her hands did not feel real as it separated into strips. It was not until she was winding the strips around his bleeding arm that things began to seem real.

"Wrap it tight," he told her. "Now put a blanket around me to keep me warm if I faint on the way."

Taking a pair of blankets, Catherine draped them over his shoulders, tying them around his waist with a strip of sheet.

"Don't worry," he told the children. "I don't think any Indians are out there, so I should come back safe."

"But what if there are Indians, and they see you?" Elizabeth asked.

"If they see me, maybe they'll take me for an Indian, the way I look with these blankets on. When I come back, I'll have some water for you."

Though almost too sick to think, Louise, Henrietta, and Helen seemed to understand, and quieted their crying. Catherine watched Mr. Kimball go downstairs, counting the moments it would take him to reach the river. Would he make it?

Suddenly she heard running footsteps outside, and voices howling. They went in the direction of the river. Then there was silence.

Helen and Henrietta were well enough to talk today. As each moment passed, they expected Mr. Kimball to be back with the water. The more they expected water, the more they wanted it. After a long while, Catherine decided he must not be coming back. She could not leave the sick children, but someone must get water.

"Elizabeth," she said, "go down for water."

"No, I'm afraid."

"The children want water. Won't you go?" Catherine looked at her pleadingly.

Elizabeth knew she had to do it. *The Indians won't kill me,* she thought. *I'm just a little girl.* But she was not entirely sure. With shaking steps she descended the stairs.

The house was deserted. Only John and Dr. Whitman were downstairs, and they were dead. Elizabeth went as with closed eyes, seeing nothing. Nowhere could she find clean water, and she was afraid to leave the house. She went back upstairs and told Catherine.

"You'll have to go down and try again," Catherine said.

Elizabeth, by now filled with a strange feeling, almost of elation, at having come back upstairs alive, went down again into the kitchen, crossing the bloodstained floor as if blinded to the sight of John lying there.

Outside the door, Mr. Rodgers lay where he had fallen. Mrs. Whitman lay in the mud, with clothes and blankets strewn about her. From the doorway Elizabeth could see the irrigation ditch. She knew river water would be cleaner, but she could see the ditch from here, and no Indians were about. She would just cross the yard and draw water from the ditch.

Then she saw Edward Tiloukaikt, Chief Tiloukaikt's son, coming towards her. Mrs. Whitman had called him Edward after her brother. As far as Elizabeth knew, he had not been involved in the massacre. He was an extremely handsome man in his early twenties, with a firm jaw, big dark eyes, and a sharp, proud nose.

"Please," said Elizabeth when he was near, "could you bring me some water?" He found a wooden bucket and a dipper and went to fill the bucket in the irrigation ditch.

While he was gone, Elizabeth peeked in the sitting room. Dr. Whitman lay on the floor with his face gashed and his blue eyes wide open and staring. Elizabeth shuddered and looked back to see Edward returning with the water. She thanked him and took it upstairs. Helen, Louise, and Henrietta drained the bucket in gulps.

It was now fully light. In the Indian room, spoons jingled in pots and pans. Indian voices called for Mr. Osborn.

"The Osborns must be alive, and they're fixing breakfast!" Catherine told Elizabeth.

At the next sound—footsteps on the stairs—the children froze, huddled together on the bed, holding their breath, looking towards the stairs. The face of Joe Lewis appeared. With him were several Indians.

"The Indians won't hurt you," said Joe. "We're sending you to Fort Walla Walla as soon as I can round up a team, so get your things ready." He turned and went downstairs.

The Indians seemed friendly, even Tamsucky. He told the girls that Francis was not killed, that he had run away. The other Indians said they thought he had gone to the fort. Elizabeth breathed a secret sigh of relief. Catherine was comforted that she was not to be head of the family after all. There was still Frank.

She stared up at the Indians and her throat felt paralyzed. What had John said about bravery? It was important! Oh, yes, now she remembered. *All I did was what had to be done for us to go on.* This was what she must do now. She summoned courage to speak. "The children want water, and we're hungry."

Tamsucky sent one Indian after water and another after food. They returned with a bowl of water and a loaf of bread. They told the girls to put part of the bread aside with their things, as Francis would be hungry when they found him. After once more telling the girls to get their things ready, they left.

"It sounds like a trick to me," said Elizabeth when they were gone. "I think they want to get us downstairs so they can kill us, like they did Mother and Mr. Rodgers. Poor Mother, she really thought they were going to help her. I'm not going down."

"Well, we can't stay here forever," said Catherine. They were all afraid to leave their retreat. The sick children drank all the water in the bowl and after a while began to cry for more.

Catherine went downstairs with the bowl and asked the Indians who had brought the food, who were now picking through the family's possessions, sorting out the best things for their women to carry back to the village, to bring water for the children. She should have taken the bucket, which sat upstairs empty, but she was still half-dreaming, dazed. Seeming to think they had done enough, they turned away.

Unable to bear going back upstairs and hearing the piteous cries for water, she decided to go for water herself, and found her shoes where she had left them before her bath yesterday. Had it been yesterday? It seemed so much longer. She only had time to slip on her dress before her whole life changed. Taking the bowl, she went out the broken sash door, towards the river, moving haltingly, starting at every sound, even at her own breathing and the heavy beating of her heart.

Filling the bowl at the nearest point on the river, she started back, shaking so much she was afraid she might spill the water.

As she neared the house, she saw three Indians sitting on the fence.

One of them aimed his rifle at Catherine. She was only a few steps from the door, but the house seemed miles away. Another Indian knocked the gun up, and it went off in the air. The Indian with the gun laughed to see Catherine jump. She did not spill all the water, though.

When she reached the others upstairs, Elizabeth looked at her with round eyes. "We thought they'd shot you," she said.

"I don't think he really meant to shoot me," Catherine answered. "He just wanted to scare me."

"Well," said Elizabeth, trying to keep her voice from quivering, "I reckon I'll go downstairs and find some food, anyway."

Once down, she went all over the house, opening door after door. In Mrs. Whitman's room the breakfast Elizabeth had brought her yesterday morning lay on the nightstand, untouched. Feeling suddenly sick at the thought of food, she turned quickly back into the sitting room, and there stood the old Chief, Tiloukaikt, scowling and motioning at her as if not to disturb anything.

The house was in complete disarray. Several Indian women roamed about, collecting things. Dr. Whitman lay on the floor in the sitting room and John in the kitchen, covered with quilts the Indian women had thrown over them. The Indians had scattered things in search of plunder, ripping straw and feathers from the settee cushions until a blizzard seemed to have struck the house.

The Indian woman who had made Elizabeth's doll, Eddie, came to her, her creased brown face covered with tears. She held a pair of Louisa's shoes and other belongings of the girls. Still crying, she pressed them into Elizabeth's hands.

Eddie, where was Eddie? Elizabeth did not want to lose him. She looked through the litter spread on the floor. Mr. Rodgers's violin, smashed in the middle, strings broken, bore mute testimony to the tuneful voice which would never sing again. Then in the corner she saw Eddie's cradleboard.

The little leather doll had been thrown out and lay nearby. One of his arms was torn off, and Elizabeth shuddered at the thought of searching through the bloodstained wreckage for it. Everything was clothed in horror; she could not have touched anything. She put Eddie and his cradleboard and the things the woman gave her on a settee where she could come back for them, and continued her search through the house.

She went into the Indian room. The Osborns were not there. Strangely enough, several floorboards were loose as if they had been pushed aside. Elizabeth opened the outside door and the pit of her stomach turned to ice.

Frank lay on the ground with a bullet hole in his head. A trickle of blood crossed his face like a single tear. She had believed the Indians who said he was still alive. Now she remembered that after Mrs. Whitman and Mr. Rodgers were killed, a single shot sounded. She had not seen him when she looked out earlier, because he was around the corner of the house.

Blindly she went upstairs and told Catherine, Mary Ann, and Helen, "They killed Frank."

Helen made a little sound as if she might cry. The others just stared, seeming to think tears would be useless. Finally Catherine said, "Matilda was with him in the schoolroom. What has happened to Matilda?"

Matilda was in the emigrant house, watching the Indians take things, wondering if they would turn and kill her yet. Yesterday, one named Powder Horn held a buffalo robe in front of the schoolchildren to shield them, but she saw anyway when an Indian by the settee where Mrs. Whitman lay beat her head with his whip. He turned the settee over, throwing Mrs. Whitman in the mud. Clothes, sheets, and blankets cascaded around her. Matilda wanted badly to help Mother, but could only stand and watch, not daring to move or say a word.

Mrs. Hall and her children, including Gertrude and Mary, who had been among the schoolchildren, Mrs. Hays and her children, and Lorinda Bewley all reached the emigrant house. Matilda, Eliza, Frank, and a few emigrant children were left behind.

Two Indians stood in front of Frank, who stood between Matilda and Eliza. One, a Walla Walla named Upps, seemed to want to spare his life. He argued fiercely with the Cayuse, Clockamus, still wearing John's straw hat. Joe Lewis came to them.

"Are you loyal to us?" Clockamus wanted to know.

"Of course I'm loyal to you."

"Then kill Frank Sager."

Tears ran down Frank's face. "Oh, Joe, please don't shoot me."

Joe looked at him and for a moment Matilda thought he could not possibly do it, no matter how mean he was.

Clockamus pulled Frank a few steps in front of Matilda and Eliza.

Joe Lewis grabbed Frank by the nose and put his pistol against his head. "You are a bad boy."

Even as he pulled the trigger, Matilda still thought he would not do it. Then Frank was falling at her feet. Eliza threw her apron over her face so she would not see the Indians shoot her, but Matilda was too stunned to do anything.

They stood a long while. Tiloukaikt's son, Edward, came and led away the emigrant children who had been lined up, leaving Matilda and Eliza standing alone, paralyzed by all they had seen. They did not go to the emigrant house, as they were taught always to ask permission before going anywhere. They could hardly comprehend that now no one was left to ask permission from.

The November evening was dark and cold. They stood close together with their heads down, not looking at anything. It seemed useless to move or speak. The Indians went back and forth past them, looting the house. Frank lay in their way, so they dragged him around the corner.

At last Upps, murmuring soothing words, took Matilda and Eliza's hands and led them to Mrs. Saunders, the teacher's widow, in the emigrant house. Mrs. Saunders fed the girls, who ate automatically, not tasting.

Mrs. Saunders took Matilda into a bedroom and spread a quilt on the floor for her. Another woman gave Eliza a place to sleep. Matilda lay down, but not to sleep until far into the night.

She and the others in the emigrant house were up early the next morning, expecting the Indians. Before daylight, some already sat on the hill, chanting the death song.

Mrs. Saunders made some white flour rolls to give them when they came, then fixed breakfast for the others. Neither she nor the other adults in the house had slept all night.

Matilda stayed close by Eliza as she had the evening before. When Mrs. Saunders asked if anyone understood the Indian language, Eliza said, "I can understand everything they say."

"Will you come with me when they come to the door?"

"Yes. When they come, you have to offer them your hand and say, '*sixtiwah*.' That means 'friend' in their language. If they won't shake hands with you, it means they're unfriendly. Tell them that if the doctor did wrong, you're sorry."

"But he didn't do any wrong!" Matilda burst out.

Eliza turned to her. "Don't you see we have to go along with them?"

"I reckon so."

They heard someone outside the door, it opened, and there stood Tamsucky. Mrs. Saunders offered him her hand. Tamsucky shook it, then took down five guns which hung on brackets over the door and handed them to Indians waiting outside. He went about the room, helping himself to whatever he wanted, including things that had belonged to Mr. Saunders, then called the other Indians in.

A few shook hands with Mrs. Saunders, but the rest stood back aloof, holding the guns Tamsucky had given them, as well as tomahawks polished like mirrors. Some of the tomahawks had wicked-looking prongs, which, Matilda well knew, might sink into her skull at any moment. She stayed very quiet.

The Indians went through the rooms, collecting whatever took their fancy. When they finished, Matilda and the others were left with only what they wore, some bedding, and small things the Indians had over-looked.

Mrs. Saunders offered them the white flour biscuits. Two of them exchanged a look, and one said in plain English, "No, you eat them and get a good heart."

The two Indians had kind faces, and although she had not seen the whole attack, Matilda knew that they were not among the murderers. Mrs. Saunders's eyes overflowed with tears. It was the first time Matilda had seen her cry. She herself was not able to cry yet. Through the whole ordeal, not one of the schoolchildren had cried out loud, or even made a sound.

"Cry, it will do you good," said one of the two.

With tears in her eyes, Mrs. Saunders turned and gave the biscuits to Matilda and the other children.

Soon Joe Stanfield lumbered in and told Mrs. Saunders that Nicholas Finley was taking John and Stephen Manson and David Malin from his lodge to Fort Walla Walla, and if she wanted to write to the fort's factor, Captain McBean, they would take the note. She wrote the note and gave it to him.

When Elizabeth came upstairs and told the others Frank was dead, she told them no Indians were downstairs. Before coming up, she had seen them leave. Catherine and Mary Ann decided to go down and look around. The three descended together.

Mary Ann pulled aside the quilt covering Dr. Whitman. Elizabeth wished she would not. "Come and see Father," she said in a breathless voice. Catherine looked. Against her will, Elizabeth found herself crossing to where the doctor lay. The sight was more horrible than she expected. Only a few gashes were on his face before, but now he was chopped beyond recognition. How could anyone have done this? They must mean it as his punishment for poisoning their people. Mary Ann slowly lowered the blanket. Silently they went into the kitchen.

John lay on the floor, and again Mary Ann lifted the quilt covering him. He was mutilated as badly as Dr. Whitman. He had poisoned no one. Mary Ann could hold back her tears no longer. Catherine wept as well, and Elizabeth sobbed with them. In one day their family life had been torn away, everything taken, gone.

A rough voice startled them. "Stop that noise! They're dead and it will do them no good." The massive form of Joe Stanfield filled the pantry door, towering over the girls. "The Indians will be mad and kill you if they see you taking on so." He glowered at them until they were silent. "Now go to the emigrant house. The women and other children are there."

The girls dried their tears. As soon as Joe saw them collecting their shawls and bonnets, he left.

Indians crowded into the kitchen, looking crossly at the girls, who retreated upstairs. In a few minutes, several Indians came up and began urging them to leave. The Indians told the girls to put their things together and they would not touch them. The girls obeyed.

Gathering up her courage, Catherine picked up Louise. "Elizabeth, you take Henrietta. Mary Ann, can you take Helen?"

"No." The measles had weakened her, the sight of the doctor and John must have drained her even more, and she was too weak to carry a ten-year-old.

"Then you'll have to stay with her until we come back."

"No, no, I want to go with you!"

"Don't leave me here alone!" begged Helen.

"We'll come back for you," said Catherine.

"That's just what Mr. Rodgers said, and I won't be left here alone!" Helen cried.

"You won't be alone. These Indians will stay with you. They're friendly." The Indians murmured agreement. "You'll be all right till we get back," said Catherine, promising to hurry.

They went downstairs, Catherine carrying Louise, Elizabeth carrying Henrietta, Mary Ann keeping up as best she could. They were afraid to go through the kitchen where the Indians were, so they started out through the Indian room instead.

Mary Ann pushed open the door. They all looked at Frank lying crumpled in the yard. It was one thing to talk about him being dead and another thing to actually see him there.

"I'm afraid to go on," said Mary Ann. "The Indians will kill us." But Elizabeth went out the door and the others followed. They stood for a moment at the edge of the yard.

Once, long ago, on the banks of a mighty river, they had been afraid to cross. That fearful crossing seemed pleasant compared to the one they now had to make. A short distance away on their right, by the woodpile, lay Mrs. Whitman and Mr. Rodgers. The girls started forward, trying not to look, although the dreadful sights seemed to call for their attention. Ahead of them was the emigrant house—surely this yard was twice as wide as the Missouri! They passed the mission house and were now in the open yard.

As they passed the blacksmith shop, to their right on the other side of the fence was the spot where the three men had been attacked at the beef. Beside the hollow carcass of the steer lay the equally hollow, disemboweled body of Jacob Hoffman. Pieces of the steer were spread about the yard. Near the steer's head lay the battered head of the schoolteacher.

Far away on their right was the mill, where the body of Walter Marsh lay. Elizabeth hardly saw any of it. It was as if she could see nothing after seeing Frank lying dead in the doorway.

A little group of people came towards them. They were the Indian, Upps, and girls from the emigrant house. Matilda was alive! She was with them. All the girls stopped and for a moment wept together. One took Louise and another Henrietta. Catherine and Elizabeth had been ready to drop under their burdens.

Lorinda Bewley said she was going on to the mission house for her brother. Upps and a few of the girls went with her. The rest went back to the emigrant house, Elizabeth leading. Mrs. Saunders met her at the door with tears and kisses. "I didn't know if any of you in the mission house were alive," she said. "Your dear mother is dead! I will be a mother to you."

The others came in, the awful crossing over with. Catherine stood in the middle of the floor, unable to believe that Frank was dead, unable to believe the rest of them were still alive. Things grew smaller, fainter, rushing away from her. She fell into a whirling black space.

When she came to, Mrs. Saunders was bending over her, looking worried. Catherine recollected where she was and asked, "Did anyone go back for Helen Mar?" She sat up. It seemed no one had. They were too worried about Catherine to think of Helen. "Oh, no! I promised her we'd be right back. Who will go with me?" Several of the girls said they would, and so for the second time they crossed the yard with its hideous sights.

They heard Helen's screams before they entered the house. Going upstairs, they found her sitting straight up in bed. Fear must have given her strength. Indians surrounded her, and she screamed for Catherine at the top of her voice. It took Catherine a minute to convince Helen she was here and stop her from screaming.

As soon as Helen calmed down, Helen Saunders picked her up. Catherine found the children's things where they had left them. The Indians had kept their promise not to touch them. Mrs. Saunders met them at the emigrant house, took Helen Mar from her daughter, and laid her on a bed. Lorinda had brought her brother and found a place for him to lie down. Now all the living had left the house to its dead.

Elizabeth entered a small dark room adjoining the larger one, and saw a man lying on a bed. "Mr. Kimball! Are you all right?" she called, and ran to him, putting her hand on his forehead. It was cold, and she saw that he was not Mr. Kimball after all, but the tailor, Isaac Gilliland. She turned and saw Matilda in the doorway, looking solemn.

"He was sewing and Frank Eskaloom shot him," she said. "I heard him moaning 'most all night. He died towards morning."

"But what happened to Mr. Kimball?" Elizabeth asked. "He went after water for us. Did he come back here?"

"We haven't seen him," said Matilda. "I reckon the Indians killed him and will do the same to us."

Mrs. Saunders came up behind Matilda and spoke softly. "They won't kill us. I spoke to them at Nicholas Finley's lodge. I said we would work for them—make clothes or whatever we can—if they'd spare us."

Elizabeth looked at her in wonder. "You went *there?* Weren't you afraid?"

"God told me to go," Mrs. Saunders said simply.

Joe Stanfield lurked about the grounds, entering the emigrant house a little after noon to report that a "Boston man" was hiding in the brush by the river. A few women wanted to investigate, but Joe said, "No, don't."

Discussion arose as to who it might be. Mr. Hall had run away. The Osborns were missing, but why would Mr. Osborn be hiding without his wife and children? Mr. Canfield had escaped, and no one had seen Mr. Kimball since he left the sick children.

Catherine was afraid to go outside, but when she saw Joe Stanfield pass the emigrant house a little later, she went to the door and asked him, "Who was hidden in the brush?"

Joe was crossing the grounds, collecting money and any other valuables he felt like taking. He stopped and told her, "It was Mr. Kimball. He wanted his wife to come to him, but I told him to stay still until dark, then he can come to the house and I'll find a way for him to escape. If she tried to go out there, or he tried to come to the house, the Indians would see them and kill him sure."

Catherine told Mrs. Kimball her husband was alive and would be there after dark.

Later that day came an interpreter named Bushman from Fort Walla Walla, wanting to know if it was true the Indians had killed "the doctor and another man."

Mrs. Saunders wanted to know how he knew. Surely her note had not had time to reach Fort Walla Walla?

"Don't know about any note," said Bushman. "Man named Hall came to the fort and told us about it."

So they knew that Mr. Hall was safe. Trembling with terror, Bushman soon left.

Joe Stanfield was digging a grave at the foot of the hill by Alice Clarissa's grave, three feet deep and wide enough to lay all the victims side by side. Two Walla Walla Indians were helping, but the only Cayuse who would help was old Beardy.

As they prepared for supper that evening, the survivors heard an outcry in the yard. Matilda was one of the first to reach the door leading out of the Halls' room. She bounded on to the lower step. Frank Eskaloom stood on the upper step holding a gun.

Matilda saw a blanket-wrapped figure atop the fence near the emigrant house. It was Mr. Kimball. A bucket sat on the ground below the fence, that he must have just placed there when the Indians saw him.

Mr. Kimball made a quick move to climb down. Frank Eskaloom raised his gun and shot over Matilda's head, deafening her for a moment. Mr. Kimball fell forward, hanging over the fence the same way the Indians dead of measles had been slung over it.

Frank Eskaloom laughed. "See how I can make a white man tumble."

With her ears still ringing, Matilda stared at Mr. Kimball. He had come to the emigrant house to see his family, but the bucket showed he had not forgotten the sick children. He hung over the fence, hands dangling limply, bleeding drop by drop into the bucket.

TWENTY-TWO

"Dr. Whitman's children must die!"

It was December 1, the day after Mr. Kimball's death. Catherine, Elizabeth, and Matilda stood huddled together in the emigrant house, with an Indian brave towering over them. Mary Ann, Helen, Louise, and Henrietta were too sick to leave bed. The other people in the room old enough, and well enough, to understand, held their breath.

The Indian had arrived early, before Old Beardy or any of the others. *He really aims to kill us,* thought Elizabeth, a sharp pain gnawing at her stomach, making her dizzy.

"You were often cross and rude to us," said the Indian. "We see by the looks you give us, how you feel. I will bring others, and we will kill you." He stormed from the house, jumped on his horse, and rode away.

"When he comes back," Mrs. Saunders told them, "you must say that he is right about your rudeness, and Mrs. Whitman made you do it."

"But that isn't true!" Catherine objected. "Mother always treated the Indians politely, and thanked them for every favor they did."

"She said we must never be rude to them or anyone," said Elizabeth.

"I know it is hard to speak that way about your mother," said Mrs. Saunders, "but it is necessary to save your lives." She urged them until they agreed.

When the Indian returned with several others, Catherine told them, "Mrs. Whitman was the one who made us be rude to you."

"But now she's gone; we won't do it no more," Elizabeth added, eyeing the Indians' hatchets.

The Indians looked at one another. A quiet ripple of talk passed between them. They seemed satisfied.

In the days that followed, those responsible for the massacre often made the children say the Whitmans were bad. They allowed none of the survivors to show grief, until they were almost bursting with pent-up tears.

Later that day, Elizabeth and Eliza Spalding were sitting underneath a table with a blanket around them. Elizabeth held her doll Eddie in her arms. She and Eliza did not talk much, though once Eliza said, in a low, sad voice, "I wonder what has happened to my father." Mr. Spalding was also a missionary, and a number of Indians wanted to kill him.

Several young Indian men entered and called on Eliza to interpret. Elizabeth felt sorry for her, always having to run here and there interpreting every little thing the Indians wanted to say. Elizabeth stayed beneath the table, which, with forty-two people in the house, was the least crowded and safest place to be.

She spent every moment fearing the Indians. They still might change their minds and kill the women and children. Many more Indians were against the massacre than for it, but they had no influence on the killers. Often the flesh on her back crept, and she thought she felt someone stealing up behind her. She jumped at any sudden movement, and started at the sound of the wind.

When the Indians finished talking, Eliza explained to Mrs. Saunders that a Catholic priest had come from the new mission on the Umatilla to baptize some sick children, and was now on his way to Waiilatpu to bury the dead. They must have his breakfast ready.

The French priest, Father Brouillet, arriving with his half-Indian interpreter, wrote down the names of everyone in the house. He and Mrs. Saunders talked about a possible rescue of the women and children. Elizabeth did not know who would do it—maybe the men from the valley.

Edward Tiloukaikt came in. Seeing the priest, he frowned, asking with suspicion what he was writing.

"He is writing Mary, my name," answered Mrs. Saunders.

Edward left, and soon afterwards his father, Chief Tiloukaikt, his face lined and sad, carried in a bolt of white cotton cloth and spoke to Eliza.

"He says we must make winding sheets for the dead," Eliza explained to Mrs. Saunders. The chief must feel deeply about this, as he had personally carried in the cloth, which was not a man's job and certainly not a chief's job.

Mrs. Saunders brought out the sewing things. Catherine and Elizabeth each took a needle and thread to help the other women sew the cloth into winding sheets. The cloth and even the needle felt heavy in Elizabeth's hands.

When the priest went to the mission house, Eliza and some others went. Catherine went out once, but soon came back because the sick children cried when she left them. Elizabeth was afraid to go. After a while, she thought better of it. They might wrap up John and Frank and she would never see them again. She remembered her last look at their parents, as if it had been yesterday.

Walking out into the cool damp mud-smelling air, Elizabeth crossed the yard beneath the cold, dreary, gray and white mottled sky. Joe Stanfield's hulking form, lugging a bucket, bent low in the yard, washing the dead.

Elizabeth took a last look at Mrs. Whitman and Mr. Rodgers, lying by the woodpile beside the kitchen door. Their faces were clean of mud and blood, but drawn and sunken, not like them at all.

Frank, lying in the Indian room door, a little apart from the others, as if neglected by everyone, was not like himself, either. Elizabeth took a quick look at his still face and went into the kitchen. Father Brouillet sat at the table, praying.

Eliza, sewing a sheet wrapped around John, stopped to give Elizabeth a needle and thread. Elizabeth threaded the needle, bit off the thread, made a few stitches in the white cloth, of the kind Mrs. Whitman had showed her, and could not go on. Everything seemed dark. She knelt, head down, while Eliza finished the sewing.

Outside, Joe Stanfield wrapped the others, and the women sewed the sheets around them. Joe Stanfield came in for John, slung him over his shoulder like a sack of potatoes, and carried him out, over the bridge across the irrigation ditch, to where a wagon stood on the trail. Bodies were piled beside it like cordwood. He came into the sitting room for the doctor, carrying him out through the Indian room door. Elizabeth stood in the kitchen door watching, feeling it was impossible that her loved ones were wrapped in those white sheets.

Joe began to load the bodies into the wagon. He had loaded several when, as he lifted another sheet-wrapped figure, the team bolted, rattling and jolting the wagon across the field, tumbling bodies to the ground. Elizabeth, unable to watch more, went into the house.

By the time Joe stopped the oxen and reloaded the bodies, Elizabeth was back in the emigrant house. She and Catherine and Matilda, afraid to go to the burial, watched from a window facing the hill. Among rye grass clumps around the grave beside Alice Clarissa's marker, dark figures loomed from gray-white mist. The black-clothed priest stood before a few women and children and several Indians, among them Beardy and Chief Tiloukaikt.

The ceremony concluding, Joe Stanfield shoveled earth into the grave, his manner as reverent as if attending one of his regular farm chores. It was not enough, Elizabeth thought. There should be more.

When the priest and his interpreter saddled their horses to leave, Eliza said to Elizabeth, "Will you come with me to talk to the interpreter?"

"Of course." Eliza was Elizabeth's good friend.

The two went out into the cold. The interpreter looked inquiringly at them.

"My father, Mr. Spalding, has been at the Umatilla," said Eliza. "He was heading back here. If you meet him on the way, please tell him not to come. The Indians will kill him for sure if he does," she finished breathlessly.

The man smiled. "I promise to let no harm come to your father," he said. He mounted his horse, and he and the priest rode away.

Edward Tiloukaikt rode up, wearing a shirt and britches of John's, and an Indian blanket. Elizabeth, furious to see him wearing her brother's clothes, could say or do to nothing about it. Stopping his horse near the girls, he drew a pistol from beneath his blanket. Elizabeth went cold, thinking he might kill them.

"I am going with the priest." Edward stared into Eliza's eyes, his own eyes and mouth hard with grim determination. "And when I meet your father, I will kill him with this," he said, tapping the pistol. Thrusting it into his waistband, he wheeled and rode through the gathering mist after the priest and his interpreter.

Eliza spent the rest of the day in dread. The next morning, Elizabeth

suggested they go to the mission house. "The Indians keep saying they'll
burn it, and I want to save some things," she said.

"All right," said Eliza, and they started.

The bodies were gone from the yard, but it was still desolate. Joe
Stanfield, Joe Lewis, and the Indians had plundered the buildings,
dropping things they did not care for outside. The survivors had not seen
Joe Lewis at all yesterday or today. Elizabeth hoped he had taken what
he wanted and left for good.

The house, which Mrs. Whitman and the girls had kept in perfect
order, was a scene of confusion. Splintered furniture and doors, spread-
eagled books, some of them torn up, and shattered pieces of Mrs.
Whitman's dishes that she had set such store by, lay mixed in one mess.
Elizabeth remembered how upset Mrs. Whitman had been a few months
ago when she and Helen broke two of those china plates.

Elizabeth also remembered how pleased she had been that the
Whitmans had a cookstove. That stove, and the small heating stove in the
sitting room, were caved in, their ashes mingled with the layer of straw
and feathers emptied from beds and settee cushions.

Standing amidst the wreckage with Eliza, Elizabeth hardly knew
why she had come. Nothing in the house, no treasures of her own, no
keepsakes of her dead mother—nothing had any interest or value. "It
would be burned"—well, what matter?

The chest in the parlor where Mrs. Whitman had kept her best things
was empty. Joe Lewis, or the Indians, someone, had those things now.
The doctor's medicine case, the cabinet of curios, where they kept their
botany specimens, and one of the bookcases, seemed undisturbed. All
else was in ruin.

Neither girl spoke as they wandered aimlessly through the sitting
room, the parlor, the kitchen, the Indian room, and back into the sitting
room, where they stood mutely. "Elizabeth," said Eliza at last, softly.
"Elizabeth—aren't you going to take anything?"

Elizabeth sighed tremulously, and began to sift through the wreckage of a happy life. Finding John's Testament facedown, open, on the
floor, she lovingly dusted it, straightening the pages. He had brought it
with him when the family left Ohio, when she was only a year old.

Thrown in a corner was her own Bible, received for being a good student, in which Mr. Rodgers had written, "Elizabeth M. Sager's Book, Oct. 20th, 1847." Was that less than two months ago? It seemed impossible for so many changes to take place in that short time.

The Indians soon put their white charges to use. Every morning the emigrant house captives finished breakfast by daylight, then the women and older girls went to work sewing for the Indians. Catherine and the others often sat on tables, for the Indians crowded the house from morning till night, leaving scarcely room to sit down.

The women made shirts from a bolt of yellow flannel, and several bales of calico taken from the doctor's stores. When these ran low, bedding, sheets, and curtains became shirts. One old fellow put Mary Marsh, the miller's eleven-year-old daughter, to knitting a pair of long-legged socks.

The younger children had to work as well. Elizabeth, Matilda, and the others took corn from the crib, and onions, potatoes, and apples from the cellar. After they sorted and sacked them, the Indian women carried them three miles to their village. They were not around much, except for carrying and other chores. Unlike the men, they cried over the doctor's children, returning things they had taken.

Sometimes the Indian women joined Catherine, Elizabeth, Matilda, and the others, in a hymn. Without Mr. Rodgers's violin, the music sounded thin, mournful, as brittle as the tall dead strands of rye grass. But the Indian women's companionship and sympathy were good, proving someone cared for them, when sometimes it seemed as if no one did. The children never feared the Indian women or their children, who showed only kindness and sympathy. Many members of the Cayuse, Umatilla, and Walla Walla tribes were in shock from the sudden deaths of their friends at Whitman Mission. Only certain young Cayuse men worried the survivors.

They said they were forming an expedition to the Dalles. Catherine knew they planned to kill Perrin and Mr. Hinman. When an Indian said he was going to the Dalles, one of the women or older girls must sew a shirt for his journey. It was terrible having to help them, knowing their intent, but any argument would bring threats of death. Several times one of them said he was going to the Dalles shortly. They always had the shirt ready on time, but in a few days the same Indian would be back with the same story.

Catherine rarely went to the mission house. Most of the survivors were terrified even to step outside. They waited until night, when the Indians had left, to draw water from the river, and made it last until the next night. They depended on Joe Stanfield for wood, but strong as he was, he fetched it so grudgingly they would often rather go without than ask him for it.

At this time, Edward Tiloukaikt came to Catherine, offering to teach her Indian if she would teach him English. Edward, like many Cayuses, had taken part in plundering the mission. He had threatened to kill Mr. Spalding, but no one knew whether he had killed him or anyone else, and no one dared ask.

An extremely handsome young man who carried himself in a proud and noble manner, Edward was usually polite and gentlemanly to Catherine and the other young girls. She dared not disagree with an Indian. Inwardly fighting them, she outwardly appeared meek and demure. She told him she would be glad to teach him her language and learn his.

He brought her Dr. Whitman's big Bible. Evenings after dinner, they cleared a small space on the table and sat side by side. By candlelight, Catherine read words and Edward repeated them. He knew enough English to translate the words into his own language. In this way, both learned quickly.

One night Edward presented Catherine with a brightly-colored cotton handkerchief. "Take this and wear it on your head or neck, all time," he told her. "Then the others will know you are my girl."

Catherine took it, thanking him as she tied it around her neck. She would feel safe as Edward's girl, glad of his protection. The intent stares of some of the young Indian men had unnerved her. Edward let it be known Catherine was his girl, and though the other young men joked with her about it, they kept their distance.

On Sunday evening, December 5, Catherine was readying to lie down before supper, when an Indian came in demanding that the women make him a shirt that night.

"Tell him it is the Sabbath. We must eat soon, and it is too late to begin the work," Mrs. Saunders told Eliza.

Eliza repeated it to the Indian, who raged and threatened in his own language until it seemed he would tear the house apart. Mrs. Saunders said, "Tell him we will do it." She took his measurements while Catherine found material and sewing things. As soon as he saw them at work, he left. Mrs. Saunders set aside the work and said, "I will tell the chief one of his warriors tried to make us work on the Lord's day."

Chief Tiloukaikt would take their part, if anyone would. Each time Catherine saw him, he seemed more conscience-stricken. His concern for the women and children brought him to the mission every few days. There he wandered among the ruined buildings, seeming ruined himself, a broken man.

He made some of the Indians return things they had taken, but his sons, Edward and Clark, and other young men of the tribe, were beyond his control. The chief told Catherine he was sorry for having killed his "best friend," Dr. Whitman. He seemed to mean it, but Catherine thought, *No matter how sorry he is, he can't bring our family back to life. Oh, why did they have to kill everybody?*

She was thinking of this when Mrs. Saunders said, "You lie down now and rest." Catherine was not sick any longer, but weak and frail. All day she sewed for the Indians and cared for Henrietta and the other sick children. Catherine went to Mrs. Saunders's room and lay on a bed with Helen. Louisa, the sickest child, lay on the bed opposite them, with Henrietta beside her. Catherine closed her eyes and drifted to sleep.

Someone shook her arm. She awakened to see Lorinda Bewley, the pretty, blonde young woman Mrs. Whitman had hired to teach the girls. "Why'd you wake me?" she asked drowsily.

"To eat your supper. You would rather sleep than eat, wouldn't you?"

"Yes. How is Louisa?"

"Better. She ate her supper and fell asleep."

Catherine sat in bed, looking at Louisa, who had never looked so peaceful. Her skin was pale except for the clusters of pink dots on her face. Her hands were thrown over her head, her hair spread across the pillow.

"How nicely Louisa sleeps!" said Miss Bewley.

"Yes," said Catherine, but something inside her said it was a sleep from which she would never awaken. Catherine arose, laying her hand on Louisa's face. It was icy cold. She put her ear to her mouth, but the breath was gone. She spoke the final words. "Louisa...Louisa is dead."

She sat back on the bed, perfectly still, looking at Louisa, while Miss Bewley spread the news throughout the house. Elizabeth and Matilda came to sit by Catherine, gazing solemnly on their departed sister. Catherine thought of how peacefully she had died. Delirious since falling sick, she had known nothing of the massacre. Now she would never have to worry about being killed.

Several Indians came in to see if the white child was really dead. When they were sure of it, every Indian in the house swiftly left. Their horses' hooves pounded away in the darkness.

Later that evening, Daniel Young, in his early twenties, came from the sawmill, where his family and another family named Smith were staying. He was looking for his older brother James, who had started to the mission with a load of wood the previous Tuesday and never returned.

Joe Stanfield told him matter-of-factly that James was ambushed by Indians and shot in the head. Joe found him, and buried him along the road where he fell. Chief Tiloukaikt entered, and he and Stanfield told Daniel to bring all the people from the sawmill to the emigrant house. Catherine felt sorry for Daniel, struggling against showing emotion in the face of the other men's lack of it.

When she saw a chance, Mrs. Saunders took him aside. "For heaven's sake," Catherine heard her say, "tell the Indians you and the rest are English. I said so, and they might kill us all if they find I have deceived them. The chief has promised to kill no one if we will work for them."

Daniel said he would tell the people at the sawmill. Mr. Smith really was English, or "King George man," as the Indians said. The others were Americans, "Boston men," the Indians called them. He started out the next day.

Edward Tiloukaikt was gone to the Umatilla to consult with a great chief about what to do with the captives, especially the two sick young men, Mr. Bewley and Mr. Sales, and the young women. Catherine missed his protection, but the Indians knew she was his girl, and did not bother

her while he was gone.

Tuesday morning they buried Louisa. Daniel Young helped Joe Stanfield build a rude coffin. Louisa Sager was not to be wrapped in a sheet like the massacre victims. Mrs. Saunders and the other women begged Catherine, Elizabeth, and Matilda not to see her buried. "It will be too upsetting," they said.

"I reckon we've seen plenty already, and ought to say good-bye to her," said Catherine. "Take care of Henrietta and Mary Ann and Helen while we're gone."

Joe Stanfield carried the little coffin through the rye grass. The three girls followed in his path, Catherine carrying a shovel, through stands of tall, damp grass to the foot of the hill, where they saw the dark, turned earth of the victims' mass grave.

Joe Stanfield had to dig through long grass and thick, tangled roots to make the grave. He had told them that he buried Dr. Whitman next to Alice Clarissa, Mrs. Whitman next to the doctor, and then John, Frank, Mr. Rodgers, and the others. Near their grave was a small, empty hole.

Catherine shivered in the cold, choking back tears. If she cried, she might not be able to stop, and it would not do to anger the Indians. As Joe placed the small box in the hole, Catherine could again see Louisa at the picnic, with the crown of flowers on her head.

Joe had to ask her twice for the shovel. He spaded in dark clods smelling of earth and damp, which rained softly on the coffin lid. Elizabeth squeezed Catherine's hand until it hurt, taking her mind from the pain in her throat.

"There," said Joe at last, for the first time seeming to show some human feeling. "I have done all I can for her. She rests by the side of her mother." Catherine looked another moment at the graves, wishing she could scatter flowers on them as they had when Joseph Finley, Mr. Rodgers's friend, died. Then she turned, the other girls following her back to the house.

That night, December 7, as the girls sat in the room where the two young men, Crockett Bewley and Amos Sales, lay sick abed, Edward Tiloukaikt and five other young Indians burst in, swarming around the sick men. Edward's eyes burned with the same dark intensity as when he had threatened to kill Mr. Spalding.

All five carried weapons. Edward grasped a bedpost from one of the spool beds in the mission house, which he had trimmed into a war club. The Indians talked all at once, like a nest of hornets buzzing. Elizabeth understood snatches: "their disease will kill us," "they may live to escape and bring others to kill us." The white men looked up bewildered, not understanding the Indians' speech.

When Edward brought his bedpost club down on Mr. Bewley's head, the children screamed and ran outside, expecting to be killed at any moment. With the Indians breaking their promise to kill no more captives, no one was safe. Edward followed and said, "Only the two young men are to be killed. Come back, you must stay until we are finished."

Elizabeth and the others returned, and though she shut her eyes, pressing her hands against her ears, she could still hear the screams of the men being beaten and tomahawked. When she dared look, the Indians were dragging the victims outside. Their heads bled, their bodies hung limp.

Afraid that all the sick ones would be killed, Elizabeth and Eliza pulled Mary Ann from bed and made her walk around, but Helen was too sick to rise.

The Indians came back into the house, asking, "Where is Crockett's sister? Does she care that he is dead, or not?"

No one knew where Lorinda was. The Indians went through and around the house a few times, and left. It was then that the others found Lorinda, under a bed, sobbing.

That night the sawmill families arrived. They were the Youngs, with two grown sons, and the Smiths, with four young boys. Horrified by the mutilated bodies in the yard, the men expected to be killed next morning, but learned that the Indians needed a few white men alive to run the gristmill. Fifty-two captives now crowded the emigrant house.

The next day, December 8, the Indians set Joseph Smith and Elam Young, Daniel's father, to work grinding wheat at the gristmill. Eliza Spalding must stay to interpret. Elizabeth went to keep her company.

The December wind was biting. The men kept warm at their work, but Elizabeth and Eliza grew cold standing still, so they dug a hole in a straw stack near the mill and crawled into the crackling straw, pulling a blanket over the hole.

Nestled in the dust-smelling straw, Elizabeth could pretend that none of the terrible events had happened. She lay on her straw tick in a measles delirium, and would awaken to Mrs. Whitman pressing a cool cloth to her head. Holding Eddie close, she could believe, until the Indians jerked aside the blanket and told Eliza to come on out and talk for them. Then the girls must stand in the cold rain until every word was said.

They were standing outside when they saw two Indians riding towards the house. Eliza broke and ran to them. Elizabeth followed wonderingly. One Indian gave his reins to the other, jumped from his horse, and caught Eliza in his arms. They talked Nez Perce so fast that Elizabeth could not understand.

Eliza turned to Elizabeth, her face bright with joy. "This is Timothy, our friend," she said, "and that one on the horse is Eagle. My mother has sent them to take me home!"

TWENTY-THREE

Timothy and Eagle told the girls that on the day of the massacre, Mr. Canfield, one of the men butchering the beef, escaped, walking the one hundred and twenty miles to Lapwai to tell Mrs. Spalding of the massacre. She wrote to Eliza and to Mrs. Canfield, and sent Timothy and Eagle to bring Eliza warm clothing and take her to her mother.

Eagle now tied the horses to a fence. He and Timothy stared in horrified disbelief at the bloodstained dead men lying in the yard. Mr. Bewley's head was almost torn from his body. Timothy shook his head, saying slowly enough for Elizabeth to understand, "So that's the way the Cayuses kill!"

The Indians who had been at the mill stood mutely at the fence. Timothy shamed them, pointing to the bodies. "Is this the way you do things here?" Then he, Eagle, Eliza, and Elizabeth went into the house.

Timothy and Eagle sat near the stove, on either side of Eliza. Elizabeth sat close by, seeing the radiance of Eliza's face as she looked from one to the other of her friends. She was happy Eliza was to be rescued, but what would she do without her company? She felt a jealous pang. The three talked slowly enough now for her to understand all they said.

"Where is your father?" Timothy asked Eliza.

"I do not know. Will you really bring me to my mother?"

Timothy looked grave. "We met some Indians on the way who say they will not let you go. We thought of stealing you, but they knew our thoughts, and said if we tried it they would search the country and murder us together. So you see, we cannot take you."

The radiance left Eliza's face, and she began to cry. Elizabeth was sorry for being jealous. Looking tearful himself, Timothy dried Eliza's tears with her apron, saying, "Don't cry, Eliza. Soon you will see your

CHIEF TIMOTHY OF THE NEZ PERCES

Eliza Spalding's good friend visiting Washington, D.C., in 1868. Courtesy of Smithsonian Institution.

mother."

Matilda looked in from the next room, where the sick children were. Catching Elizabeth's eye, she quietly said, "We think Helen is dying."

Elizabeth jumped up, but Timothy, with long strides, was ahead of her. He and Eagle fell on their knees by Helen's bed. Helen lay terribly still, her eyelashes very dark against her skin, her hair dark against the pillow. Elizabeth could barely see her ribs rise and fall with each breath.

Timothy prayed in his own language, his voice the only sound in the room. Elizabeth watched his mouth as he prayed, eyes closed, face uplifted towards heaven. She watched Helen breathe in and out. Then the breath went out and did not go back in again. After a still moment, Timothy rose and pointed upward to show that the spirit had flown. A quiet awe filled Elizabeth.

That evening Joe Stanfield took Helen away and buried her. He and Daniel Young buried Mr. Bewley and Mr. Sales. Not long after, Mrs. Hays's baby died, adding another grave to the foot of the hill.

One gray day, Catherine answered a knock on the door. A young

Indian woman, her face showing great distress, began to speak as soon as the door was open. She pulled on Catherine's sleeve, speaking rapidly in her own language, so upset Catherine could not understand her.

"Eliza," she called, "come tell me what she says."

Eliza came and listened a few moments. "She says the wolves have dug up the doctor and his wife."

"Oh, no! Watch Henrietta for me, will you?" She called to the others, telling what had happened. Joe Stanfield and the other men grabbed up the shovels Joe kept handy, and started out. One of them called to Catherine not to go, but she was already hurrying down the path through the rye grass, heart pounding with each step. The men followed close behind her. When they were close enough to have a clear view of the grave, they all stopped.

Catherine reeled with horror. She had seen the carcasses of antelope and buffalo pulled apart on the plains by wolves and coyotes. She knew her father's remains had been scattered by coyotes, but had never imagined anything this horrible....

She stared dizzily, hearing one of the men behind her make a small, sick sound. The others said nothing. Then Daniel Young said, "Yonder come the women. For mercy's sake, don't let them see it!"

They went to work with their shovels. Before the women arrived, the job was done. "Go back to the house, little lady," old Elam Young told Catherine. "You've seen enough."

Catherine turned, stomach twisting, and, feeling weak and jumpy all over, went slowly back to the house.

The wolves visited the grave many more times. Each morning Catherine heard their snarling and saw from a distance the large, shaggy gray beasts, scratching at the ground and worrying at something, but she never took a close look again.

"The Indians have buried their hatchets and are sorry," Joe Stanfield said. "If you do not wish to be friends, they can dig up their hatchets. Do you want that?" Joe Stanfield, the hulking French Canadian, was in good with the Indians. All the captives knew by now that he had known of the massacre plans three days in advance. When they asked why he had not warned the Whitmans, he said, "It would have done no good."

Nicholas Finley sat near Stanfield. Although Finley's lodge had been a meeting place for the massacre plotters, Finley himself seemed sympathetic towards the doctor and the survivors. He was also sympathetic about the decimation of the Cayuse tribe. He took no part in the massacre and looting, was always ready to do the Cayuses and their white captives a good turn, and was respected by both sides.

Catherine and the other girls listened to Joe's speech in terrified silence. It was December 11. A number of young chiefs were holding a council over the girls, who were lined up according to size. Old Tiloukaikt, who had upheld their right not to work on the Sabbath, was not there to protect them. Neither were Eliza's friends, Timothy and Eagle. Edward had taken them to stay in the Indian village. Nicholas Finley, though he would do them no harm, would make little effort toward protecting them. He had his own life to consider.

Edward stood with the young chiefs, his expression unreadable. Catherine still taught him English words from the Bible, although terrified to be near him after what he did to Mr. Bewley and Mr. Sales.

Mrs. Saunders entered.

"Go away. This does not concern you," said Joe.

She ignored him and spoke to Edward. "Edward, you do not want a wife of eleven snows."

"No," said Edward. "Eleven snows too young."

She pointed to her daughter. "Helen," she said, "eleven snows. Helen, you go home."

Helen rose and went into her mother's room. Catherine knew Helen was fourteen, but the Indians did not. Now Helen's younger sisters, and her own, were safe. But what of herself? She was twelve, would be thirteen in April, and since she had lived here for three years, the Indians knew her age. Indian girls sometimes married that young.

She feared to call attention to herself by looking at the Indians, so she looked at her shoes, which were not moccasins, but real hard-soled shoes from a missionary barrel. She wore them day and night because of the Indians' habit of taking things.

One of the chiefs began to speak. Nicholas Finley translated his words to Joe Stanfield in French and Joe, who spoke better English than Nicholas, repeated them to the girls. The Indian told them they were helpless young women needing protection.

Protection! Catherine thought. He had strange ideas of protection. Two days earlier, the servant of Chief Five Crows carried Lorinda Bewley away. Five Crows had sent for her, and she had no choice but to go. Eliza Spalding turned pale when she saw one of the horses the Indian had. "Oh, there is Tashe—my horse," she said. "Now I know the Indians have killed my father." Lorinda rode away weeping. What was happening to her now was too horrible to think about. The other girls were terrified of sharing her fate.

The night after Lorinda was taken, Tamsucky and Joe Lewis, carrying ropes, ransacked the house for her, not believing she was gone. Joe grinned at Catherine, asking if she had been sick lately. When she said no, he replied, "I think you have. Why, you look as pale as a ghost."

She was pale now, listening to the chief's speech while she twisted her cold hands in her lap, unable to warm herself, even by the fire. Fear chilled her from within.

"One girl has already been taken," the chief said, "but by a chief, not a vagabond. Vagabonds have no home, no property. They will drag a girl all over the country, beating and starving her. These young men—" he gestured to five standing near him—"want white wives. They will protect you. If you do not wish to marry, say no." Then he spoke to the Indians in their language, and they left the room.

"I'd sooner be killed than marry an Indian," said sixteen-year-old Susan Kimball when they were gone. She looked ready to cry.

"I won't insist on living, knowing the terrible sacrifice you'd have to make," said her mother, "but the decision is yours."

The girls did not know what to do. The Indians might kill them if they said no. Once started, they would spare no one.

The Indians filed back in. The air crackled with charged silence. Catherine knew the other girls were going to refuse them. She tried so hard not to breathe it seemed her lungs would catch fire.

A number of vagabonds straggled in behind the young chiefs. Lean, dirty, and ragged, they wore a desperate, hungry look, like half-starved wolves. The young chiefs, some wearing fine buckskins, others in clothing taken from the white men, stood a little apart, scorning the wretched vagabonds.

"What have you decided?" asked the chief. "Will you take Indian husbands, or not?"

The girls lowered their eyes and shook their heads. "No," they whispered.

The vagabond Indians collected in a corner, whooping and laughing. The others looked grave. Again the chief, with Nicholas and Joe as interpreters, spoke to the girls. "You have not considered well before answering. Once you cast off the protection of the chiefs, you cannot expect their help in trouble. What now is your answer?"

"Yes," said the miserable girls. Catherine trembled inside.

"Now you are wise. Those wanting white wives, come forward. The girls may take their choice."

Five young men stepped forward. Three were Frank Eskaloom, Edward Tiloukaikt, and his brother Clark. Mary Smith, a fifteen-year-old with a trim figure, curly black hair and dark, flashing eyes, stepped up to Clark and said, "I choose him."

Nicholas and Joe consulted her father, who said, "I would prefer a rich Indian for a son-in-law over a poor white man." Catherine knew he was suffering, but must approve or risk death.

Susan Kimball was the only older girl left, because Ellen Canfield was too sick to rise from bed, and the others were too young. Everyone waited tensely to see who she would choose.

Frank Eskaloom strode forward and grasped her arm. "I killed your father. You belong to me." Susan burst into tears, sobbing as the chief told them that they must teach their husbands to read, and the men must provide well for their wives. Catherine was grateful not to be chosen. She could not imagine how dreadful a forced marriage would be. The things she had been through were bad enough.

Mary Smith shed no tears, standing with head held high, emotions showing only in quickened breathing, snapping eyes, and heightened color. The Indians nodded approval. "You have a brave heart." Clark Tiloukaikt said he would bring a priest from the Umatilla to marry them, and the others as well.

Old Elam Young stepped up to Mary Smith. "Congratulations on your marriage," he said.

This was too much for poor Mary, who hid her face in her hands, sobbing. The Indians called derisively at him for making her cry, and her father hurled a barrage of harsh words upon the old man, telling him to mind his own business in the future. Mr. Young scowled in reply.

It was tragic, yet funny in an odd, heartbreaking way, like the time Catherine saw an Indian brave using the schoolroom's map of the world as a saddle. It almost covered his little pony, draping far down either side of it. Catherine and the other girls could not help laughing at him for riding on the world, although it reminded them of the destruction of their schoolroom.

The two couples took rooms in the upper part of the house. Clark Tiloukaikt seemed happy with his new wife at first, but before long became ill at ease, seldom visiting Mary, paying little attention to her when he did.

One day when Catherine was out, she passed an abandoned wagon and was surprised to see Clark lying in it, staring into the cold gray sky. She approached with caution.

"What ails you?" she asked.

"I am sick." He did not look at her, but kept staring into the sky as if searching for an answer.

"What made you sick?" She hoped it was not another case of measles.

"My father talked to me. He say it no good take white wife." He continued to look skyward, with an expression of deep sorrow. Knowing of no way to comfort him, Catherine went into the house, leaving him to his thoughts.

Not long afterwards, Clark abandoned Mary entirely. At their evening lessons one day, Edward asked Catherine if she would mind him taking Mary as his wife, since his brother no longer wanted her.

"I don't mind. I'm too young to be a wife," said Catherine. Here at last was a way to rid herself of Edward.

"If you are my girl, I will not leave you."

"It is all right. Ask Mary if you want. Here's your handkerchief back, to give to her." Catherine drew the handkerchief, the symbol of Edward's protection, from around her neck and put it in his hand.

Edward asked, and Mary accepted. She kept up a cheerful appearance in his presence, and soon he became quite fond of her, striding in with great importance to demand, "Where is my wife?" He studied English with determination, and as they sat together evenings, Mary spoke earnestly of how well her father ran the mill, and how he was English and not a "Boston man." Catherine knew she was trying to protect him in case of another attack.

When Edward left with the other Indians, around eleven or twelve each night, Mary dropped her pretenses, sobbing to Catherine that she was miserable being his wife. Catherine listened, offering what comfort she could, and soon the two were good friends.

Some nights, a number of Indians stretched out on the beds until morning. Whoever had the bed they wanted, slept on the floor that night.

Not long after the forced marriages, a young vagabond named Istulest led an unkempt group to the door. Rapping thunderously, they stormed through the house, brandishing tomahawks, raging at the captives. Catherine and her sisters cowered together until they left.

Though weary from strain and sickness, Catherine could scarcely close her eyes to rest any longer. When she did, she saw the shadow of a tomahawk descending, its sharp edge seeking her skull. She whipped her eyes open to find nothing there.

The day after Istulest burst in, Mrs. Saunders spoke to old Beardy, the Indian who had strenuously protested the massacre, doing everything in his power to protect the captives. She hired him and several other men to stay each night until the rest left. With old Beardy's calming influence, Catherine thought they might be safe.

Catherine stayed in one room with Mrs. Saunders, Eliza Spalding, and her sisters. Lorinda Bewley had been with them. Every day Catherine missed Lorinda, Louisa, and the others. Mary Ann stayed with Mrs. Hall, and the other captives stayed in the other two downstairs rooms.

Mrs. Hall had a fireplace, and Catherine sat by it evenings before joining the other children. Looking at the yellow and orange and blue flickerings, thinking of nothing, she could relax enough to fall to sleep.

One night she was staring with unfocused eyes at the flames when a rough hand on her arm jerked her from her trance, and she looked up to see Istulest, who dragged her from her seat.

He aims to take me away, thought Catherine, clinging to the chair with all her might, regretting for the first time having cast off Edward's protection.

Istulest jerked and tugged until he pried her clinging hands from the chair. Catherine screamed as loud and long as she could. *Where are those Indians hired to protect us?* she wondered desperately as he dragged her through the door into the next room.

Though she struggled till he could hardly hang on, still his strength prevailed. He sat her in a chair in the room where Elizabeth and her friend Eliza, Matilda, and Henrietta lay.

"Hush noise," he told her. "I have friend wants to marry you."

Before long the friend appeared, as ragged and ill-cared-for as Istulest, wearing two long, greasy black braids, clothing soiled and stained, smelling as bad as he looked. In broken English he wooed Catherine. She dared not express her opinion of his love speeches, but inside her a kettle simmered, rising to a boil. Outwardly she grew colder until she was shivering.

"I'm cold," she said at last. "Won't you let me sit by the fire?"

Istulest grabbed a blanket off the bed and his friend wrapped it around Catherine and went on talking to her. The children did not seem to waken, but possibly were awake and too frightened to let the Indians know.

Nicholas Finley, the French interpreter, stepped in and said, "Don't you take that girl."

"We won't," Istulest's friend replied. "This is all in fun." Catherine could not see the fun. The moment Nicholas left, the vagabond dragged Catherine to the bed and forced her in next to the wall, pushing the children aside. Then the Indian crowded in next to her. She could smell his rank body and feel his rough hands on her shoulders.

At that moment Catherine could stand no more. She was wearing her hard-soled shoes, as always. All the tension in her body seemed to flow into her legs and out through her feet as she kicked the Indian's shins again and again. He hollered and tried to hold on to her, but she kicked until he jumped from the bed, dancing with pain. He and Istulest beat a swift retreat. Drained of energy, Catherine was asleep before their horses' hoofbeats died away.

TWENTY-FOUR

The next day, Catherine talked to the adults about what to do if the two Indians came after her again.

"Why don't you sleep in the straw stack by the mill?" Joe Stanfield suggested.

The women shook their heads. "Don't trust that Joe."

Looking insulted, Joe left.

"Maybe you could go to Nicholas Finley's lodge," Mrs. Young, a grandmotherly woman, suggested. "He seems nice enough. One of my boys could go with you."

"I couldn't leave the children," said Catherine, "but before I'd be taken off, I'd jump in the mill pond!" Leaving the children would be terrible, being carried away by those wretches would be worse. The mill pond's icy waters closing over her head might end all her sorrows. Concerned as the adults were, it still seemed that no one cared enough.

"There's no need for such talk," said old Elam Young. "I have a plan. Every evening before we take down the pile of mattresses to spread on the floor, I lie down on them and have me a nice nap. What if you were to lie down behind them until those fellows went away?"

This seemed like a good plan to everyone. A few nights later, Istulest and his friend were back, casting sly glances at Catherine. As usual, the women cooked dinner for all the Indians. They had to taste each dish as the Indians watched intently, still fearing poison.

During this, Mary Smith took Catherine's hand and led her out the door and around the side of the house. On their way, they met Edward. "We're going to hide," Mary told him. "Don't worry," she told Catherine as they entered the Youngs' room. "He won't tell on you."

"Here you are, dear." The old lady motioned to the pile of mattresses. Catherine crawled between them and the wall, and Mrs. Young

239

passed her a blanket. The old man lay down upon the mattresses as usual.

Catherine pulled the blanket around herself. The pile of mattresses made a warm, cozy nest. For the first time since the massacre she felt momentarily safe, and relaxed, sleep enfolding her.

"You should have seen how they tore up the house looking for you," Mary told her later. "For a while we were afraid they'd find you. One young brave kept pointing out places to look, and laughing when they didn't find you there. Finally your suitor left. I'm surprised you didn't hear him yelling and firing his pistol."

"I didn't hear anything," said Catherine. "I was asleep."

Catherine hoped she was rid of her pursuer, but he returned yet again. When he came in, she dodged into Mrs. Kimball's room. Joe Stanfield made signs at her which she didn't understand. Heart pounding, she crawled on to a mattress in the dark under the stairs leading to the loft. When the Indian did not come after her, she drifted to sleep.

She awakened late. Firelight flickered on the walls, voices murmured. Creeping from beneath the stairs, she saw Mary Smith sewing with several others. "Is he gone?" Catherine asked.

Mary frantically motioned her to hush, but too late. A movement in the shadows on the other side of the fire revealed the face she had hoped never to see again, staring straight at her. With a gasp, she dodged back under the stairs. Still the Indian did not pursue her. *Most likely he knows the ones we hired to protect us will stop him,* thought Catherine. Calmed, she went to her usual bed with the children, and to sleep once more.

In the middle of the night she felt a tug on her arm. She awoke to find it was her enemy.

"Sit by fire," he said, "talk with me."

"I will not."

"I will make you." He jerked her arm roughly. Catherine grabbed the covers, using all the strength in her body to cling to the bed. She screamed for the Indians hired for protection, but none came.

"If you do not come, I whip you!"

"I'd like to see anyone whip me!" Catherine yelled, losing all fear in her desperation. He tried again to pull her from bed, and she found his arm with her teeth and bore down hard, tasting salt and hoping she had drawn blood.

Yelling in rage, he tried to climb in bed with her, since he was having no success in pulling her out. There was no room for him, so he grabbed Matilda by the arm and flung her on the floor, where she sat wide-eyed as the Indian demanded again that Catherine sit by the fire with him. "Then I go off and not bother you."

"I won't sit by the fire, or go any place with you. I hate you! I never hated anyone so much, except Joe Lewis!" She did not care who knew it. She was tired of being good, and sweet, and demure. Fear was replaced by burning, all-consuming anger.

"I—am going—to take—you!" The Indian's words came out in gasps as he tugged at Catherine. She fought with nails, teeth, and feet, gouging his flesh. Still he hung on.

She raised the biggest racket she ever had in her life, yelling and pounding frantically. Finally she heard Joe Stanfield yelling at the men to "drive that Indian off." Joseph Smith and Elam, Daniel, and John Young bounded into the room. They had been too afraid to help before, but now, with Stanfield's permission, they meant to attack. Seeing himself outnumbered, the Indian raced into the night.

After that, the Indians looked on Catherine as a brave girl. They laughed and talked about her whipping an Indian man, and no one tried again to carry her away.

On Christmas morning, Mrs. Saunders, who had a store of white flour, baked white bread and a large batch of pies using dried peaches. The peach pies filled the house with a warm, delicious, summery scent. The children ate in secret in her room when no Indians were about, the emigrant children talking of past Christmases.

Catherine and Elizabeth remembered Christmases with their parents, but Matilda did not. This was the first Christmas she remembered being allowed to celebrate. It felt a little bit naughty, even though Mrs. Saunders and the others acted as if it were all right.

This Christmas was unlike any the captives had known. They had crossed the plains bound for a land where they could enjoy freedom and prosperity. Captivity was a trial on their proud spirits, but today they sang and prayed in thankfulness at being alive.

Old Beardy was an honored guest at the feast. For his valuable friendship, everyone saw he had all the peach pie he wanted, even if they had to go without. He sat by the stove eating slice after slice, juice dribbling down his stubbly chin. He wiped his face and passed his dish for more. Mrs. Saunders laughed indulgently and heaped more helpings upon the dish.

Later that day, several Indians came in and told Mrs. Saunders they wanted bread, as they were going to see the big white chief at Fort Walla Walla. They did not know what was to happen, but said no one would be killed. Mrs. Saunders gave them food, and they left.

At sundown a young Indian the captives called "Good Samuel" came to the door. When Catherine looked out the window and saw his expression, she said, "Good news," and opened the door. She had not seen anyone look so happy since before the killings.

Good Samuel called all the captives together before telling his news. "I know something that will make you smile," he said. "'Uncle Pete' has come from Fort Vancouver. He is at Fort Walla Walla, to buy you with blankets, tobacco, and other things, and take you to the valley."

A flood of joy burst within Catherine. For a few moments the captives were wild with happiness, crying and hugging each other. A few, swept away with joy, even hugged Good Samuel. He had ridden twenty miles at sundown to tell them that 'Uncle Pete' had paid for all the captives, even the girls taken as wives, that he would pay half the ransom now and half when they were delivered to the fort.

'Uncle Pete,' since he was from Fort Vancouver, was British. This was a further cause of joy for the captives. They knew that when news of the massacre reached the Willamette Valley, a party of Americans would pursue the Indians. The Indians had talked of this, saying they would kill the captives if the Americans came after them. Now they need no longer fear. After almost a month of waiting, expecting every day to be killed, they were to be rescued!

Their happiness lasted only overnight. The next morning Good Samuel entered, looking grave. "What is the matter?" Catherine asked him.

"They are coming to kill the white women," he replied.

"Old Beardy will stop them!"

"He is leading them."

Catherine studied his face to see if this could be some horrible joke. The sadness in his eyes told her that he spoke the truth. The captives' hour had come. Silently Catherine went to the children's room and gathered up Henrietta. She sat behind the stove holding her, determined to meet her fate with her little sister in her arms.

About noon, they heard someone at the door. *That's the Indians come to kill us,* thought Catherine. Mrs. Saunders opened the door. There stood a lone Indian woman. Mrs. Saunders asked her in.

The woman's name was Katherine. Her husband was a Frenchman. She had been at Fort Hall when she heard of the massacre, and rode night and day to the mission to see if she could help.

"You can help us, if you can convince the Indians not to kill us," said Mrs. Saunders.

Shortly the door burst open. Beardy strode in, his whiskered face grim and angry. Catherine, peering from behind the stove, had never seen the mild old Indian look like that. His companions were equally wrathful, and all were armed with knives, clubs, guns, and tomahawks.

Catherine's stomach shrank to a tight knot as Beardy sat on the floor right by the stove she was hiding behind. Mrs. Saunders was sitting by the stove, too, and Good Samuel sat in front of her with pity on his face.

The white captives silently looked at the Indians. Old Beardy, his stubbly face contorted with rage, Tamsucky, and Frank Eskaloom, who had wanted to kill the captives all along, and others now angry enough to kill, were tensed for the final slaughter.

Good Samuel and Old Jimmy, the Nez Perce who at the beginning of the year had fooled others into paying him to bring about a thaw, looked on the whites with regret. Eliza's two Nez Perce friends, failing to rescue her, had left. Indian Katherine was in the next room. For a moment, everyone was frozen, each waiting for someone to take action.

At last Good Samuel arose and spoke long to Beardy. Catherine squeezed her eyes shut, pressing her face against Henrietta's warm body. At any moment the killing might begin.

Beardy leaped to his feet. He spoke wild, loud, and fast. "I was almost killed last night! The white women poisoned my food! I was always their friend, now I am their enemy. They must die before they kill us all!"

More speeches followed, the word "poison" a continuous thread running through each. Captives who did not know Nez Perce looked on uncomprehendingly. Catherine understood enough. She heard Tamsucky say, "Just kill them; that will be the easiest way to get rid of them."

Old Jimmy sprang up, scathing Tamsucky. Tamsucky's cringing before the onslaught reminded Catherine of the expression "he could have crept through a knothole."

Beardy made a speech, brandishing a war club. He said his food had been poisoned, and the blankets that 'Uncle Pete' had traded for the captives, were poisoned. Then he struck the stove with violent force. The clang of metal almost deafened Catherine, who shrank against the wall, trembling. Henrietta whimpered, and Catherine hushed her.

At that moment, Indian Katherine, who had been listening from the next room, entered, saying, "These women have not poisoned you, and neither has 'Uncle Pete.' It would be well if you stopped acting the fool."

The warriors stood dumbfounded. It was absolutely forbidden for a woman to speak in public, or to contradict a man. Had she been of their tribe, she would have been severely punished.

Finding his voice, Beardy insisted that he had been deathly ill after eating the peach pies the day before. He had vomited blood. The white women must have poisoned his food.

"Are you sure it was blood, and not peaches? How much pie did you eat?"

Taken aback, Beardy stammered awhile, finally admitting he had eaten a good deal of pie—he could not remember exactly how much.

"It was your own fault you were sick. No one else is to blame."

Beardy's shoulders drooped. The war club hung limply in his hand. He looked thoroughly ashamed and dejected. Tamsucky and Frank Eskaloom scowled darkly, others looked relieved. The Indians returned to their village for more councils. When the captives saw Beardy, he treated the incident as a joke. Tamsucky was too ashamed to show his face. Some Indians said he had died, others said not, until the captives declared, "Old Tamsucky can die and come to life when he's a mind to."

Late that day, Chief Tiloukaikt decided the story about the poisoned blankets was merely a story, and he would accept 'Uncle Pete's' terms of ransom. When they heard that, the captives thought they were safe.

Near sunset, bright yellow streaked the horizon beneath dark blue clouds. Night closed in. After darkness fell, the captives were horrified by the sound of hoofbeats and wild yells in the yard. Catherine looked out the cold window pane and could make out the dim shapes of braves hideously decorated with war paint.

One called that a band of American soldiers was coming to the fort. The Cayuse braves would meet and kill them, then return and leave not one captive alive. They wheeled and rode in the direction of Fort Walla Walla. Another band of Indians arrived to guard the captives. Frank Eskaloom leaned his gun in a corner where he could reach it in a moment.

All night the runners came and went, calling, "News! News!" Catherine and the others had little rest.

The next day they waited tensely for whatever might come. Ears strained for the sound of hoofbeats. At last, far away among the rye grass, the sound came, closer and closer, like the thunder of an approaching storm. Then lightning flashes of gunfire split the air.

The Indian guards went wild. Frank Eskaloom grabbed his gun and rushed into the yard, ready to fight. The others yelled and grabbed the children to kill them. Catherine snatched up Henrietta and dodged through the rooms, seeking a safe place. An Indian grabbed Matilda and swung his tomahawk at her head, but she ducked and the blade passed through the hair by her ear.

From outside came another sound—the rainfall of cascading laughter. The Indians in the house froze. One still held his arm tight around Matilda's middle and his tomahawk poised above her head. Catherine stood shivering, holding Henrietta, looking at the motionless Indians and captives standing in tableau.

In a moment the Indians released their intended victims and went outside. Through the open door, Catherine saw Indians in the yard sitting on their horses, laughing and talking. One came to the door and said, "The Americans are not at the fort, only 'Uncle Pete.' He has bought you, and you will leave in three days."

-FIVE

"Are you forgetting to yoke our oxen?" asked Catherine for at least the tenth time.

"We are trying. Stop being a nuisance," said Mr. Smith.

It had seemed that Joe Stanfield, in his sluggish indifference, would never round up the oxen. Now it seemed the men would never yoke them.

It was the twenty-ninth of December, 1847. Catherine sat in the wagon under the dark sky, holding Henrietta and shivering. No canvas covered the wagon. An Indian had thought the wagon canvas would make a fine coat lining, and others demanded the same, till all the canvas was gone, and the wagon bows arched like bare ribs against the sky.

Catherine's breath steamed out in white mist. Points of starlight hung above her, brightest white and incredibly cold. Beside her were Elizabeth, Matilda, Eliza Spalding, Mrs. Saunders's oldest and youngest girls, Mrs. Canfield and Mrs. Kimball, each holding her youngest. All eleven huddled together for warmth in the cramped wagon bed; still they shivered.

In a nearby wagon were the older Kimball and Canfield children, Mary Marsh and her two-year-old nephew, Alba Lyman, Mrs. Young, and Mrs. Saunders's three middle children.

Joe Stanfield and Mr. Smith hitched the best oxen to Mr. Smith's wagon, and his family started out with Mrs. Hays and her child. Joe Stanfield had taken a liking to Mrs. Hays despite her violent objections, and when distributing food among the captives gave her the largest share. This had caused much quarreling, but no one felt like quarreling today.

Clark Tiloukaikt was in high spirits the night he heard of the ransom. He had been uneasy about holding white captives ever since his father talked to him, but still he did not mind joking about it. He told Catherine that 'Uncle Pete' had bought all but her, having given her to him.

246

"We'll settle that question in the fort," said Catherine, and Clark laughed as if she had told a brilliant joke.

One by one, the men hitched up the five wagons. Catherine and the others rode in the last one. Elam, Daniel, and John Young yoked the oxen, and Daniel and John went on to drive other wagons.

Elam Young started the wagon in which rode his wife and the Canfield, Kimball, Saunders, and Marsh children. Mrs. Saunders climbed in beside the Sagers and, with a weary sigh, gathered her youngest, a two-year-old who bore her name, into her lap. She had been up all night finishing a coat for an Indian, preparing for the journey, and helping others. The middle-of-the-night preparations reminded Catherine of the Jews' flight from Egypt. Haste and secrecy were necessary, in case any Indians changed their minds.

Finally Mrs. Saunders spoke one quiet word of complaint. "You'd think those others could have given us some of the best oxen and at least waited till we'd started before going off."

The other wagons pulled ahead, and they were left with only a boy for a driver—twelve-year-old Nathan Kimball, the son of the man shot climbing the fence. He was the man of his family, just as Catherine, at twelve, was the head of her family. He cracked his whip and the lumbering oxen started. The four beasts pulled, steaming in the frosty air.

Catherine looked back at the mission lying desolate beneath the star-filled sky. The shattered windows stared blank and empty. A cat that had been her pet ran by the house. The cats would turn wild now. The mission buildings would rot and collapse, if the Indians did not burn them, and turn to dirt mounds amid the rye grass. The mill pond and irrigation ditches would fill in. For eleven years the Whitmans had fought off nature. Now nature would reclaim the place once known as Whitman Mission.

Catherine remembered the fear and dread with which she first approached the mission, riding in an ox-drawn cart. Now, three years later, riding in an ox-drawn wagon, she felt even more fear and dread. Once again she was leaving behind loved ones' graves, to face an uncertain future. Tears filled her vision, hiding the buildings from sight, pouring bitterly cold down her cheeks. She cried in silence, hoping that in the darkness the others would not notice.

The wagon creaked on through mud, the oxen's hooves crunching through grass. As they passed an Indian lodge, a woman hurried out, distress on her face. "Keep going, hurry all the way," she told Nathan. "The young men are sorry they sold you." The wagon driven by Elam Young was a little ahead. She must have told him the same thing. The other three wagons were far ahead, out of sight.

Clouds hid the stars. The day dawned gray and cheerless, but each step of the oxen brought them farther from danger. Their spirits lifted a little.

At noon they reached the Touchet River and stopped to rest. The others were there, also having their noon stop. Just as they were about to eat the food Mrs. Saunders had prepared, a group of people rode towards them. They were Chief Tiloukaikt, old Beardy and his wife, Good Samuel, and Nicholas Finley. Mr. Finley talked with Joe Stanfield. Then Beardy and Tiloukaikt told the drivers, "Hurry, hurry, no camp. Get to fort."

Catherine nearly cried. Hungry and cold, she wanted badly to eat. The river was so muddy and swollen, lapping up beyond its banks, they could hardly find a place to cross. Joe Stanfield and the others crossed the roaring water and outdistanced the last two wagons again. Old Beardy and Samuel swam their horses across. Elam Young drove his wagon over, and lastly Nathan floundered through the cold brown water as best he could, driving the oxen as hard as they would go.

The water ran so high the oxen had to swim in the middle. The chill current seeped through the cracks in the wagon bed, soaking Catherine's dress. She shivered violently, teeth chattering. Henrietta wailed. Catherine and the others managed to hold the food in the air so it was not completely drenched. Elizabeth held up her doll Eddie, to keep him and his cradleboard from being ruined.

They ate the bread and meat and cake in the wagon, shivering miserably in clinging, clammy garments. Catherine's fingers were cold and red, so stiff she could hardly hold her food. The wind cut her until she expected to bleed at any moment.

The other wagons pulled up a steep incline, but Nathan's oxen stalled. By the time Mrs. Saunders ran up the hill to seek help, the other wagons were nowhere in sight. Old Beardy and Good Samuel helped drive the oxen up the hill, then rode ahead to join the other wagons.

Left behind, the lone wagon creaked on through skeleton woods, then across sand, sagebrush, and bunch grass, crackling across dead gray stems. Rain drizzled until there was no hope of drenched clothes drying. The brown-gray sand ripples darkened; the wheels dug deep and came up encrusted. After a while of following in Mr. Young's tracks, one of the lead oxen began to falter.

Old Beardy galloped over a rise, down towards the wagon. Coming up on the off side, he whipped the oxen and called to Nathan, "*Hia klatawa! Muchus cocol, muchus cocol!*" Nathan cut at the oxen with his whip as Beardy wheeled to catch the other wagons, disappearing once more over the rise.

Still the ox staggered, collapsing on the sand. Nathan kneeled by it, his hair clinging around his face in wet spikes. Water-darkened clothes hung heavy on his body. Rain water and tears streamed down his cheeks. His jaw trembled as he said, "Get up, please."

The beast half-sighed, half-groaned, and seemed to sink into the sand. Catherine had seen death enough to know it would not rise again.

"Leave it, Nathan," said Mrs. Saunders, her voice calm. "We can manage without it." She climbed down and helped him unhitch the ox. They left it lying beneath the gray-white sky, and pressed on. The wheels sank deeply, wet clumps of sand falling behind the wagon. The air was cold and wet. The three remaining oxen labored to pull through the soft wet sand. Further on, they passed one of Mr. Young's oxen, which had dropped dead in its yoke.

Night set in, deepening the surrounding cold. Finally they could no longer see the other wagons' tracks. Nathan climbed in beside the others, letting the oxen have their head. They all sat, saying little, not knowing if they were in the right way or not. At last a yellow-orange glow warmed the edge of the sky. Bright sparks danced above it.

"Those are the fires at the fort!" said Mrs. Saunders. "We made it!" They saw that the gate was open and a wagon was passing through.

At that moment, a piercing yell split the air. Catherine whipped around and looked back. A band of Indians, dimly seen in the fires' glow, topped a distant rise and raced towards them. Nathan and the women leaped from the wagon and drove the oxen with renewed energy. As they neared the fort, the stout figure of a man stepped from the shadows. "Thank God you are safe," he said. "I thought you had all been killed."

They drove the wagon through the gates and several men shut the Indians out. A huge fire in the center of the yard cast orange light on the rain-slick stockade walls. Raindrops sizzled on the flames. The fire was too big to be doused by the rain. Catherine would have been content to stay there, but the stout man said to another man, "Mr. Charles, take these children in to the fire." The word sounded good.

From the shadows came another man. It was Josiah Osborn, who had been missing since the day of the massacre! Catherine had never thought to see him alive again. He told Mrs. Saunders, "My wife wants you to come and stay with her." So she was alive, too.

Mrs. Saunders went with Mr. Osborn. Mr. Charles led the rest of the women and children into one of the wooden buildings standing within the stockade. In the smoke-smelling room was a fireplace and a long table. Several men sat in the fire's glow.

"I wonder which one is 'Uncle Pete'?" Matilda asked Catherine. They were very curious as to who this 'Uncle Pete' was.

The stout man who had met them at the gate came in. Looking at him with round eyes, Matilda asked, "Are you 'Uncle Pete'?"

The man looked at Matilda, then at Catherine, his expression perplexed. "What does she mean?"

"She wants to know if you're the man who rescued us," Catherine explained.

The man responded with a hearty, booming laugh. "I am Peter Skene Ogden, Chief Factor of the Hudson's Bay Company. I bought you from the Indians. Now, with your permission, little girl," he said, looking at Matilda, "I would like to make sure you have warm food and a place to sleep."

That night Mr. Ogden, and Mr. McBean, the factor of Fort Walla Walla, put all the captives in one room. The Sagers were reunited with the Manson boys and David Malin. They were surprised and delighted to see Lorinda Bewley. Mr. Ogden had insisted on "all, every one, or no pay," and an Indian named Camaspelo brought her to the fort.

The Osborns were also there. Mr. Osborn told them of how, on the night of the massacre, he and his family hid under loose floor boards in the Indian room. Escaping after dark, they reached the fort in three days, only to be turned away. Mr. McBean did not want to invite trouble with the Indians by sheltering Americans. Unable to go farther, they returned and pleaded until he let them in.

With them was John Mix Stanley, the artist who the girls became so fond of when he visited the mission in October. He related his narrow escape. "I would be dead now if not for my Indian guide, Solomon, and a Cayuse woman and boy who warned us as we neared the mission.

"We turned towards Fort Walla Walla, but a Cayuse warrior stopped us, asking if I were a 'Boston man.' I told him a Buckeye, since I lived most recently in Ohio. Thinking I was English, he let me pass. Laugh if you will," he said, but no one laughed. He planned to go to the valley with the ransomed captives.

"We're from Ohio, too," Elizabeth told him. "My brothers and sister Katie and I were all born in Ohio."

Mr. Ogden ordered the captives, "Stay in your room and open the door for no one."

"I reckon some of the Indians who killed my brother are out there," said Daniel Young, "and if I knew who they were I would kill them yet."

Catherine cringed to hear him talk so recklessly, when they were not yet out of danger.

Mr. McBean snapped, "Take care what you say. *The very walls have ears.*" He and Mr. Ogden left. The room was crammed till the people in it could scarcely lie down. After a long conversation with Lorinda, Catherine lay in a corner with Henrietta and closed her eyes. All around she heard coughing, shuffling, the murmur of adult voices, and whimpers from the younger children.

What made sleep the most difficult was wondering what tomorrow would bring. Would they be freed...or killed? In the past month, Catherine had been forced to live in uncertainty many times. She had learned that no matter what happened, she must continue as if things would turn out all right. Now she prayed, *Dear God, please take things into your hands.* Sending the prayer comforted her, and after a while she fell asleep.

TWENTY-SIX

The next day, when the Indians were to collect the rest of their ransom, Mrs. McBean let Catherine and some other girls stay in her room. Mr. McBean came in and locked the door and closed the blinds. "Do not let the Indians see you on any account," he said.

A short while later the voice of 'Uncle Pete' Ogden, raised in loud and scolding tones, neared the door. Mrs. McBean opened it, and Mr. Ogden shooed in Elizabeth, Eliza, and Matilda, their cheeks red with cold and shame. "I found these mischiefs playing outside the fort gates," he said. "Keep an eye on them, please. The Indians will be here any time."

"How could you be so naughty?" Catherine asked when he had left.

"It was dark inside the gates, and we wanted to be out in the sun," said Elizabeth.

Catherine would have liked to see the sun, too, but none dared leave the room.

Three times Mr. McBean came in and told Mary Smith, "Edward wants you to go out and see him." He probably would have stopped her if she had wanted to go, but as it was she refused each time. Catherine saw angry sparks flare in her dark eyes.

The third time, Mr. McBean returned and laughingly said, "You are a hard-hearted girl to treat that poor fellow so. He seemed heartbroken, and wept freely."

"I care nothing for his tears," Mary replied. When Mr. McBean left, she said under her breath to Catherine, "Only a man would find that funny."

Mr. Ogden took a census of the captives before paying the Indians. Mr. Canfield and the people from Lapwai were traveling towards the fort. A Nez Perce band went to accompany them, telling Mr. Ogden he would have to pay them for the protection, to which he agreed. The question of ransom seemed to be settled; still, fearing the Indians might change their minds, he kept the captives inside until that night.

The Indians received their pay in the form of fifty blankets, fifty cotton shirts, ten guns, one hundred rifle balls and powder, twelve flints, ten handkerchiefs, and ten fathoms (twisted ropes) of tobacco, all valued at five hundred dollars by the Hudson's Bay Company. They had already received the first half of these things. On December 30, the day after the captives arrived, they received the second half.

The Indians were willing to listen to Peter Skene Ogden. The Hudson's Bay Company had always dealt fairly with them. Many Hudson's Bay men, including Ogden himself, had Indian wives and half-Indian children. He made the Cayuses no false promises. Later, the captives learned what he had told them.

"We have been among you for thirty years, without the shedding of blood. We are traders, and of a different nation from the Americans. But, recollect, we supply you with ammunition, not to kill Americans...whose cruel fate causes our hearts to bleed....

"If you wish it, on my return I will see what can be done for you; but I do not promise to prevent war. Deliver me the prisoners to return to their friends and I will pay you a ransom, that is all."

Chief Tiloukaikt replied, "Chief, your words are weighty—your hairs are gray! In life there are ties of blood between us; in death your Company has allowed our dead to sleep beside yours. We have known you a long time." He told Mr. Odgen that because of his long and difficult journey to rescue the American families, he would turn them over to him, "which I would not do to another younger than myself."

The young men, stirred by the talk of war, gathered inside the fort gates, chanting war songs nearly all night. The drums beat so loudly that Catherine's heart shook with each blow. The yells and shouts sent shivers down her spine. Cramped inside with the other captives, listening to the wild shrieks, she could hardly sleep.

The additional ransom for Mr. Canfield, Mr. Spalding's family, and the people with them was to be twelve blankets, twelve shirts, two guns, two hundred rifle balls and powder, twelve handkerchiefs, five fathoms of tobacco, and some butcher knives. Mr. Odgen told the ransomed captives that the others should arrive any time.

The next day Nancy, the Osborns' seven-year-old daughter, told Catherine, "I'll tell you something if you promise not to tell."

"I promise. What is it?"

"Nancy McBean and I were playing between a building and the wall, and she showed me Mr. Hall's pants back there."

Catherine did not know what to make of this. When they arrived at the fort, she had heard Mr. McBean tell Mrs. Hall that her husband had traveled down the river, insisting on going to the valley.

"Maybe Mr. McBean gave him new clothes before he went down the river," Catherine said.

Nancy shook her head. "When we got here, my father asked him for blankets because my little brother was awful sick. At first he wouldn't give us any, and finally made Father pay for them."

The realization of what had happened, what still might happen, chilled Catherine through. "This is a secret, Nancy. I promise not to tell a living soul, and you must promise, too."

Nancy promised.

Clearly, Mr. Hall was killed at the fort, and Mr. McBean did not know about it, or pretended not to know. Remembering his statement about the very walls having ears, Catherine dared say nothing until much later.

As the days passed, the Indians became increasingly uneasy about the rumors of American soldiers coming to kill them. A large number of Cayuses camped outside the fort gates.

Mr. Ogden became uneasy for the safety of his "large family," as he termed the ransomed captives. The big, jovial man was like an uncle to them. Matilda was his special favorite. Finally he said, "If the people from the Nez Perce Mission do not arrive by Saturday, I will not take chances of staying any longer, but will start without them."

This terrified Eliza Spalding, and nothing Elizabeth or the others could say would comfort her.

Saturday, New Year's Day, 1848, a Nez Perce rode to the fort to give word of the Spalding party's approach. That night Elizabeth and Eliza waited together inside the house until they arrived.

Eliza could hardly sit still. Every five minutes she peered through the blinds to search for her family. When they rode through the fort gates, the first thing Elizabeth noticed was Mr. Spalding riding with them. He and the others entered the house, and Eliza threw herself into her father's arms. "I thought Edward had killed you!"

"He nearly did," her father said. "It was by the grace of God I escaped. Edward fired his pistol to light his pipe and forgot to reload it. When he saw me coming, he went back down the trail to reload. That's when the priest told me Edward intended to kill me."

"But why did the Indians have my horse?"

"Tashe escaped when I was resting on the way towards Lapwai, and I dared not go after him. I was nearly seen as it was. I had to walk the rest of the way. My blankets were heavy and my shoes tight, so I went on without blankets, shoes, or food."

Eliza's mother clung to her, and they wept. Her mother was deeply distressed to see the healthy little girl she had sent away a month ago, reduced almost to a skeleton from all the care that had fallen upon her.

The Canfields also were having a reunion. All five of Mr. Canfield's children were climbing over him, voices raised in joyous babble.

The next day was the Sabbath, and the Spaldings were extremely reluctant to travel. The day after Mr. Canfield arrived at Lapwai bringing news of the massacre, Mrs. Spalding refused to travel even a short distance on Sunday to save her life, for, as she said, "He that obeyeth the commandment shall be rewarded."

Mr. Ogden, however, insisted, and early Sunday morning, January 2, 1848, the ransomed captives marched towards three bateaux waiting on the banks of the Columbia. Mr. Spalding was in the center of the group, because many Indians still wanted to kill him. Tamsucky had waited with his gun at the gate the day he arrived, but the escort of about forty armed Nez Perces frightened him off. Now the Nez Perces, the men from the fort, and a few friendly Cayuses, watched closely as the captives walked towards the boats.

Catherine, Elizabeth, Matilda, Henrietta, and the others walked across a thin coating of snow. Yellow weeds and pale, drained sagebrush showed through the white. The river was silvery green. The black basalt hills faded into misty blue distance.

Four years ago, part of their lives began on a riverbank where green grass and buds overflowed with the new life of spring. They had lived in

Left: Peter Skene Ogden.
Photo courtesy of Oregon Historical Society.

Below: 1853 sketch of Fort Walla Walla, by John Mix Stanley.
Courtesy of Northwest and Whitman College Archives.

the summer warmth of a happy family, with a river flowing past their back door. Now, part of their lives was ending on a riverbank hard with rocks and snow and dead, dried plants.

They heard lapping water, the crunching sounds of their feet, and the calls of the French oarsmen, six to each boat. Above these sounds rose the heartbroken wails of David Malin, who was being left behind. The people at Fort Walla Walla said he belonged to them, since his father had worked for the Hudson's Bay Company. He was eight, Matilda's age, and his cries pierced her heart.

When they reached the bateaux, Mr. Odgen put an arm each around Elizabeth and Matilda. "You two ride with me," he said. Matilda had been his special favorite ever since asking if he were 'Uncle Pete.' He handed her into one of the bateaux, which was a big open boat. She felt it rock treacherously beneath her feet and felt the cold wind slice past her face. The oarsmen kept up a steady stream of French as they assisted Elizabeth, Mr. Stanley, and others into the boat. Catherine and Henrietta boarded another boat.

Matilda hardly knew who to trust any more, but Mr. Ogden seemed nice, and they all loved Mr. Stanley. Before eating, Mr. Stanley made sure they had enough food, and before he sat down to the fire, he saw to it that the Sager girls had a good seat. With over sixty people traveling in the three bateaux, most of the children having at least one parent to look after them, four orphan girls could easily be neglected.

As the boat shoved off, Matilda looked back at the outlines of the fort, the people on the bank. The watchers were silent, except for David, who was half bent over with grief, eyes shut and mouth wide open, howling. A Hudson's Bay man laid hands on his shoulders. David shook him off and stood alone, begging hoarsely to go with the others.

Mr. Ogden's eyes misted over. "Poor little fellow," he said. Quickly he turned his attention to his oarsmen. "Pull towards the north bank," he ordered, "in case some unruly Cayuses should fire at us." The north bank was on their right. The Cayuses were camped on the left, or south, bank.

The words had scarcely left his mouth when a huge, booming roar resounded, echoing off the hills. Matilda and Elizabeth grabbed each other and dived for the bottom of the boat, too frightened to scream. Then they heard Mr. Ogden's great booming laugh. He helped Elizabeth up, saying, "You are all right, little girl. The Indians haven't killed you yet."

Mr. Stanley helped Matilda to a seat beside him. He put his arm around her and said, "That's only the cannon, saluting the boats." In memory Matilda heard Mrs. Whitman say, "Hush, child. They are firing the cannons to salute the boats. Everything is all right." Leaning against Mr. Stanley, her face resting on the rough fabric of his coat, she felt comforted for a moment.

The boats sailed off away down the wide river. When Matilda looked across, the water was a cold blue-green, but when she looked straight down, it was greenish-black, with flecks of white foam on top from the oars dipping in. She heard the oars' sloshing and the rapid, incomprehensible sound of the oarsmen's voices. Cold breezes skimmed the water, cutting through her clothing. David's wails became higher and thinner, at last muffled by a curtain of softly falling snow.

The flakes slid against Matilda's thin clothing and melted, looking like tears. The terraced cliffs were black rock dusted with white snow, fading into gray nothingness. Her future lay somewhere ahead in that gray distance, through which she could not see.

"Look up there." Mr. Stanley's arm moved against her as he pointed. Matilda looked toward the left bank, where two dark basalt columns stood sharply against the sky, ridged on top like teeth. "Do you know what those are?"

Matilda shook her head. All was uncertain; she knew nothing. "Those are called the Two Sisters," Mr. Stanley continued. "The Indians tell many stories about a character named Coyote. One is that Coyote had three wives, and, becoming jealous, he turned two into these rock pillars. The other he changed into a cave downstream. Then he changed himself into a rock so he could watch them forever."

Matilda looked up at the pillars and thought it would be nice to be a rock and be able to sit outside all winter and not feel cold. At last the rock pillars were lost in the curtain of snow.

Matilda leaned against Mr. Stanley's shoulder. The cold, and the boat's rocking motion, numbed her until she thought of nothing for a long while. War whoops on the south bank shook her from her trance. Indians rode there, voices thinned by distance, but still angry. Smoke plumes rose as they fired their guns in the air, but they were too far away to attempt a shot. Finally they, too, were hidden in the falling snow.

The boats traveled down the Columbia all day, to the sound of oars, and the French oarsmen singing boatmen's songs. Though Matilda did not understand the words, the beautiful music of blending voices sent chills through her, making her forget the chill winds.

Each night the boats had to be pulled ashore to keep from freezing in the ice. Mr. Stanley assisted with this task, then gave Catherine his guns and took Henrietta in his arms. "You be my armor bearer while I carry the little one," he told her. Then he wrapped the girls in his surwrapper and lit a fire of crackling dead sagebrush.

Mr. Ogden thought of portaging at the Deschutes rapids, but they would lose a day, the women and children would have to walk nine or ten miles, and Indians might lurk on the banks. "We will have to shoot the rapids," Mr. Ogden told them. "Everyone must duck under the canvas and keep your heads covered."

He was strict in that pronouncement, keeping close watch and yelling, "Duck that head!" whenever one appeared.

Matilda sat between Mr. Stanley's knees with a blanket wrapped around her. He put one arm tight around her waist and the other around Elizabeth's. Crouching in the boat with canvas pulled over her head, Matilda still managed to glimpse the rapids out the side. White water foamed between steep, high bluffs. It flattened out over huge dark rocks, in places shooting high in the air, throwing spray. The boat's lurching and bucking, and the sight of the huge rocks, was terrifying.

Matilda remembered when a toad had frightened her. That was now extremely long ago and far away. After all she had passed through, even the rapids lost some of their terror. She had nearly been tomahawked. How could water hurt her?

At the Dalles, the river was so rough the boatmen had to recaulk and pitch the boats, then let them shoot the rapids by themselves while the passengers walked. Each child had to carry a bundle. Matilda had saved such few things that all her belongings were wrapped in a handkerchief. Mr. Stanley carried Henrietta during the portage. Elizabeth carried Eddie on her back and a bundle in her arms. She, Catherine, and Matilda walked close behind Mr. Stanley.

The rough black rocks were etched with frost, frilled with lichen, and frozen to the ground. When the girls felt cold and miserable, Mr. Ogden told stories or jokes to cheer them. Seeing how Mr. Stanley looked after the girls, he laughed, asking, "How do you like your new family, John? You remind me of a mother quail with her babies following behind."

During this portage, they met the first company of the American soldiers they had heard so much about. The men were volunteers, since Oregon Country had no regular army.

"I am glad I arrived first," said Mr. Ogden, "else none would be left alive to rescue."

Catherine learned from the volunteers that Perrin was not killed. A band of Cayuses rode to the Dalles to attack the Waskopum mission, as she had suspected, but as they reached the door, a band of Nez Perces appeared, running them off and saving Perrin and the others at the mission.

The party made a similar portage at the Cascades, another company of volunteers helping the women and children.

On Friday afternoon, January 6, 1848, Elizabeth heard someone call out that Fort Vancouver was in view. Through the mist she saw a long high stockade with roofs showing above it and an octagonal turret at the far end. Smoke plumed from the turret as cannon fire boomed across the water, but this time the children did not dive to the bottom of the boat. The French oarsmen tuned up their voices and launched joyously into a Canadian boat song.

Fort Vancouver was a large and busy place. Its stockade walls housed a bakery, blacksmith's shop, laundry, trade shop, and other buildings.

The Chief Factor's huge house, with its brown-shingled roof, white clapboard siding, and dark green shutters, was by far the most elegant the Sagers had ever seen. A front porch ran its length, with white picket railing lining it and the flowerbed in front. Dead grape vines clung to iron trellises. Two cannons stood sentinel, a cannon ball pyramid by each.

In this house, the Sager girls and Mary Ann Bridger stayed, with the Douglas family. James Douglas, a Scotsman, was as dark as his half-Indian wife, Amelia. Like Mr. Odgen, he was a Chief Factor of the Hudson's Bay Company, which disappointed Elizabeth. When Mr.

Ogden said he was Chief Factor, Elizabeth thought there was only one, like the President.

Mrs. Douglas wore long skirts in the English fashion, but when she walked, Elizabeth saw moccasins and leather leggings. The Douglases had five girls, aged from nearly two to thirteen. A half-Indian girl named Helen looked after them.

Mrs. Spalding and her children, the Sagers, and Mary Ann ate with Mrs. Douglas and her children. Mr. Douglas and Mr. Spalding ate in another room with the men. Cecilia, the oldest Douglas girl, explained it was not "proper" for gentlemen and ladies to eat at the same table. This seemed strange to Elizabeth, but she liked the Douglases and showed her best manners, trying very hard to be polite and good.

Later that day, Mrs. Douglas said she would like to adopt Elizabeth and Matilda. An English lady named Mrs. Covington wanted to adopt Catherine and Henrietta. "How would you like that?" Mrs. Douglas asked Elizabeth. "We'll give you the finest education."

Elizabeth felt herself turn bright pink. "Oh, very much, thank you, ma'am."

"Then I will ask Mr. Ogden about it."

Deep down, Elizabeth thought, *Maybe they'll adopt Mary Ann, too, and David can come from Fort Walla Walla, and we can all be a family again.*

Elizabeth wanted badly to stay with the Douglases in the beautiful house with its honey-colored wood paneling, polished floors covered with reed mats and real woven carpets, and furniture carved and upholstered. She longed to have a home again.

The Douglases were wonderfully nice, and served good bread and cake, and owned beautiful blue-patterned china dishes that reminded her of Mrs. Whitman's. Elizabeth remembered her saying that her dishes came from England. Many of the supplies at Waiilatpu were bought at Fort Vancouver, so the things seemed familiar to Elizabeth.

Matilda was soon at home with the Douglases, chattering, telling the girls, as they sat together in one of their rooms, that Mrs. Whitman had taught them to sing.

"Oh," said Cecilia, turning to Elizabeth, "Please sing some of the songs she taught you."

Elizabeth, barely at ease, shrank back. She looked down, fingering the fringes on Eddie's cradleboard. Misery nearly drowned her as she remembered Mrs. Whitman. "I don't know how to sing," she whispered.

"That is all right. I'm not so good at it either," the other girl said.

When Mrs. Douglas asked Mr. Ogden about adopting the girls, he said, "It is my intention to keep the Americans together, and deliver them all into the American governor's hands without fail." Elizabeth crept away to a quiet corner where they would not see her cry.

On Monday afternoon, the captives again boarded boats, rowing towards Portland. Catherine, Elizabeth, Matilda, and Henrietta carried packages, presents from Mr. Stanley. At the Trade Shop where furs and shiny powder horns and crisp new fabrics were sold, he had bought enough calico to make each girl a badly needed dress. The small amount of clothing they had saved was becoming worn.

As the boats neared the wharf, Elizabeth saw many men. To her horror, they raised guns and fired. She and the other children scrambled to the bottom of the boat. *They aim to kill us, after all,* she thought, expecting the thought to be her last.

"Now, now, little girl," said Mr. Ogden, patting her shoulder. "That is twice you have been fooled in the same way."

"It's all right, girls," said Mr. Stanley. "They're firing the guns in your honor."

This seemed to be true, Elizabeth realized as she stood shakily, for now the men on shore were cheering, and the people in the boats cheered back.

Portland was a town of two frame houses and a few log cabins. Twenty-five volunteers stood on the sloping bank with arms presented. In their midst was George Abernethy, governor of Oregon.

Mr. Ogden stepped ashore. He and Governor Abernethy clasped hands. Over their heads the alternate red and white horizontal stripes of the American flag seemed to change places as they waved in the breeze, while the twenty-nine stars stood brilliant white against one dark blue corner. When all the freed captives were gathered, Mr. Ogden presented the governor with some papers. Then he turned to the group of Americans and said, "Now you are a free people. You can go where you please."

TWENTY-SEVEN

Years passed, in which change swept Oregon Country. The Oregon Volunteers, fearing an Indian uprising, vengefully pursued the Cayuse tribe. Many killed during the Cayuse War knew nothing of the massacre until it was over, many knew and were against it. They were killed just the same, for being Cayuses.

At last, to halt the slaughter of their people, five Cayuse leaders surrendered. Chief Tiloukaikt, Tomahas, Clockamus, Frank Eskaloom, and Kia-ma-sump-kin were tried at Oregon City in May, 1850.

Fifteen-year-old Catherine and twelve-year-old Elizabeth Sager, and Eliza Spalding, also twelve, were among the witnesses. Answering questions about the massacre while feeling the Indians' hate-filled gaze upon them was a frightening ordeal. Only old Tiloukaikt did not look at them with hate. He seemed wise, sad, resigned.

An estimated fourteen to eighteen Indians actually participated in the killing during the massacre, others being looters or merely bystanders. Many of the killers died in the Cayuse war. As for the plotters, Joe Lewis and Nicholas Finley escaped. Their fate was never certain, though several unconfirmed stories stated Lewis was killed for later crimes. Joe Stanfield was arrested upon arriving in Oregon City in 1848, but was released and reportedly died before the 1850 trial.

After the fifteen-day trial, the five Indians were sentenced to hang. They pleaded to be shot, saying that to hang was to die as a dog and not a man. Shooting meant an honorable passage to the Land of the Dead, hanging caused the disturbed spirit to roam the earth, but hanging was the law.

Shortly before his death, Chief Tiloukaikt answered a questioner about why he gave himself up: "Did not your missionaries teach us that Christ died to save his people? So we die, to save our people." But it was

263

too late to save the broken Cayuse tribe. The few Cayuse survivors joined other tribes, never again to be the proud band of warriors who once roamed the place of the rye grass.

In the passing years, as more and more settlers poured in over the Oregon Trail, the Willamette Valley fulfilled its promise as rich farm land. Faint trails became roads, towns sprang up in the wilderness, connecting railroads and telegraph wires crisscrossed the land, bringing communication in place of isolation. Oregon country was divided into territories, then states: Oregon in 1859, Washington in 1889, Idaho in 1890. Fifty years after the captives' release from Waiilatpu, the little flag of twenty-nine stars bore forty-five. A crowd of American settlers overwhelmed the British and pushed the Indians aside. The surviving Sager girls witnessed these years of change.

On a bleak November day in 1897, three aging women walked up a small incline towards a crowd gathered around a platform. Behind the platform, a hill covered with rough clumps of rye grass rose sharply against the gray sky.

Matilda, walking between Catherine and Elizabeth, saw the rye grass waving, smelled wet earth, and heard the wind blowing mournfully. The wind sounds brought memories as nothing else could, of the wagon journey, life at the mission, the terror of the massacre, and the open boat ride down the Columbia.

After the arrival in Portland back in January of 1848, Mr. Stanley took the Sager girls to Oregon City to visit a man he knew, Dr. John McLoughlin. Matilda learned later that Dr. McLoughlin was an important shaping force in Oregon's history, but as a girl of eight she saw him only as a strange man with startlingly white locks and pale, glittering eyes. His home was large and elegant, greatly impressive to a small girl used to frontier living.

Mr. Stanley took them up a wide staircase with a dark, polished banister, to see a room where his paintings were, beautiful pastel-colored landscapes and vivid portraits. He wanted to paint portraits of the girls, but they shyly said no.

When Mr. Stanley took them downstairs, Dr. McLoughlin fastened

Elizabeth Sager Helm, (top), Catherine Sager Pringle, and Matilda Sager Delaney at the time of the 50th anniversary of the Whitman Massacre in 1897.

Courtesy, Northwest and Whitman College Archives.

A group of massacre survivors stands around the Great Grave at Whitman Mission on the day of its dedication, November 30, 1897.

Courtesy, Northwest and Whitman College Archives.

A group of massacre survivors. Left-right, front row: Elizabeth Sager Helm, Lorinda Bewley Chapman, Gertrude Hall Denny. Back row: a Kimball (Susan or Sarah), Nancy Osborn Jacobs, Mina Kimball Megler. Courtesy, Northwest and Whitman College Archives.

the doors and said, "Now you are my prisoners."

Matilda shrank against Mr. Stanley in terror. The round patterns on the wallpaper became a net waiting to draw tight, and the dark draperies seemed to close in, choking her. Dr. McLaughlin looked at the terrified girls with his colorless eyes, so pale they were almost white, with sharp black points in the middle. Then he said, "I did not mean it. I was only joking."

Matilda could hardly realize it was true. Even now, fifty years after the massacre, a sudden shout or sharp noise brought the terror back. Worst of all was the wind's wailing in winter time, as it wailed now. In the daytime she could stand it, but at night the sound never failed to take her back to the night of the massacre. She would lie awake listening, only to fall into nightmare-troubled sleep.

On that autumn day in 1897, the crowd gathered, the three elderly

MATILDA and first husband, LEWIS MACKEY HAZLITT
Taken around 1855.
Courtesy, Northwest and Whitman College Archives.

sisters among them. In their midst was a pit, covered with wooden planks. This was the new grave, the reinterment place of the Whitman massacre victims, at the end of the hill farthest from where the mission buildings once stood. The wood was in place of a marble slab to arrive later.

The mission buildings had long since been burned. Wandering the grounds with the others today, Matilda could hardly believe finding the place they had called home sunk away to nothing, even some of the graves gone. They had tried in vain to locate Louisa and Helen's graves. Beneath the stark gray sky, through the cold wind, she heard the rye grass whispering beyond the hushed voices of the crowd. The voices of wind and rye grass would be here long after the people went away.

The crowd, like Catherine, Elizabeth, and Matilda, were dressed in somber black. Matilda felt the people's stares. She and her sisters were different. Although many had passed over the Oregon Trail in the years since their journey, and a few massacre survivors besides the Sagers were present, none had survived an ordeal such as theirs. Tragedy, and survival of tragedy, set them apart.

A minister offered up a prayer. Fifes keened a dirge as solemn drums kept a steady beat. Matilda and the others filed around the grave. People laid flowers upon the wood, the only bright things in the gray and brown and black day.

Others ought to share this final resting place: David Malin, who Matilda had not seen since leaving Fort Walla Walla long years ago, and Mary Ann Bridger, who died the spring after the massacre, and Matilda's little sister Henrietta, dead at age twenty-six and laid in an unknown grave in California.

Catherine took the platform. The people drew close, eyes fixed on her, attentive, respectfully silent. "Ladies and Gentlemen of Walla Walla: I cannot express to you the feelings of my sisters, myself, and these survivors as we view this scene."

Catherine spoke briefly of the massacre and captivity, while many in the crowd wept, moved not so much by her words as by the day's somber aspect. Matilda stood dry-eyed as the words went on: "—no hope of escape—all dark and despair. But Providence made a way of escape and we stand here today."

Catherine closed her speech by saying, "We desire to thank the people of Walla Walla and the Northwest for their presence here, for their kindness in burying our dead, and for their royal entertainment. We desire also to thank the O. R. & N. Co. for the generosity that enables us to be here and to see the dream of many years consummated. These acts of kindness will be told to our children's children and be carried down to the future generations in grateful remembrance as each recurring anniversary passes."

As Catherine stepped down, Matilda felt deep, contented happiness and pride. After all these years, after Catherine and many others had worked hard for this day, the Whitmans were at last to have a monument.

The minister gave a benediction, the crowd drifted into the waiting trains. The thin steel rails carried them back towards town, away from the lonely graves in the rye grass.

Catherine, Elizabeth, and Matilda had all married young. Matilda was fifteen when she married Lewis Mackey Hazlitt in 1855. When he

Above, left: Earliest known photograph of Catherine Sager Pringle.

Above, right: Elizabeth Sager Helm.

Left: Henrietta Naomi Sager Cooper Sterling.

Catherine and Elizabeth courtesy of Northwest and Whitman College Archives. Henrietta courtesy of Oregon Historical Society.

CATHERINE SAGER
PRINGLE
Taken around 1908.
Courtesy, Northwest and
Whitman College Archives.

MATILDA SAGER
DELANEY

Courtesy, Northwest and
Whitman College Archives.

died eight years later, leaving her with five children, she took in washing to support them, marrying again in 1865. Her second marriage was to Matthew Fultz, who had been a great help after Lewis died. They had three children.

Elizabeth was married at the age of eighteen, also in 1855, to William Fletcher Helm, a man she met at a revival meeting. They had nine children.

When Catherine, at the age of sixteen, married Clark Pringle in 1851, they took in seven-year-old Henrietta, who, being too young to work much, was considered a burden by the people she was living with. She stayed with Catherine and Clark until her uncle, Solomon Sager, visited the family in Salem, Oregon, five years later. Uncle Solomon's plan was to travel among the California miners, entertaining them with the Sager Dramatic Troupe.

Although she did not remember her father and barely remembered brother Frank, twelve-year-old Henrietta had inherited her father's wanderlust and Frank's free spirit. A life on the road sounded fine to her. "I can sing with Uncle Solomon's troupe," she said. "You always tell me I have a good voice."

"You have a good voice for singing hymns in church, not for singing goodness knows what for a pack of miners," Catherine said.

"Mining camps are rough, wild, and dirty, no place for a young girl," Clark said.

Ignoring their protests, Henrietta went on tour with Uncle Solomon and family, marrying twice before her life ended in 1870, when, at the age of twenty-six, she was accidentally shot by a man aiming for her husband.

As far as anyone knew, Henrietta had no children. Catherine and Clark had eight, and outlived five of them. Many of the Sager sisters' children were named for lost loved ones: Catherine's Frank, Marcus, Annie Louise, and Lucia Naomi, Elizabeth's Edwin Whitman, and Matilda's Henry Sager and Sarah Naomi.

Despite many sad experiences, the Sagers never grew bitter, and never forgot how to laugh. "That was one of my sins—to laugh," Matilda recalled in later years.

After the massacre, she lived with the Geiger family. William Geiger had taught the Whitman Mission school in 1846. The Geigers burdened Matilda with jobs much too hard for her. In the bitterly cold winter of 1848-1849, many of their sheep froze. Matilda had to pull the icy wool from the dead sheep and wash it in freezing creek water, a heartbreaking job for a nine-year-old. Mrs. Geiger knit the wool into socks to sell. Her husband was in California digging for gold, and the family must survive.

No tragedy could defeat Matilda. Not long before the fiftieth anniversary of the massacre, rheumatism crippled her. She lay drawn up in bed for five months. Her children gathered, nursing her as Mrs. Whitman had after she ate the poison plant.

Like her father, Matilda had earned a reputation for medical knowledge. Neighbors she had doctored now came to help her. A Chinese cook steeped her limbs with brewed herbs, and at last she walked, at first with crutches, and finally unaided.

Matilda, who had made many friends, was never without them, often

MATILDA and one of her daughters, MATTIE HYE
Courtesy, Northwest and Whitman College Archives.

inviting Indian girls into her home. Around Matilda, the normally shy girls became merry and outgoing.

After her second husband, Matthew Fultz, died in 1883, she ran their hotel in Farmington, Washington, by herself until marrying David Delaney in 1889. She was then fifty years old.

While on a visit to Perrin Whitman, she received word that her hotel, and everything she owned, was burned to the ground. Again her children offered assistance.

Like Matilda, Catherine had Indian friends, and spoke to them in their own language. None of the Sager girls felt any bitterness toward Indians. Catherine spent her time caring for others, whether visiting the sick, raising money to buy a memorial shaft for the hill at Whitman Mission, assisting in the birth of children, or anything else she was called upon to do.

When her sons died, leaving families, she cared for her grandchildren. Remembering the pain of being an orphan, she would not hear of them being sent to an orphanage. She also took in needy youngsters until they found a place to stay. Catherine was a great favorite with neighborhood children, who loved her stories.

The only stories her grandchildren refused to hear were those about the massacre. To think of their own grandmother suffering such things gave them the cold shudders. Catherine, proud of being a survivor, told the stories often and vividly. Recalling her ordeal did not bother her, and eventually she wrote of her life, in between caring for others.

Even on the day she died, her thoughts were of others. On that day, her four-year-old granddaughter Celista Collins, and Celista's cousin John Bentley, three months younger, were swinging on a cupboard door in the pantry. The cupboard crashed down, pans clattering out. Hearing the noise, Catherine knew the children were into mischief and might be punished because their grandmother was trying to rest. She told the adults with her, "Don't punish the children."

Catherine died on August 7, 1910, in Spokane, Washington.

Elizabeth lived in Portland, Oregon, until her death on July 19, 1925. The town she had first seen as a tiny collection of houses had grown to a thriving city.

Matilda was active until the last. The year after Elizabeth's death, Matilda's daughter, Sarah Naomi Swan, told her of an article about the Sager family written by Honoré Willsie Morrow, published in the January issue of *Cosmopolitan* magazine. This article claimed that the Sagers' wagon train broke up after the deaths of their parents and others. Left without adult guidance, the seven children were forced to continue alone.

It contained a ridiculous description of the oldest girl, who the author mistakenly called Matilda, riding on the back of an emaciated cow after breaking her leg, while a younger sister supported the leg and the other children walked. Supposedly they staggered, alone and half-starved, to Whitman Mission.

The story was an insult to the Sagers and those who had helped them on their journey. Matilda and her sisters had stayed close to Dr. Degen and Uncle Billy and Aunt Sally as long as they lived, exchanging visits and letters.

Incensed, she wrote Mrs. Morrow, "I positively forbid you to use either the name of Sager and its family history." She told Mrs. Morrow that she would have helped, had she wished to write a true account. "I do not feel pleased or gratified by your story in the *Cosmopolitan,* quite the contrary," Matilda wrote.

Mrs. Morrow, however, paid no heed. Later that year a book, *On to Oregon!* was published, with some mistakes corrected and others added. The story put forth in this book lived on in other books, articles, and, many years later, in movies and television. Matilda fought the false story the rest of her life.

In later years, Matilda moved to the warm, dry climate of Southern California. Her children were devoted to her, at least one staying by her at all times. She died in Reseda, California, on April 13, 1928, but chose as her final resting place to lie by her second husband, Mat Fultz, on a peaceful hill overlooking Farmington, Washington.

The Sagers' lives were a long struggle, but it brought them wisdom. Catherine, Elizabeth, and Matilda each wrote accounts of their lives.

Matilda wrote her book, *A Survivor's Recollections of the Whitman Massacre,* at the age of eighty. Her life began before ox teams traveled the Oregon Trail, and she lived to ride in automobiles and see airplanes cross the skies. She witnessed the days of the Civil War, First World War, and Charles Lindbergh's solo flight across the Atlantic.

In her recollections she said, "Surely if the way of the pioneer is hard and beset with dangers, at least the long years bring at last the realization that life, patiently and hopefully lived, brings its own sense of having been part and parcel of the onward move to better things—not for self alone, but for others."

MATILDA SAGER DELANEY
In her final years, taken 1927 or 1928. Courtesy, Northwest and Whitman
College Archives.

Bibliography

Part 1: Books Consulted

Catherine Sager Pringle, Elizabeth Sager Helm, and Matilda Sager Delaney left many accounts of their lives, some of which were collected in *The Whitman Massacre of 1847*. Others are listed in Part 2, "Individual Accounts."

Besides the books and articles listed below, I consulted a number of sources on Native American tribes, flora and fauna, and many maps to retrace the Oregon Trail.

Allen, Durward L. *The Life of Prairies and Plains.* New York: McGraw-Hill, 1967.

Applegate, Jesse A. *A Day with the Cow Column in 1843. Recollections of my Boyhood.* Chicago: The Caxton Club, 1934.

Bennett, Robert A., ed. *We'll All Go Home in the Spring.* Walla Walla, Washington: Pioneer Press Books, 1984.

Binns, Archie. *Peter Skene Odgen: Fur Trader.* Portland: Binfords & Mort, 1967.

Bowen, William A. *The Willamette Valley: Migration and Settlement on the Oregon Frontier.* Seattle: University of Washington Press, 1978.

Cannon, Miles. *Waiilatpu, Its Rise and Fall.* Fairfield, Washington: Ye Galleon Press, 1969.

Drury, Clifford M. *First White Women over the Rockies, Vol. 1.*

Glendale: The Arthur H. Clark Company, 1963.

_____. *Marcus and Narcissa Whitman and the Opening of Old Oregon, Volumes I* and *II*. Glendale: The Arthur H. Clark Company, 1973.

Eells, Rev. Myron, D. D. *Marcus Whitman: Pathfinder and Patriot.* Seattle: The Alice Harriman Company, 1909.

Franzwa, Gregory M. *The Oregon Trail Revisited.* Rev. ed. St. Louis: The Patrice Press, 1978.

Frazier, Neta Lohnes. *Stout-Hearted Seven.* Seattle: Pacific Northwest National Parks & Forests Association, 1984.

Haines, Aubrey L. *Historic Sites along the Oregon Trail.* Gerald, Missouri: The Patrice Press, 1981.

Hussey, John A. *Champoeg: Place of Transition.* Portland: Oregon Historical Society, 1967.

Lockley, Fred. *Oregon Trail Blazers.* New York: The Knickerbocker Press, 1929.

Marcy, Randolph B. *The Prairie Traveler.* New York: Harper & Brothers, 1859.

Mattes, Merrill J. *The Great Platte River Road.* Nebraska State Historical Society Publications, 1969.

Miles, Charles and Sperlin, O. B. *Building a State: Washington, 1889-1939.* Tacoma: Washington State Historical Society Publications, 1940.

Mintonye, Edna A., comp. *They Laughed, Too.* San Antonio: The Naylor Company, 1968.

277

Moeller, Bill and Jan. *The Oregon Trail: A Photographic Journey.* Wilsonville, Oregon: Beautiful America Publishing Co., 1985.

Morrow, Honoré Willsie. *On to Oregon!* New York: Morrow, 1926.

National Geographic Society, Special Publications Division. *Trails West.* Washington, D. C.: National Geographic Society, 1979.

Phelps, Netta Sheldon. *The Valiant Seven.* Caldwell, Idaho: The Caxton Printers, Ltd., 1942.

Place, Marian T. *Westward on the Oregon Trail.* New York: American Heritage Publishing Co, Inc., 1962.

Ramsey, Jarold, ed. *Coyote Was Going There: Indian Literature of the Oregon Country.* Seattle: University of Washington Press, 1977.

Relander, Click. *Drummers and Dreamers.* Caldwell, Idaho: The Caxton Printers, Ltd., 1953. Reprint Seattle: Pacific Northwest National Parks & Forests Association, 1986.

Ruby, Robert H. and Brown, John A. *The Cayuse Indians: Imperial Tribesmen of Old Oregon.* Norman, Oklahoma: The University of Oklahoma Press, 1972.

Sager, Catherine, Elizabeth, and Matilda. *The Whitman Massacre of 1847.* Fairfield, Washington: Ye Galleon Press, 1981.

Thompson, Erwin N. *Shallow Grave at Waiilatpu: The Sagers' West.* Rev ed. Portland: Oregon Historical Society, 1973.

Warren, Eliza Spalding. *Memoirs of the West.* Portland: Marsh Printing Company, 1916.

Part 2: Individual Accounts

Interviews are listed by the name of the interviewee, the interviewer's name following. Matilda Sager Delaney appears under two married names, Fultz and Delaney. Many of the Fred Lockley interviews were collected in abbreviated form in his book, *Oregon Trail Blazers*, and in the Lockley Files, *Conversations with Pioneer Women*, edited by Mike Helm. Eugene: Rainy Day Press, 1981.

Besides these sources, materials, letters, and interviews supplied by Mrs. Celista Collins Platz, a granddaughter of Catherine Sager Pringle, helped immensely.

The Yamhill County Assessor, Yamhill County Clerk, and Ruth Stoller of Dayton, Oregon, were most helpful in supplying documents relating to the John Perkins family. The 1850 census and John Perkins's land claim record in the Oregon State Archives, Salem, were useful sources.

Bewley, Lorinda. "Statement of Miss Lorinda Bewley." Gray, *Oregon.*

Bottoms, Debbie. "Indian Children." Article courtesy of Whitman Mission National Historic Site.

_____. "Traditional Games." Article courtesy of Whitman Mission National Historic Site.

Canfield family. "Refugees from the Tomahawk," by Mrs. N. G. Day. *Up-to-the-Times Magazine,* January, 1909, pp. 1728-1731. Reprinted as "Oscar Canfield" in Bennett, *Spring.*

Canfield, Oscar. "Oscar Canfield's Pioneer Reminiscences." *Washington Historical Quarterly,* October, 1917, pp. 251-256.

Cason, Mary Marsh. "Bits for Breakfast," by R. J. Hendricks. *The Oregon Statesman,* 6 November 1936, p. 6.

Church, Helen M. Saunders. "The Massacre at Whitman Mission." *The Whitman College Quarterly, volume 2, #4*, 1898, pp. 21-26.

Crockett, Samuel Black. "Diary of Samuel Black Crockett, 1844." Carstensen, Vernon, ed., in Miles and Sperlin, *Building a State*.

Delaney, Matilda Sager. "Told by a Survivor." *The Oregonian* (Portland), 1 December 1897, p. 6.

_____. "Mrs. Delaney, Who Crossed Plains in 1844, Tells of Pioneer Days," by Wilbur Kirkman. *The Spokesman-Review* (Spokane), 27 June 1920, p. M3.

_____. "Observations and Impressions of the *Journal* Man," by Fred Lockley. *The Oregon Daily Journal*, 24-25 December 1921.

_____. Letter to Honoré Willsie Morrow, 21 June 1926, in Eells Northwest Collection, Penrose Memorial Library, Whitman College.

Denny, Gertrude Hall. "An Interview With a Survivor of the Whitman Massacre." *Oregon Native Son*, June, 1899, pp. 63-65.

_____. "Survivor of Whitman Massacre may be in Walla Walla for the Frontier Days Celebration; Tells of Experiences," by Fred Lockley. *Walla Walla Evening Bulletin*, 9 September 1914.

Feightner, Mia Mae. "Clothing and accessories available to pioneers of southern Indiana, 1816-1830." Master of Science Thesis, Iowa State University, Ames, Iowa, 1977.

Fultz, Matilda Sager. "Newspaper Find Said Big Break for Mission," by Vance Orchard. *Walla Walla Union-Bulletin*, 5 January 1969, p. 9. Letter reprinted from *Walla Walla Daily Journal*, 19 September 1888.

Gilliam, Washington Smith. "Reminiscences of Washington Smith Gilliam." *Transactions of the Thirty-First Annual Reunion of the Oregon Pioneer Association for 1903*, pp. 202-220.

Helm, Elizabeth Sager. "The Last Day at Waiilatpu," by Mrs. E. M. Wilson. *Transactions of the Twenty-fourth Annual Reunion of the Oregon Pioneer Association for 1896*, pp. 120-128.
Reprinted in *The Whitman College Quarterly,* April 1897, pp. 17-28.

_____. "The Massacre of the Whitman Party." *Yates County Chronicle* (Penn Yann, New York), 18 March 1914, pp. 1, 6.

_____. "The Oregon Country in Early Days," by Fred Lockley. *Oregon Journal,* 14-27 March 1915, 17-19 August 1915.

_____. "Saw Massacre at Waiilatpu," by David W. Hazen. *The Evening Telegram* (Portland), 29 November 1916, Section Two, p. 9.

_____. "Impressions and Observations of the *Journal* Man," by Fred Lockley. *Oregon Journal*, 23-27 July 1923, 4-6 September 1923.

Jacobs, Nancy Osborn. "Nancy Osborn (Kees) Jacobs" in Bennett, *Spring.*

Kimball, Nathan. "Recollections of the Whitman Massacre." *Transactions of the Thirty-first Annual Reunion of the Oregon Pioneer Association for 1903*, pp. 189-195.

Lavadour, Maynard. "Cayuse People of the 1800s." Article courtesy of Whitman Mission National Historic Site.

Majors, Harry M. "Notes to the Sager 1844 Oregon Trail Journey" in Sager, *Massacre.*

Minto, John. "Antecedents of the Oregon Pioneers and the Light These Throw on their Motives." *The Quarterly of the Oregon Historical Society, V,* 1904, pp. 38-63.

_____. "Reminiscences of Honorable John Minto, Pioneer of 1844." *The Quarterly of the Oregon Historical Society,* March 1901-December 1901, pp. 119-244.

Morrow, Honoré Willsie. "Are Our Boys Soft?" *Hearst's International Cosmopolitan,* January 1926, pp. 48-49, 172-174.

Parrish, Rev. Edward Evans. "Crossing the Plains in 1844." *Transactions of the Sixteenth Annual Reunion of the Oregon Pioneer Association for 1888,* pp. 82-122.

Pringle, Catherine Sager. Typed copy of original handwritten account in Whitman College.

_____. account in Clarke, *Pioneer Days.*

_____. account in Eells, *Marcus Whitman.*

_____. Letters to W. H. Gray, dated 21 May 1878 (?) and 12 February 1882, in Whitman College.

_____. "Letter of Catherine Sager Pringle." *The Oregon Historical Quarterly,* December, 1936, pp. 354-360.

_____. "Mrs. Pringle's Address." *The Whitman College Quarterly, I,* 1897, pp. 30-31.

Saunders, Mary. *The Whitman Massacre.* Fairfield, Washington: Ye Galleon Press, 1981.

Shaw, T. C. "Capt. William Shaw." *Transactions of the Fifteenth Annual Reunion of the Oregon Pioneer Association for 1887,* pp. 49-51.

Sprague, Roderick. "Plateau Shamanism and Marcus Whitman." *Idaho Yesterdays*, Spring/Summer 1987, pp. 55-56.

Walker, Cyrus H. "Occasional Address." *Transactions of the Twenty-Eighth Annual Reunion of the Oregon Pioneer Association for 1900*, pp. 35-48.

Warren, Eliza Spalding. "The First Woman Born in the West," by Claud Alfred Clay. *The Ladies' Home Journal,* August, 1913, pp. 14, 38-40.

Whitman, Marcus. "From Dr. Whitman." *Transactions of the Twenty-First Annual Reunion of the Oregon Pioneer Association for 1893*, pp. 64-65, 68-70.

_____. "Additional Letters," *op. cit.,* pp. 109-110, 142-143, 194-195, 198-203.

_____. "Copy of Letter Written by Marcus Whitman to H. F. Wisewell, Naples, Ontario County, N. Y." *The Whitman College Quarterly, vol. 2., #4,* 1898, pp. 26-29.

Whitman, Narcissa. "Mrs. Whitman's Letters." *Transactions of the Twenty-First Annual Reunion of the Oregon Pioneer Association for 1893*, pp. 53-61, 66-68, 70-82, 86-93.

_____. "Additional Letters," *op. cit.,* pp. 104-108, 111-142, 143-194, 195-198, 203-219.

_____. "Letter from Oregon." *Oregon Historical Quarterly, XXXIX,* 1938, pp. 119-122.

_____. *My Journal.* Fairfield, Washington: Ye Galleon Press, 1984.

Williams, Marjorie. Interview at Whitman Mission National Historic Site, 27 March 1988. Tapes in author's collection.

_____. "Their Call Was Answered." Article courtesy of Whitman Mission National Historic Site.

Winchell, Jack. Interview at Whitman Mission National Historic Site, 27 March 1988, and on phone, 17 April 1988. Tapes in author's collection.

_____. "Cayuse Culture." Article courtesy of Whitman Mission National Historic Site.

Young, Daniel. "Deposition of Mr. Daniel Young relative to the Wailatpu *(sic)* Massacre," in Gray, *Oregon*.

Sager Sources

A number of stories, some true, many false, are based on Sager family history. Listed below are those this author knows of. Further information would be much appreciated, for a planned pamphlet titled *The Sagers: Fact and Myth.*

In his book *Shallow Grave at Waiilatpu: The Sagers' West,* historian Erwin N. Thompson noted that Mrs. Morrow's book was "plagiarized by a number of less creative writers." This author has located only one false book besides Mrs. Morrow's published before Mr. Thompson's, so presumably others exist.

If you have information about any sources listed below, or any other sources on the Sager family, please write Cornelia Shields, Green Springs Press, 217 East Oak Street, Dayton, Washington, 99328-1595.

Part 1: Books: Non-Fiction

Sager, Catherine, Elizabeth, and Matilda. *The Whitman Massacre of 1847.* Fairfield, Washington: Ye Galleon Press, 1981.

Thompson, Erwin N. *Shallow Grave at Waiilatpu: The Sagers' West.* Portland: Oregon Historical Society, 1969. Rev ed. 1973.

These are the only factual published sources completely devoted to the Sagers. For other sources, see the Bibliography.

Part 2: Books: Fact-Based Fiction

Dye, Eva Emery. *The Soul of America: An Oregon Iliad.* New York: The

Press of the Pioneers, Inc., 1934.

Frazier, Neta Lohnes. *Stout-Hearted Seven.* New York: Harcourt Brace Jovanovich, Inc., 1973.
Reprint Seattle: Pacific Northwest National Parks & Forests Association, 1984.
Excerpted in *Cobblestone, the history magazine for young people,* December 1981. Peterborough, New Hampshire: Cobblestone Publishing, Inc.

Phelps, Netta Sheldon. *The Valiant Seven.* Caldwell, Idaho: The Caxton Printers, Ltd., 1941, 1942, 1945, 1947.

Shields, Cornelia. *Seven for Oregon.* Dayton, Washington: Green Springs Press, 1986, 1988.

These books, though fiction, are mostly true retellings of the Sager story.

Part 3: Books: False Fiction

Hays, Wilma Pitchford. *For Ma and Pa; on the Oregon Trail, 1844.* New York: Coward, McCann & Geoghegan, 1972.

Morrow, Honoré Willsie. *On to Oregon!* New York: Morrow, 1926.
Reprinted as *The Splendid Journey.* London: William Heinemann, Ltd., 1939, 1947, 1950, 1952, 1955, 1957.
Revised by Phyllis Braun and reprinted as *Seven Alone.* New York: Scholastic Book Services, no date.

Rutgers van der Loeff-Basenau, Anna. *De Kinderkaravaan.* Amsterdam: Uitgeverij Ploegsman, 1954.
English translation by Roy Edwards reprinted as *Children on the Oregon Trail.* London: University of London Press, 1961.
Same condensed and reprinted as *Oregon at Last!* New York:

Morrow, 1962.

Mrs. Morrow's book, though extremely distorted, bears traces of fact. The others are complete fabrications. All three feature the seven Sager children striking out alone across the wilderness after their parents' deaths.

Part 4: Articles: Non-Fiction

Bundy, Rex. "Star-Crossed Orphans of the Trail." *The West*, December 1969, pp. 22-25, 54-58.

Orchard, Vance. "Pioneer descendant protests movie facts." *Walla Walla Union-Bulletin*, 20 March 1975, p. 11.

Part 5: Articles: False Fiction

Morrow, Honoré Willsie. "Are Our Boys Soft?" *Hearst's International Cosmopolitan,* January 1926, pp. 48-49, 172-174.
Reprinted as "Child Pioneer." *The Reader's Digest*, December 1940, pp.6-10.
Reprinted in Wagner, Guy W., *et. al. Reader's Digest Reading Skill Builder, Part two.* Pleasantville, New York: Reader's Digest Services, 1958, pp. 27-33.
Reprinted in *The Reader's Digest*, August 1960, pp. 210-216.

Part 6: Pamphlets

Comic book format adaptation, "He Never Quit." *Bible-In-Life Pix*, February 1978. Elgin, Illinois: the David C. Cook Publishing

Company.

Bartholomew, Barbara. "Pioneer Journey." *Bible-In-Life Pix*, May
1982. Elgin, Illinois: the David C. Cook Publishing Company.

The first story, based on Mrs. Morrow's book, drew protests from
outraged historians. The Cook Company then published a first-person
account based on Catherine Sager Pringle's story of her life. Of all the
distributors of false Sager stories, the David C. Cook company is so far
the only one to correct itself, replacing falsehood with factual material.

Part 7: Plays

Play titled "The Charm of the Seventh Orphan," marked "Dorothy Elliott
Estate," in Eells Northwest Collection, Penrose Memorial Library,
Whitman College, Walla Walla, Washington. Author and produc-
tion history unknown.

The Sagers were also portrayed in pageants based on local history.

Part 8: Movies and Television

Seven Alone. Doty-Dayton Productions, 1974.

Go-USA two-part episode titled "Oregon Bound," telecast several times
in 1975 and 1976.

The first was a theatrical movie, the second a children's television show.
Both shows were based on Mrs. Morrow's book and have appeared on
television. The movie featured seven Sager children, the TV show, five.
Seven Alone was issued on videocassette by Children's Video Library in
1983.

About the Author

Cornelia Shields, the author of *Seven for Oregon*, was born on September 14, 1961, in Kennewick, Washington, and moved to nearby Dayton in July of 1969. Both of her home towns are within forty miles of Whitman Mission, and her grandparents' farm in upstate New York, where she spent several summers, was not far from Marcus and Narcissa Whitman's birthplaces.

She researched six years, 1980-1986, on *Seven for Oregon*, much of it in Holland Library at Washington State University, where she graduated in 1984 with a major in English and a minor in history. The writing took three years, 1983-1986. Besides reading documents in the form of diaries, books, interviews, and letters, she also visited many of her story's locales. Second edition revisions were completed in 1987-1988.

She set the book's type and did artwork using a Macintosh 512K with the Microsoft Word, MacDraw, MacPaint, and Aldus PageMaker programs.